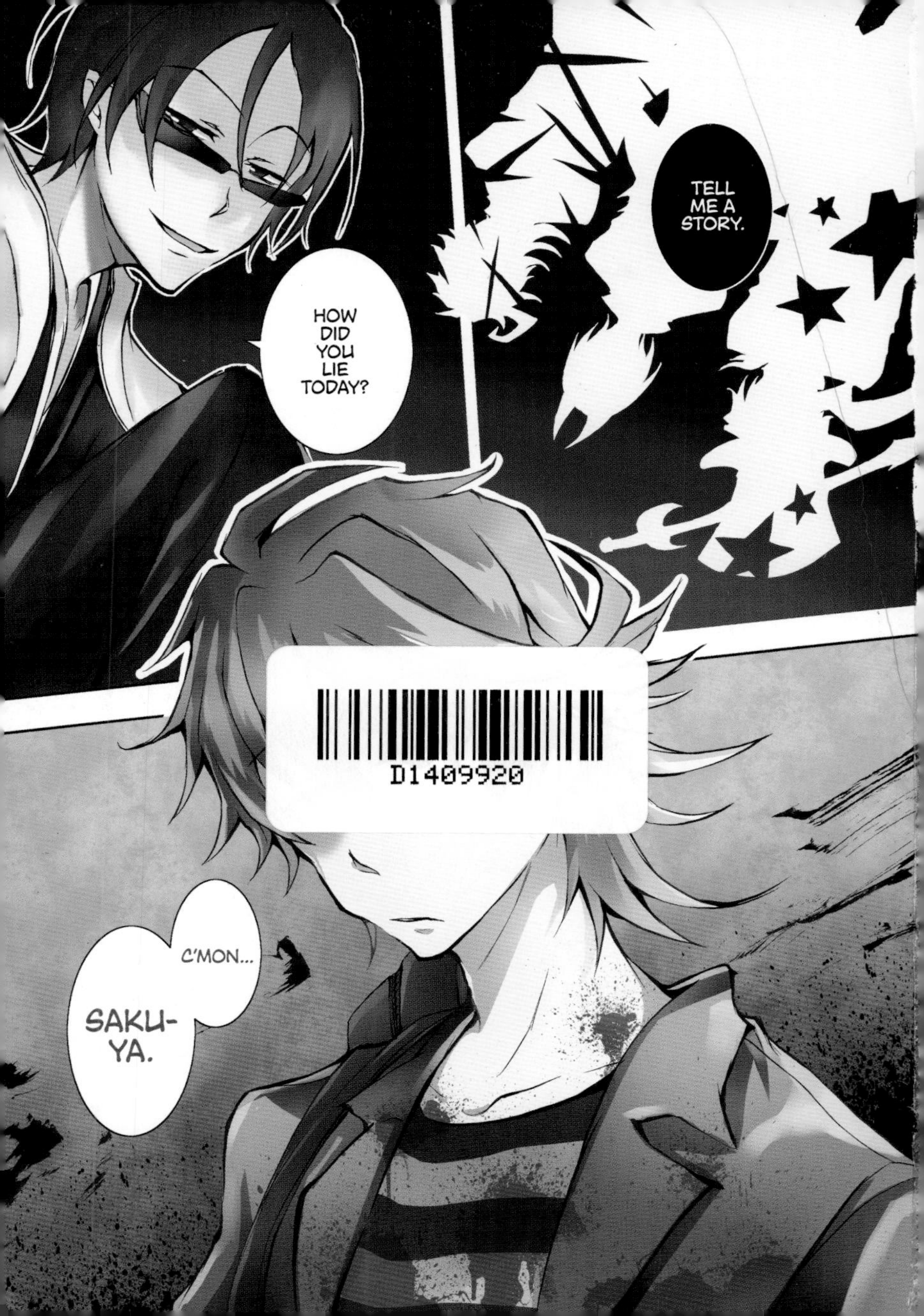
TELL ME A STORY.
HOW DID YOU LIE TODAY?
C'MON...
SAKU-YA.

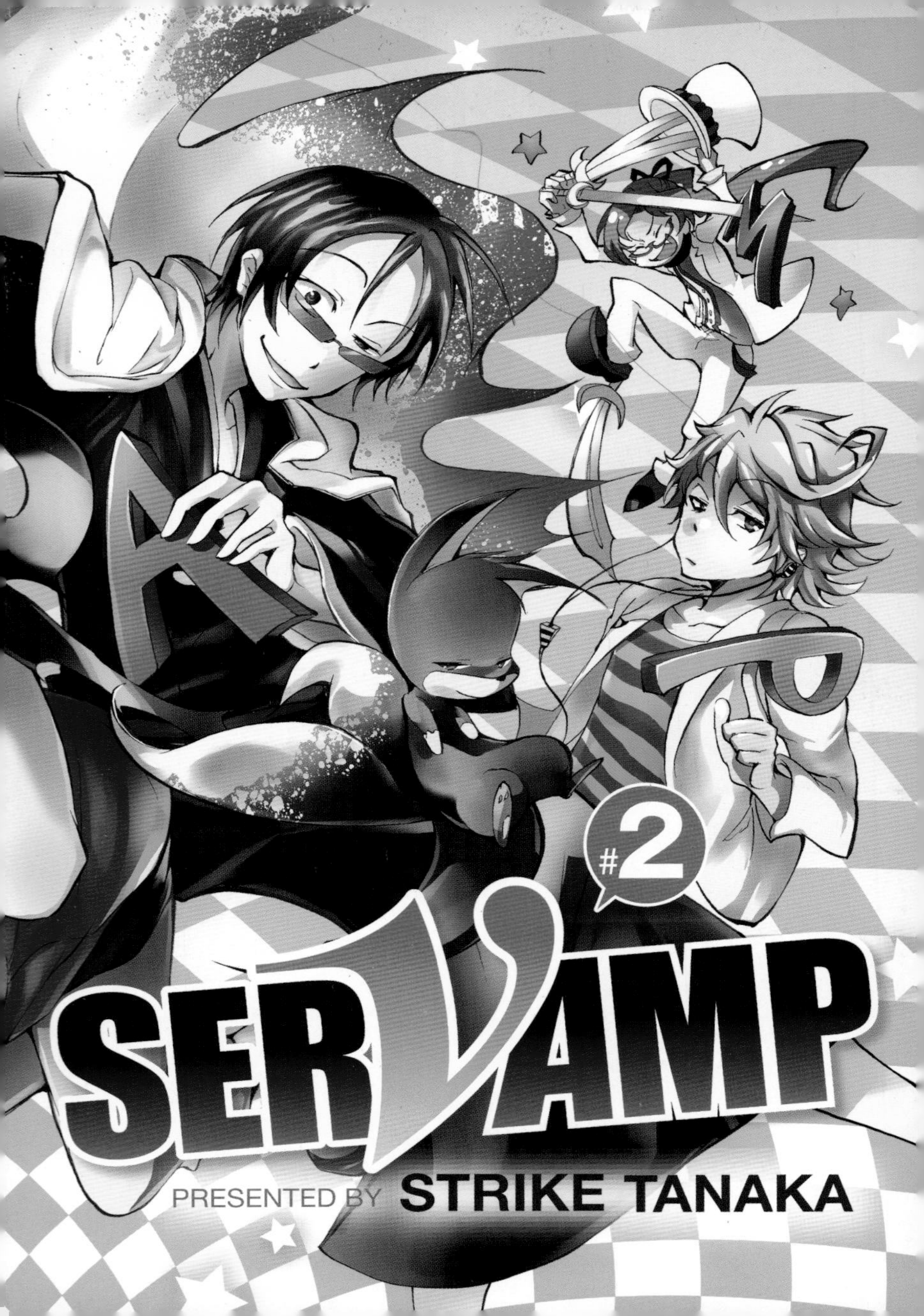
#2
SERVAMP
PRESENTED BY STRIKE TANAKA

06 WHO'S THE LIAR?

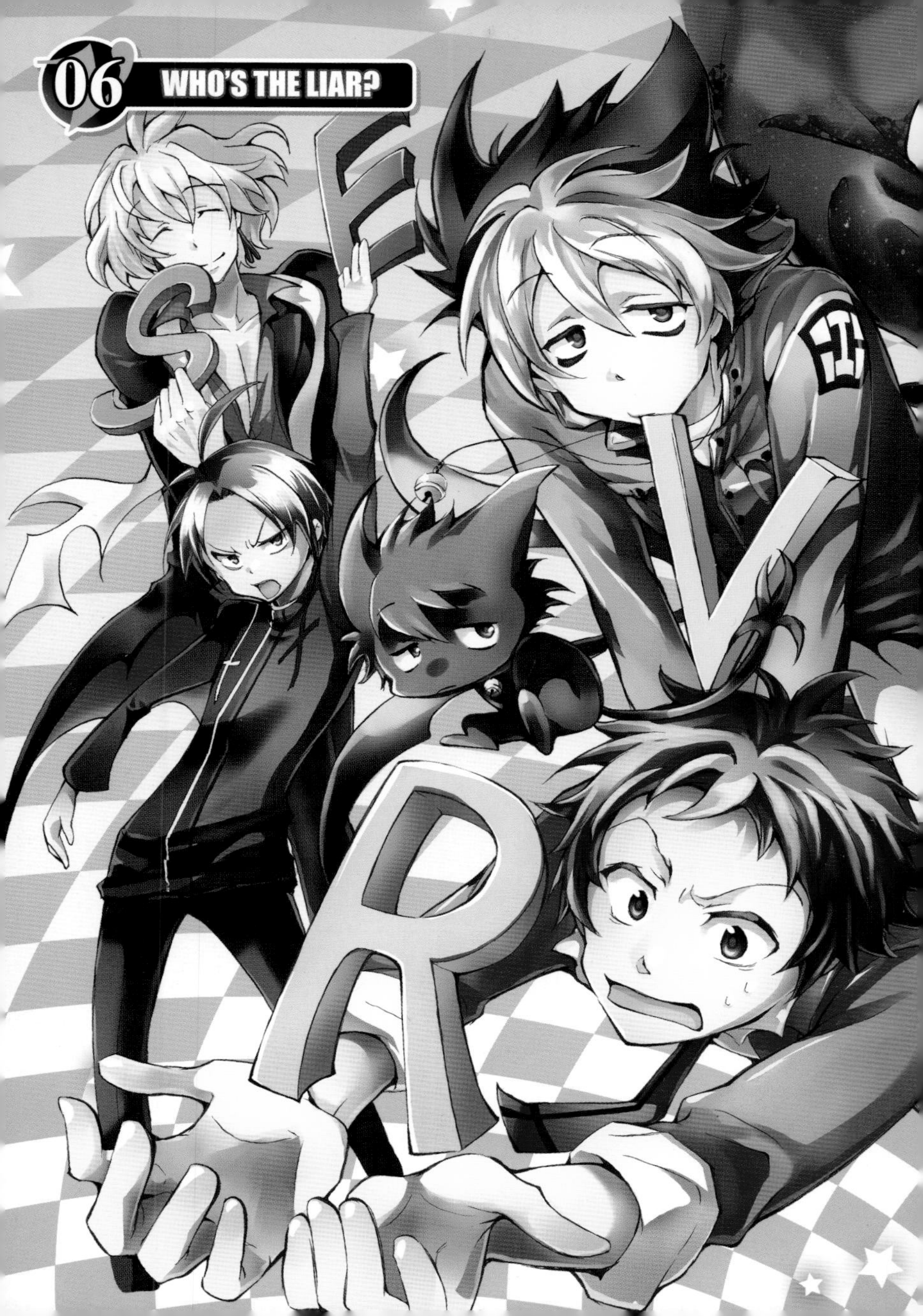

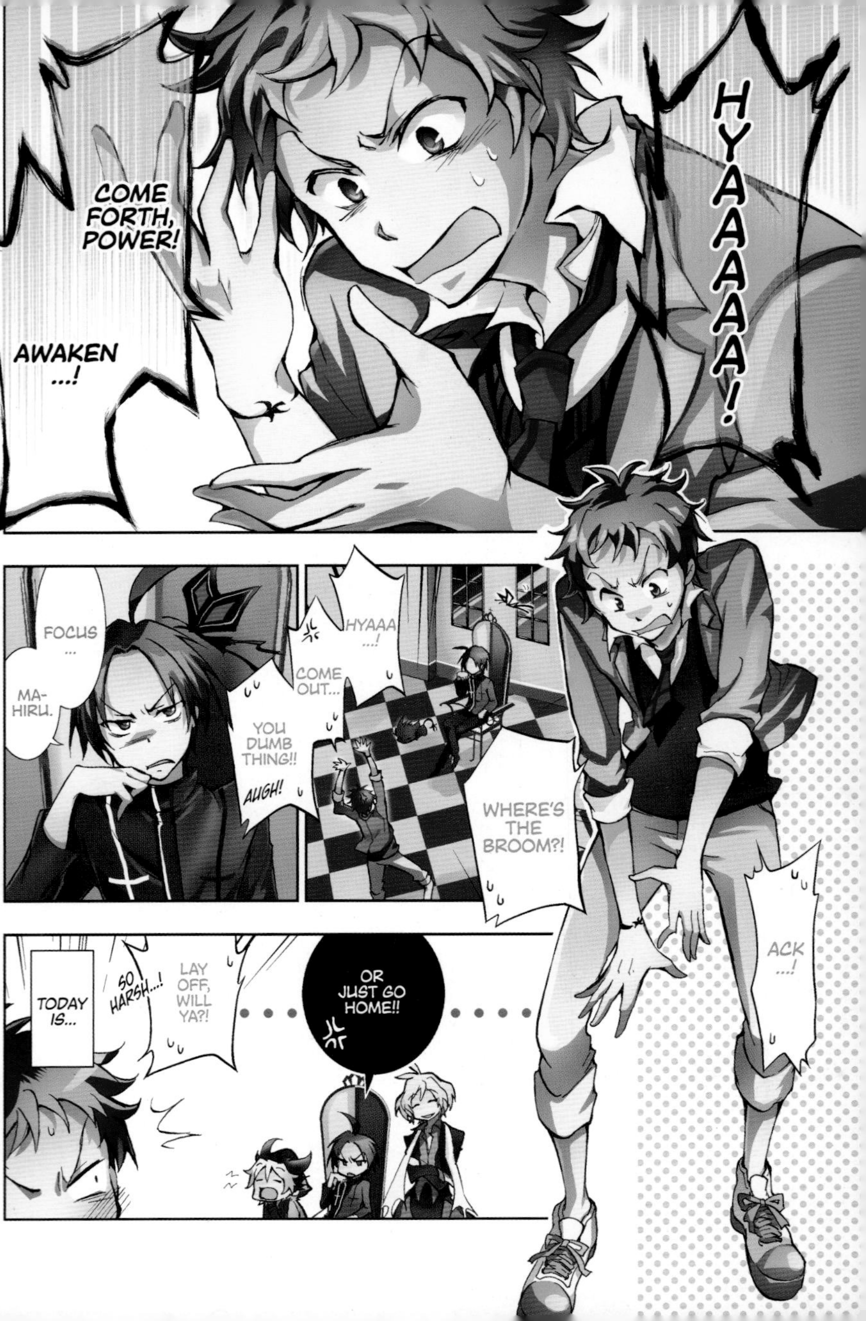

HYAAAAAA!
COME FORTH, POWER!
AWAKEN ...!
WHERE'S THE BROOM?!
ACK ...!
HYAAA ...!
COME OUT...
YOU DUMB THING!!
AUGH!
FOCUS ...
MA-HIRU.
OR JUST GO HOME!!
LAY OFF, WILL YA?!
SO HARSH...!
TODAY IS...

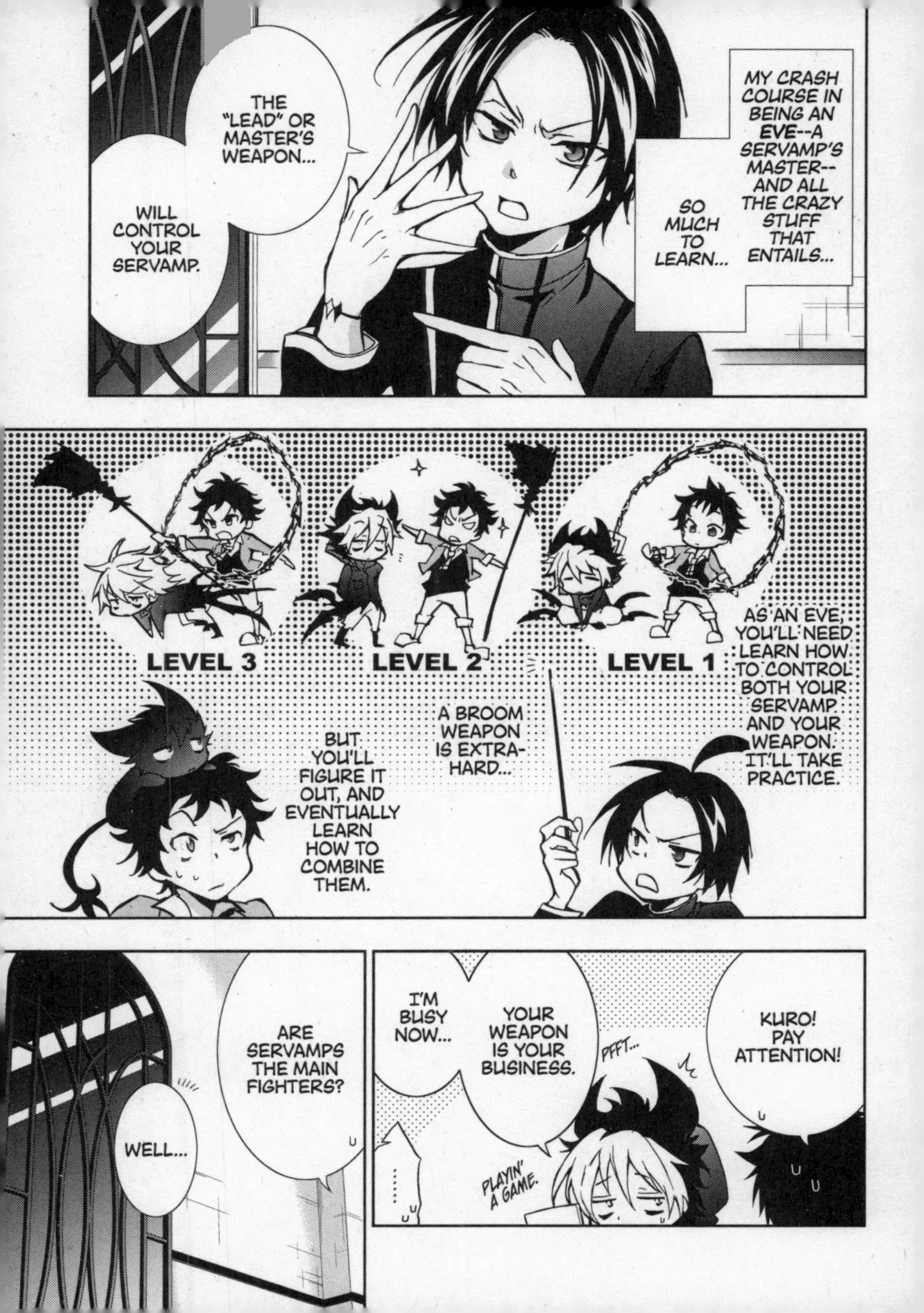
MY CRASH COURSE IN BEING AN EVE--A SERVAMP'S MASTER--AND ALL THE CRAZY STUFF THAT ENTAILS...
SO MUCH TO LEARN...
THE "LEAD" OR MASTER'S WEAPON...
WILL CONTROL YOUR SERVAMP.
AS AN EVE, YOU'LL NEED LEARN HOW TO CONTROL BOTH YOUR SERVAMP AND YOUR WEAPON. IT'LL TAKE PRACTICE.
LEVEL 1
LEVEL 2
LEVEL 3
A BROOM WEAPON IS EXTRA-HARD...
BUT YOU'LL FIGURE IT OUT, AND EVENTUALLY LEARN HOW TO COMBINE THEM.
KURO! PAY ATTENTION!
PFFT...
YOUR WEAPON IS YOUR BUSINESS.
I'M BUSY NOW...
PLAYIN' A GAME.
......
ARE SERVAMPS THE MAIN FIGHTERS?
WELL...

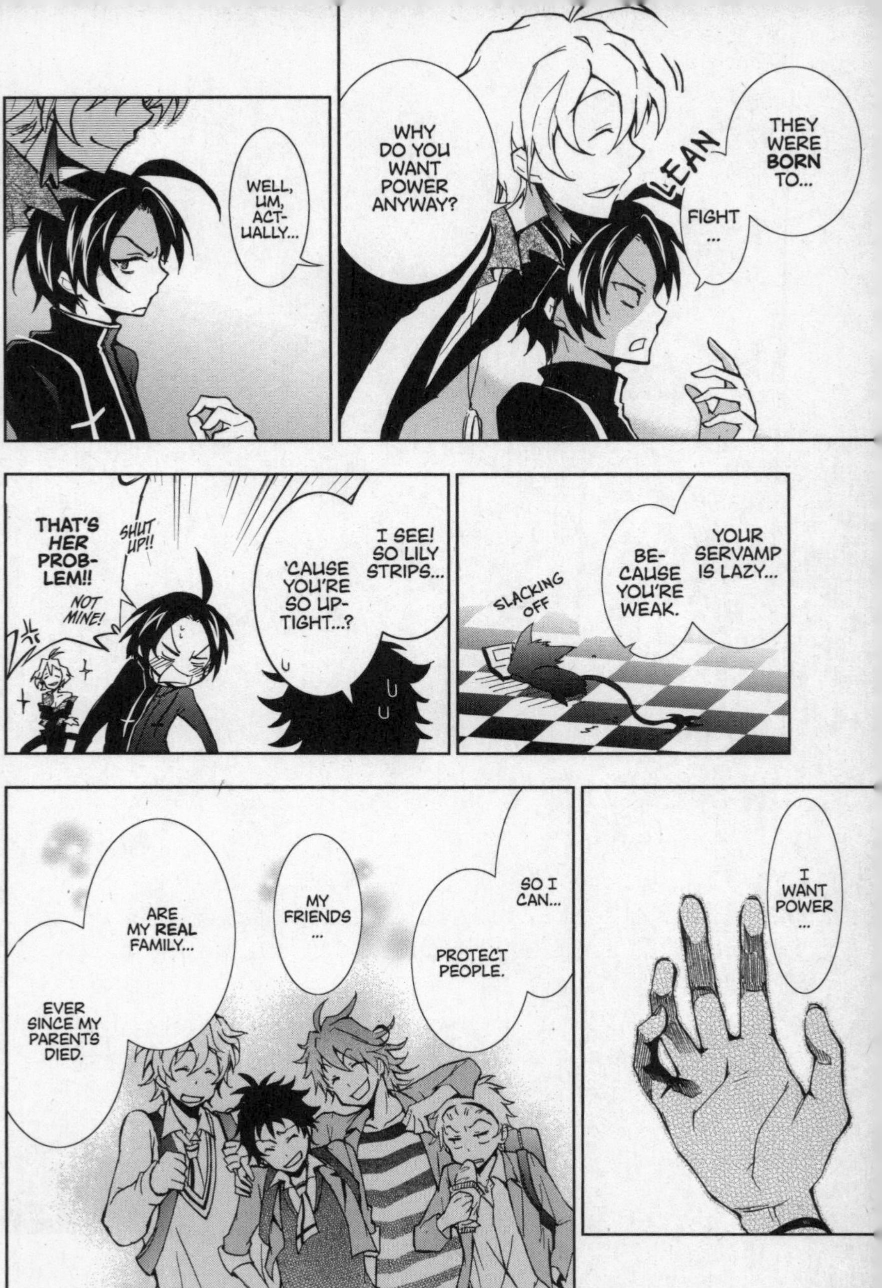
THEY WERE BORN TO...
FIGHT...
LEAN
WHY DO YOU WANT POWER ANYWAY?
WELL, UM, ACT-UALLY...
YOUR SERVAMP IS LAZY...
BE-CAUSE YOU'RE WEAK.
SLACKING OFF
I SEE! SO LILY STRIPS...
'CAUSE YOU'RE SO UP-TIGHT...?
SHUT UP!!
THAT'S HER PROB-LEM!!
NOT MINE!
I WANT POWER...
SO I CAN...
PROTECT PEOPLE.
MY FRIENDS...
ARE MY REAL FAMILY...
EVER SINCE MY PARENTS DIED.

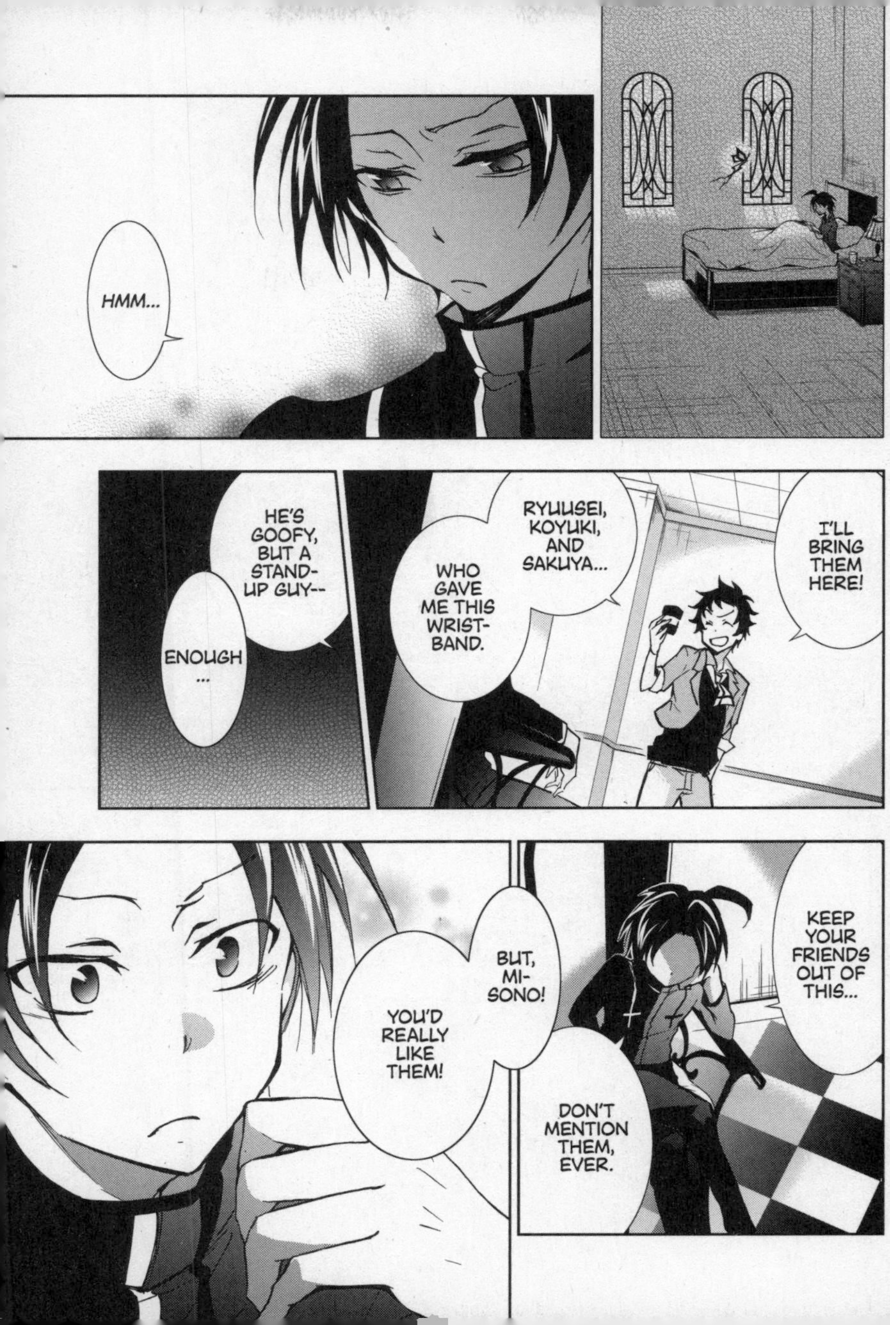
HMM...
I'LL BRING THEM HERE!
RYUUSEI, KOYUKI, AND SAKUYA...
WHO GAVE ME THIS WRIST-BAND.
HE'S GOOFY, BUT A STAND-UP GUY--
ENOUGH...
KEEP YOUR FRIENDS OUT OF THIS...
DON'T MENTION THEM, EVER.
BUT, MI-SONO!
YOU'D REALLY LIKE THEM!

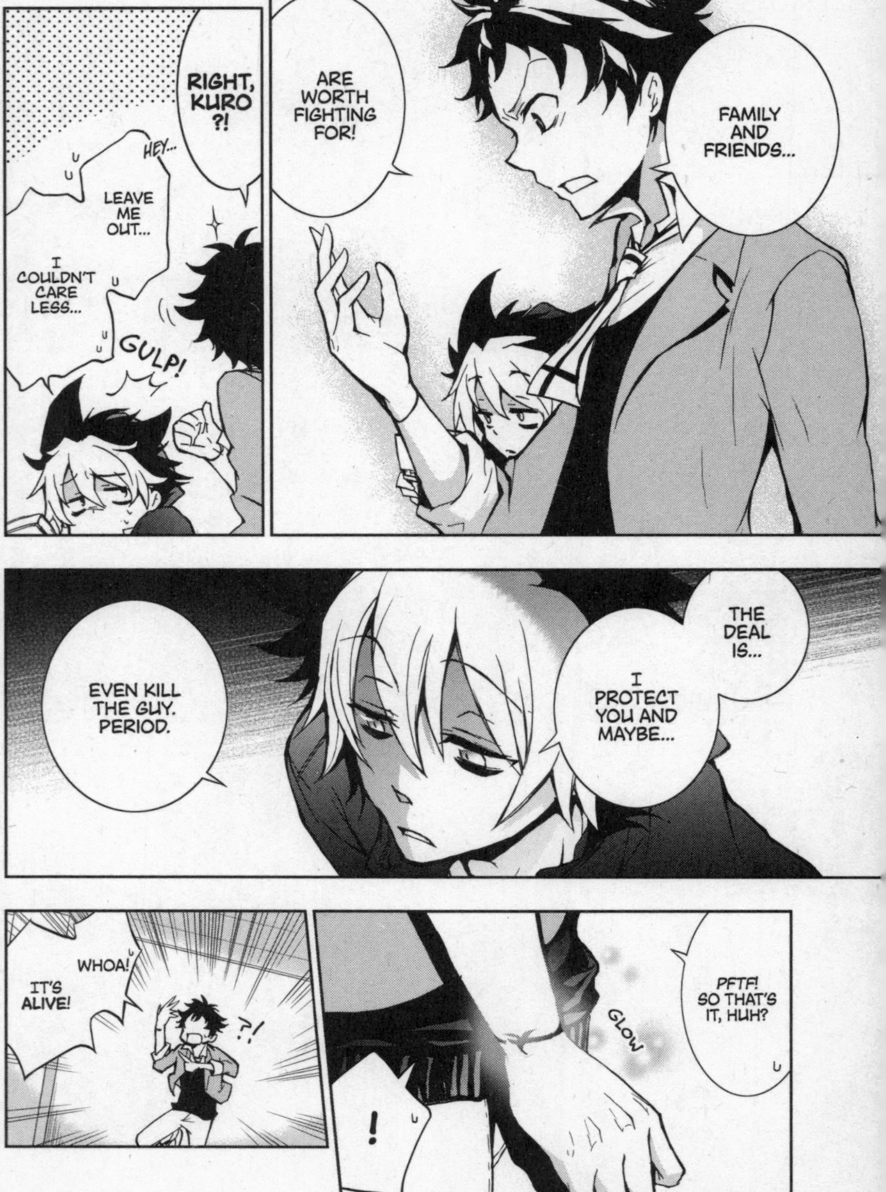
FAMILY AND FRIENDS...
ARE WORTH FIGHTING FOR!
RIGHT, KURO ?!
HEY...
LEAVE ME OUT...
I COULDN'T CARE LESS...
GULP!
THE DEAL IS...
I PROTECT YOU AND MAYBE...
EVEN KILL THE GUY. PERIOD.
PFTF! SO THAT'S IT, HUH?
GLOW
!
WHOA!
IT'S ALIVE!
?!

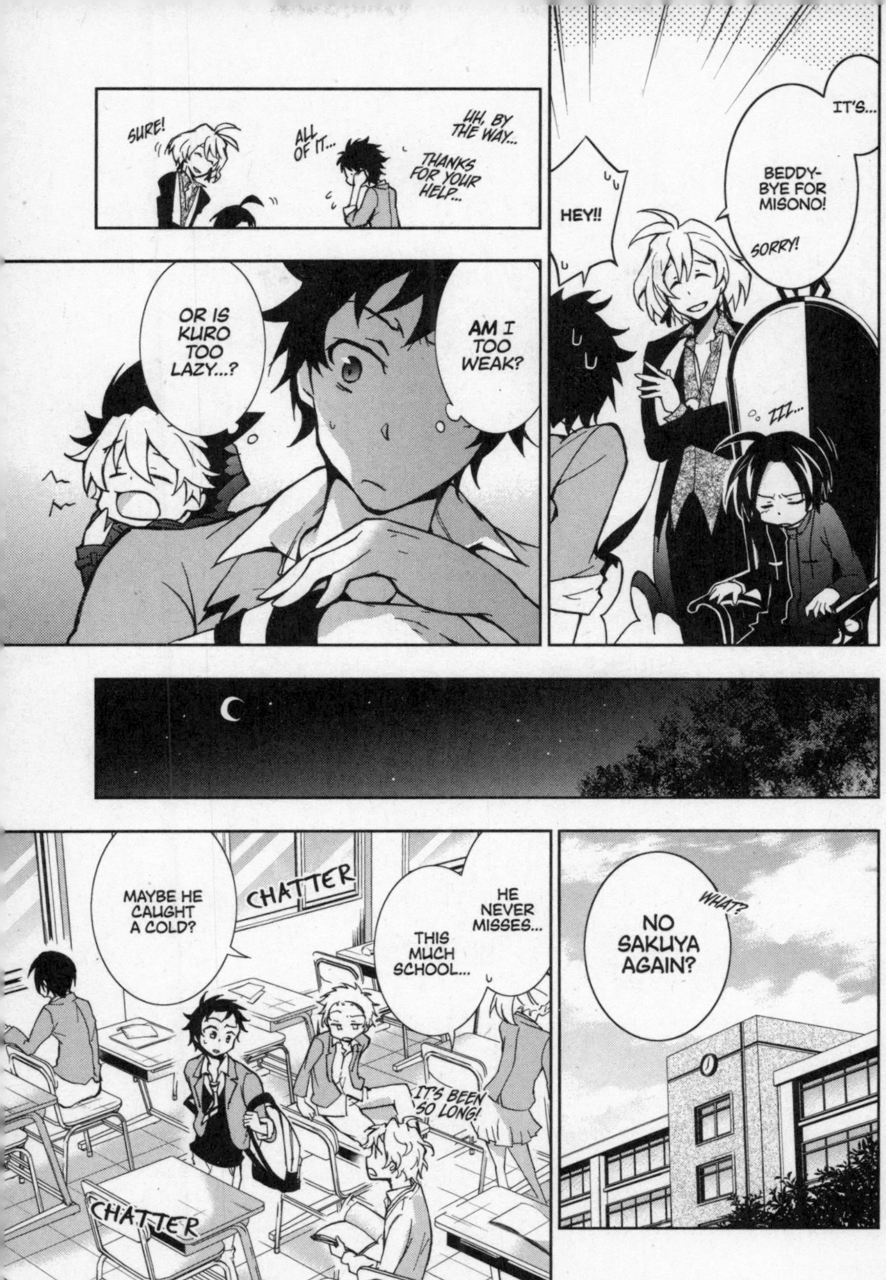
IT'S...
BEDDY-BYE FOR MISONO!
SORRY!
HEY!!
ZZZ...
UH, BY THE WAY...
THANKS FOR YOUR HELP...
ALL OF IT...
SURE!
AM I TOO WEAK?
OR IS KURO TOO LAZY...?
WHAT?
NO SAKUYA AGAIN?
HE NEVER MISSES...
THIS MUCH SCHOOL...
CHATTER
MAYBE HE CAUGHT A COLD?
IT'S BEEN SO LONG!
CHATTER

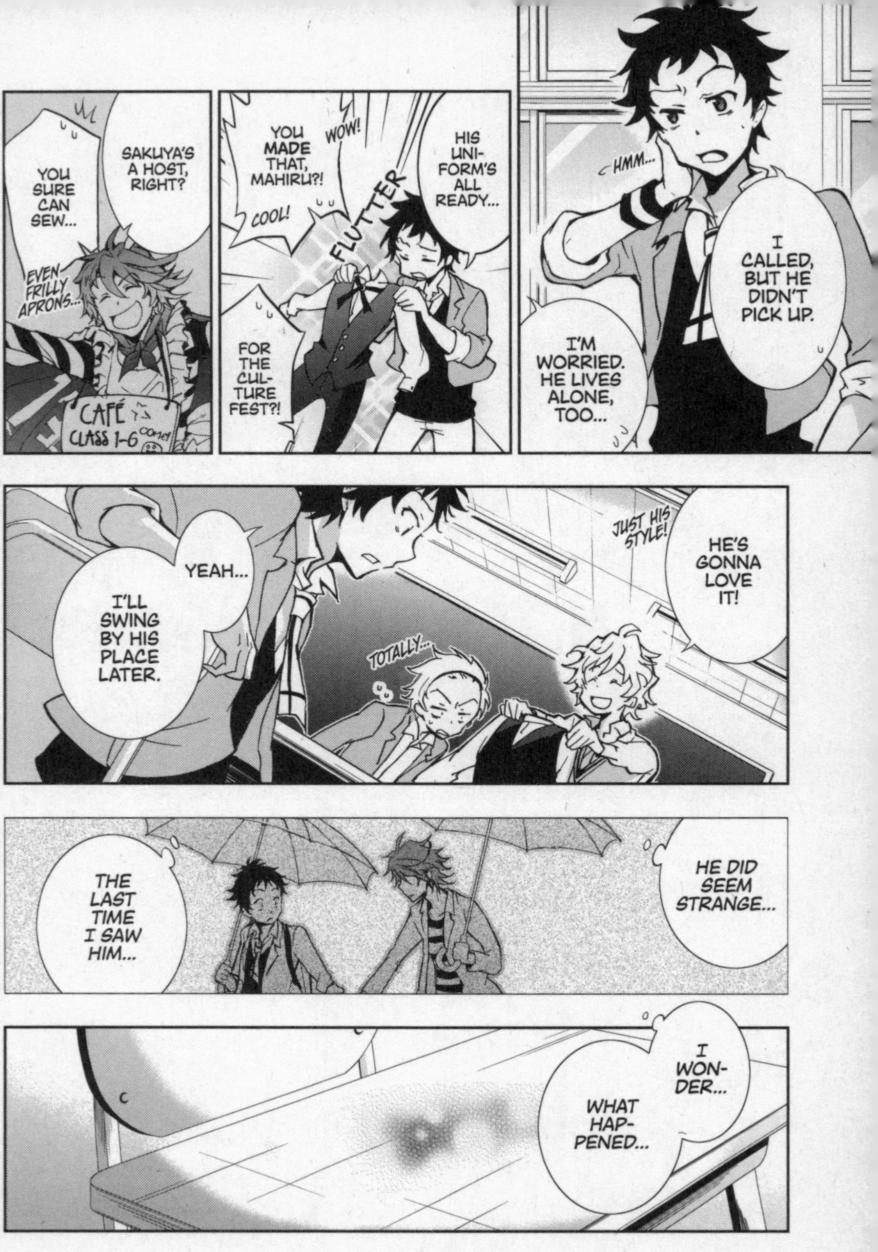
HMM...
I CALLED, BUT HE DIDN'T PICK UP.
I'M WORRIED. HE LIVES ALONE, TOO...
HIS UNIFORM'S ALL READY...
FLUTTER
WOW!
YOU MADE THAT, MAHIRU?!
COOL!
FOR THE CULTURE FEST?!
SAKUYA'S A HOST, RIGHT?
YOU SURE CAN SEW...
EVEN FRILLY APRONS...
CAFÉ
CLASS 1-6
come!
HE'S GONNA LOVE IT!
JUST HIS STYLE!
TOTALLY...
YEAH...
I'LL SWING BY HIS PLACE LATER.
HE DID SEEM STRANGE...
THE LAST TIME I SAW HIM...
I WONDER...
WHAT HAPPENED...

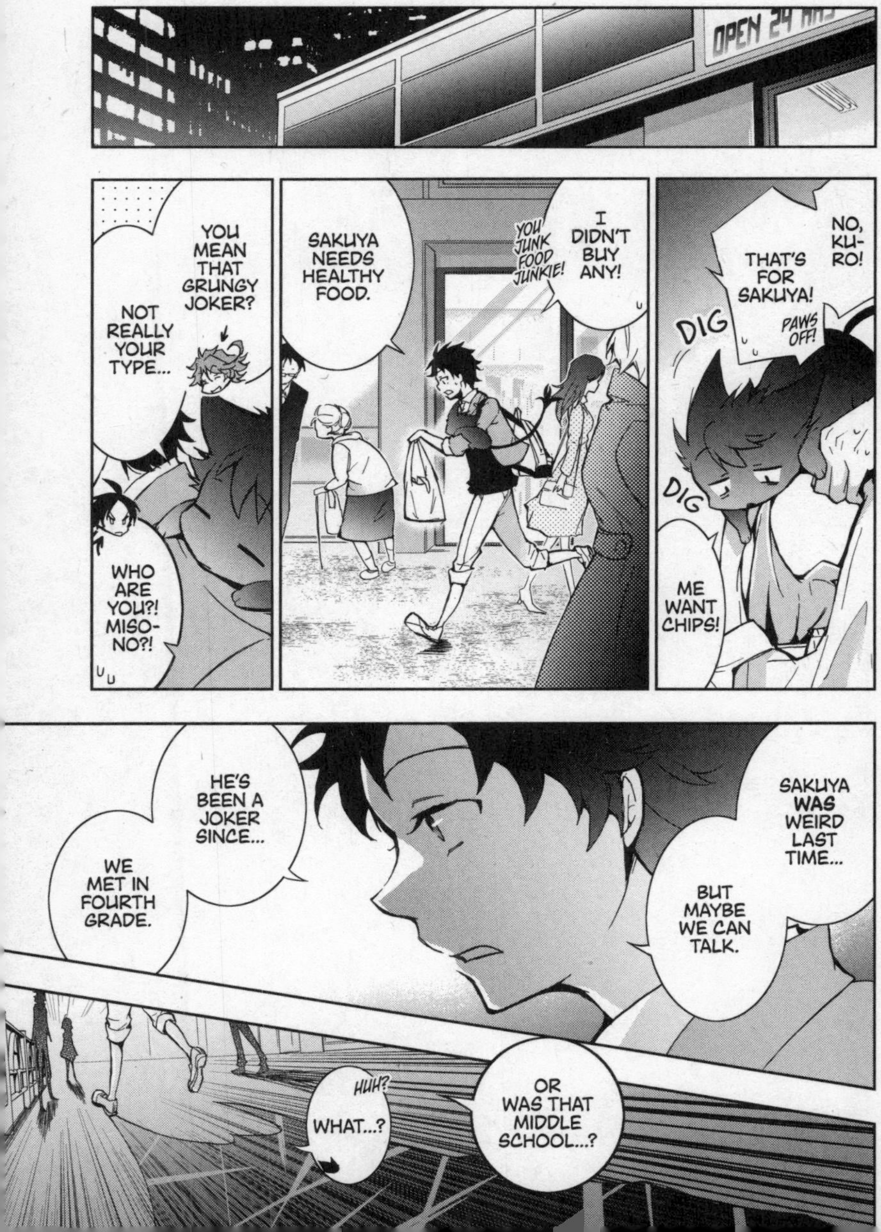
OPEN 24
NO, KU-RO!
THAT'S FOR SAKUYA!
PAWS OFF!
DIG
DIG
ME WANT CHIPS!
I DIDN'T BUY ANY!
YOU JUNK FOOD JUNKIE!
SAKUYA NEEDS HEALTHY FOOD.
YOU MEAN THAT GRUNGY JOKER?
NOT REALLY YOUR TYPE...
WHO ARE YOU?! MISO-NO?!
SAKUYA WAS WEIRD LAST TIME...
BUT MAYBE WE CAN TALK.
HE'S BEEN A JOKER SINCE...
WE MET IN FOURTH GRADE.
OR WAS THAT MIDDLE SCHOOL...?
HUH?
WHAT...?

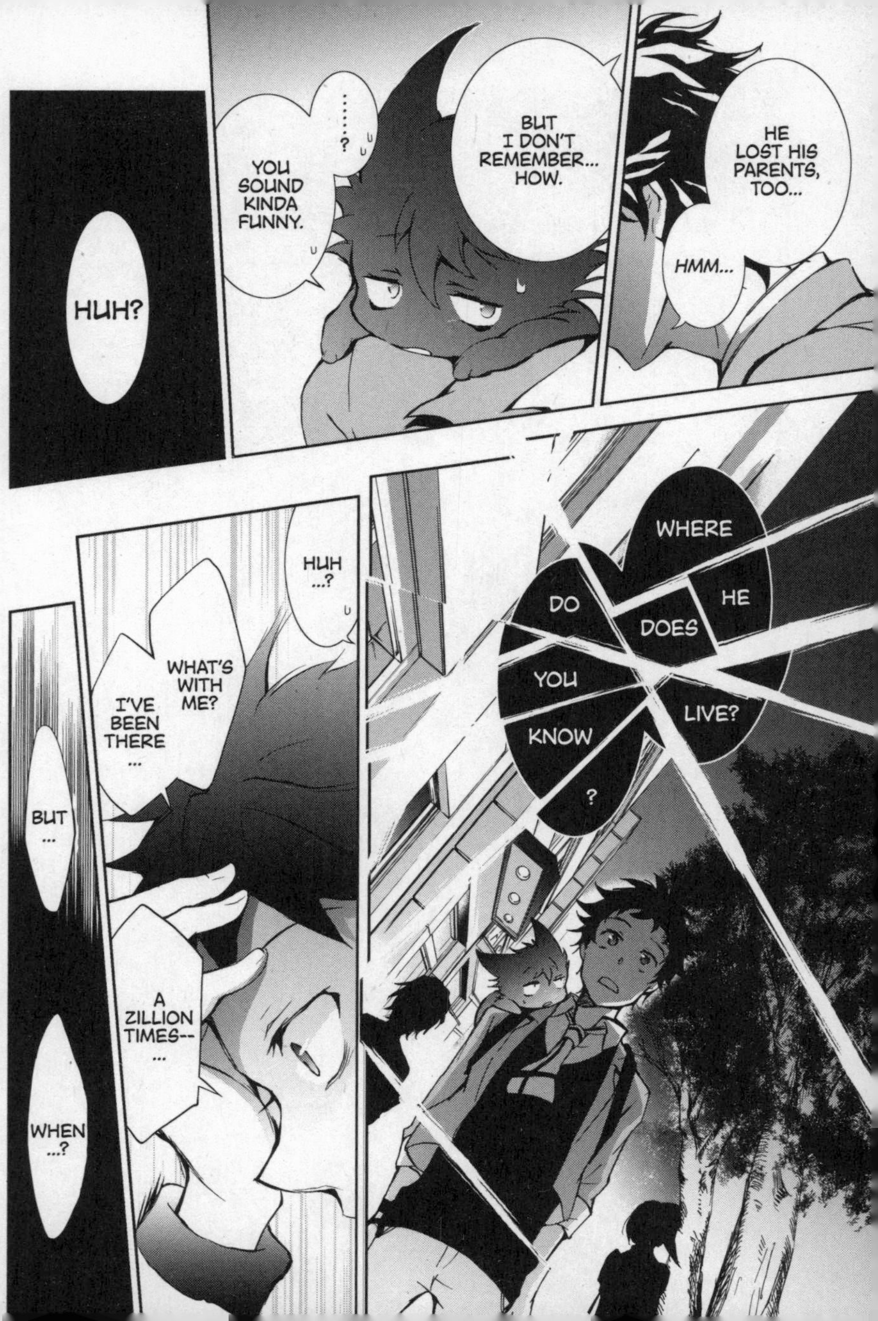
HE LOST HIS PARENTS, TOO...
HMM...
BUT I DON'T REMEMBER... HOW.
......?
YOU SOUND KINDA FUNNY.
HUH?
WHERE DOES HE LIVE?
DO YOU KNOW ?
HUH ...?
WHAT'S WITH ME?
I'VE BEEN THERE ...
A ZILLION TIMES-- ...
BUT ...
WHEN ...?

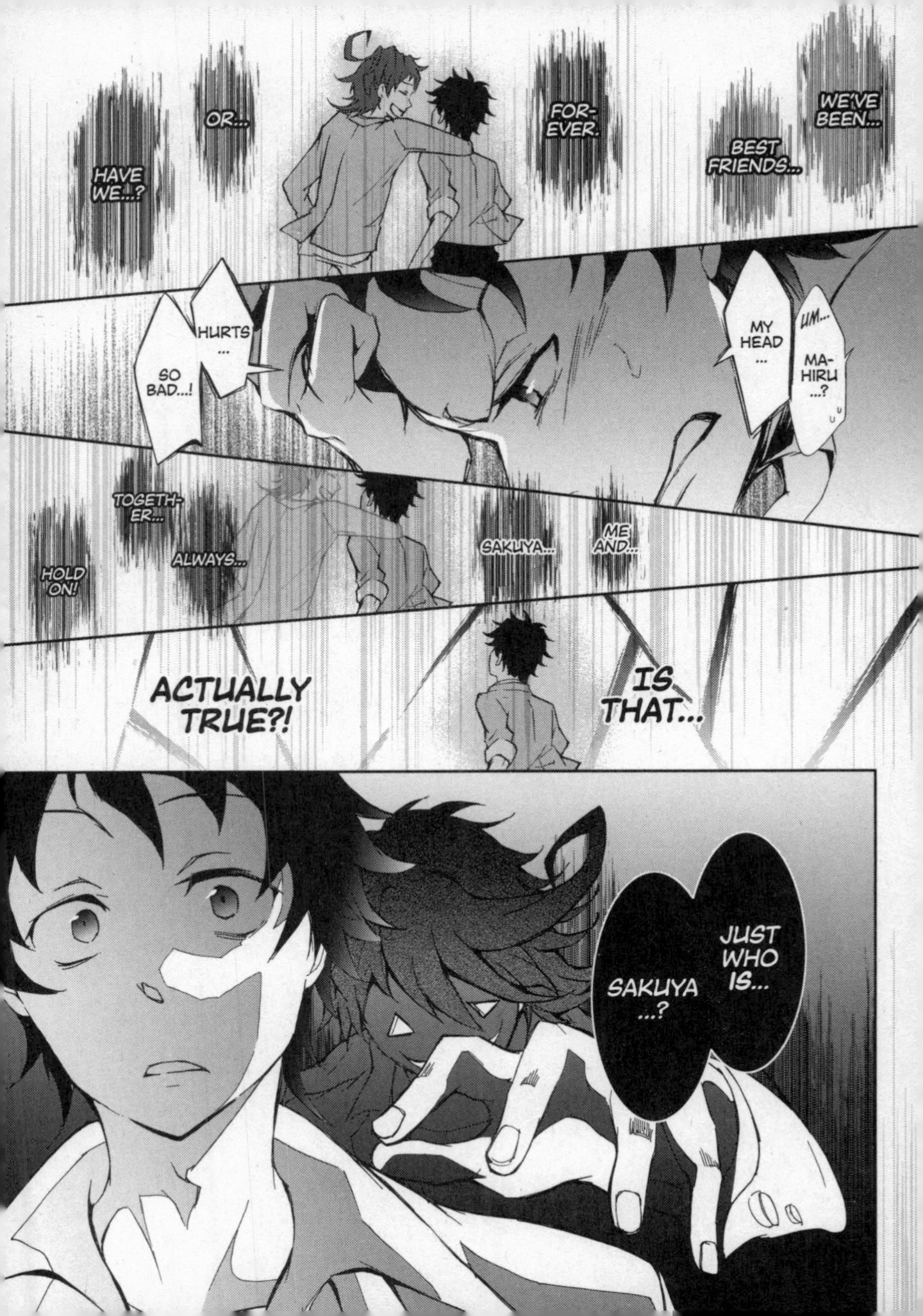
WE'VE BEEN...
BEST FRIENDS...
FOR-EVER.
OR...
HAVE WE...?
UM... MA-HIRU...?
MY HEAD...
HURTS... SO BAD...!
ME AND...
SAKUYA...
TOGETH-ER...
ALWAYS...
HOLD ON!
IS THAT...
ACTUALLY TRUE?!
JUST WHO IS...
SAKUYA...?

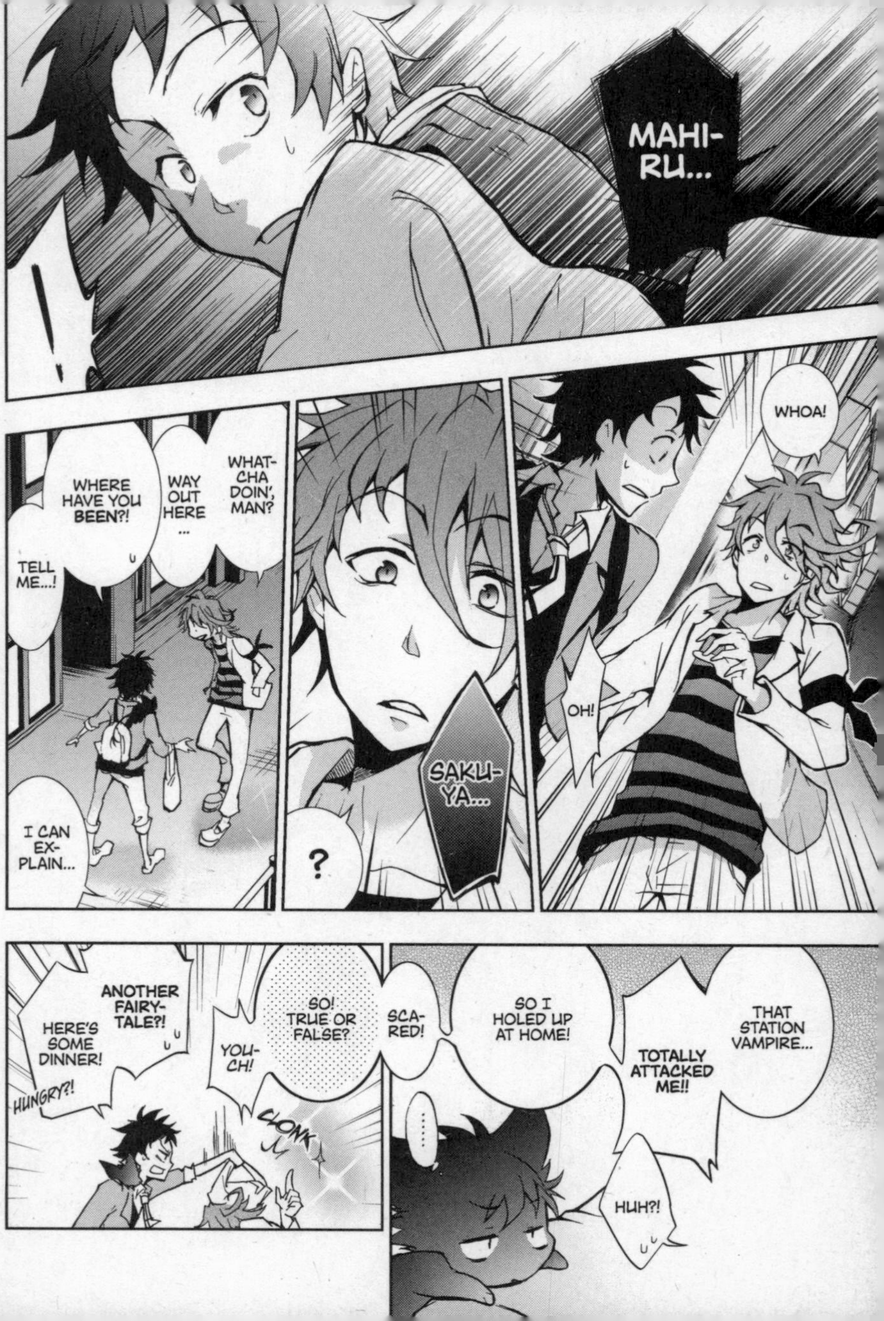
MAHI-RU...
!
WHOA!
OH!
SAKU-YA...
?
WHAT-CHA DOIN', MAN?
WAY OUT HERE...
WHERE HAVE YOU BEEN?!
TELL ME...!
I CAN EX-PLAIN...
THAT STATION VAMPIRE...
TOTALLY ATTACKED ME!!
SO I HOLED UP AT HOME!
SCA-RED!
......
HUH?!
SO! TRUE OR FALSE?
YOU-CH!
CLONK
ANOTHER FAIRY-TALE?!
HERE'S SOME DINNER!
HUNGRY?!

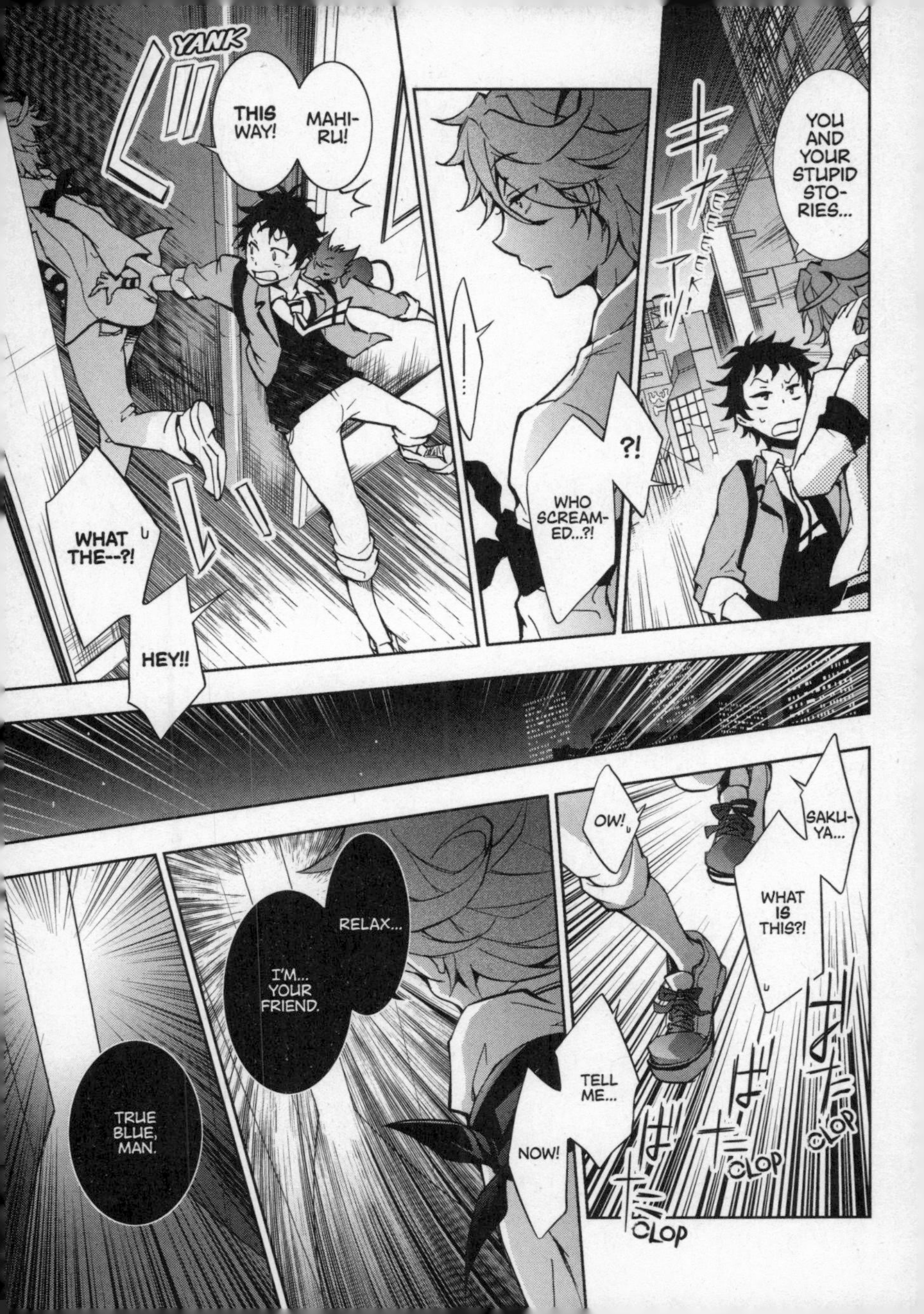
YOU AND YOUR STUPID STORIES...
EEEEEEK!
!...
?!
WHO SCREAMED...?!
YANK
MAHI-RU!
THIS WAY!
WHAT THE--?!
HEY!!
SAKU-YA...
OW!
WHAT IS THIS?!
TELL ME...
NOW!
CLOP
CLOP
CLOP
RELAX...
I'M... YOUR FRIEND.
TRUE BLUE, MAN.

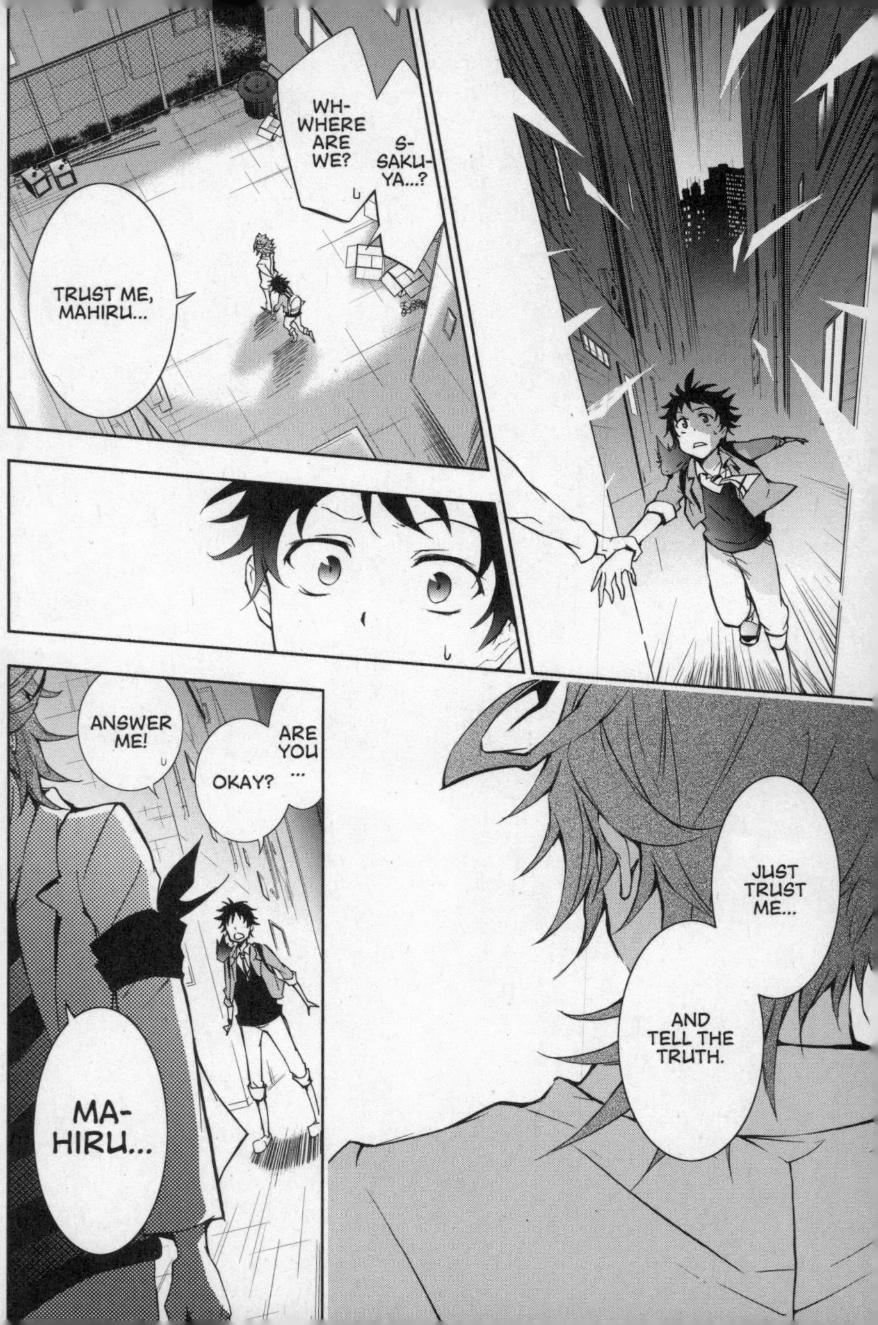
S-SAKU-YA...?
WH-WHERE ARE WE?
TRUST ME, MAHIRU...
JUST TRUST ME...
AND TELL THE TRUTH.
ARE YOU ... OKAY?
ANSWER ME!
MA-HIRU...

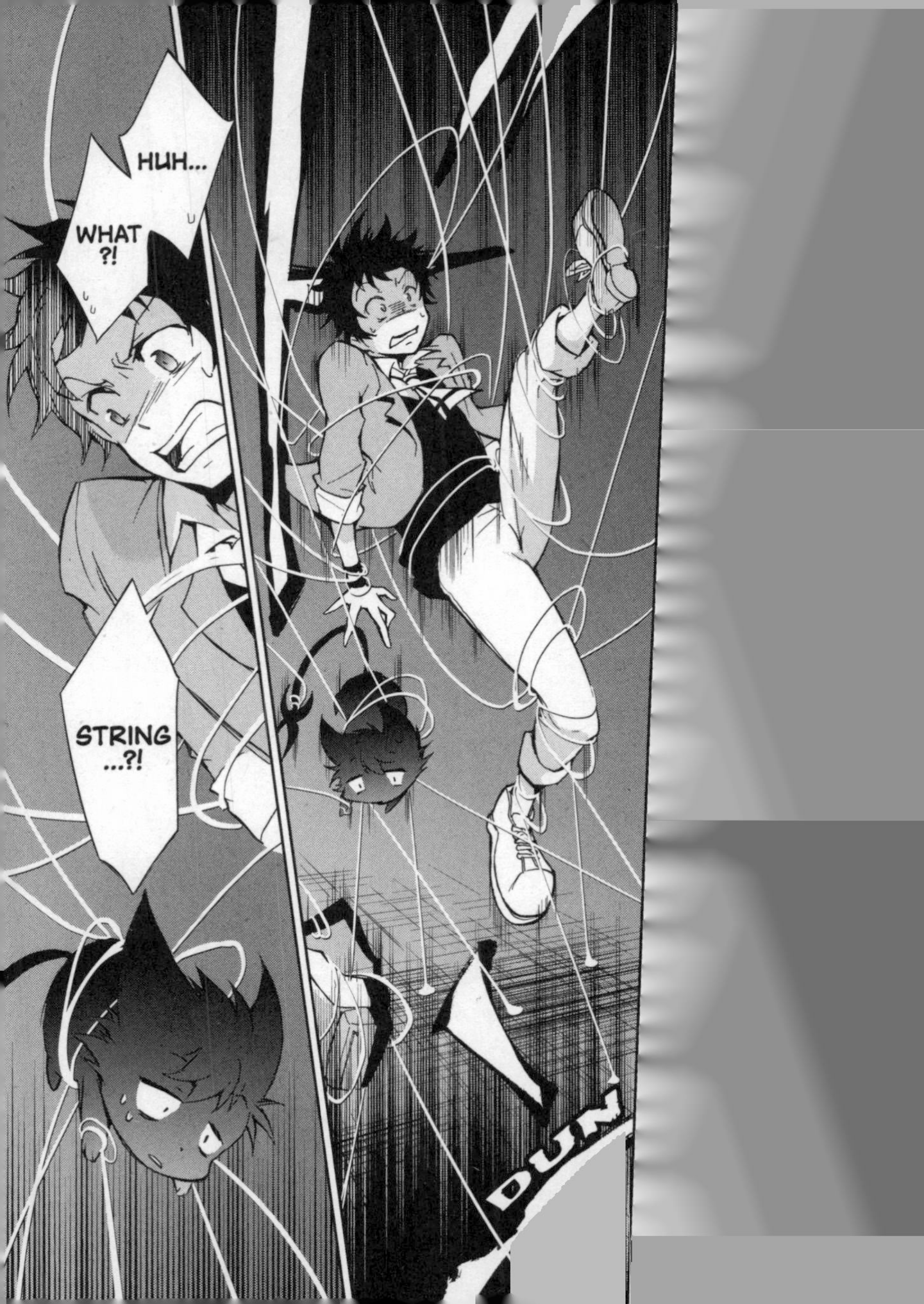
DUN
HUH...
WHAT ?!
STRING ...?!

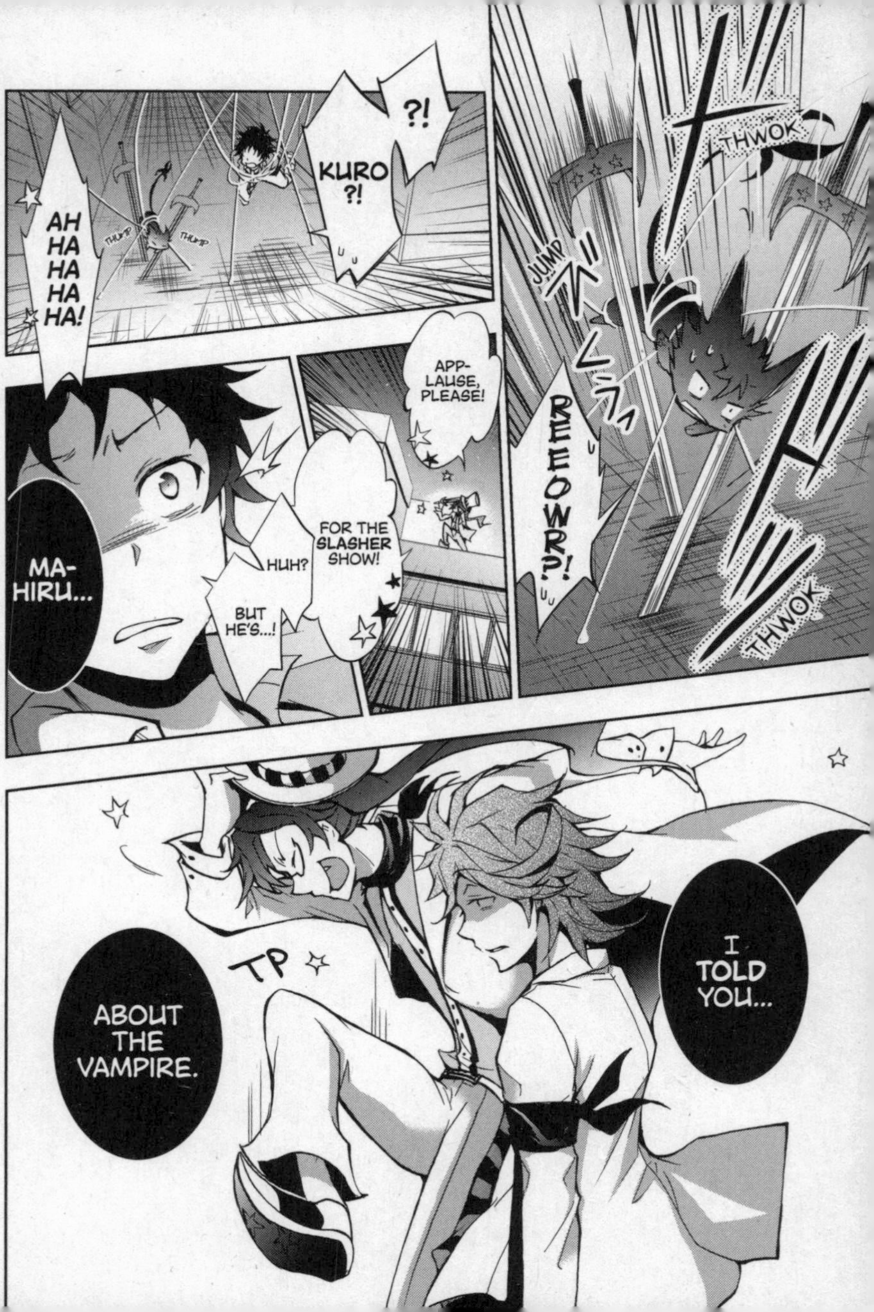
THWOK
JUMP
REEOWR?!
THWOK
?!
KURO ?!
AH HA HA HA HA HA!
THUMP
THUMP
APP-LAUSE, PLEASE!
FOR THE SLASHER SHOW!
HUH?
BUT HE'S...!
MA-HIRU...
I TOLD YOU...
ABOUT THE VAMPIRE.
TP

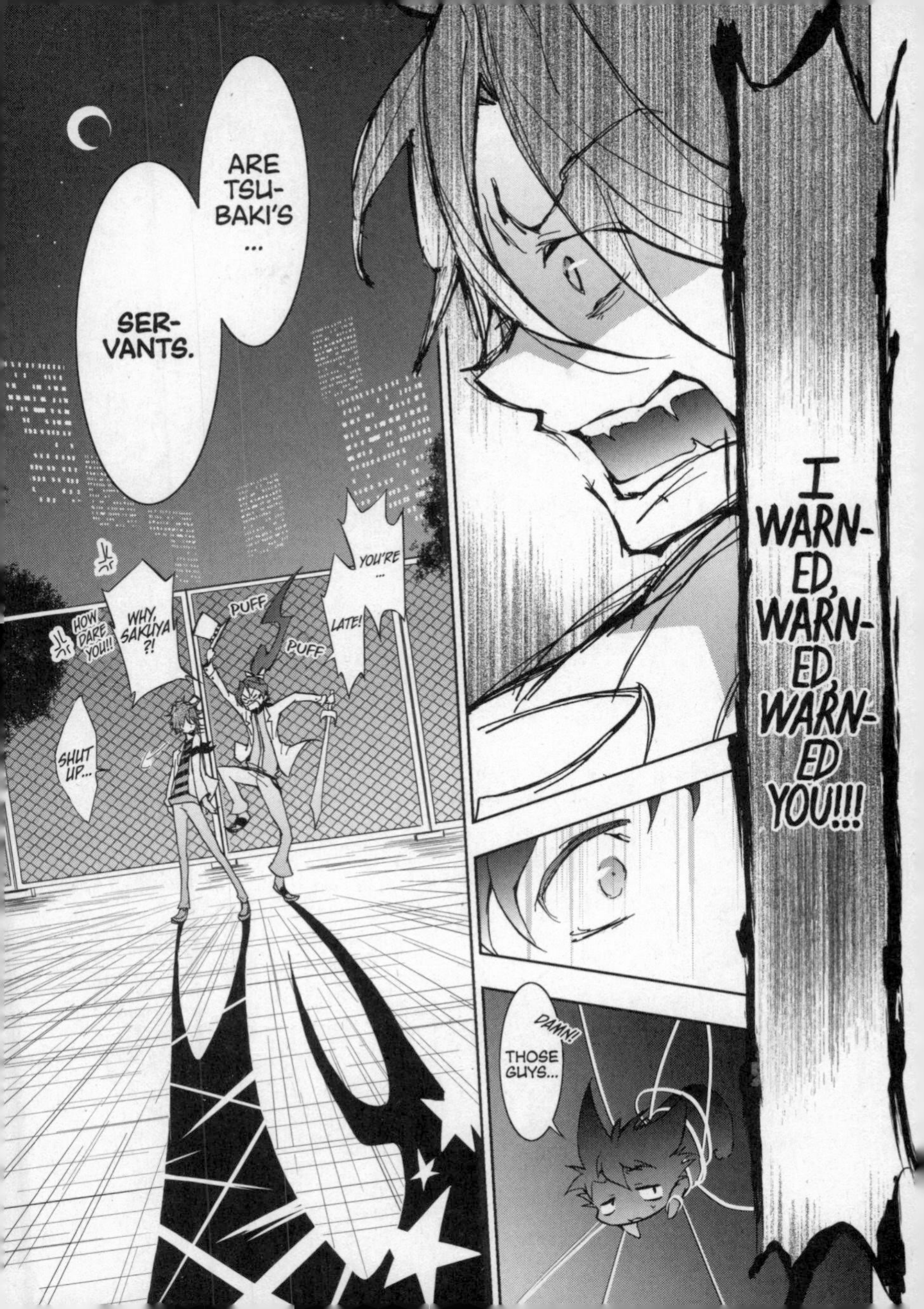
I WARNED, WARNED, WARNED YOU!!!
DAMN! THOSE GUYS...
ARE TSUBAKI'S ... SERVANTS.
YOU'RE ... LATE!
PUFF
PUFF
WHY, SAKUYA?!
HOW DARE YOU!!
SHUT UP...

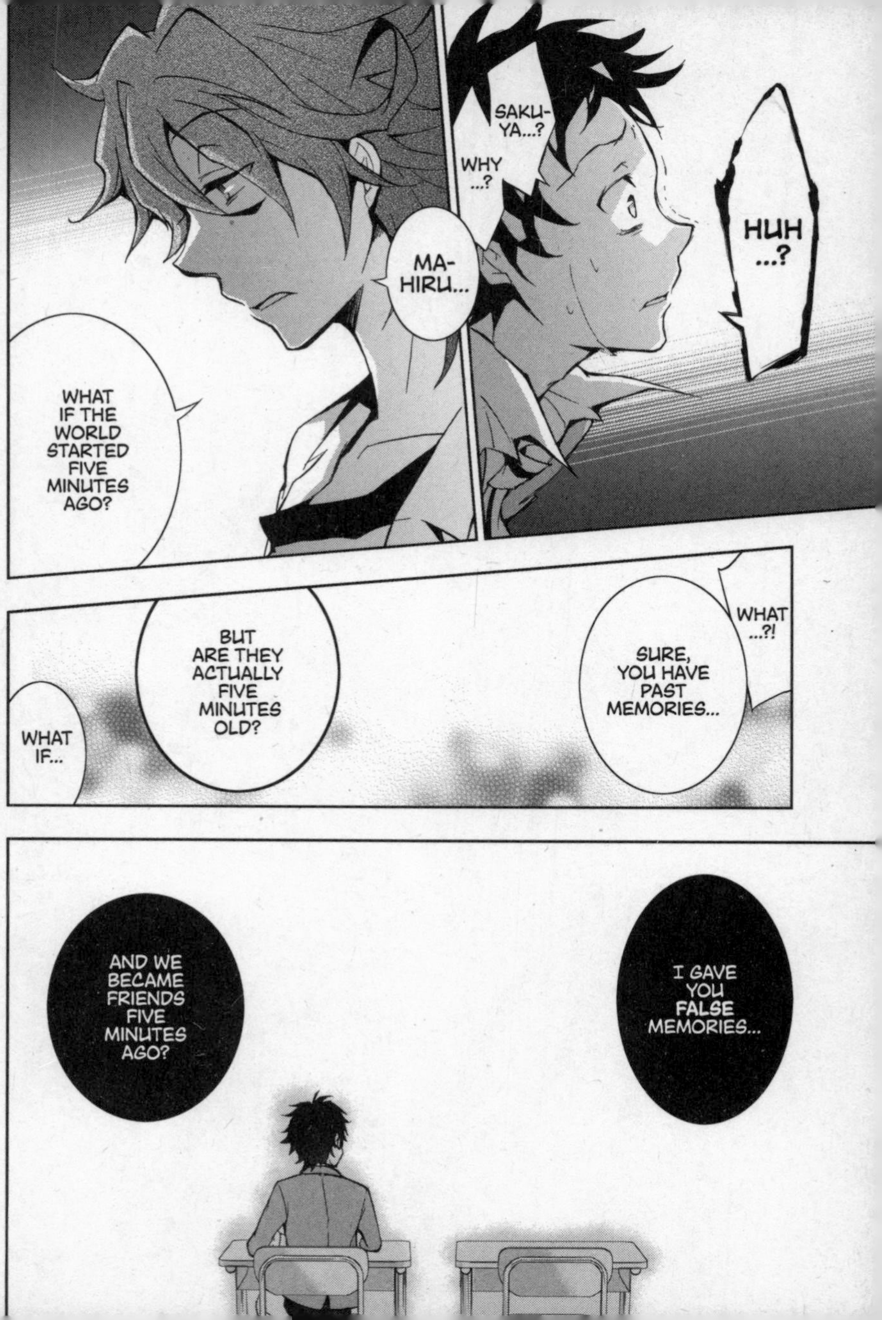
HUH ...?
SAKU-YA...?
WHY ...?
MA-HIRU...
WHAT IF THE WORLD STARTED FIVE MINUTES AGO?
WHAT ...?!
SURE, YOU HAVE PAST MEMORIES...
BUT ARE THEY ACTUALLY FIVE MINUTES OLD?
WHAT IF...
I GAVE YOU FALSE MEMORIES...
AND WE BECAME FRIENDS FIVE MINUTES AGO?

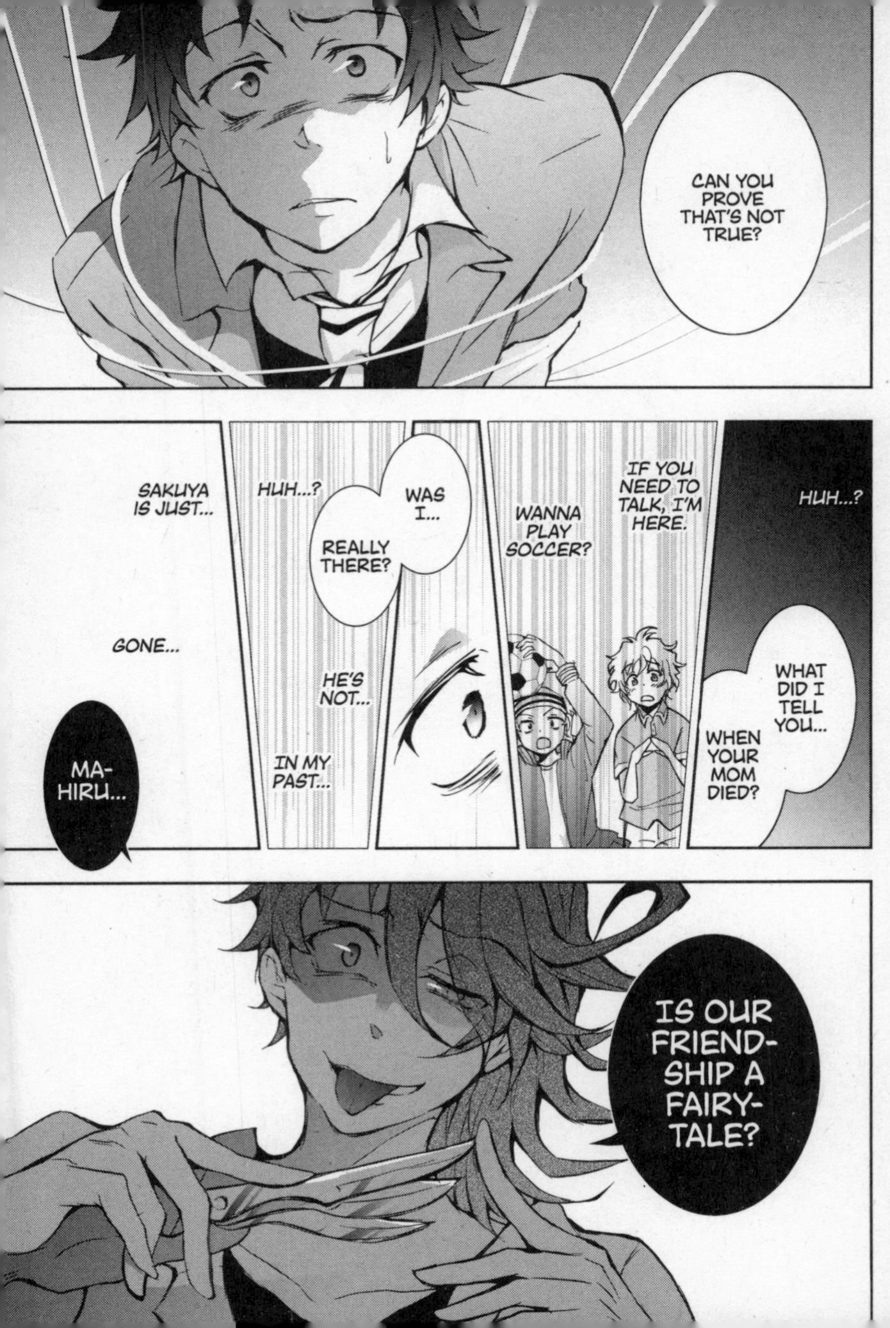
CAN YOU PROVE THAT'S NOT TRUE?
HUH...?
WHAT DID I TELL YOU... WHEN YOUR MOM DIED?
IF YOU NEED TO TALK, I'M HERE.
WANNA PLAY SOCCER?
WAS I... REALLY THERE?
HUH...?
HE'S NOT... IN MY PAST...
SAKUYA IS JUST... GONE...
MA-HIRU...
IS OUR FRIEND-SHIP A FAIRY-TALE?

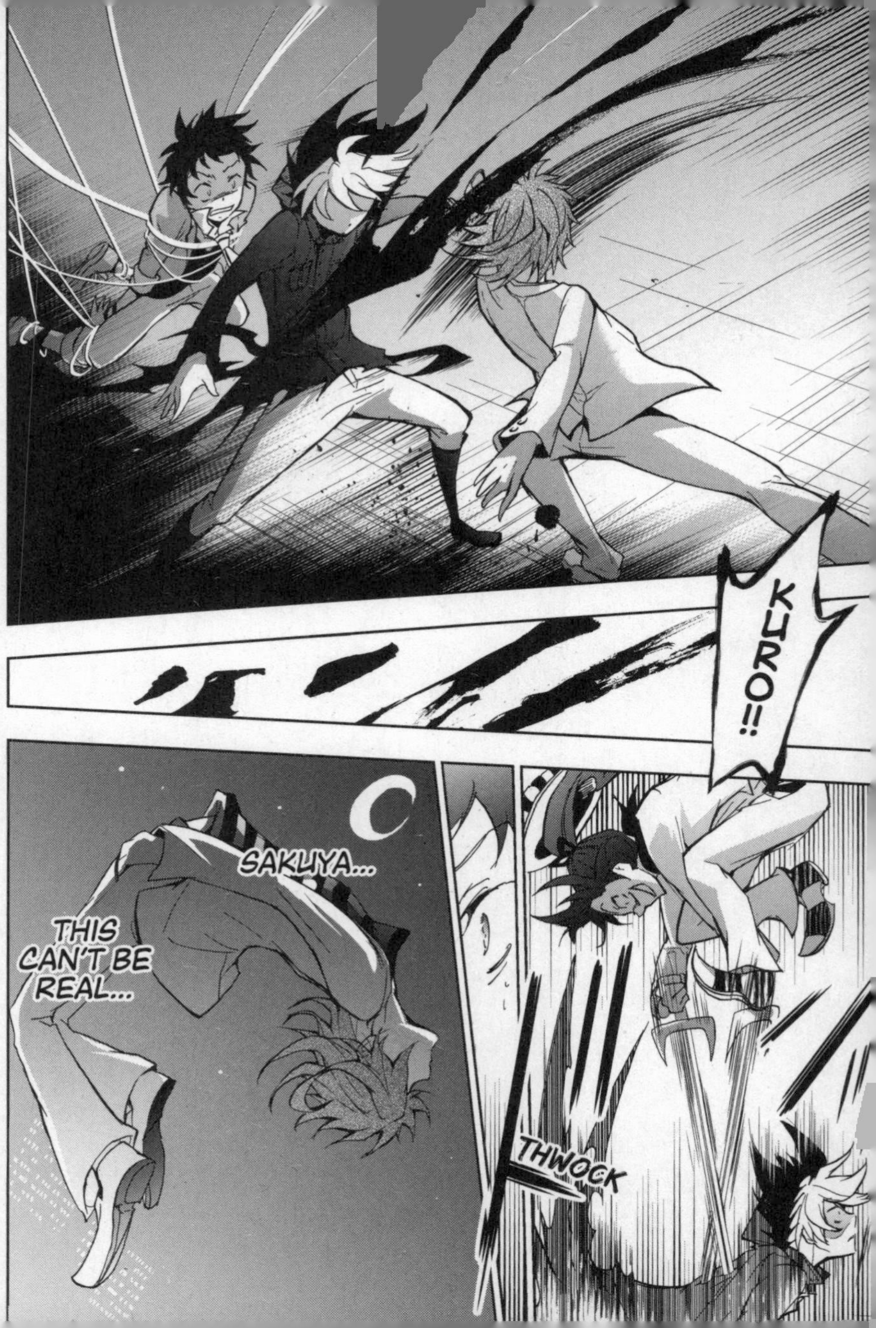
KURO!!
THWOCK
SAKUYA...
THIS CAN'T BE REAL...

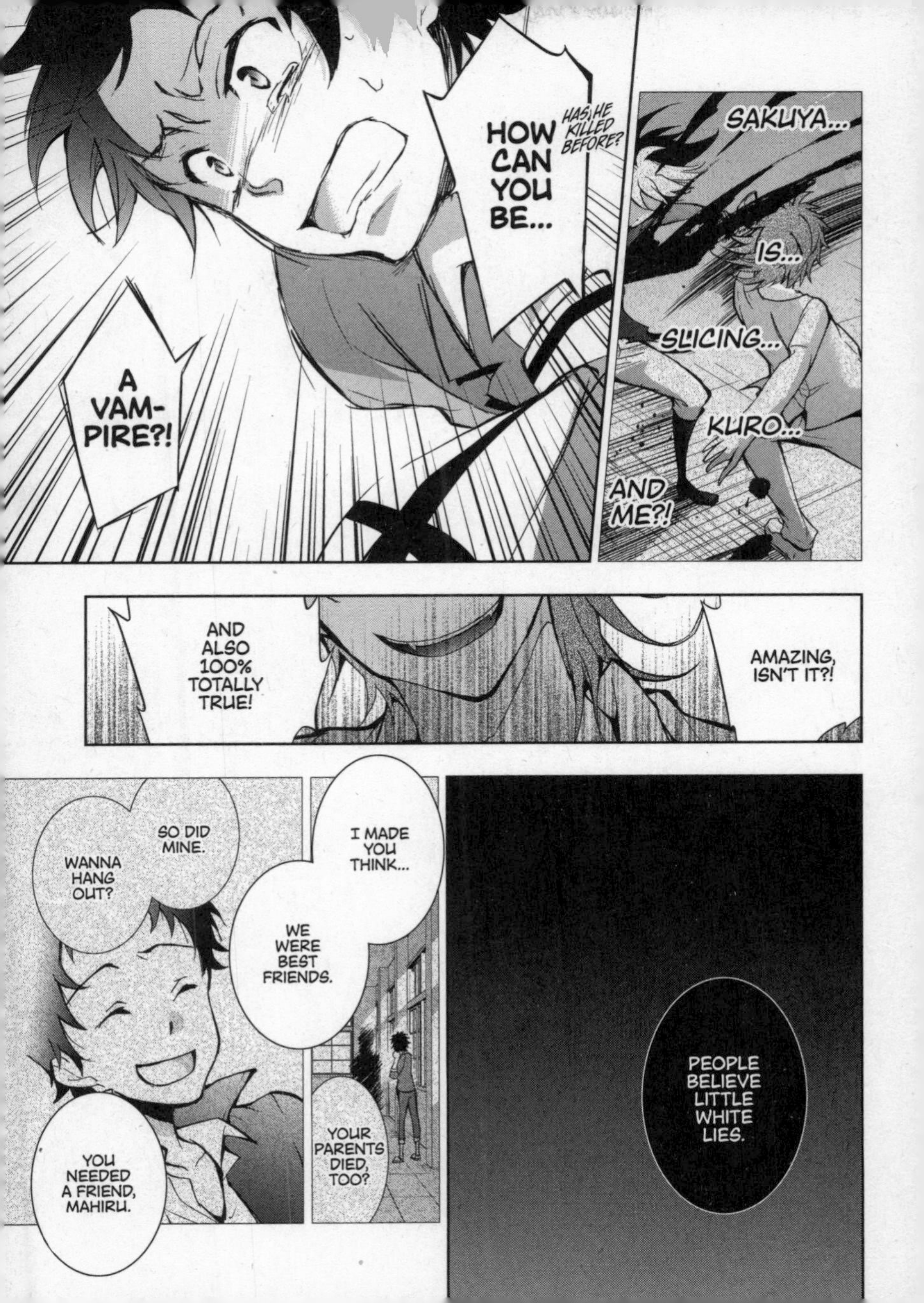
SAKUYA...
IS...
SLICING...
KURO...
AND ME?!
HAS HE KILLED BEFORE?
HOW CAN YOU BE...
A VAMPIRE?!
AMAZING, ISN'T IT?!
AND ALSO 100% TOTALLY TRUE!
PEOPLE BELIEVE LITTLE WHITE LIES.
I MADE YOU THINK...
WE WERE BEST FRIENDS.
YOUR PARENTS DIED, TOO?
SO DID MINE.
WANNA HANG OUT?
YOU NEEDED A FRIEND, MAHIRU.

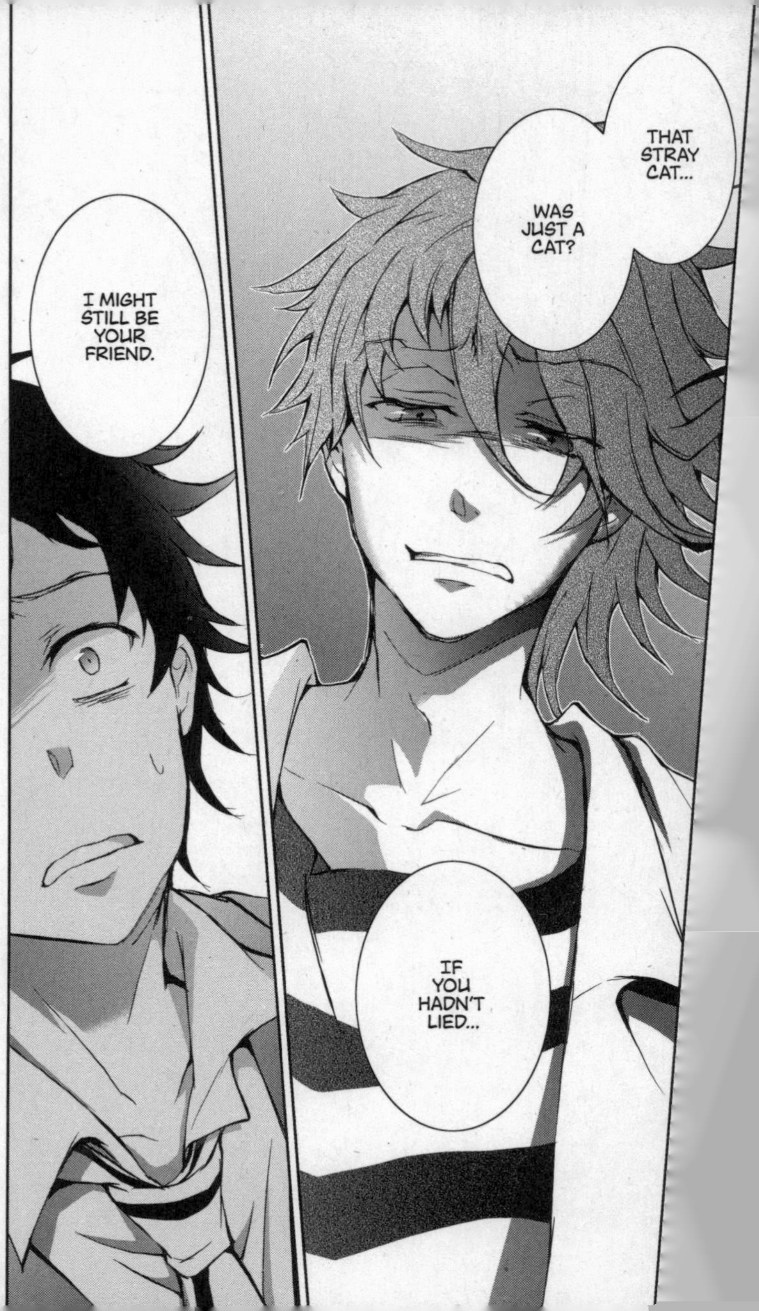
THAT STRAY CAT...
WAS JUST A CAT?
IF YOU HADN'T LIED...
I MIGHT STILL BE YOUR FRIEND.

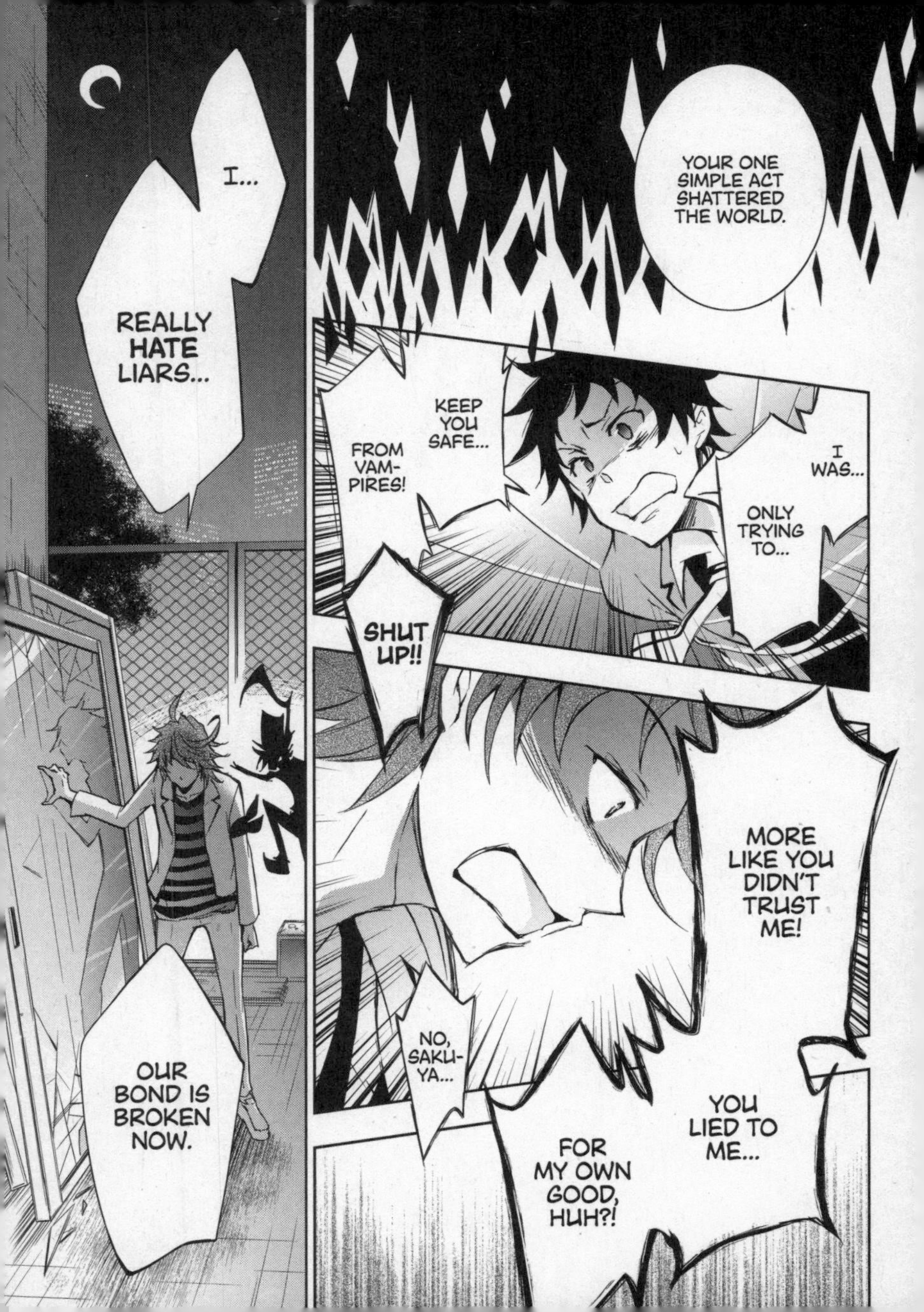
YOUR ONE SIMPLE ACT SHATTERED THE WORLD.
I WAS...
ONLY TRYING TO...
KEEP YOU SAFE...
FROM VAM-PIRES!
SHUT UP!!
MORE LIKE YOU DIDN'T TRUST ME!
NO, SAKU-YA...
YOU LIED TO ME...
FOR MY OWN GOOD, HUH?!
I...
REALLY HATE LIARS...
OUR BOND IS BROKEN NOW.

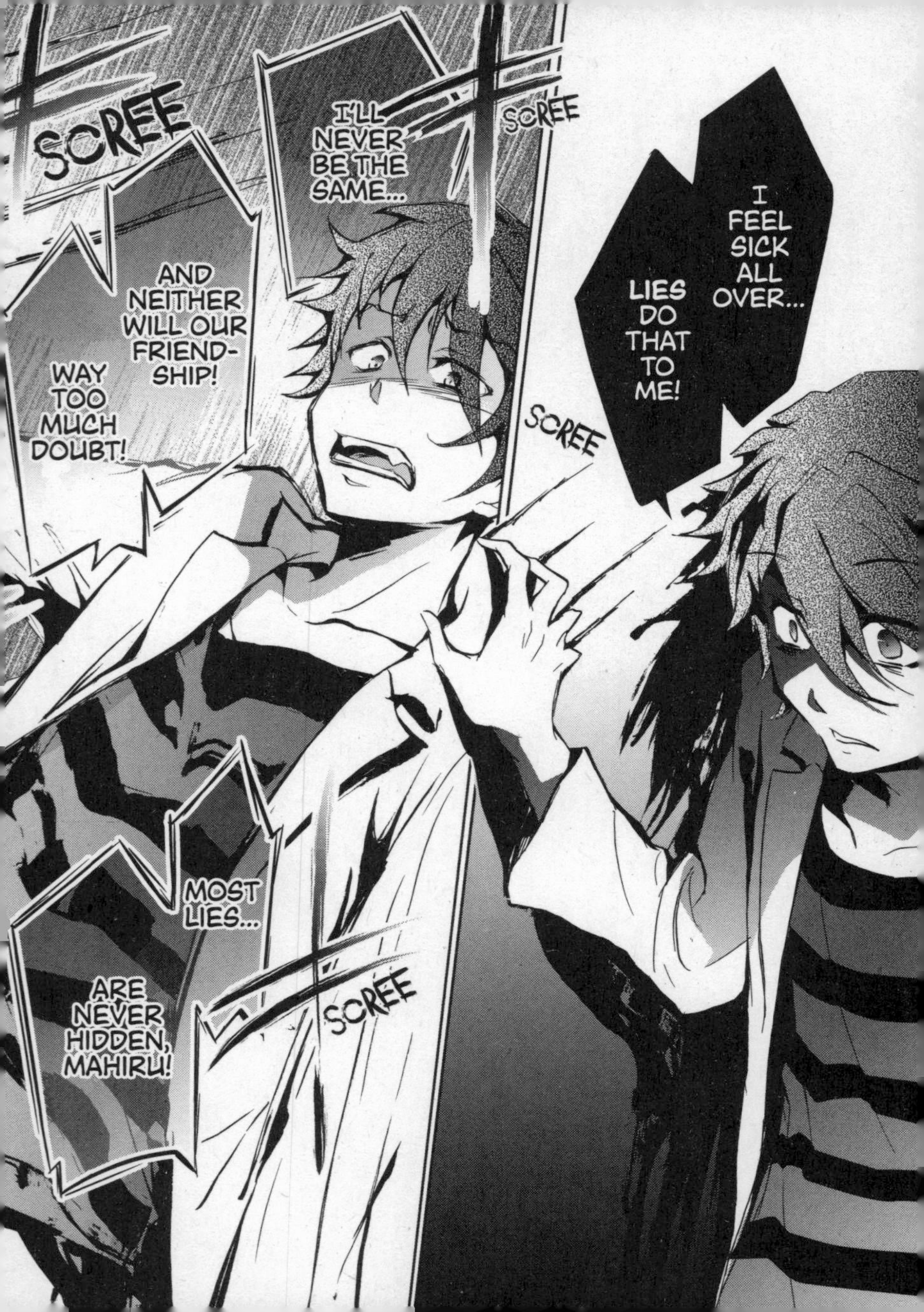
SCREE
I FEEL SICK ALL OVER...
LIES DO THAT TO ME!
I'LL NEVER BE THE SAME...
SCREE
AND NEITHER WILL OUR FRIEND-SHIP!
WAY TOO MUCH DOUBT!
SCREE
MOST LIES...
SCREE
ARE NEVER HIDDEN, MAHIRU!

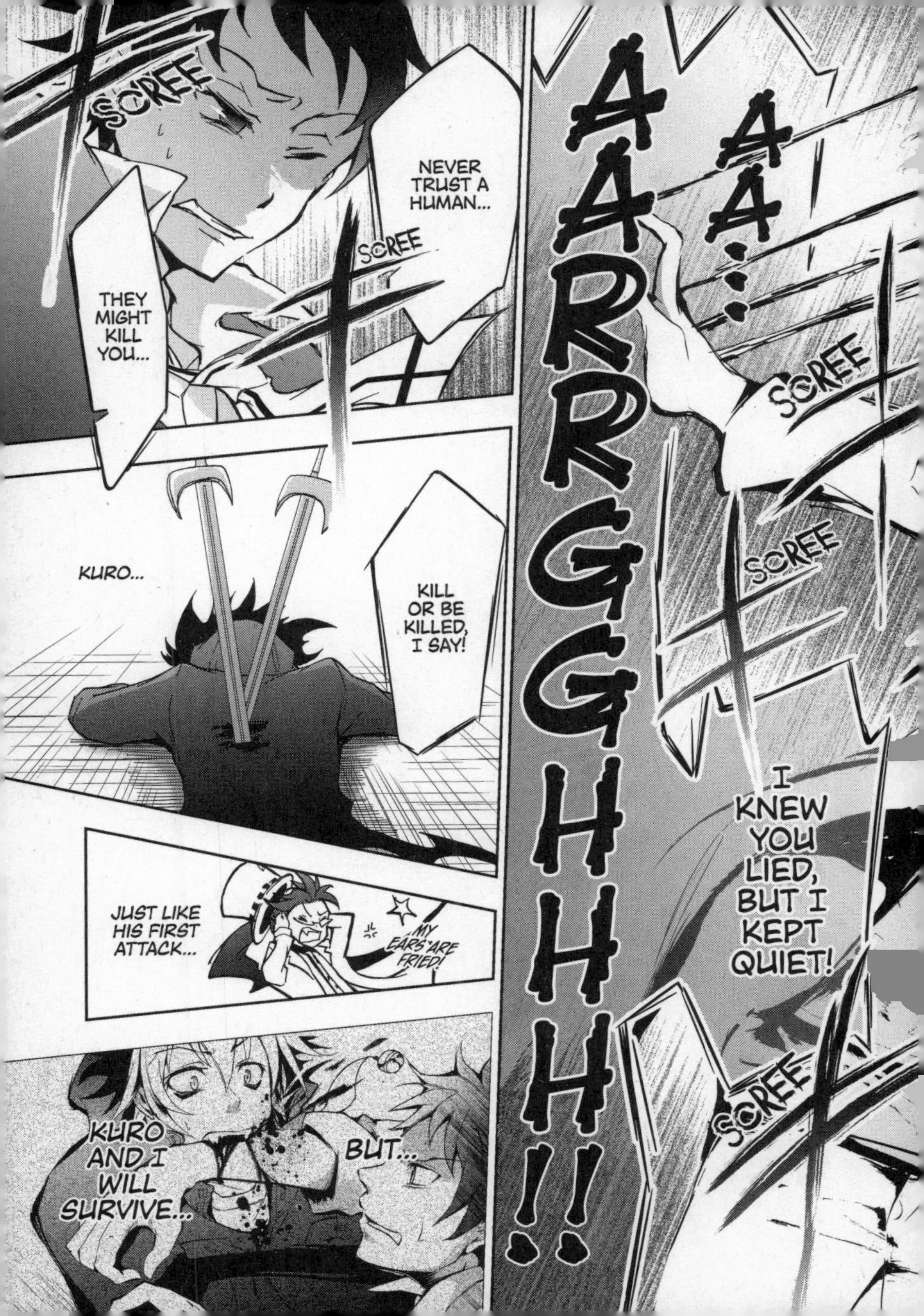
AA...
AARRGGHHH!!
SCREE
SCREE
I KNEW YOU LIED, BUT I KEPT QUIET!
SCREE
SCREE
NEVER TRUST A HUMAN...
THEY MIGHT KILL YOU...
SCREE
KILL OR BE KILLED, I SAY!
KURO...
MY EARS ARE FRIED!
JUST LIKE HIS FIRST ATTACK...
BUT...
KURO AND I WILL SURVIVE...

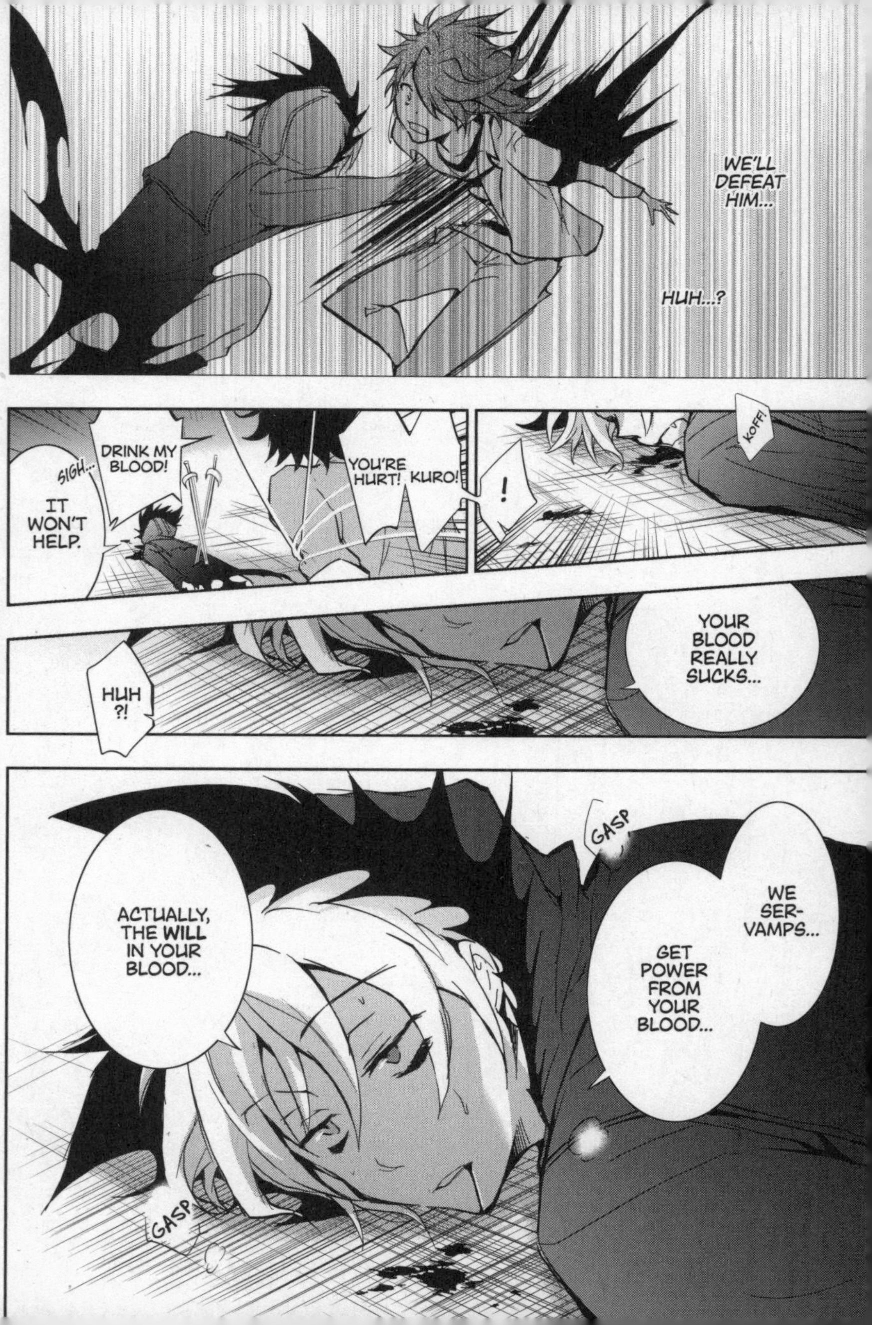
WE'LL DEFEAT HIM...
HUH...?
KOFF!
!
YOU'RE HURT! KURO!
DRINK MY BLOOD!
SIGH...
IT WON'T HELP.
YOUR BLOOD REALLY SUCKS...
HUH ?!
GASP
WE SER-VAMPS...
GET POWER FROM YOUR BLOOD...
ACTUALLY, THE WILL IN YOUR BLOOD...
GASP

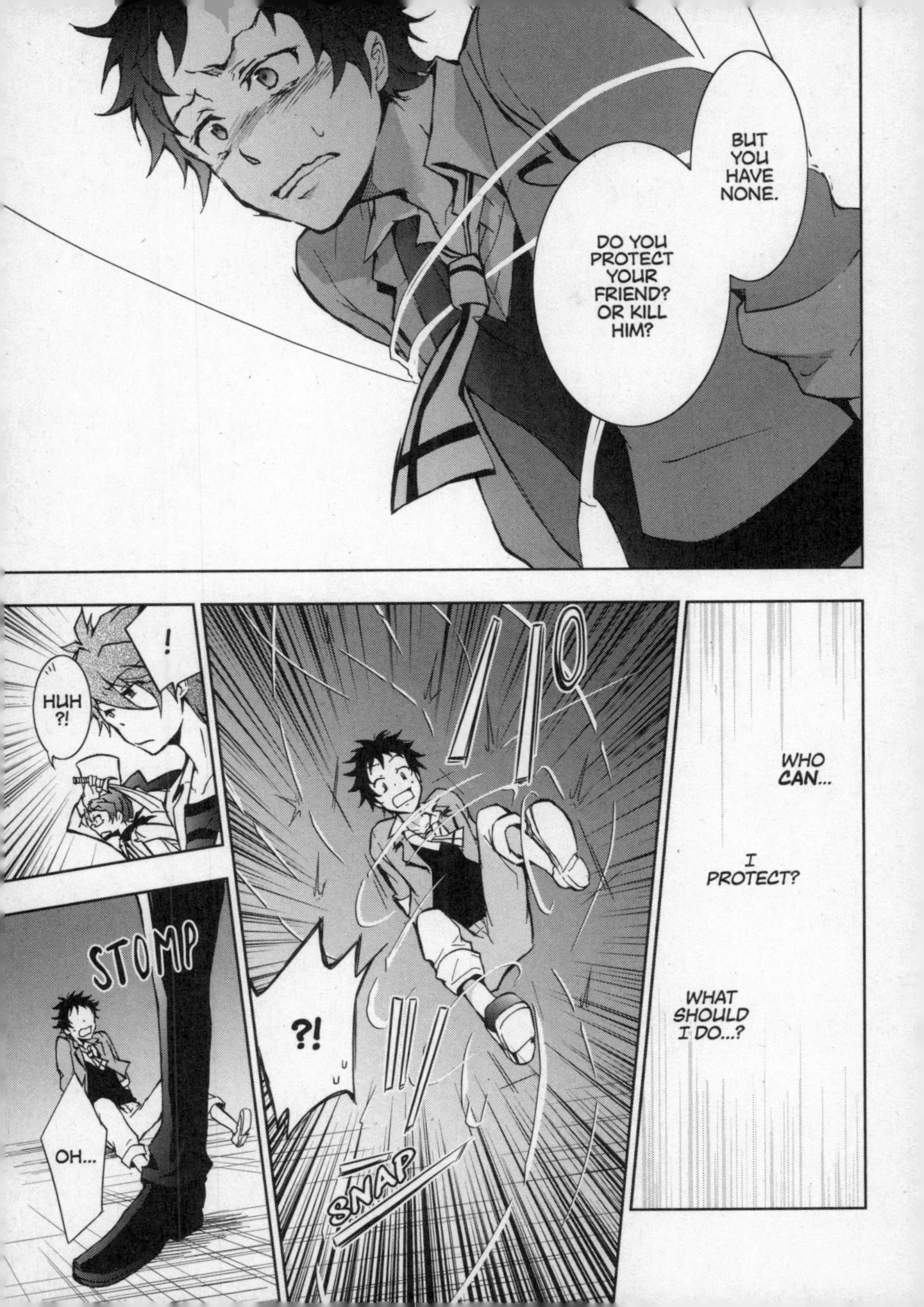
BUT YOU HAVE NONE.
DO YOU PROTECT YOUR FRIEND? OR KILL HIM?
WHO CAN...
I PROTECT?
WHAT SHOULD I DO...?
?!
SNAP
!
HUH?!
STOMP
OH...

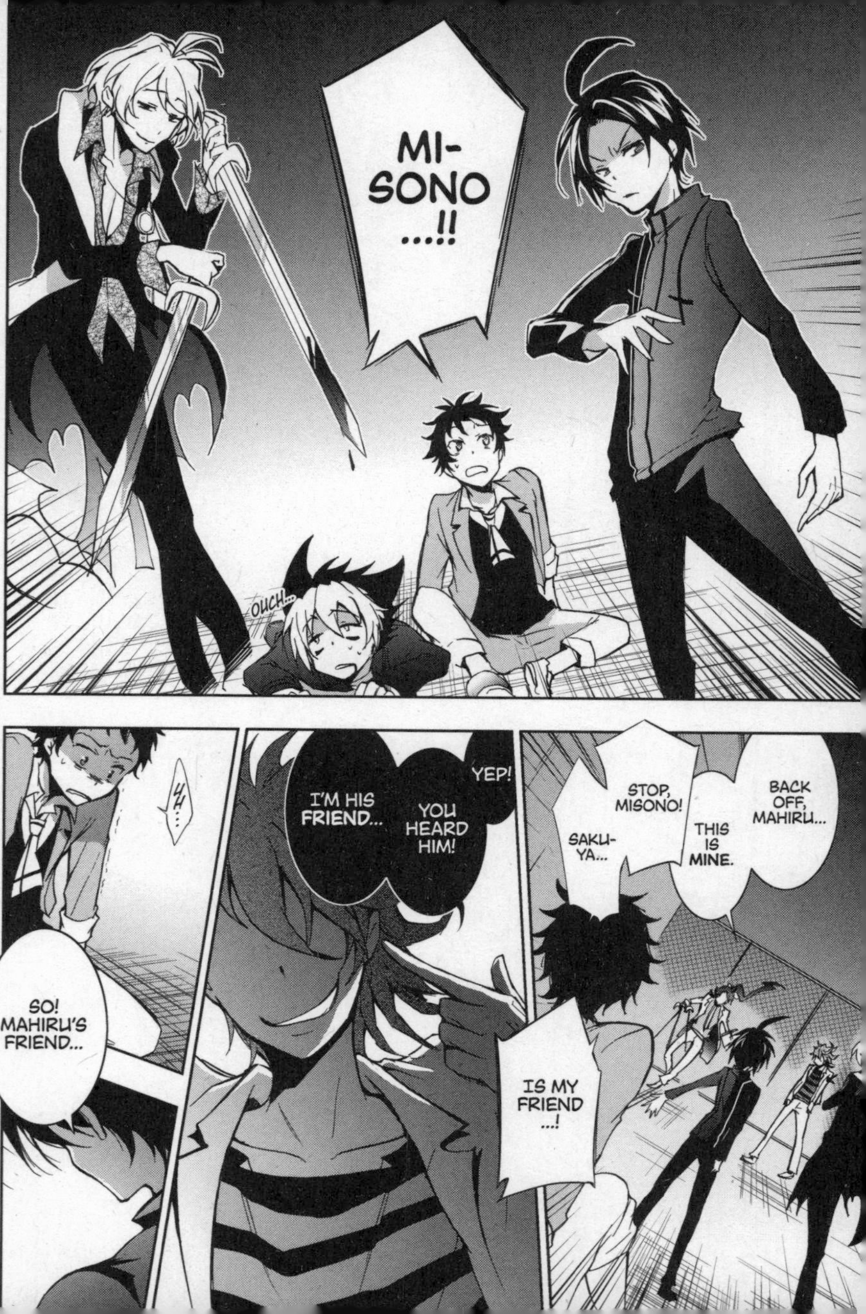
MI-SONO ...!!
OUCH...
BACK OFF, MAHIRU...
THIS IS MINE.
STOP, MISONO!
SAKU-YA...
IS MY FRIEND ...!
YEP!
YOU HEARD HIM!
I'M HIS FRIEND...
UH...
SO! MAHIRU'S FRIEND...

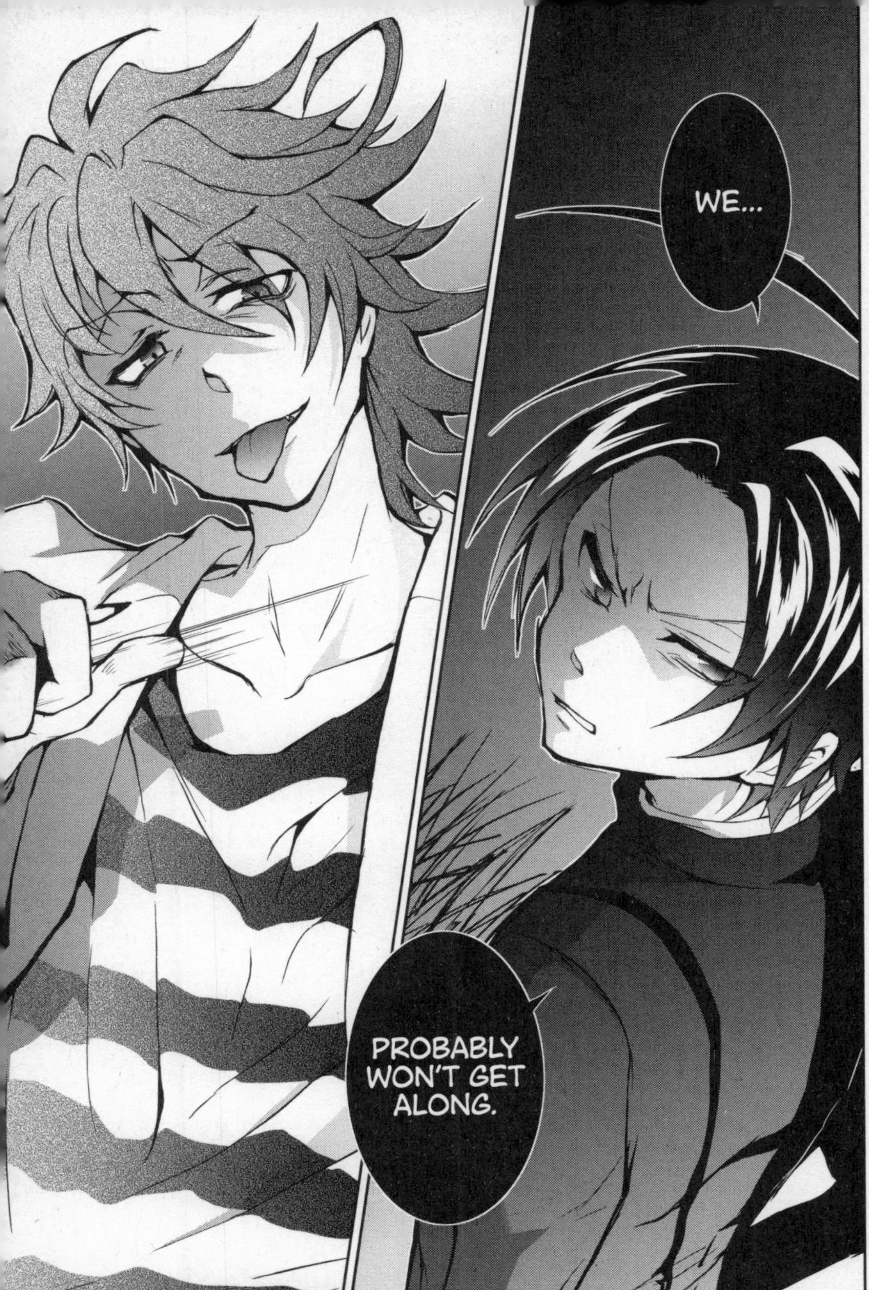
WE...
PROBABLY WON'T GET ALONG.

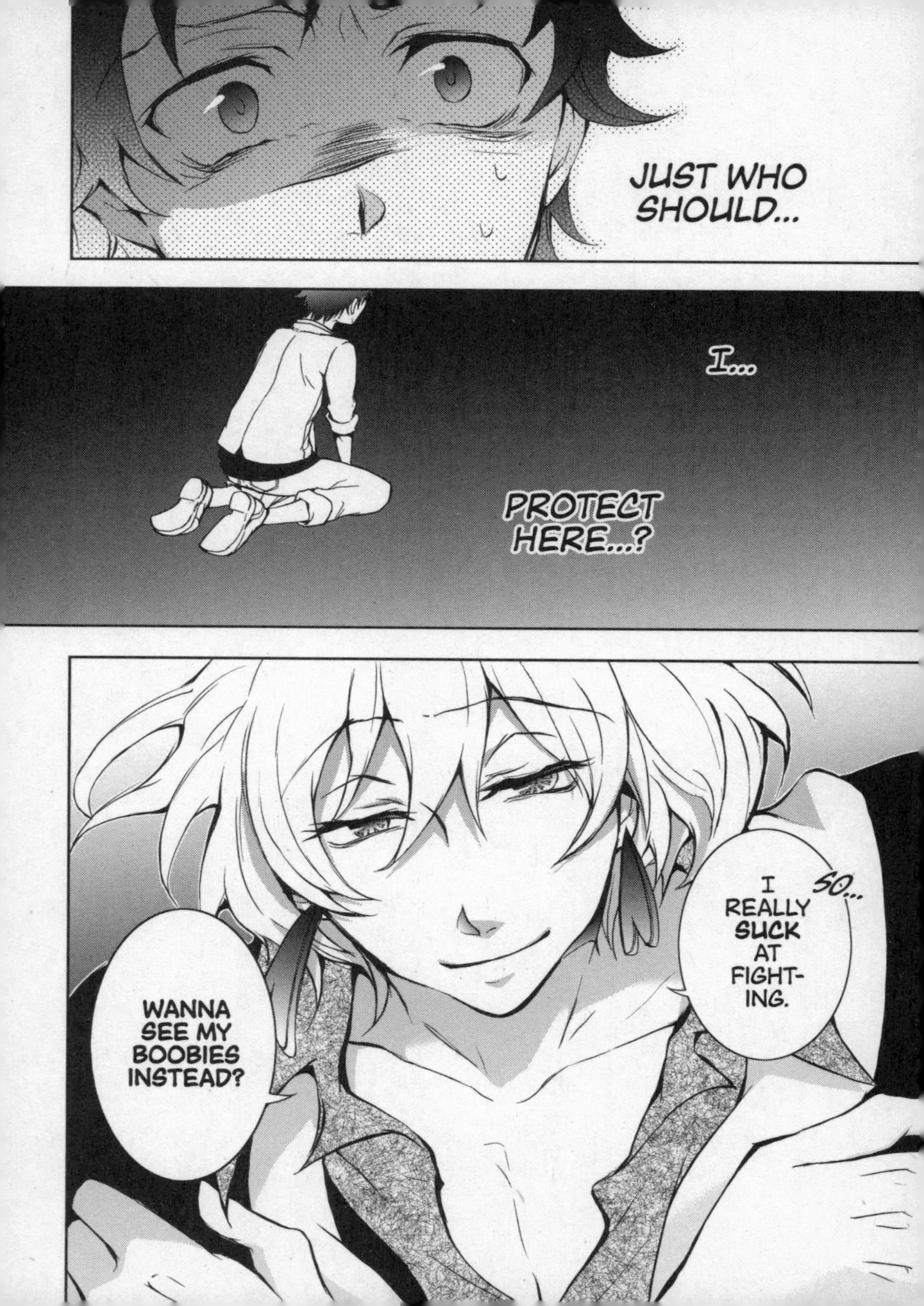
JUST WHO SHOULD...
I...
PROTECT HERE...?
SO...
I REALLY SUCK AT FIGHT-ING.
WANNA SEE MY BOOBIES INSTEAD?

07 THE LOST FUTURE

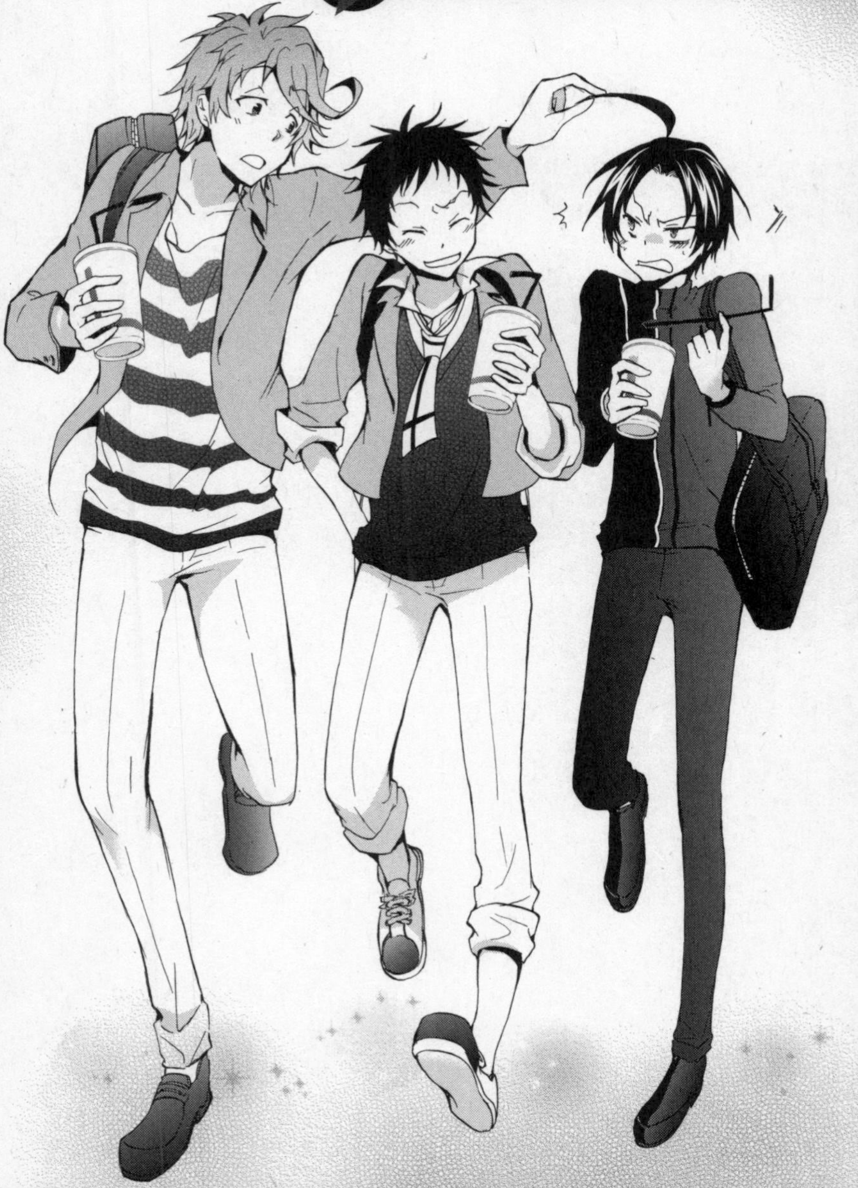

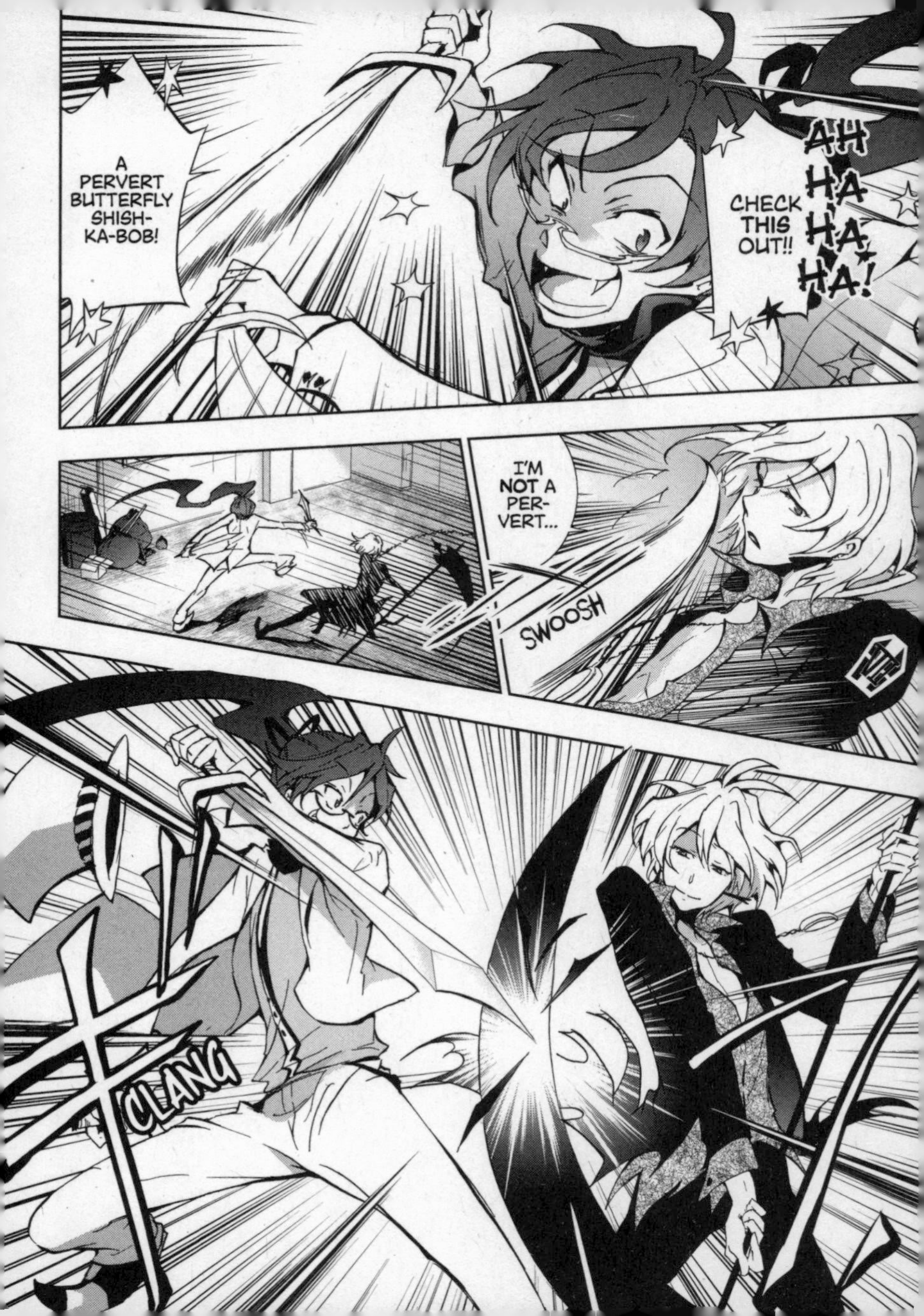
AH HA HA HA HA!
CHECK THIS OUT!!
A PERVERT BUTTERFLY SHISH-KA-BOB!
I'M NOT A PER-VERT...
SWOOSH
CLANG

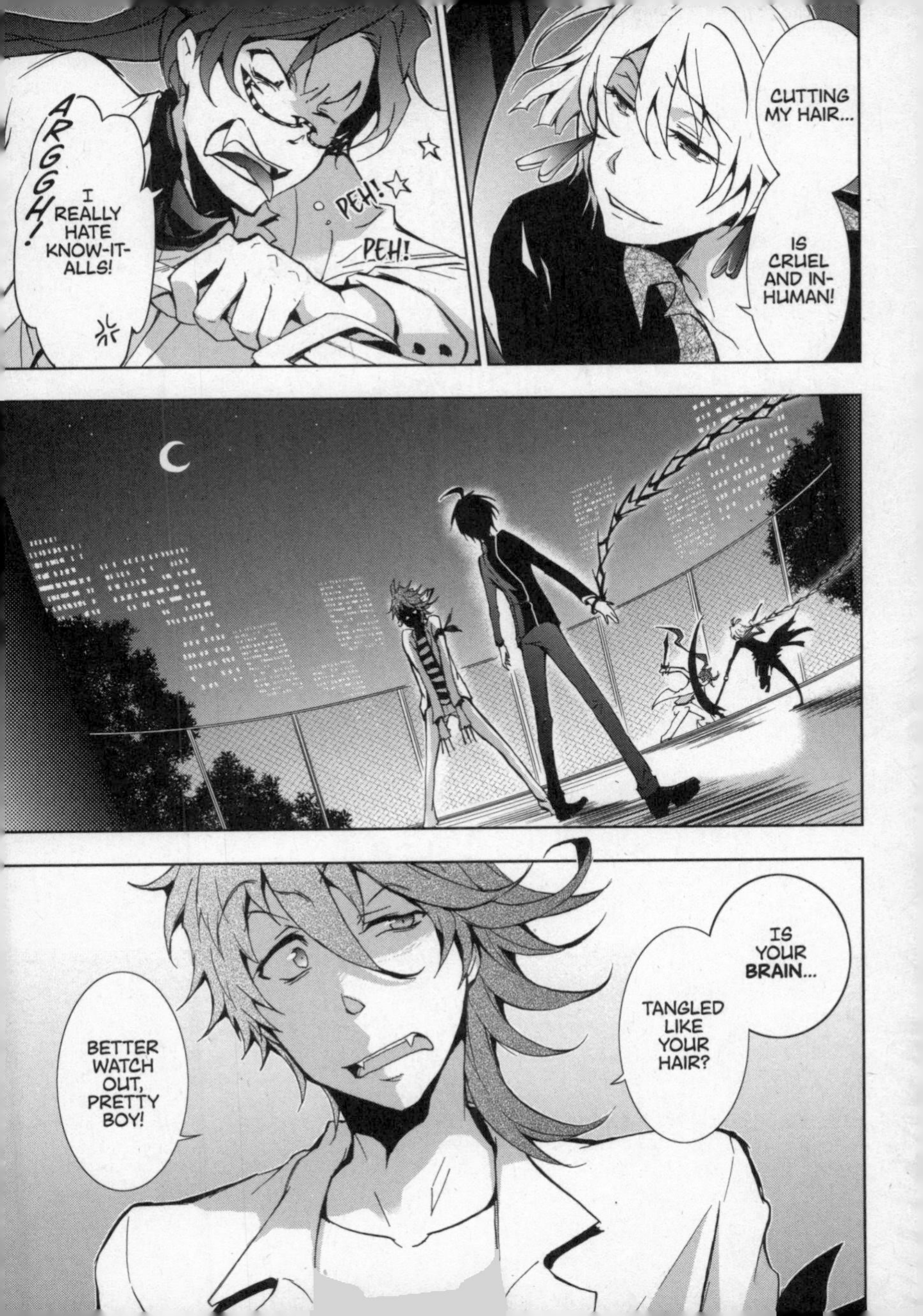
CUTTING MY HAIR...
IS CRUEL AND IN-HUMAN!
ARGGH!
I REALLY HATE KNOW-IT-ALLS!
PEH!
PEH!
IS YOUR BRAIN...
TANGLED LIKE YOUR HAIR?
BETTER WATCH OUT, PRETTY BOY!

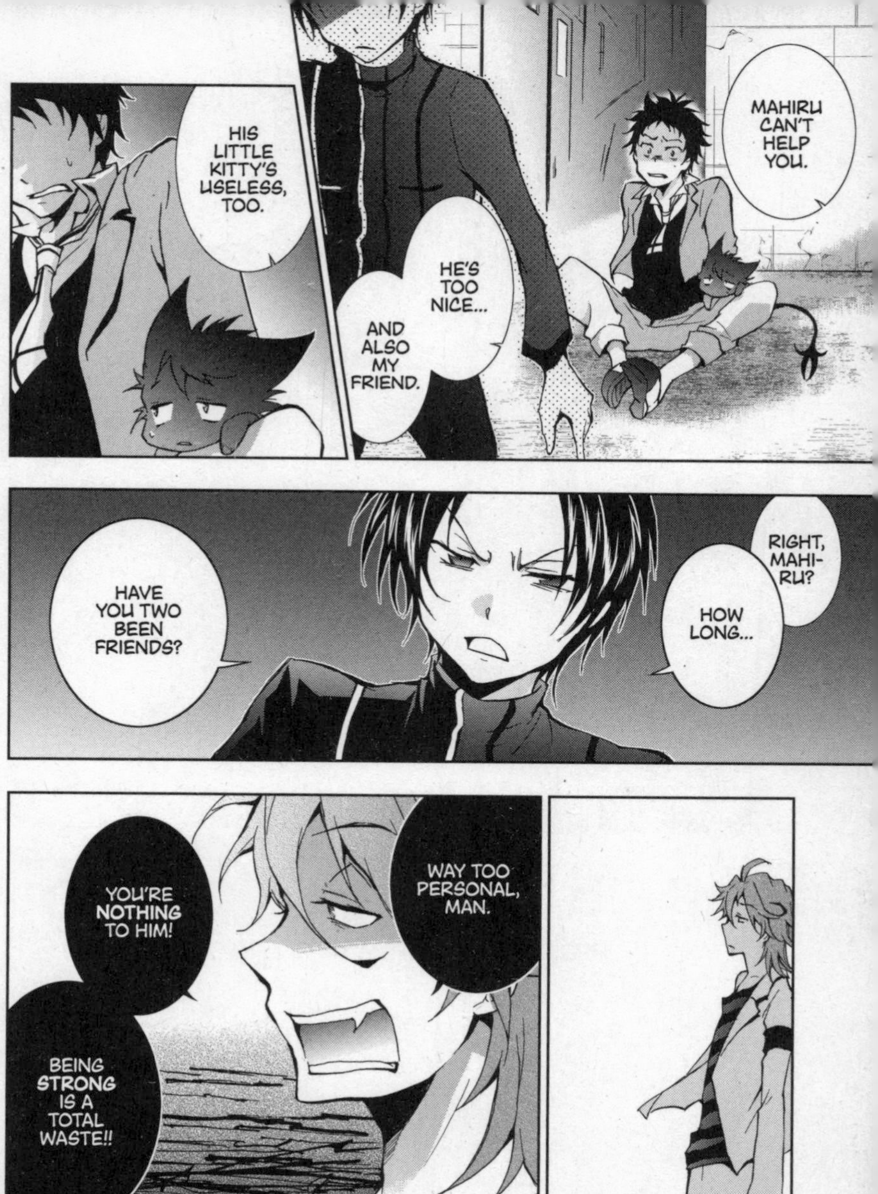
MAHIRU CAN'T HELP YOU.
HE'S TOO NICE...
AND ALSO MY FRIEND.
HIS LITTLE KITTY'S USELESS, TOO.
RIGHT, MAHIRU?
HOW LONG...
HAVE YOU TWO BEEN FRIENDS?
WAY TOO PERSONAL, MAN.
YOU'RE **NOTHING** TO HIM!
BEING **STRONG** IS A TOTAL WASTE!!

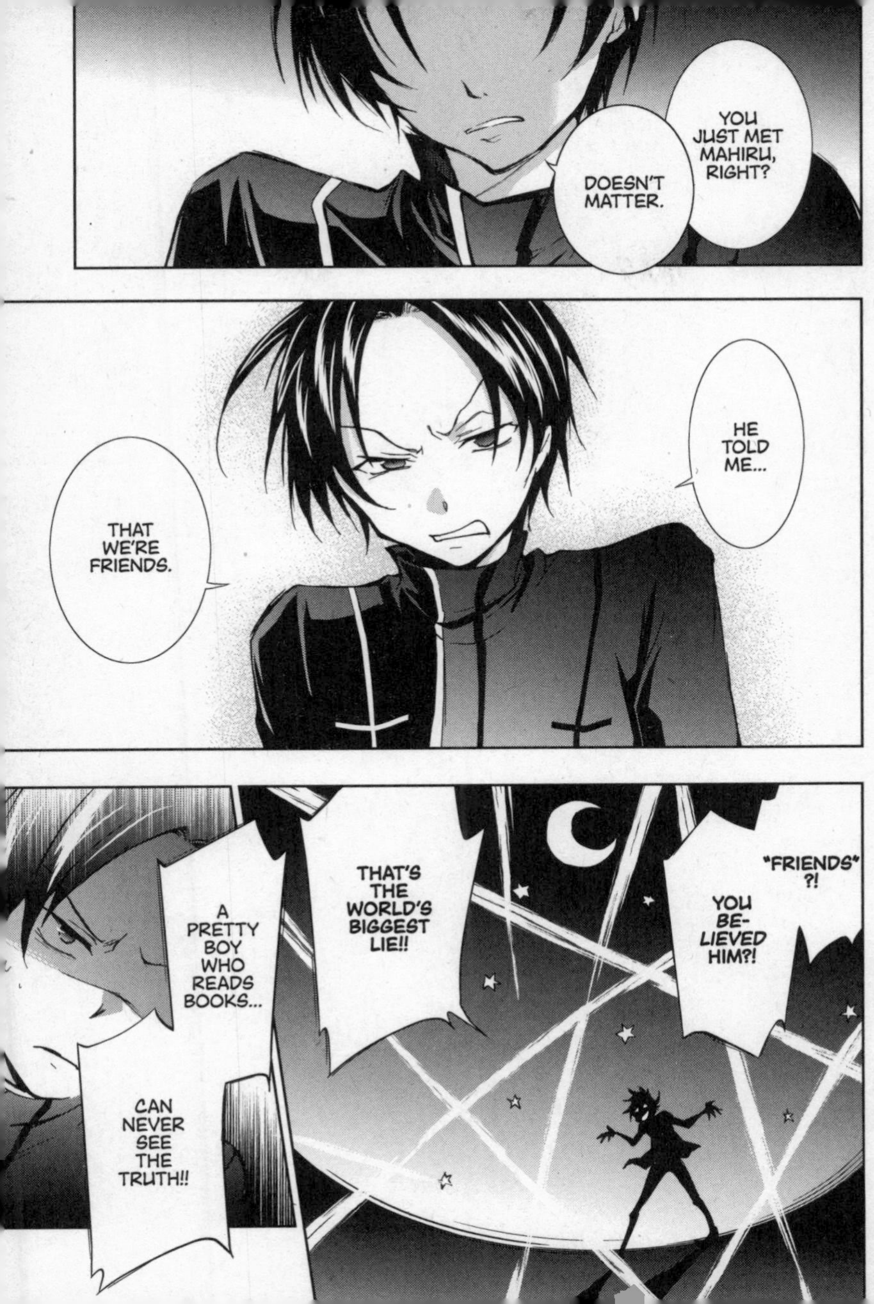
YOU JUST MET MAHIRU, RIGHT?
DOESN'T MATTER.
HE TOLD ME...
THAT WE'RE FRIENDS.
"FRIENDS" ?!
YOU BE-LIEVED HIM?!
THAT'S THE WORLD'S BIGGEST LIE!!
A PRETTY BOY WHO READS BOOKS...
CAN NEVER SEE THE TRUTH!!

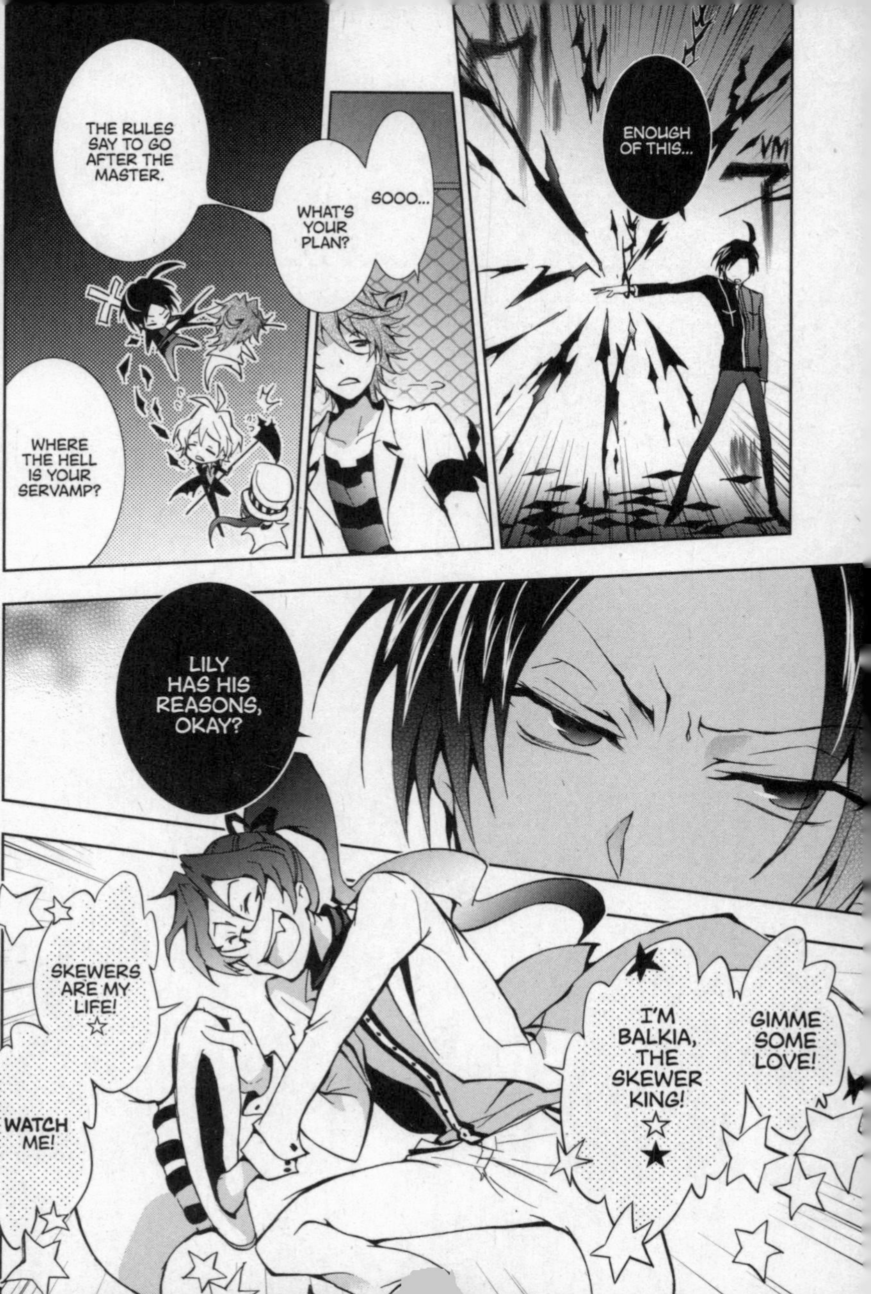
ENOUGH OF THIS...
SOOO...
WHAT'S YOUR PLAN?
THE RULES SAY TO GO AFTER THE MASTER.
WHERE THE HELL IS YOUR SERVAMP?
LILY HAS HIS REASONS, OKAY?
GIMME SOME LOVE!
I'M BALKIA, THE SKEWER KING!
SKEWERS ARE MY LIFE!
WATCH ME!

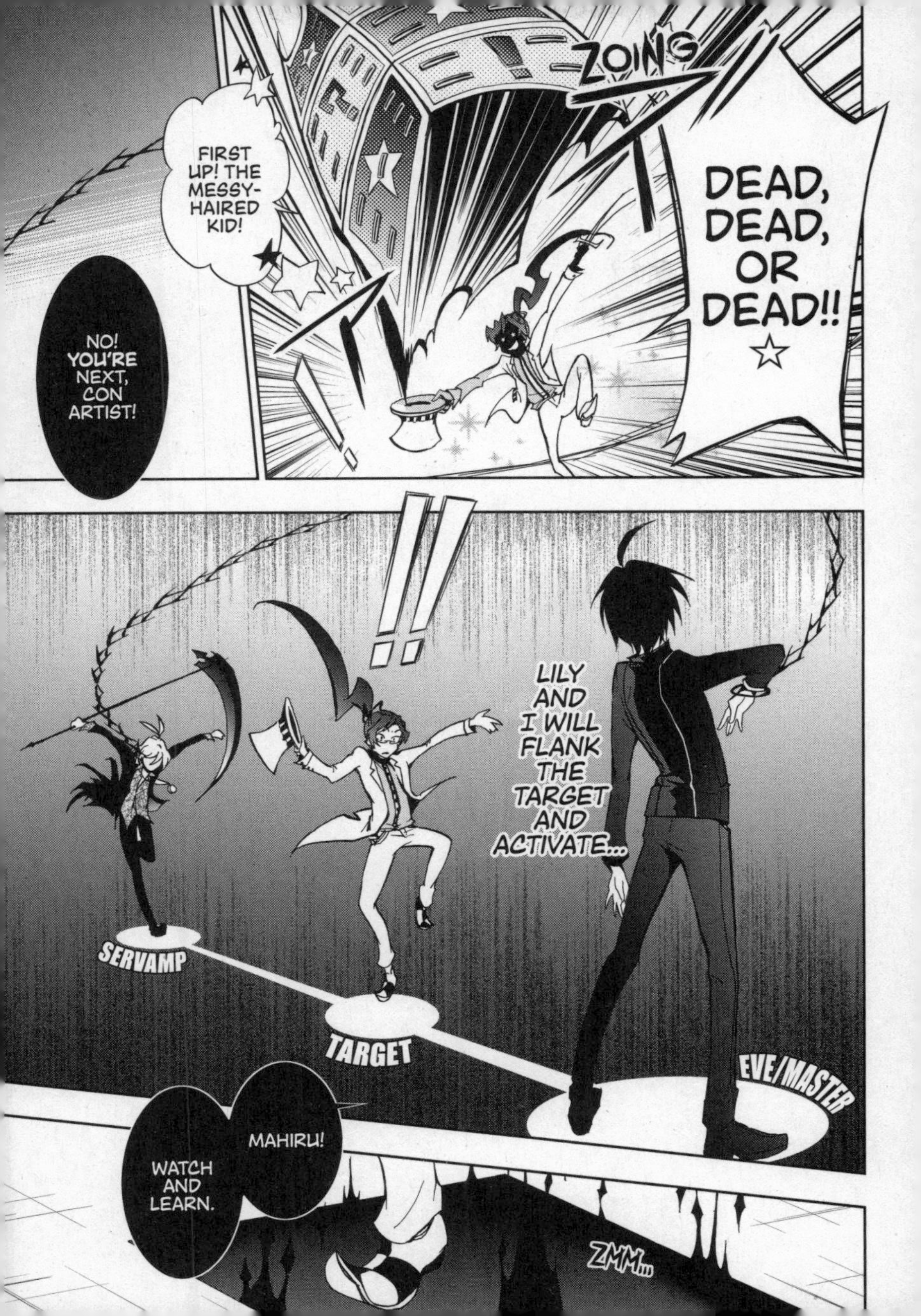
ZOING
DEAD, DEAD, OR DEAD!! ☆
FIRST UP! THE MESSY-HAIRED KID!
NO! YOU'RE NEXT, CON ARTIST!
!!
LILY AND I WILL FLANK THE TARGET AND ACTIVATE...
EVE/MASTER
TARGET
SERVAMP
MAHIRU!
WATCH AND LEARN.
ZMM...

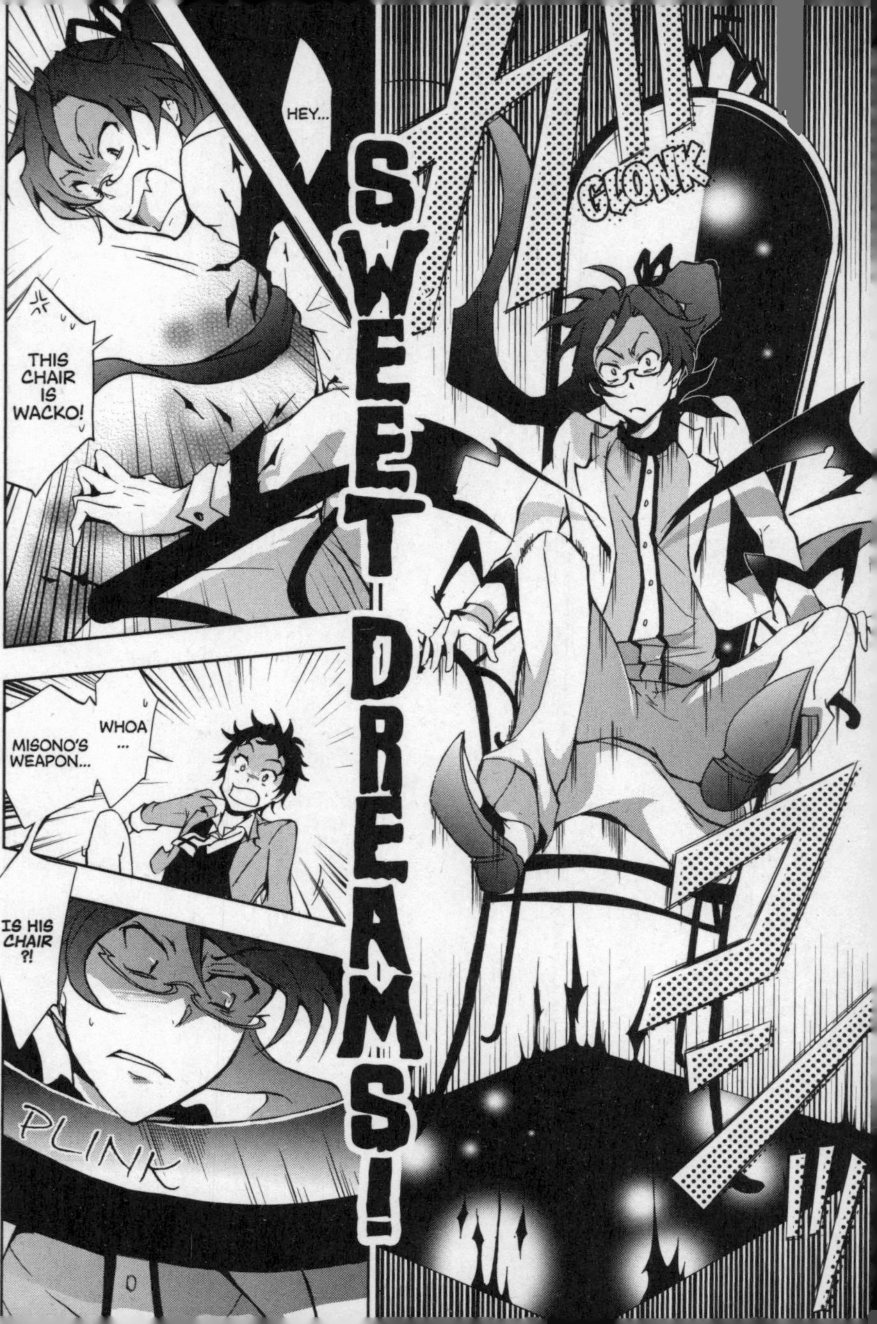
GLONK
SWEET DREAMS!
HEY...
THIS CHAIR IS WACKO!
WHOA...
MISONO'S WEAPON...
IS HIS CHAIR?!
PLINK

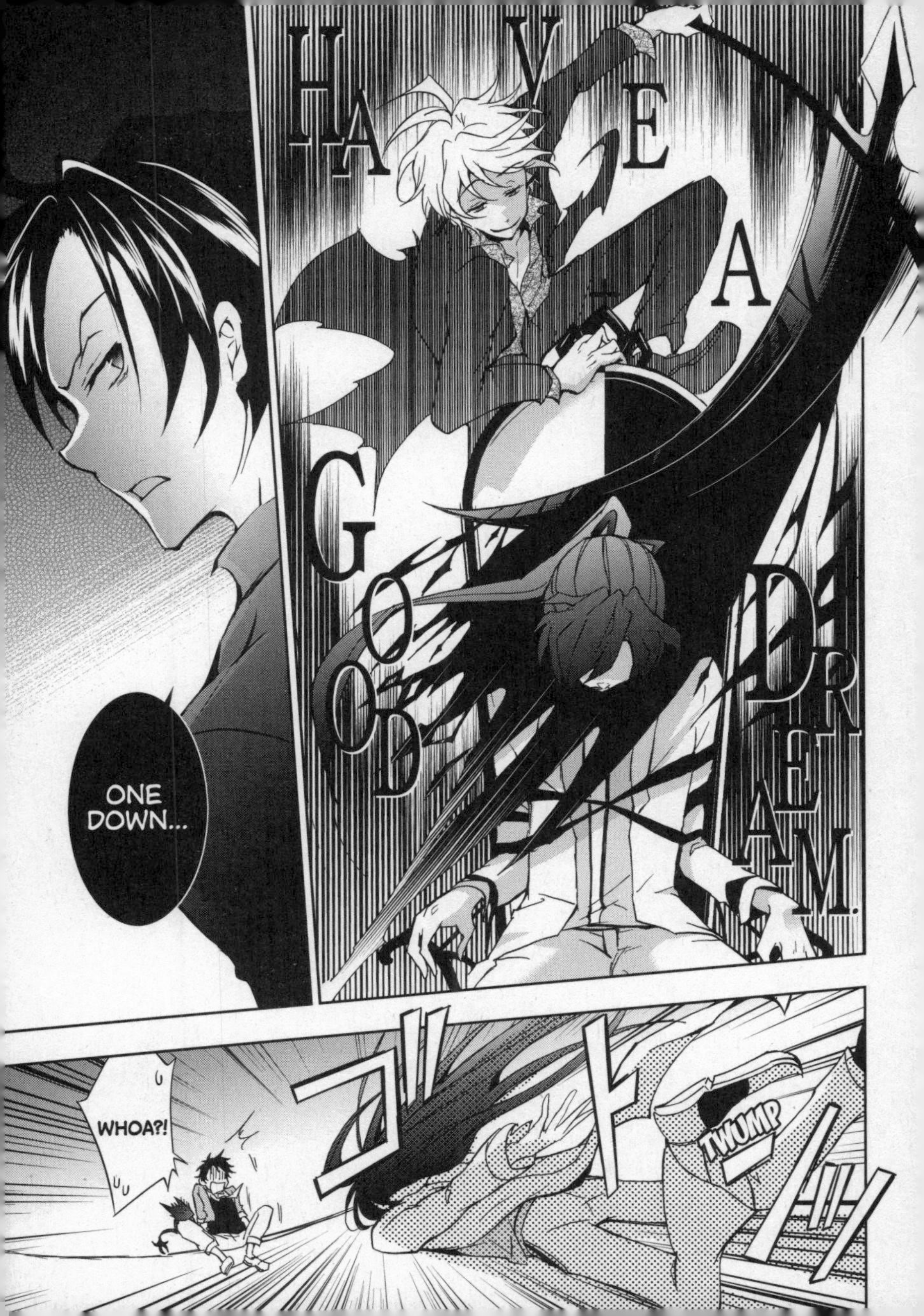
HAVE A GOOD DREAM.
ONE DOWN...
TWUMP
WHOA?!

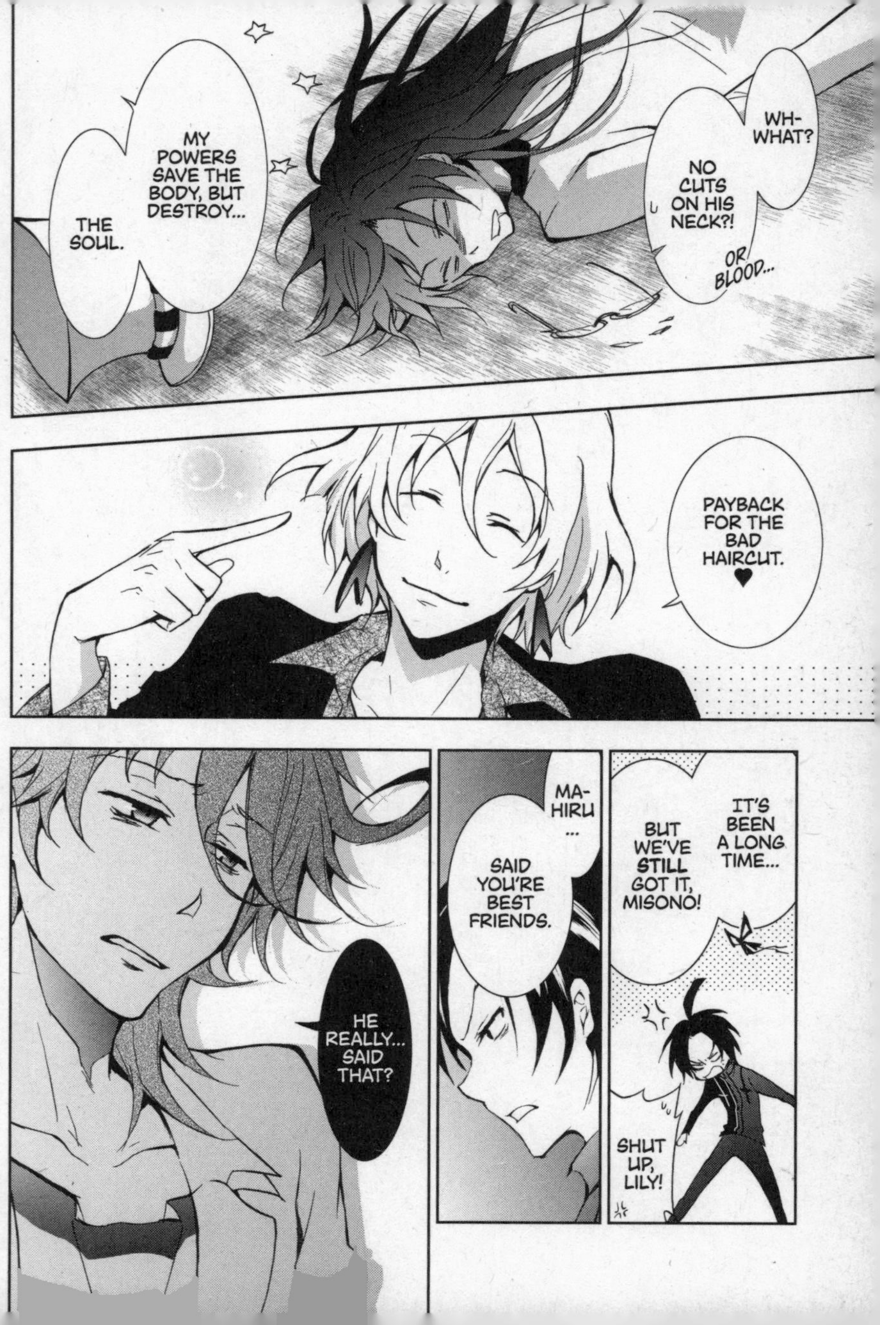
WH- WHAT?
NO CUTS ON HIS NECK?!
OR BLOOD...
MY POWERS SAVE THE BODY, BUT DESTROY...
THE SOUL.
PAYBACK FOR THE BAD HAIRCUT. ♥
IT'S BEEN A LONG TIME...
BUT WE'VE STILL GOT IT, MISONO!
SHUT UP, LILY!
MA-HIRU ...
SAID YOU'RE BEST FRIENDS.
HE REALLY... SAID THAT?

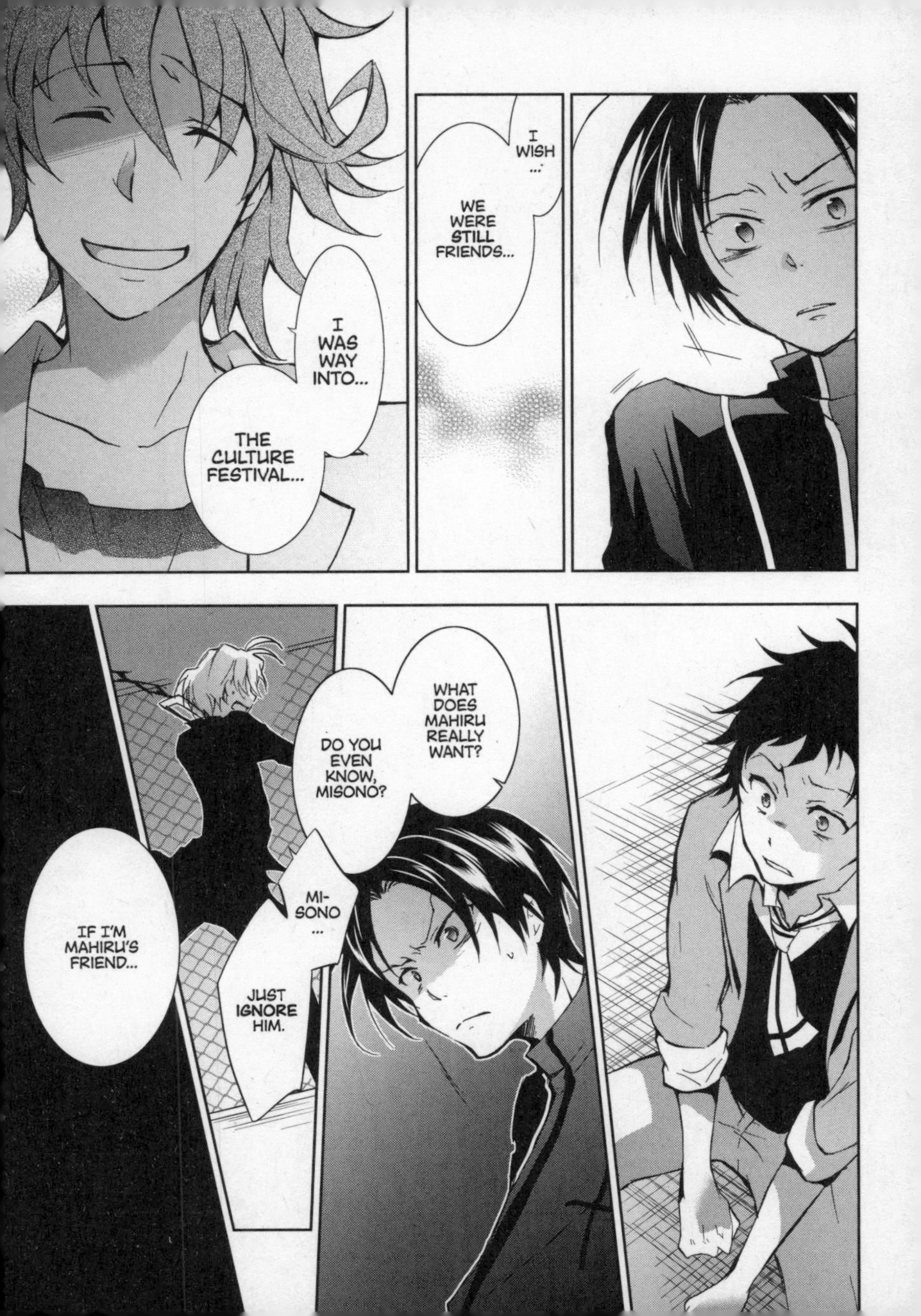
I WISH...
WE WERE STILL FRIENDS...
I WAS WAY INTO...
THE CULTURE FESTIVAL...
WHAT DOES MAHIRU REALLY WANT?
DO YOU EVEN KNOW, MISONO?
MI-SONO...
JUST IGNORE HIM.
IF I'M MAHIRU'S FRIEND...

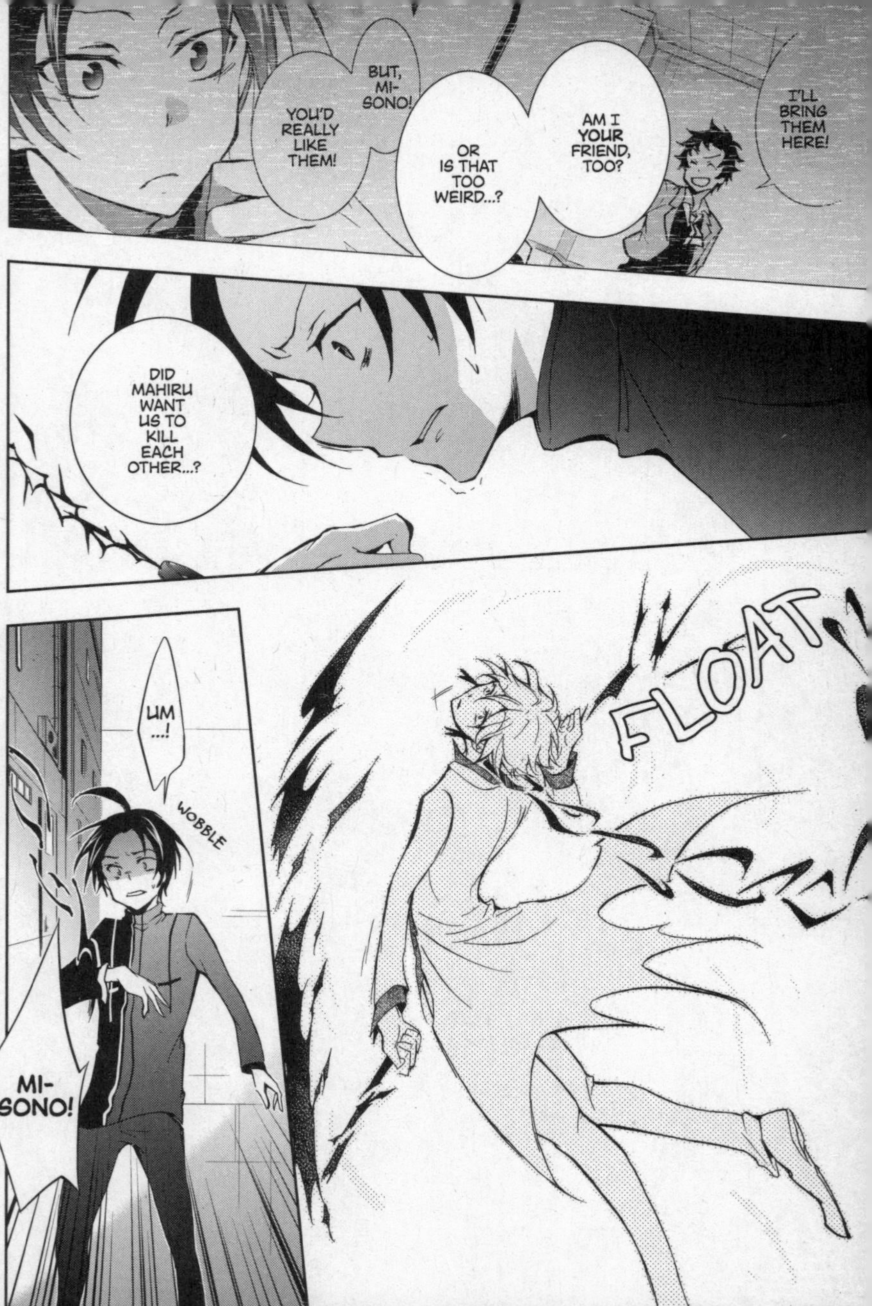
I'LL BRING THEM HERE!
AM I YOUR FRIEND, TOO?
OR IS THAT TOO WEIRD...?
BUT, MI-SONO!
YOU'D REALLY LIKE THEM!
DID MAHIRU WANT US TO KILL EACH OTHER...?
FLOAT
UM ...!
WOBBLE
MI-SONO!

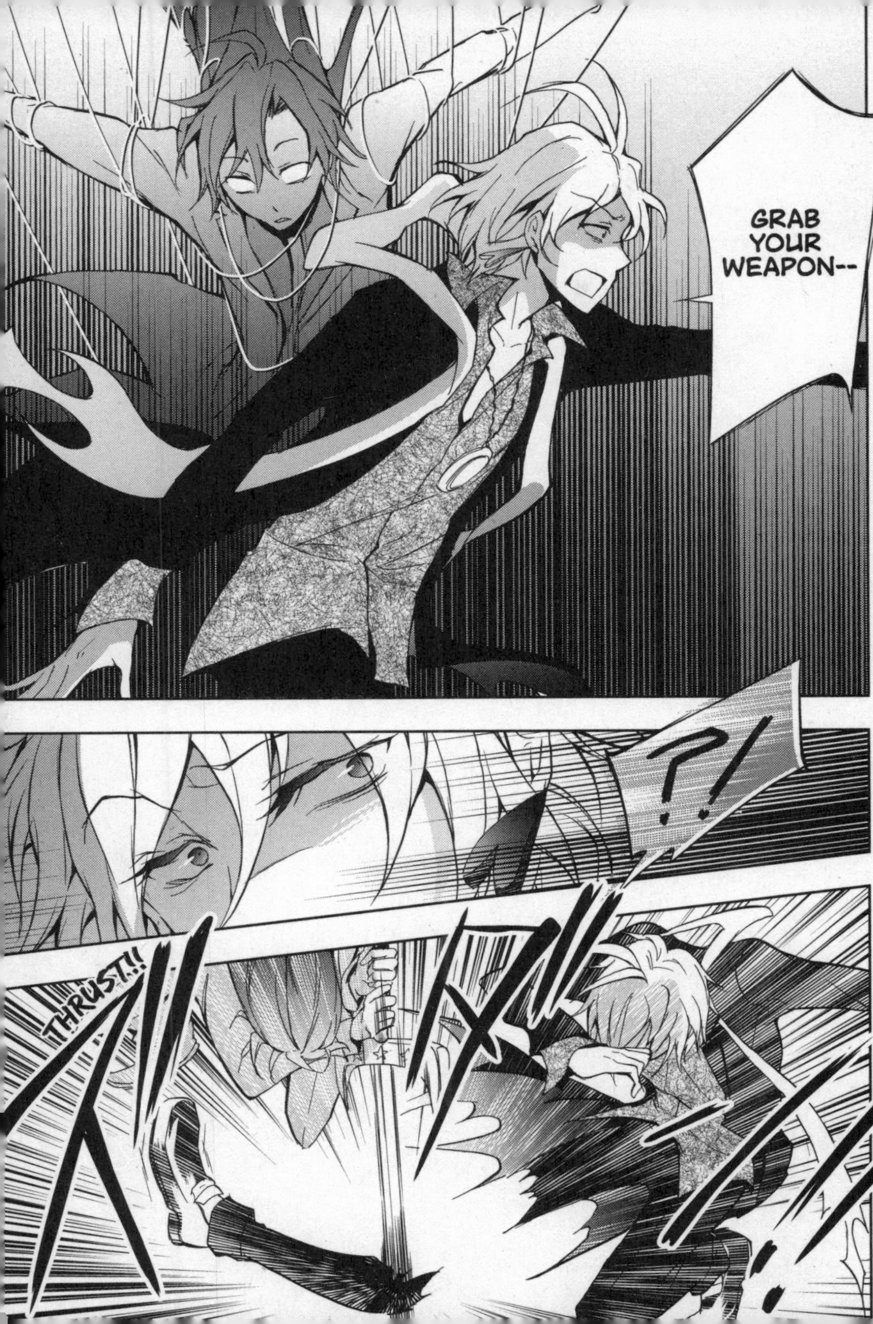
GRAB YOUR WEAPON--
?!
THRUST!!

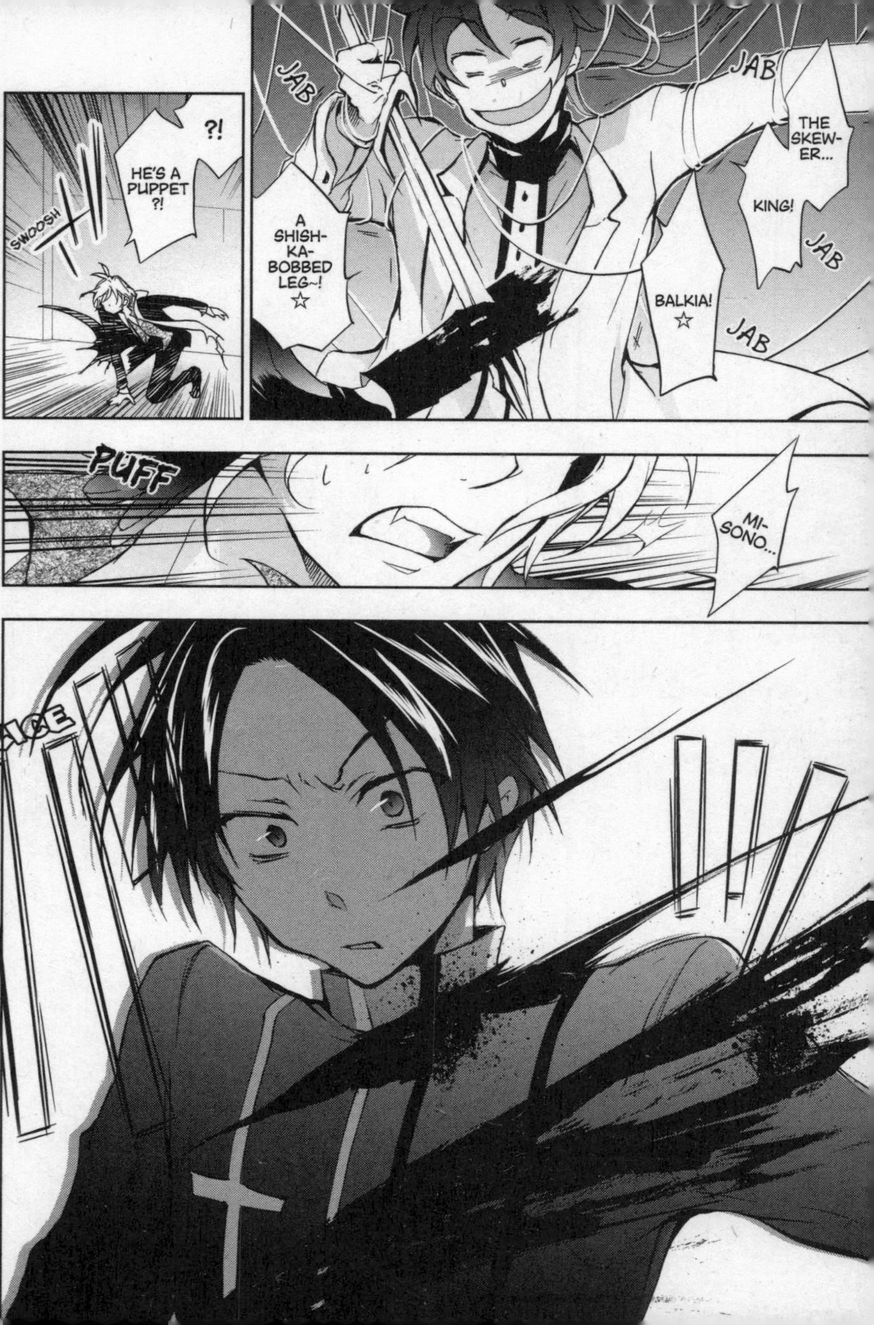
JAB
THE SKEWER...
KING!
JAB
BALKIA! ☆
JAB
A SHISHKABOBBED LEG~! ☆
JAB
?!
HE'S A PUPPET ?!
SWOOSH
MI-SONO...
PUFF
SLICE

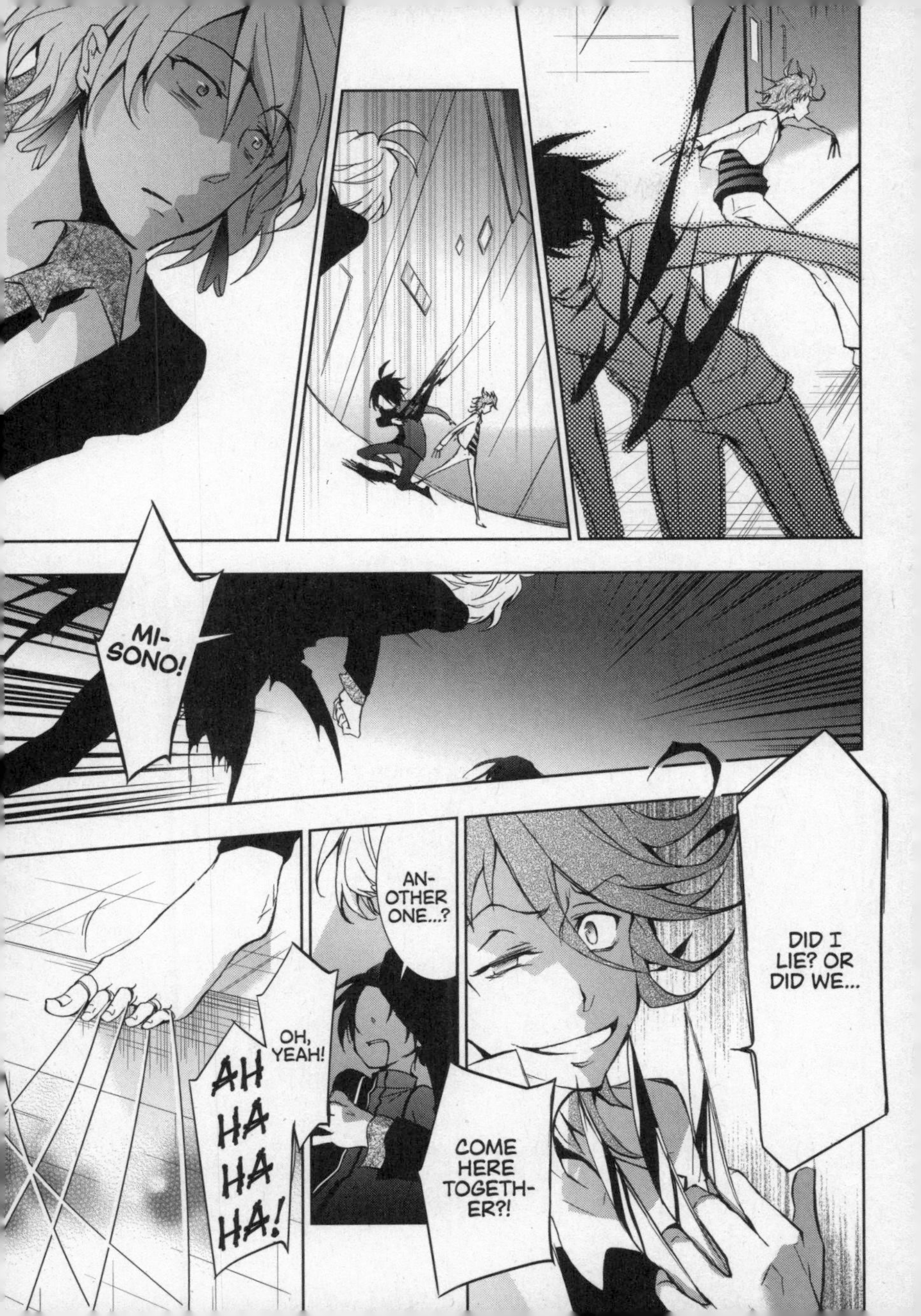
MI-SONO!
DID I LIE? OR DID WE...
COME HERE TOGETH-ER?!
AN-OTHER ONE...?
OH, YEAH!
AH HA HA HA HA!

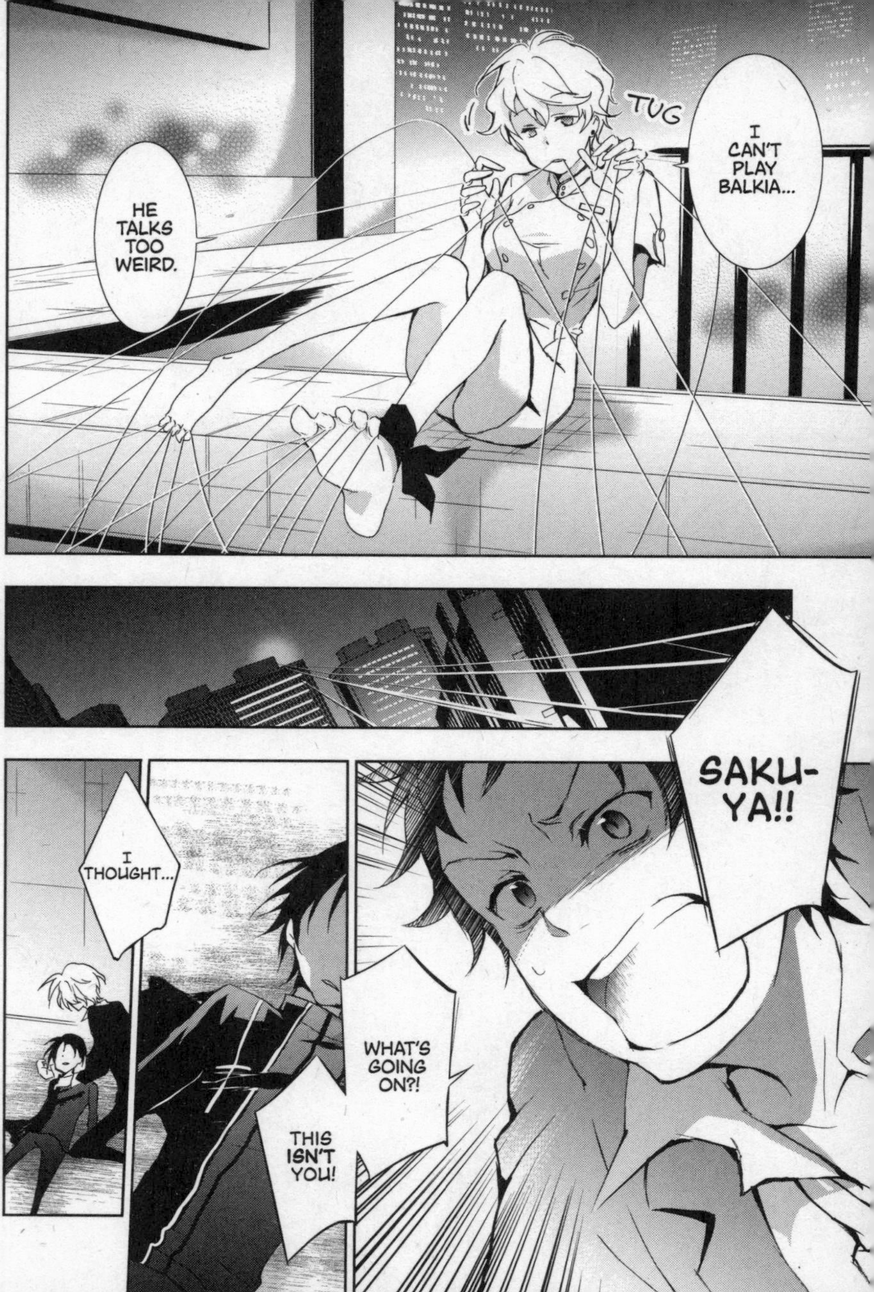
TUG
I CAN'T PLAY BALKIA...
HE TALKS TOO WEIRD.
SAKU-YA!!
WHAT'S GOING ON?!
THIS ISN'T YOU!
I THOUGHT...

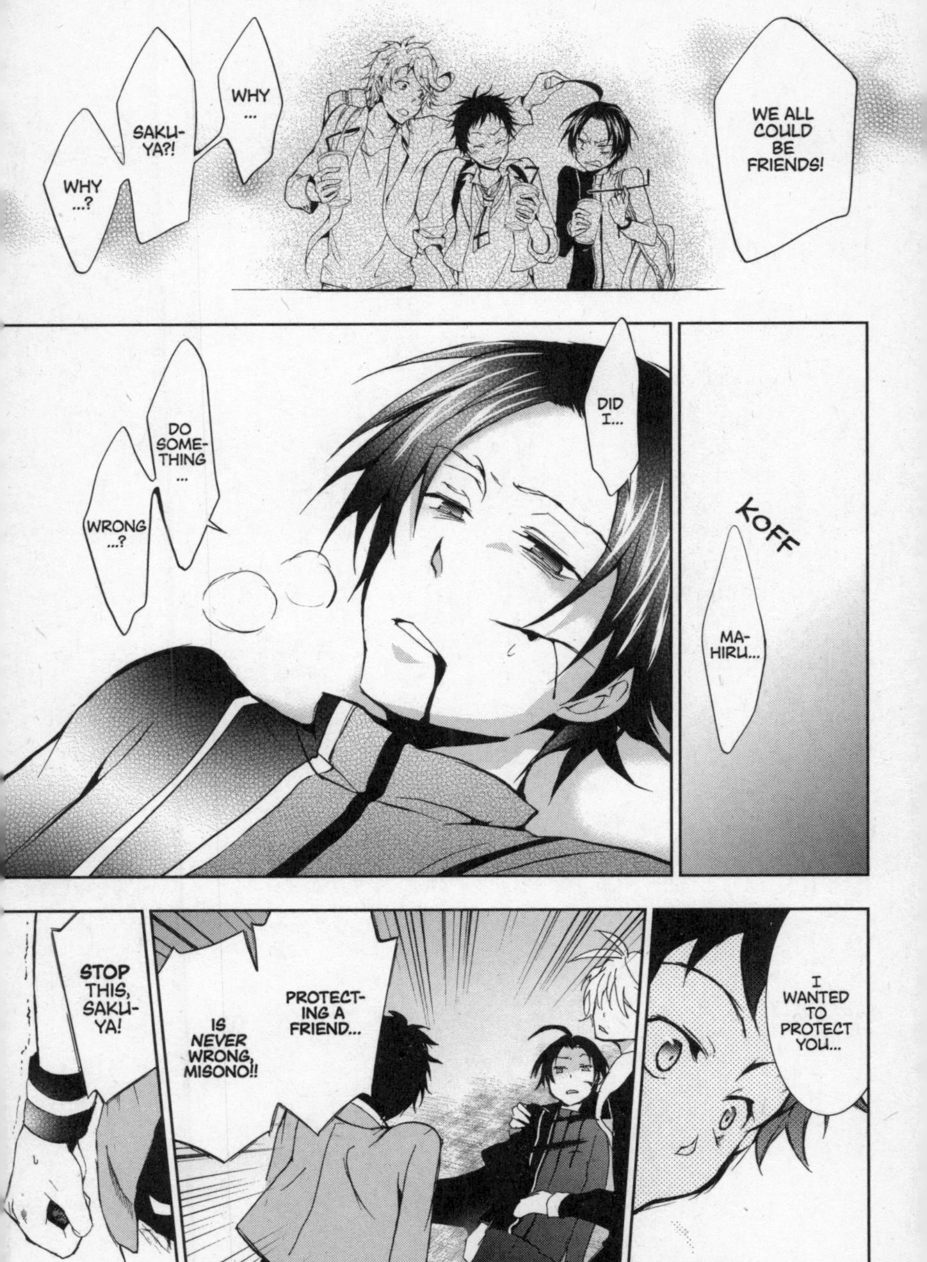
WE ALL COULD BE FRIENDS!
WHY ...
SAKU-YA?!
WHY ...?
KOFF
MA-HIRU...
DID I...
DO SOME-THING ...
WRONG ...?
I WANTED TO PROTECT YOU...
PROTECT-ING A FRIEND...
IS NEVER WRONG, MISONO!!
STOP THIS, SAKU-YA!

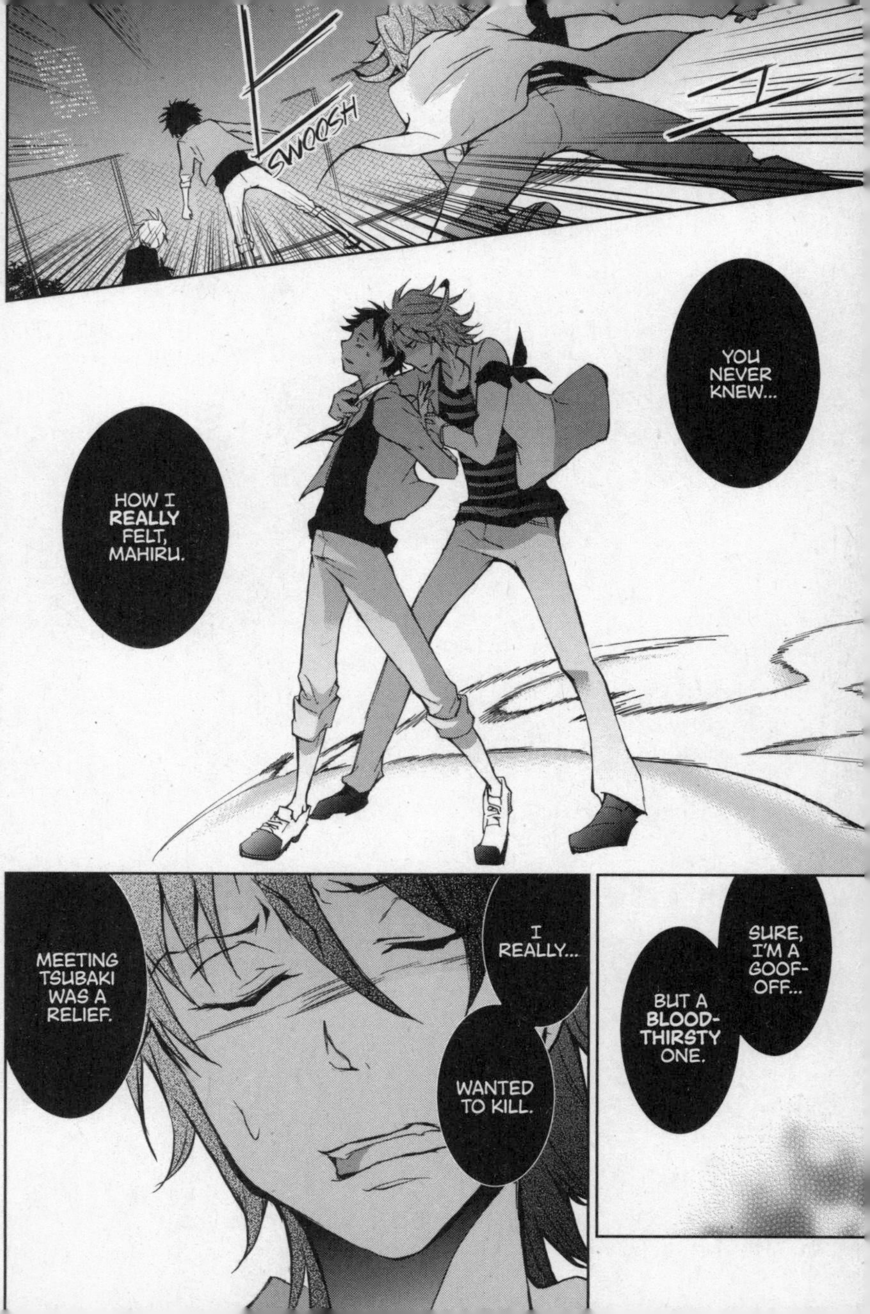
SWOOSH
YOU NEVER KNEW...
HOW I REALLY FELT, MAHIRU.
SURE, I'M A GOOF-OFF...
BUT A BLOOD-THIRSTY ONE.
I REALLY...
WANTED TO KILL.
MEETING TSUBAKI WAS A RELIEF.

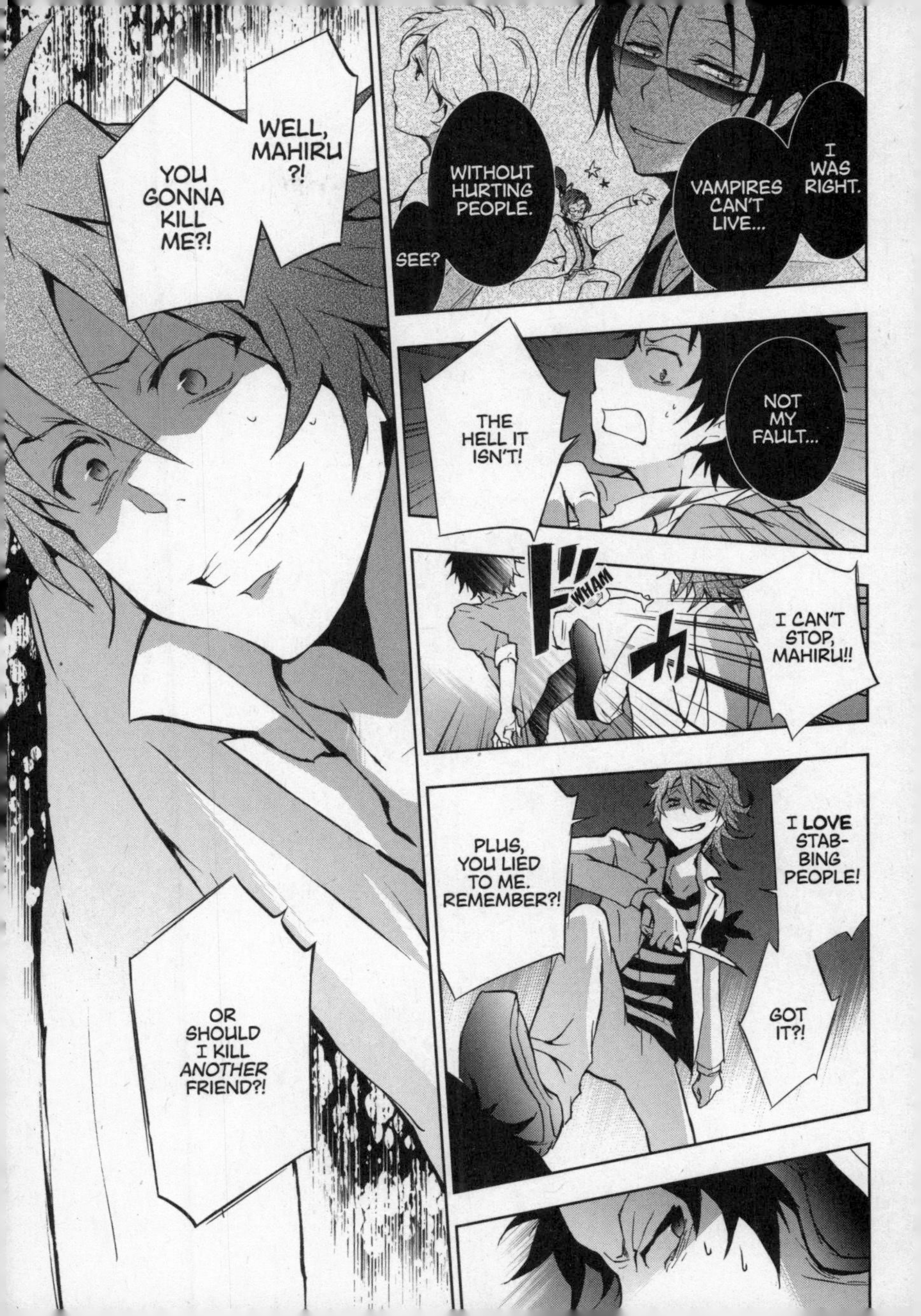
I WAS RIGHT.
VAMPIRES CAN'T LIVE...
WITHOUT HURTING PEOPLE.
SEE?
NOT MY FAULT...
THE HELL IT ISN'T!
ドッ
WHAM
I CAN'T STOP, MAHIRU!!
I LOVE STAB-BING PEOPLE!
GOT IT?!
PLUS, YOU LIED TO ME. REMEMBER?!
WELL, MAHIRU?!
YOU GONNA KILL ME?!
OR SHOULD I KILL ANOTHER FRIEND?!

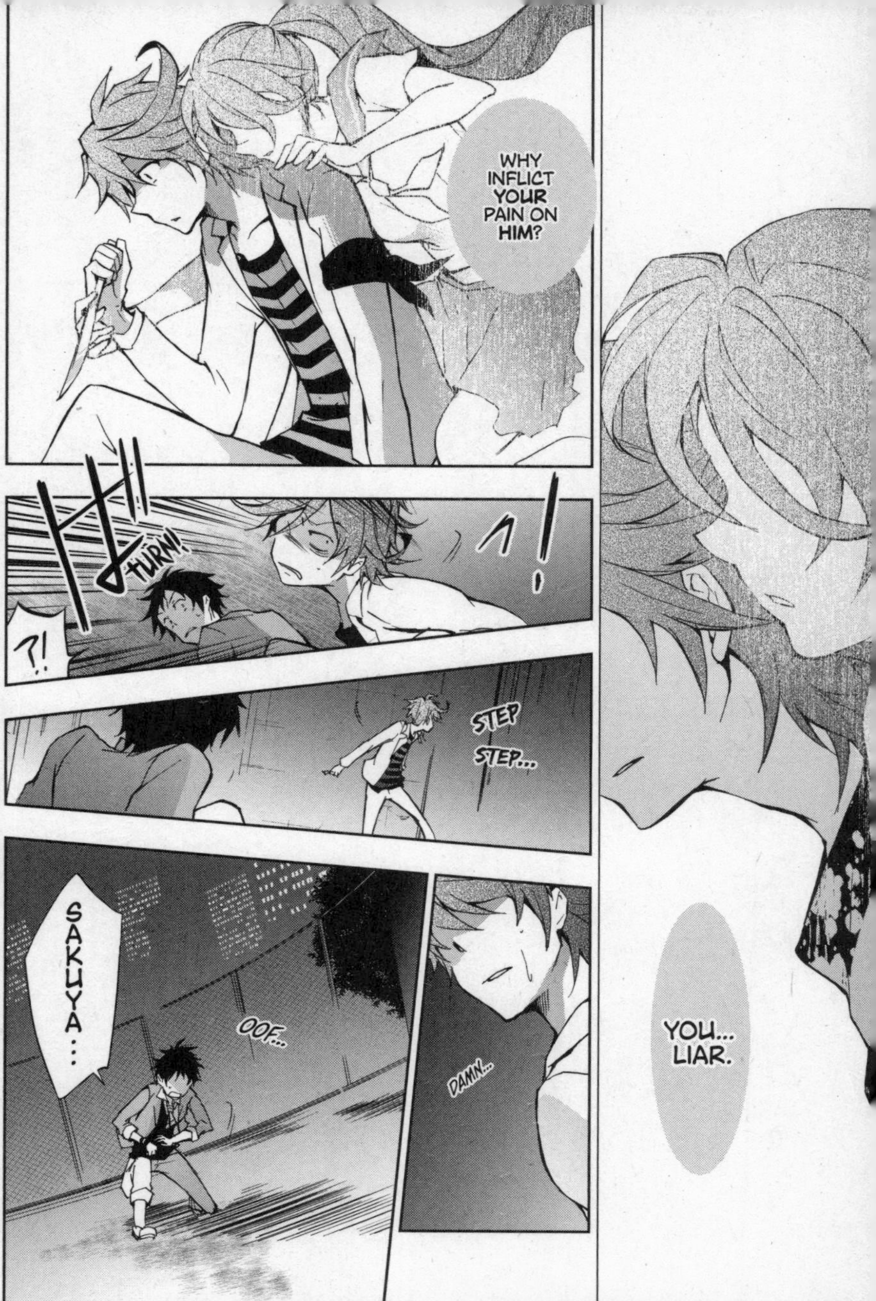
YOU... LIAR.
WHY INFLICT YOUR PAIN ON HIM?
!
TURN!
?!
STEP
STEP...
DAMN...
SAKUYA...
OOF...

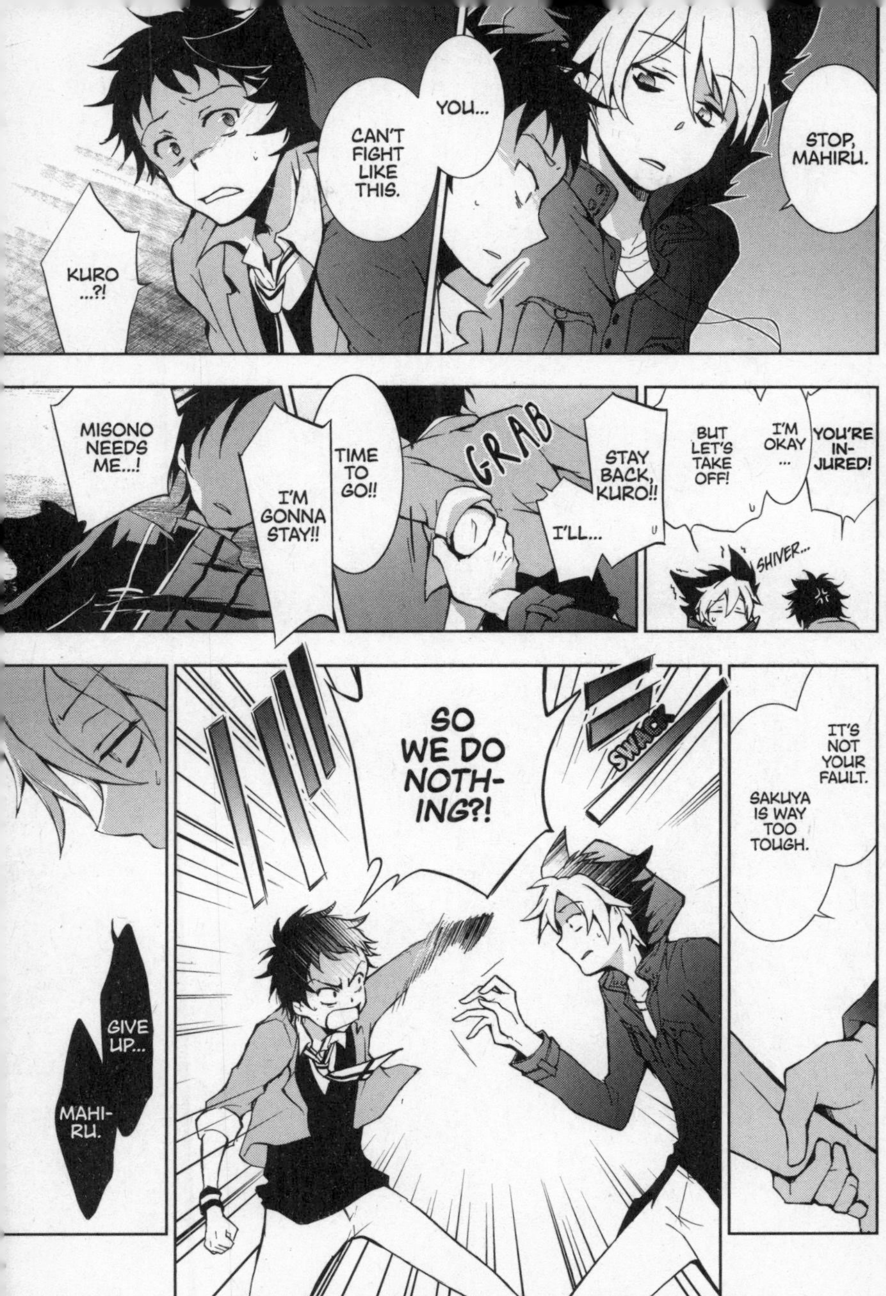
STOP, MAHIRU.
YOU... CAN'T FIGHT LIKE THIS.
KURO ...?!
YOU'RE IN-JURED!
I'M OKAY ...
BUT LET'S TAKE OFF!
SHIVER...
STAY BACK, KURO!!
I'LL...
GRAB
TIME TO GO!!
I'M GONNA STAY!!
MISONO NEEDS ME...!
IT'S NOT YOUR FAULT.
SAKUYA IS WAY TOO TOUGH.
SWACK
SO WE DO NOTH-ING?!
GIVE UP...
MAHI-RU.

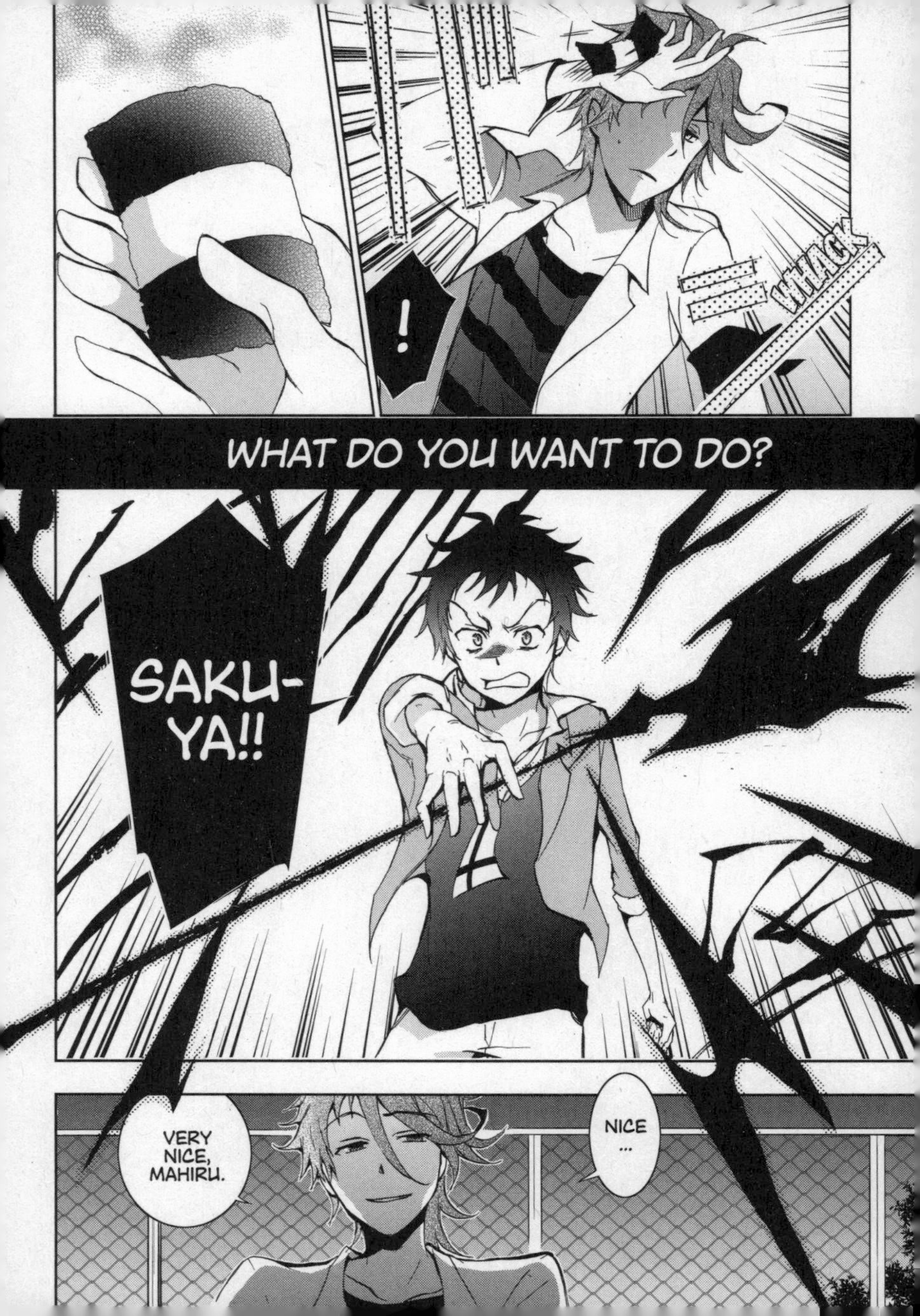
WHACK
!
WHAT DO YOU WANT TO DO?
SAKU-YA!!
NICE ...
VERY NICE, MAHIRU.

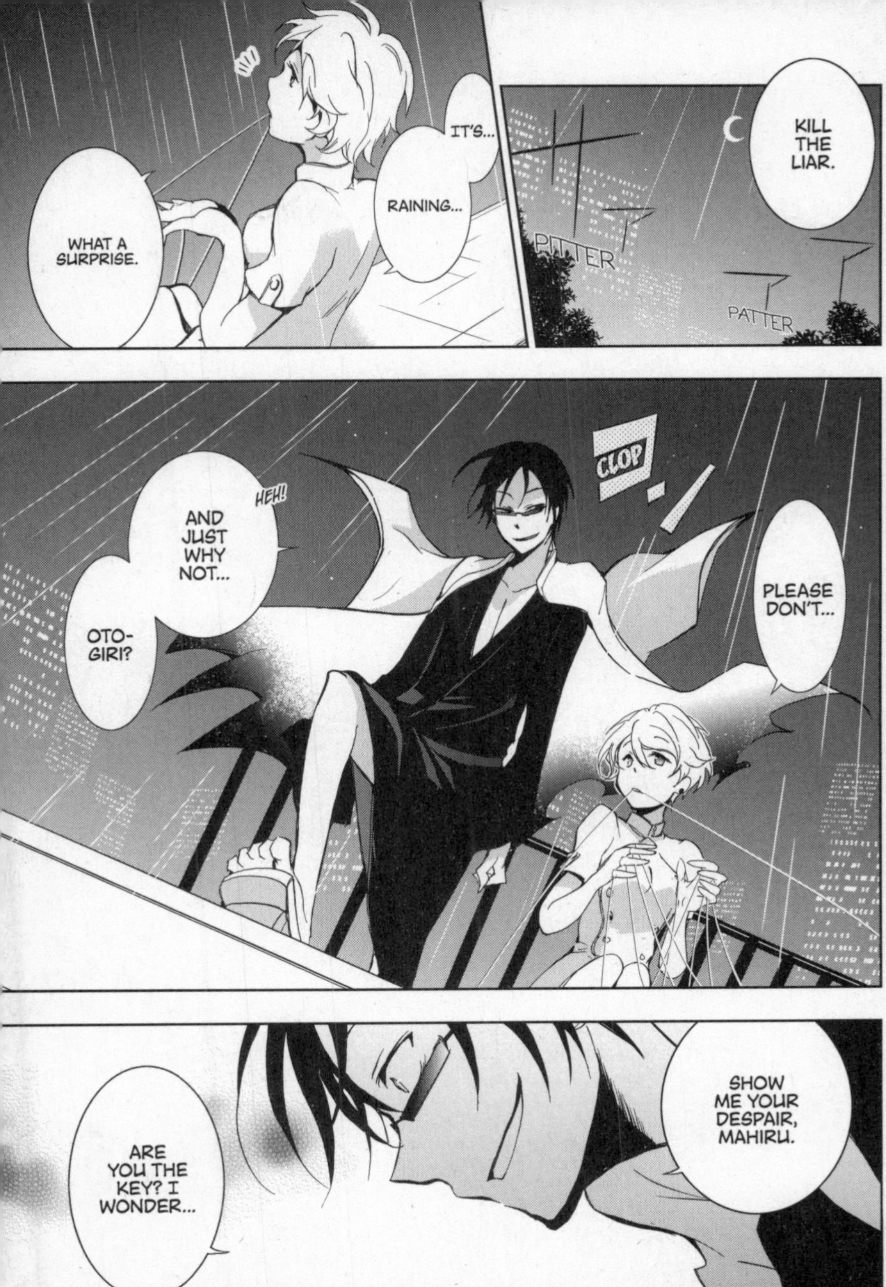
KILL THE LIAR.
PATTER
PATTER
IT'S... RAINING...
WHAT A SURPRISE.
PLEASE DON'T...
CLOP
HEH!
AND JUST WHY NOT...
OTO-GIRI?
SHOW ME YOUR DESPAIR, MAHIRU.
ARE YOU THE KEY? I WONDER...

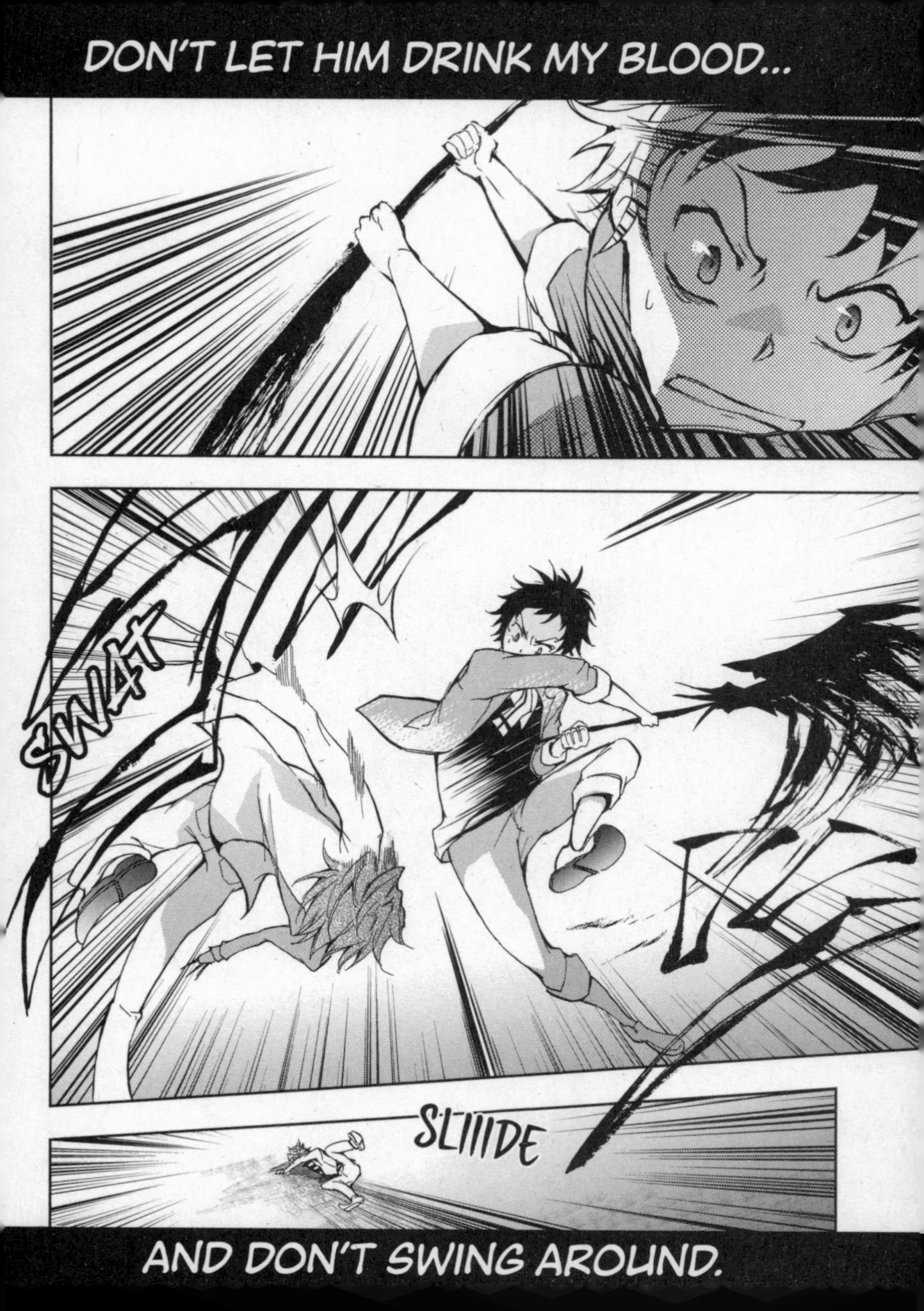
DON'T LET HIM DRINK MY BLOOD...
SWAT
SLIIIDE
AND DON'T SWING AROUND.

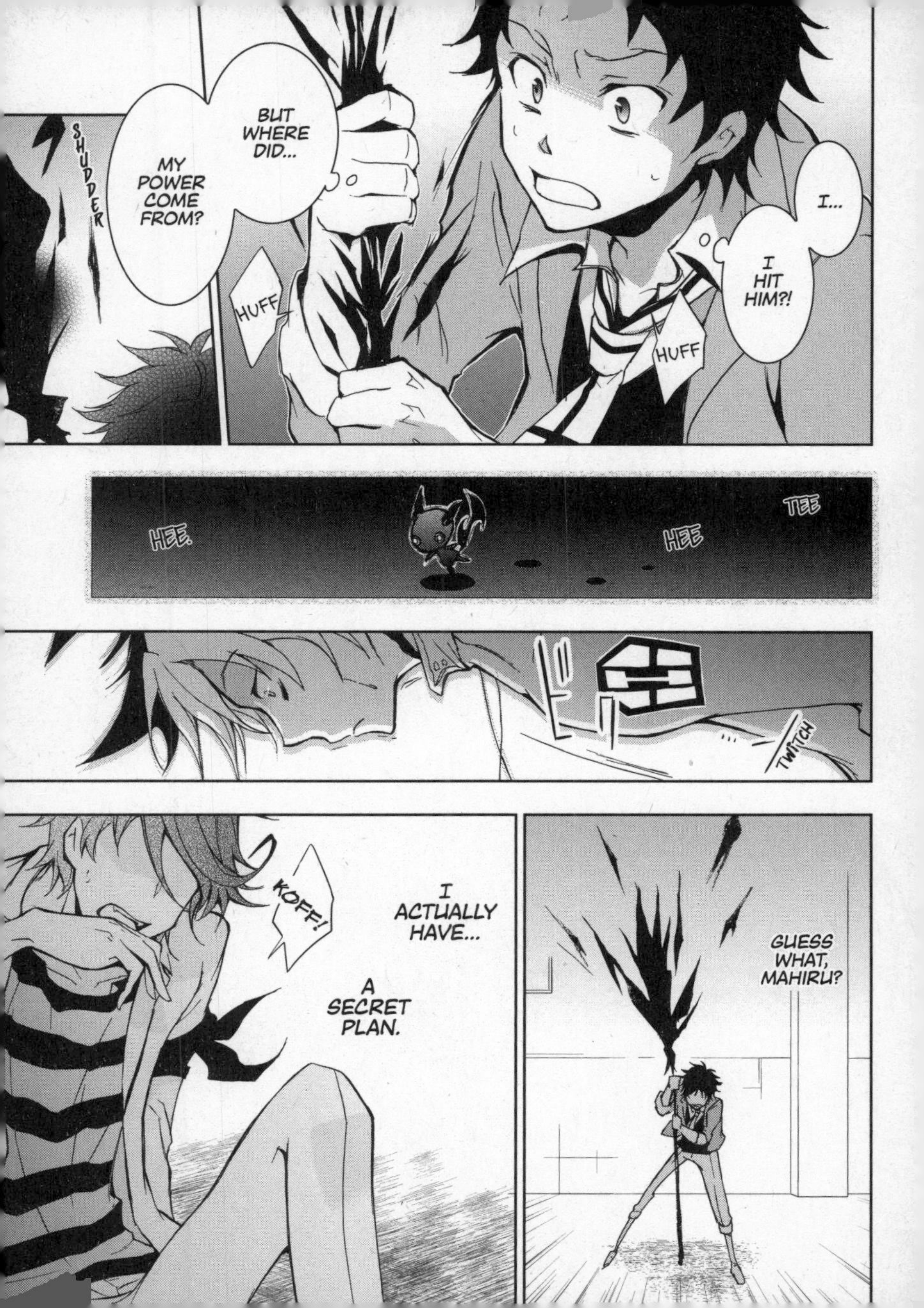
I...
I HIT HIM?!
HUFF
BUT WHERE DID...
MY POWER COME FROM?
HUFF
SHUDDER
TEE
HEE
HEE.
TWITCH
GUESS WHAT, MAHIRU?
I ACTUALLY HAVE...
A SECRET PLAN.
KOFF!

SO...

SINCE I'M IMMORTAL...

I'D NEED TO VANISH FROM YOUR LIFE...

RIGHT AFTER HIGH SCHOOL.

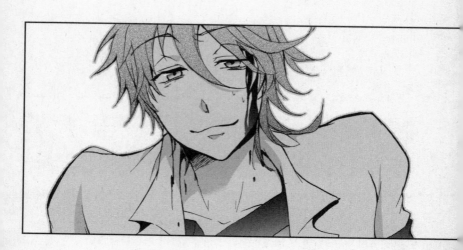

NO HAPPY ENDINGS FOR US! NONE AT ALL...

KEEP TRACK OF HIM...

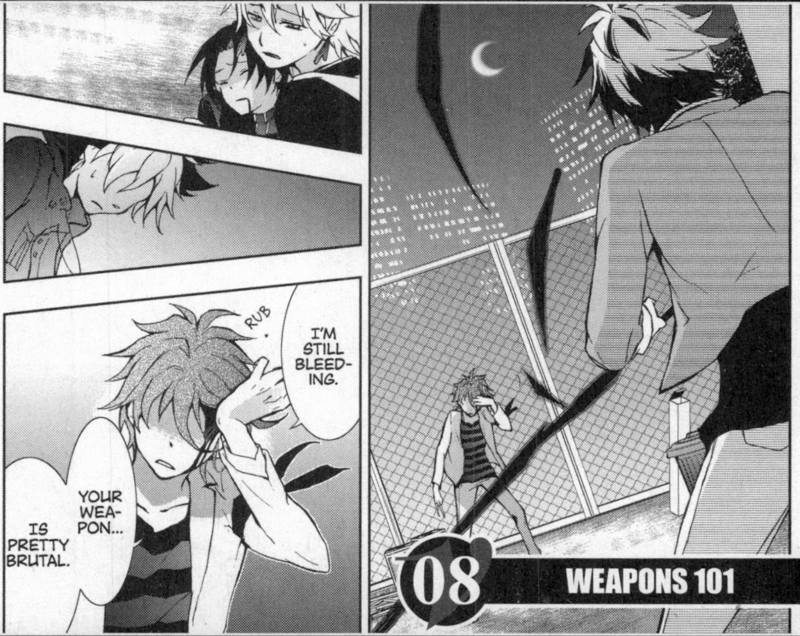
08
WEAPONS 101
RUB
I'M STILL BLEEDING.
YOUR WEAPON...
IS PRETTY BRUTAL.

KEEP AWAY! DON'T GO NEAR HIM!

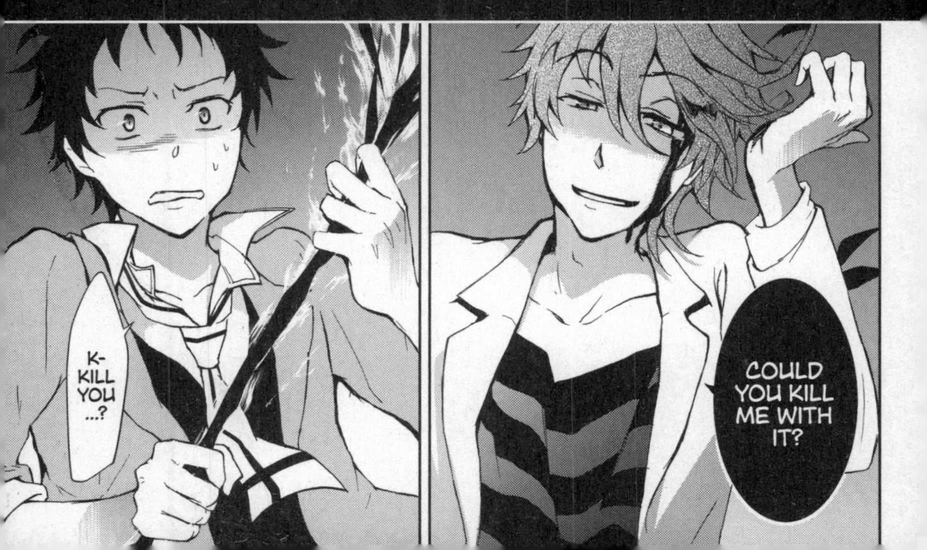
COULD YOU KILL ME WITH IT?
K-KILL YOU ...?

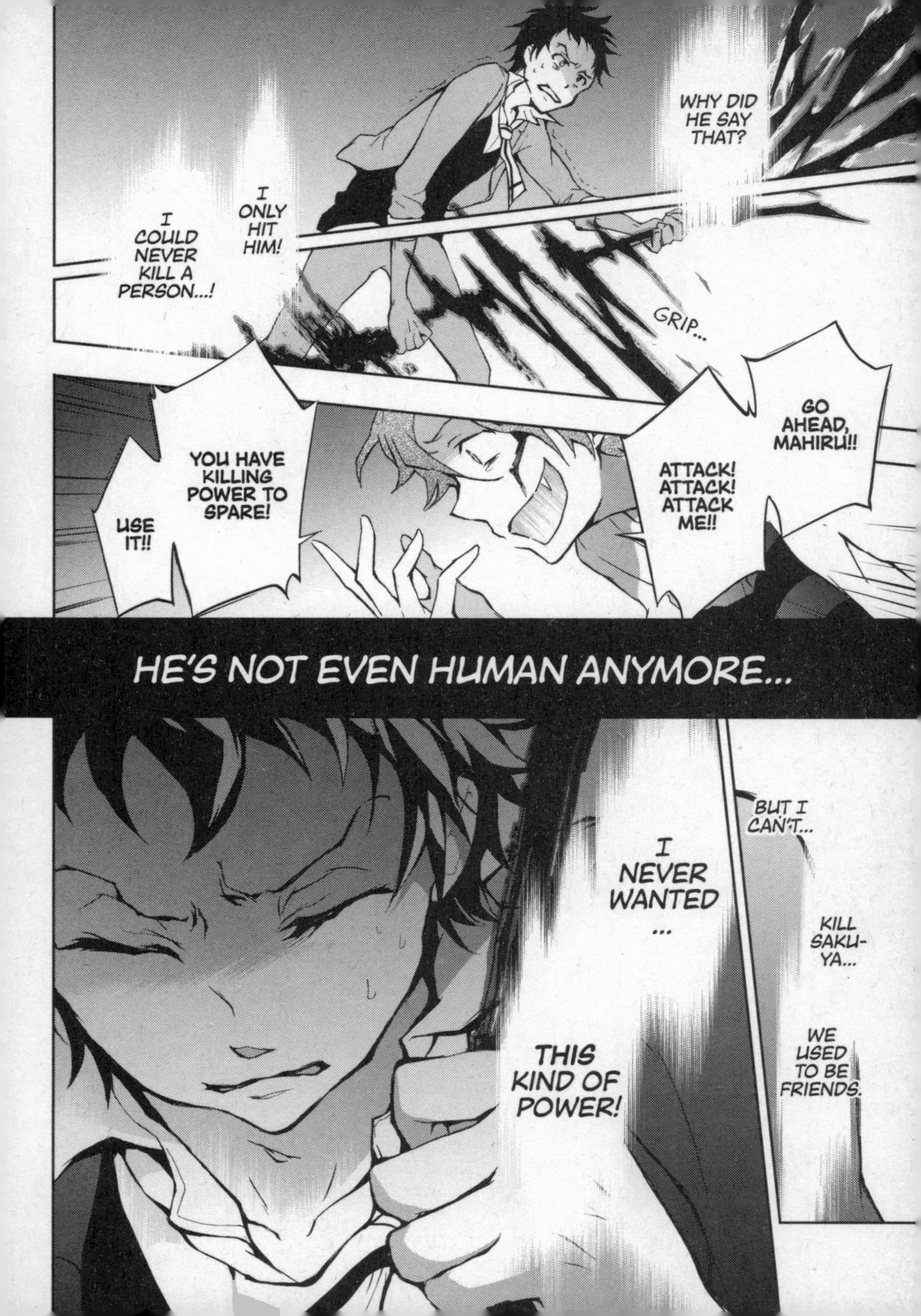
WHY DID HE SAY THAT?
I ONLY HIT HIM!
I COULD NEVER KILL A PERSON...!
GRIP...
GO AHEAD, MAHIRU!!
ATTACK! ATTACK! ATTACK ME!!
YOU HAVE KILLING POWER TO SPARE!
USE IT!!
HE'S NOT EVEN HUMAN ANYMORE...
BUT I CAN'T...
KILL SAKU-YA...
WE USED TO BE FRIENDS.
I NEVER WANTED ...
THIS KIND OF POWER!

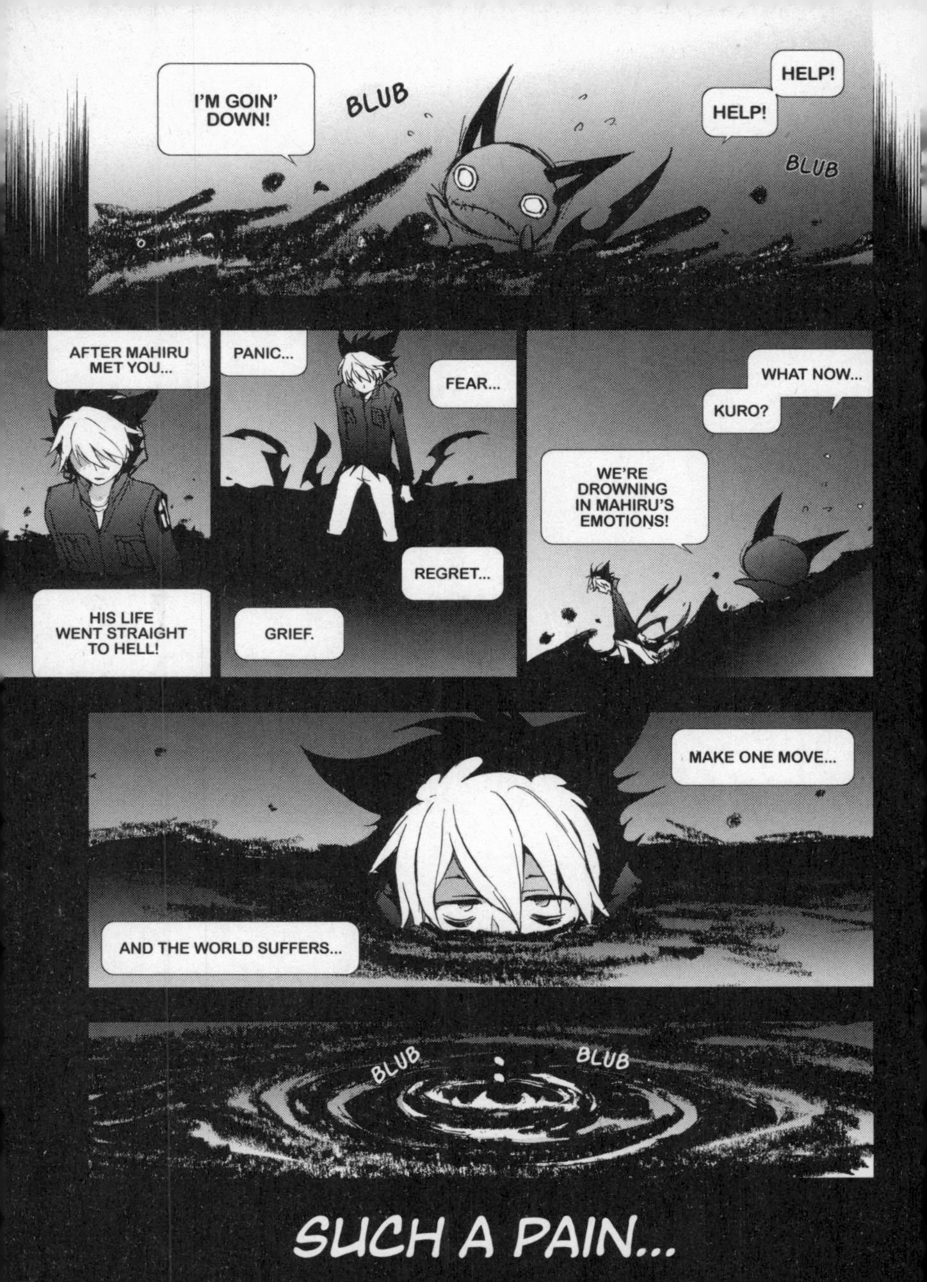
HELP!
HELP!
BLUB
BLUB
I'M GOIN' DOWN!
WHAT NOW...
KURO?
WE'RE DROWNING IN MAHIRU'S EMOTIONS!
PANIC...
FEAR...
REGRET...
GRIEF.
AFTER MAHIRU MET YOU...
HIS LIFE WENT STRAIGHT TO HELL!
MAKE ONE MOVE...
AND THE WORLD SUFFERS...
BLUB
BLUB
SUCH A PAIN...

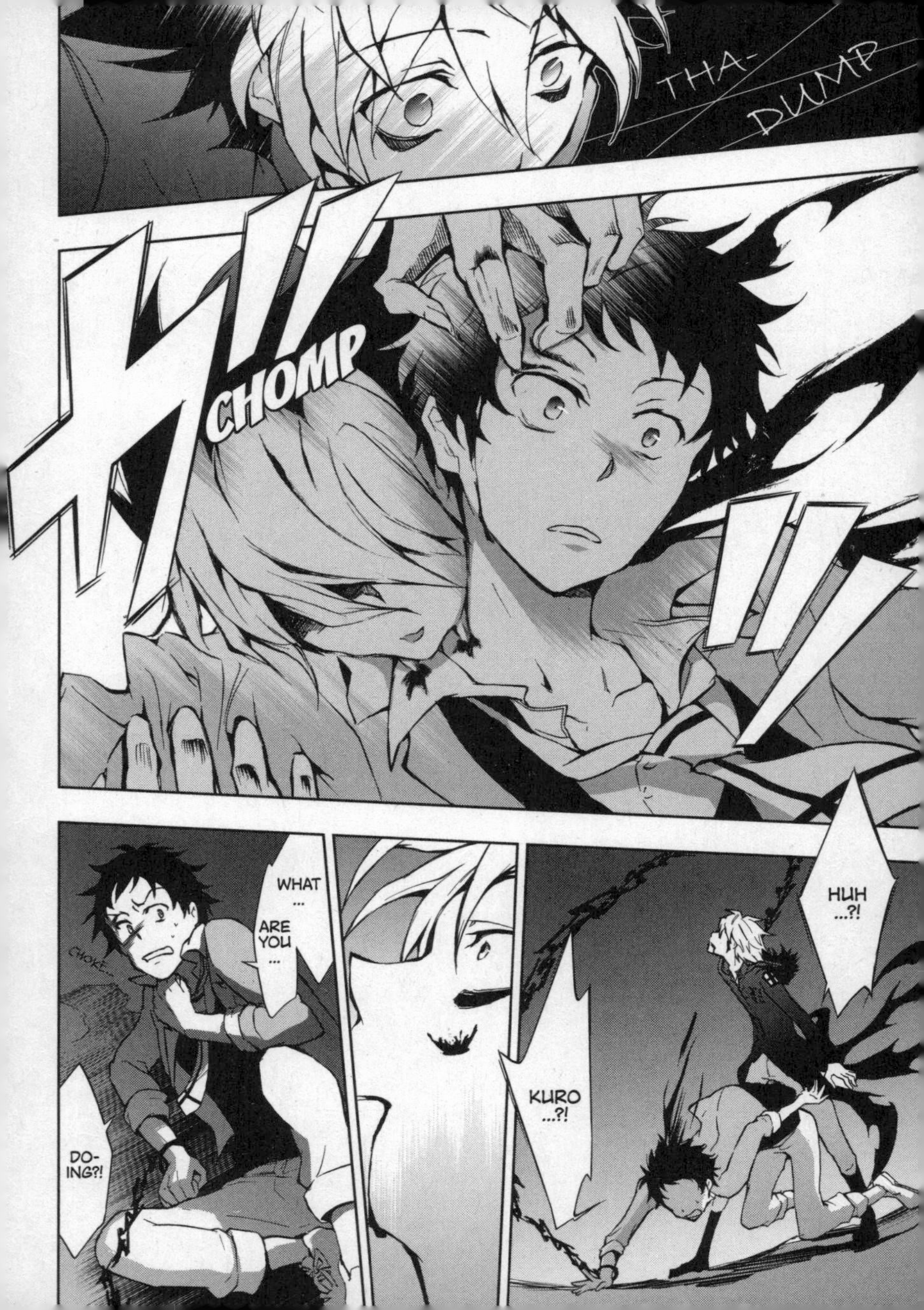
THA-DUMP
CHOMP
HUH ...?!
KURO ...?!
WHAT ... ARE YOU ...
CHOKE...
DO-ING?!

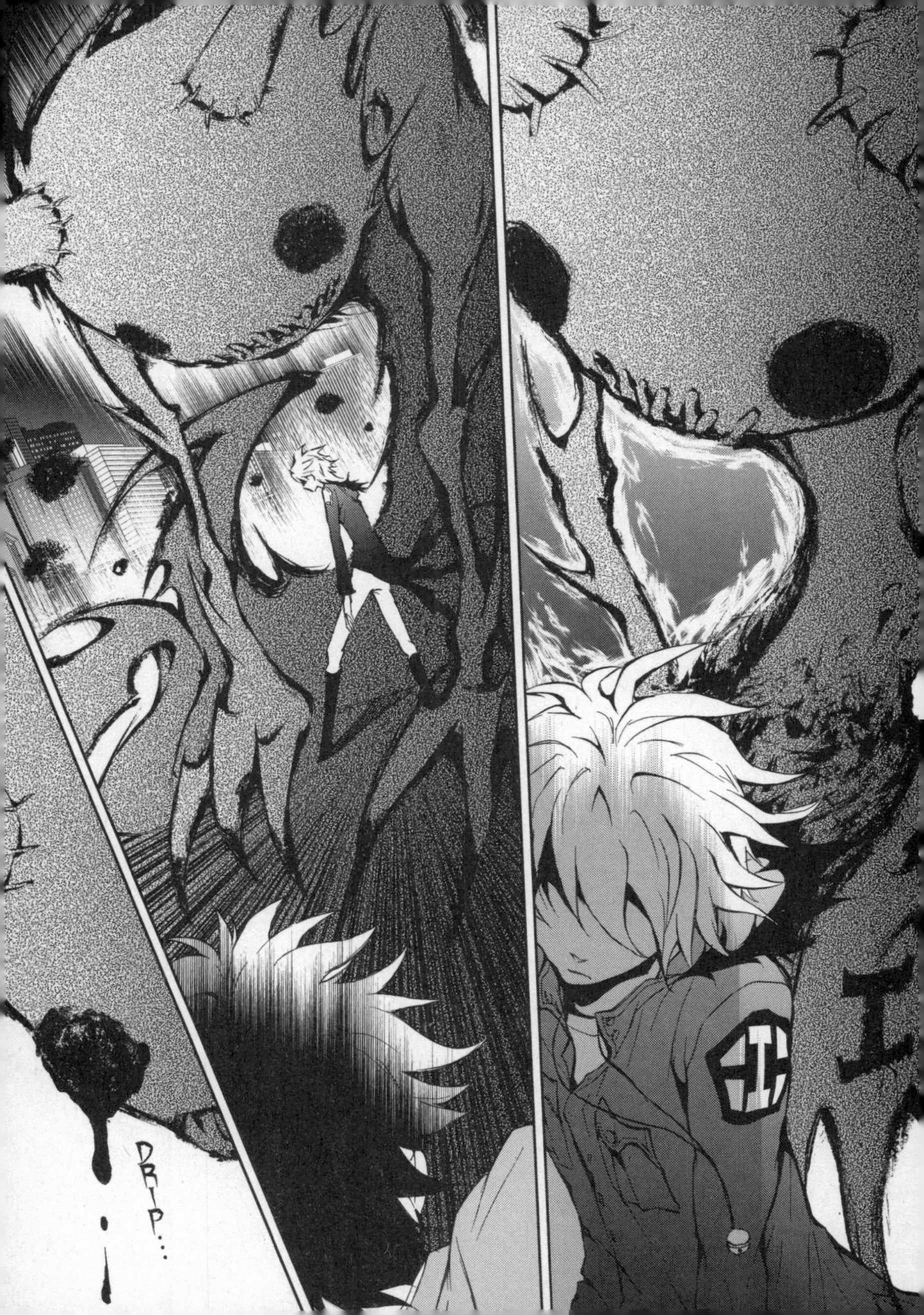
DRIP...

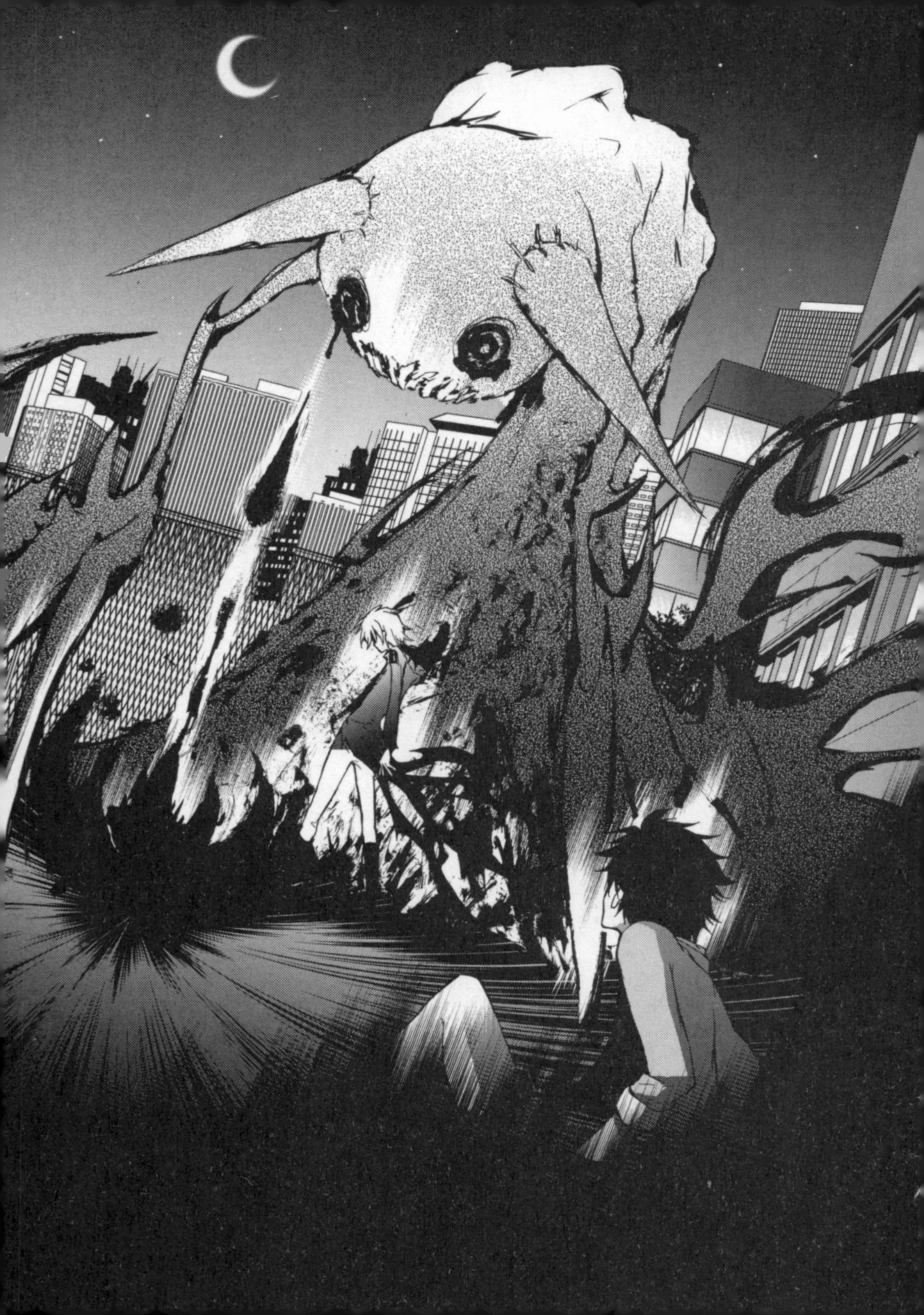

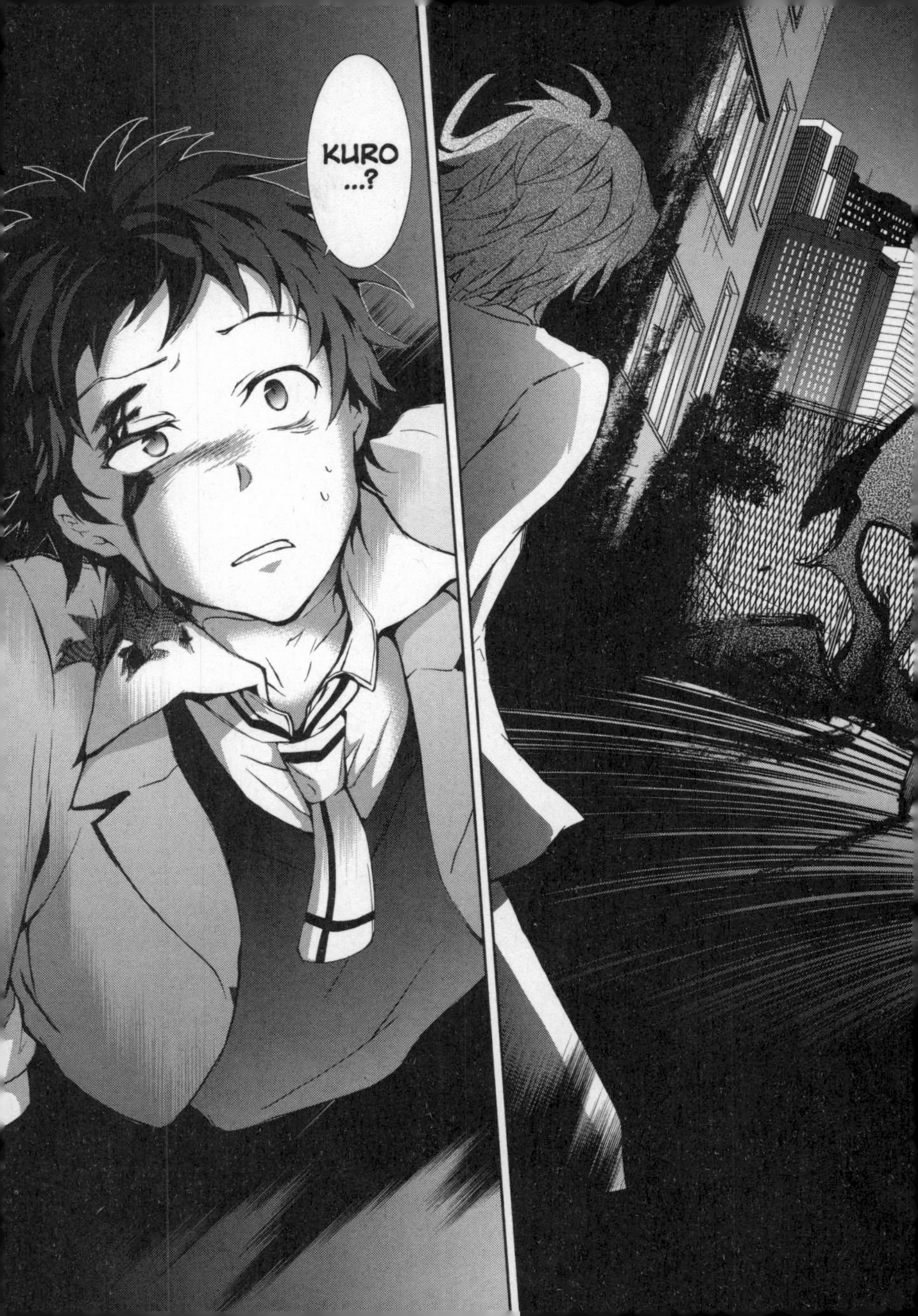
KURO ...?

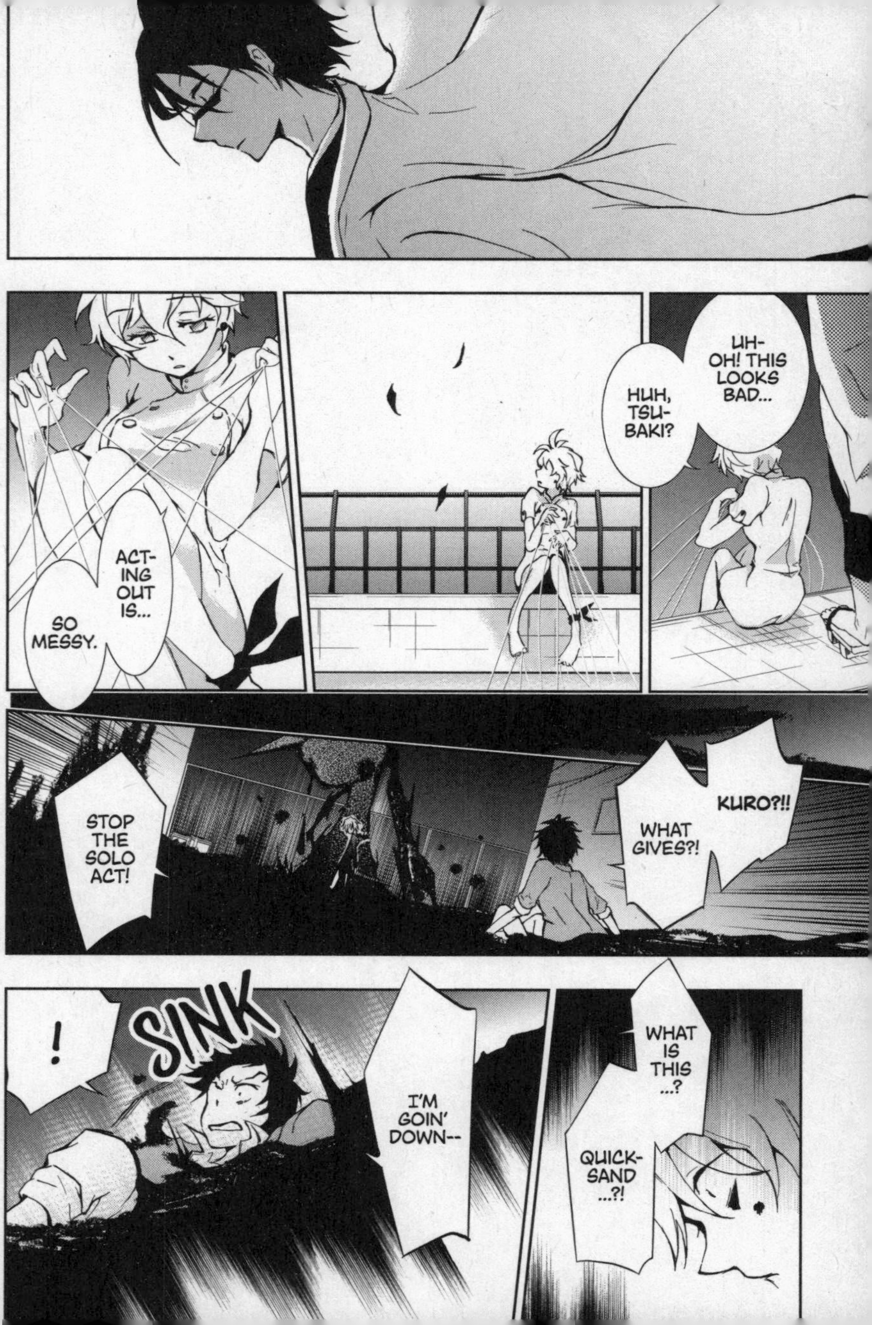
UH-OH! THIS LOOKS BAD...
HUH, TSU-BAKI?
ACT-ING OUT IS...
SO MESSY.
KURO?!!
WHAT GIVES?!
STOP THE SOLO ACT!
WHAT IS THIS ...?
QUICK-SAND ...?!
I'M GOIN' DOWN--
SINK
!

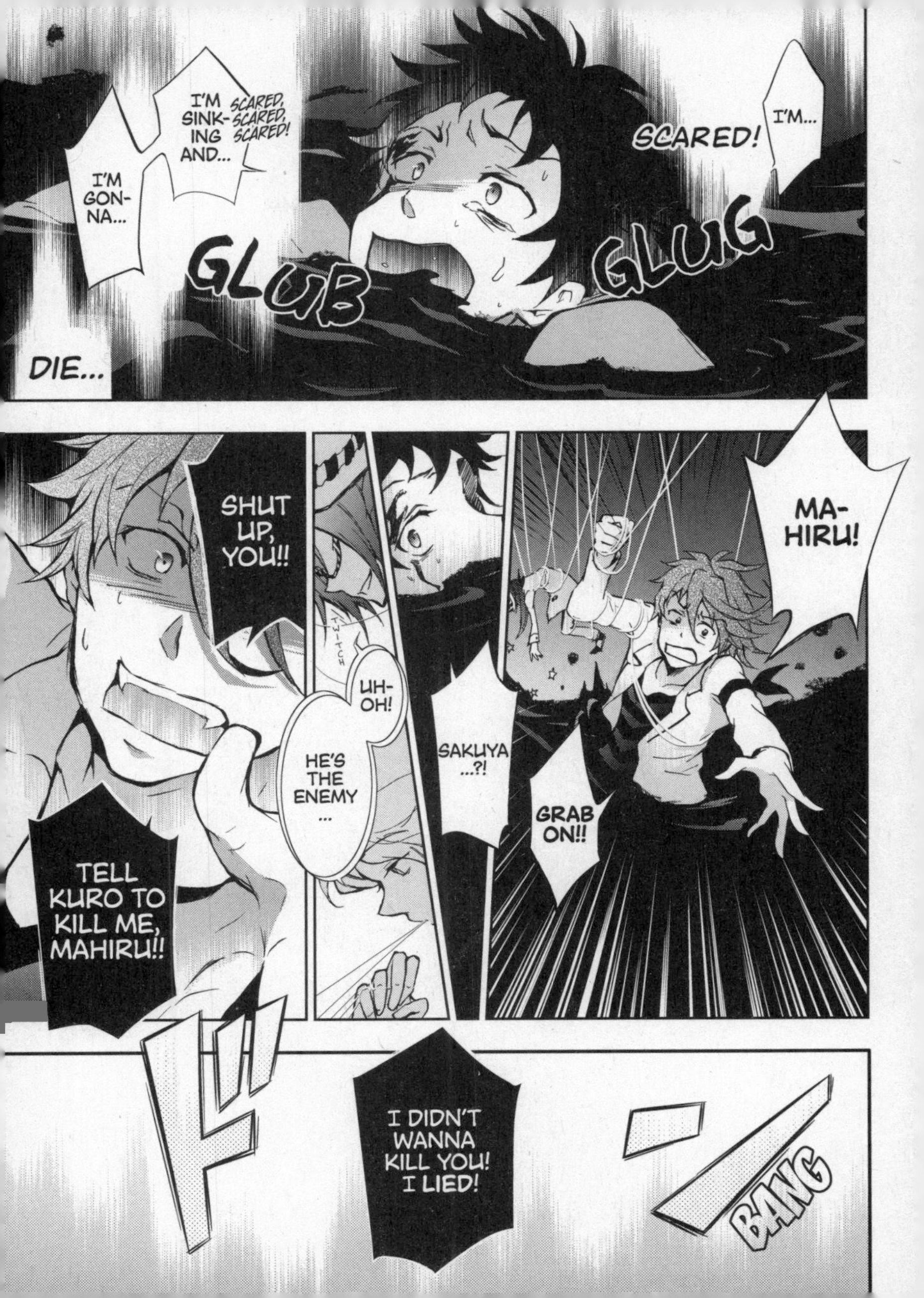
I'M...
SCARED!
GLUG
GLUB
I'M SINK-ING AND...
SCARED, SCARED, SCARED!
I'M GON-NA...
DIE...
MA-HIRU!
GRAB ON!!
SAKUYA ...?!
TWITCH
UH-OH!
HE'S THE ENEMY ...
SHUT UP, YOU!!
TELL KURO TO KILL ME, MAHIRU!!
BANG
I DIDN'T WANNA KILL YOU! I LIED!

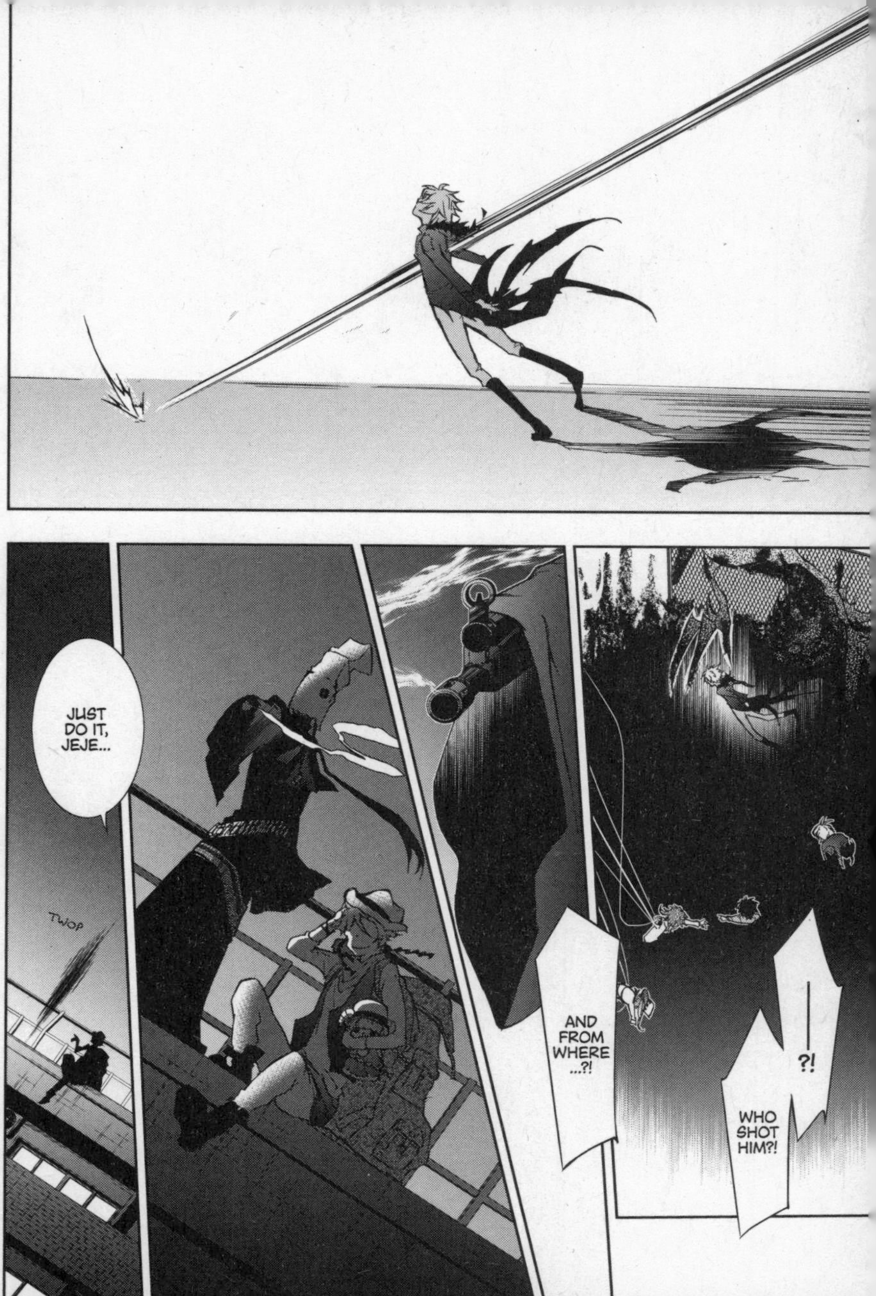
——?!
WHO SHOT HIM?!
AND FROM WHERE ...?!
JUST DO IT, JEJE...
TWOP

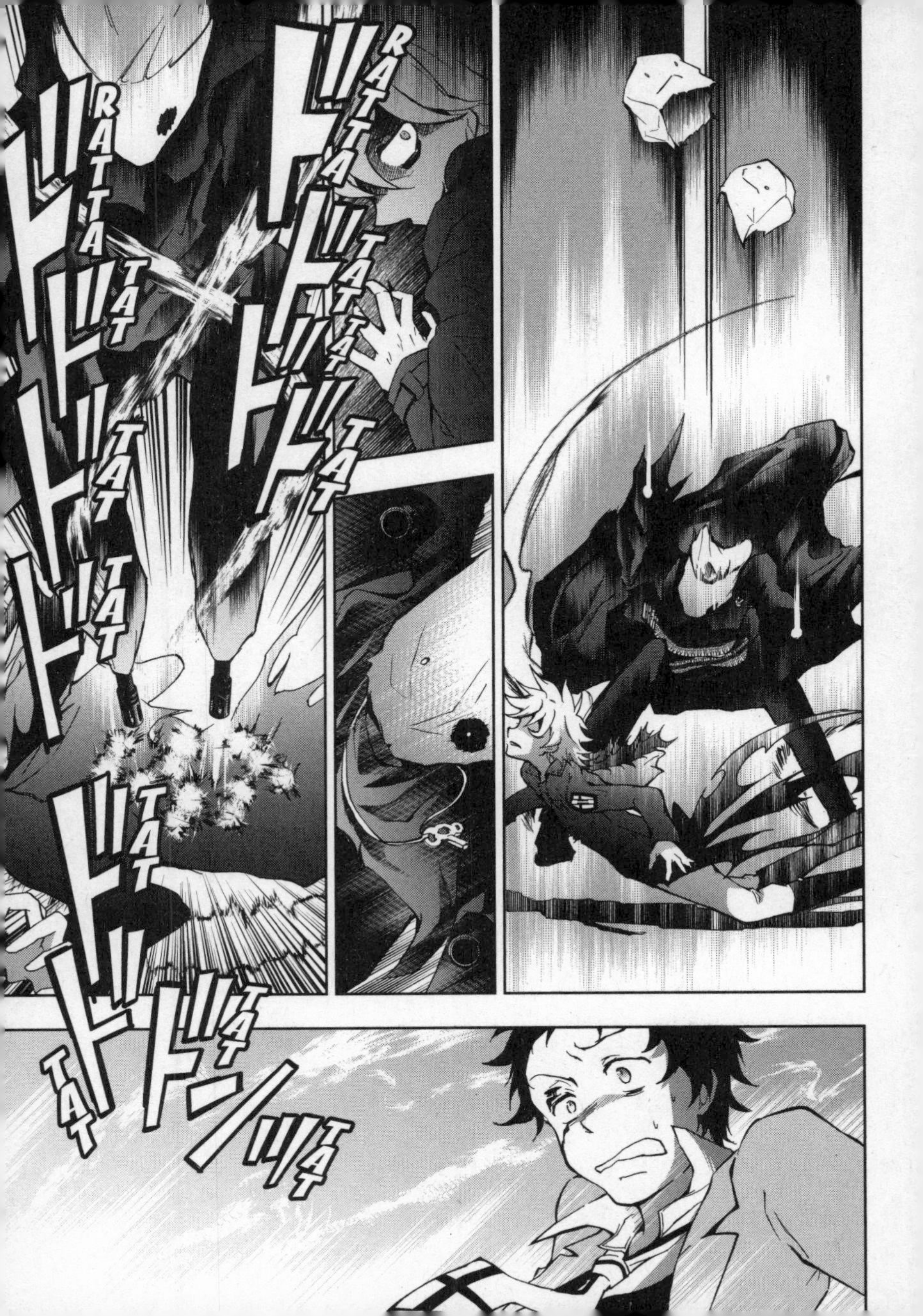
RATTATATATAT
TAT
RATTATA
TAT TAT
TAT TAT
TAT TAT
TAT TAT
TAT TAT
TAT TAT

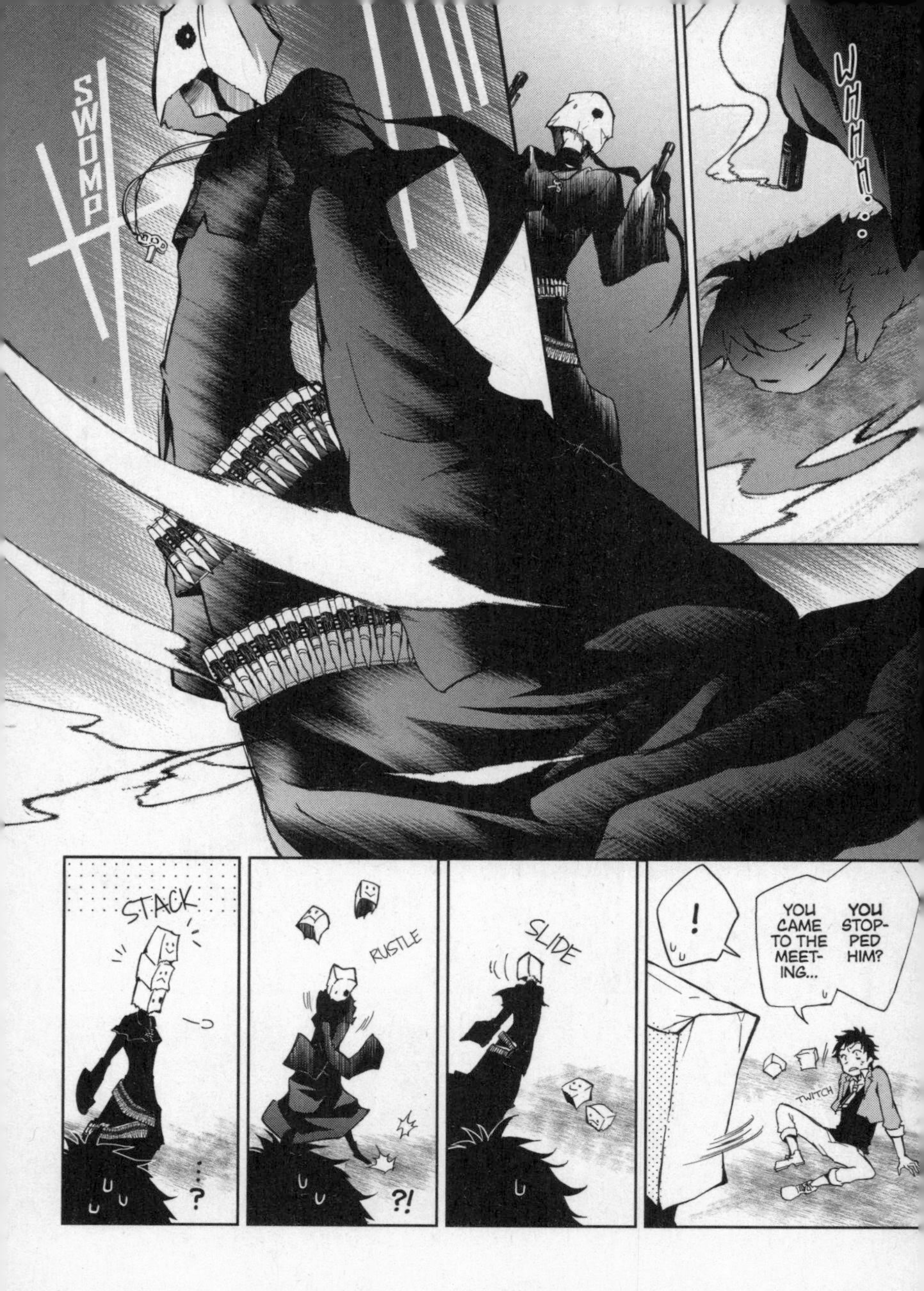
WHHHH!...
SWOMP
!
YOU STOPPED HIM?
YOU CAME TO THE MEETING...
TWITCH
SLIDE
RUSTLE
?!
STACK
...?

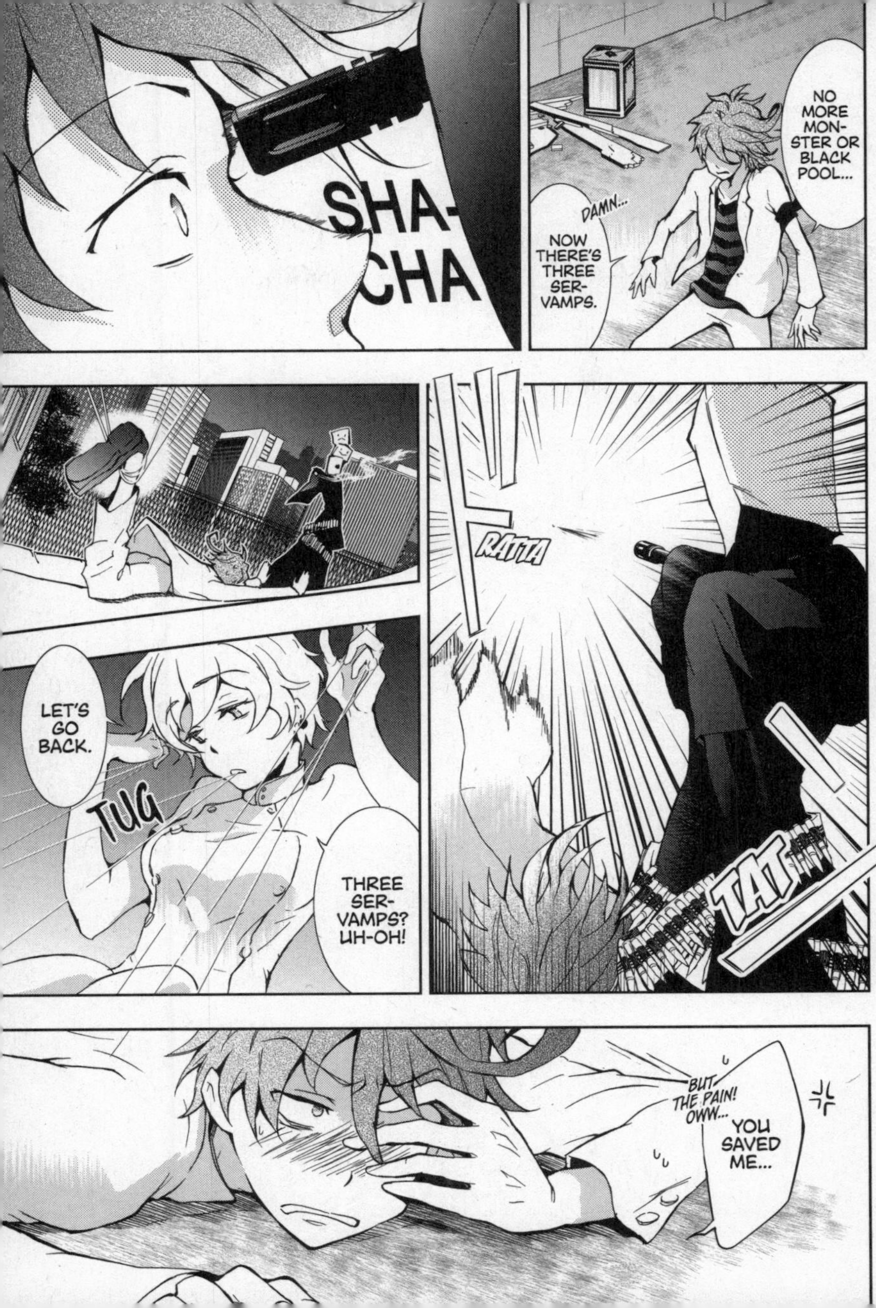
NO MORE MON-STER OR BLACK POOL...
DAMN...
NOW THERE'S THREE SER-VAMPS.
SHA-CHA
RATTA
TAT
LET'S GO BACK.
TUG
THREE SER-VAMPS? UH-OH!
BUT THE PAIN! OWW...
YOU SAVED ME...

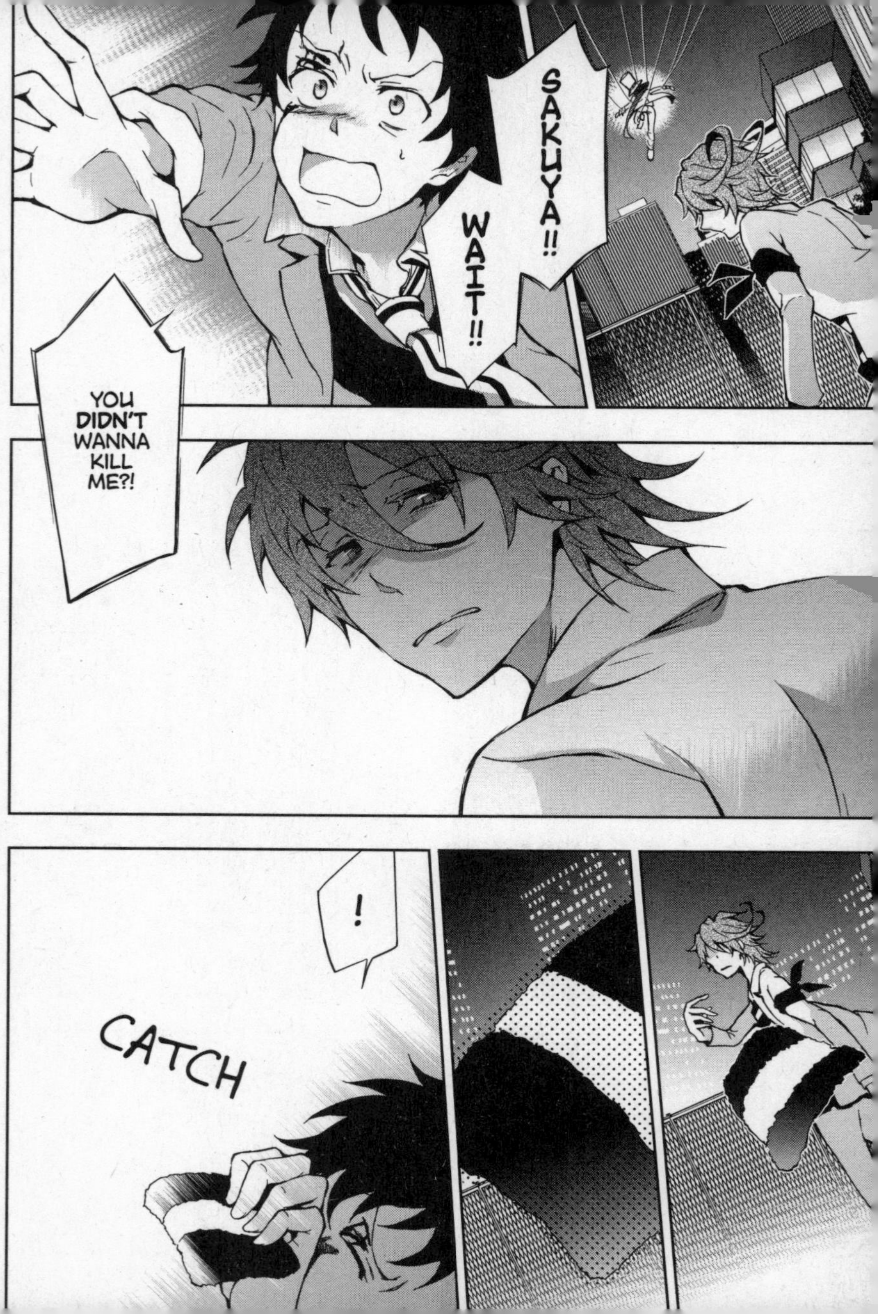
SAKUYA!!
WAIT!!
YOU DIDN'T WANNA KILL ME?!
!
CATCH

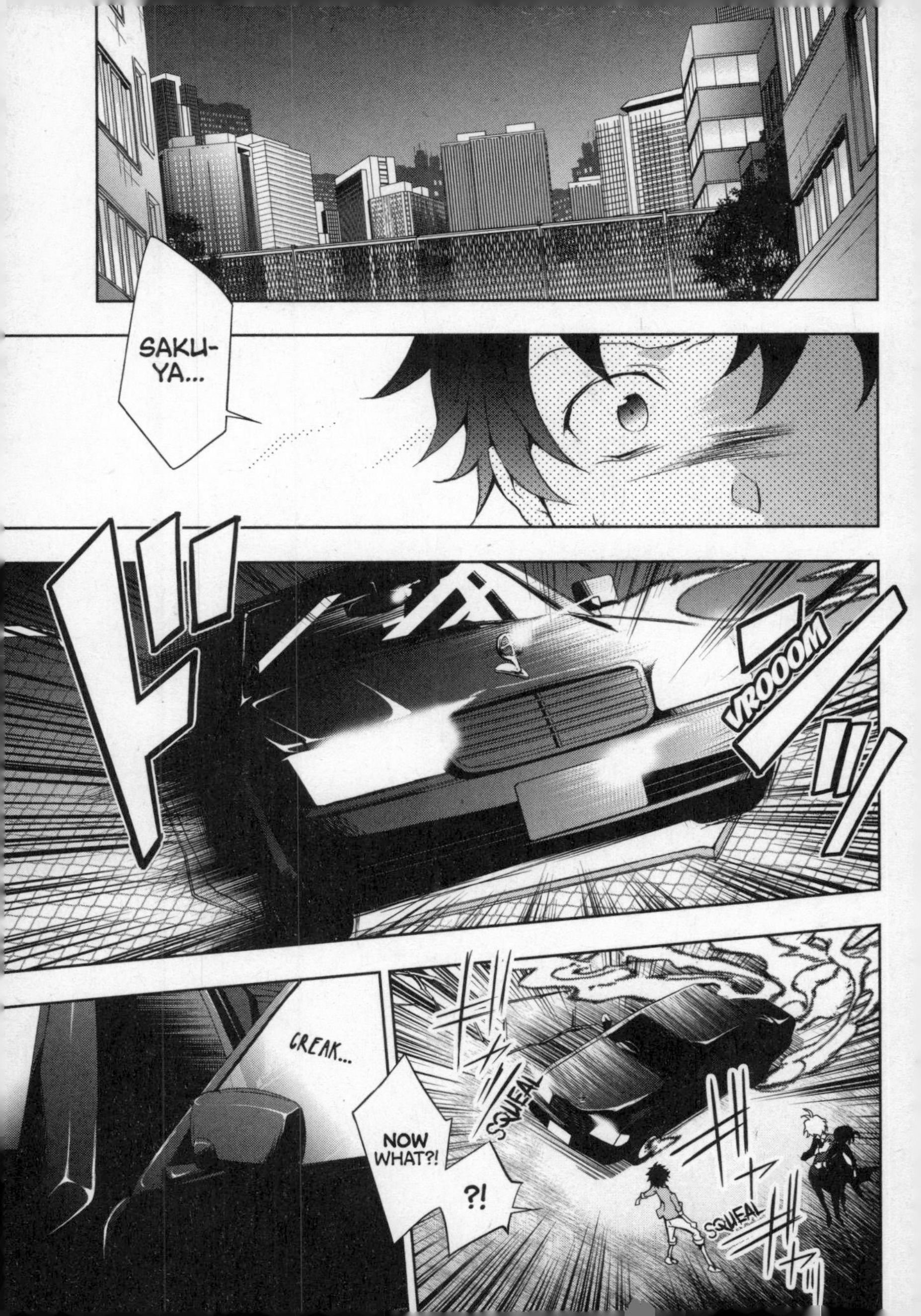
SAKU-
YA...
VROOOM
SQUEAL
NOW WHAT?!
?!
SQUEAL
CREAK...

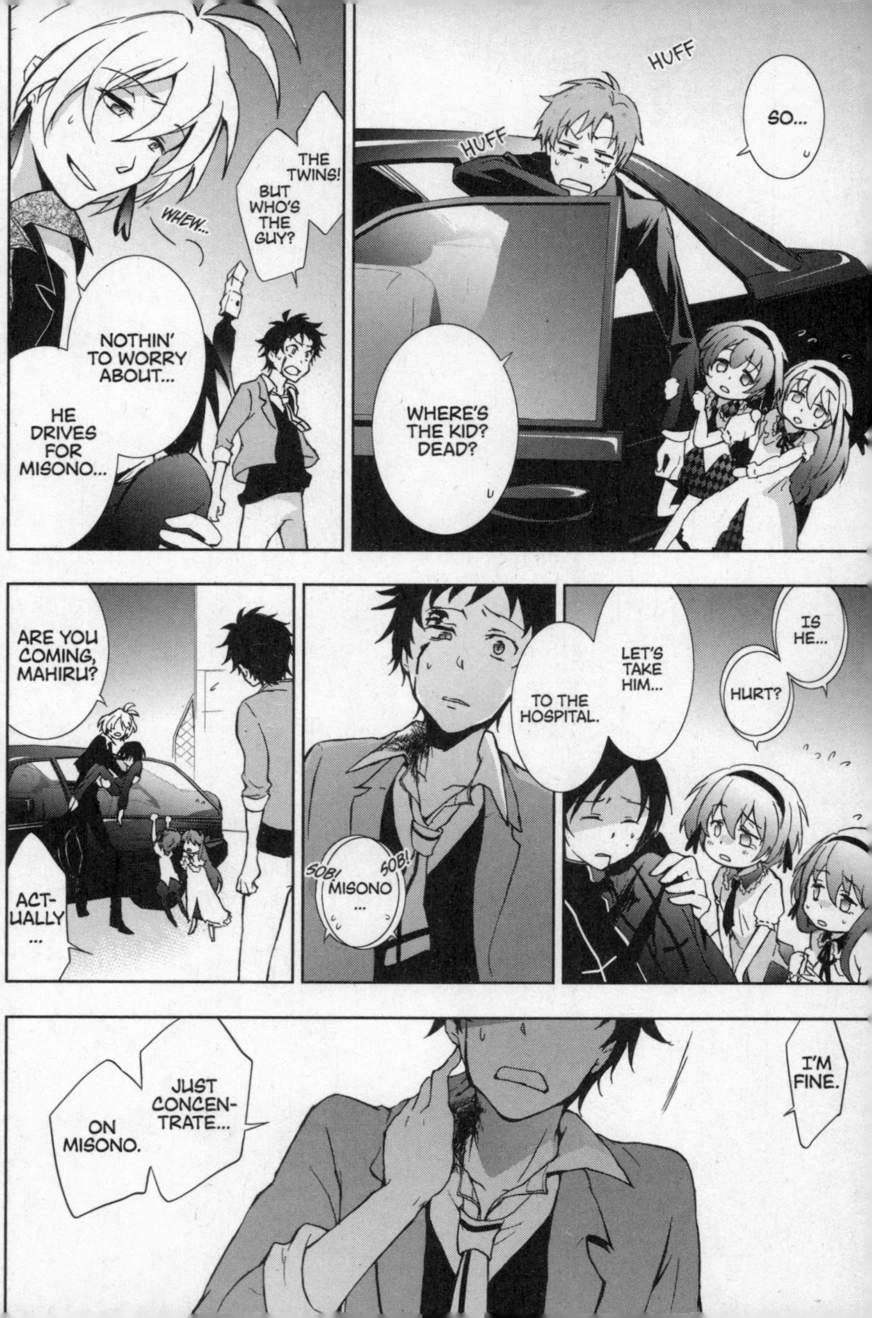
HUFF
SO...
HUFF
WHERE'S THE KID? DEAD?
THE TWINS! BUT WHO'S THE GUY?
WHEW...
NOTHIN' TO WORRY ABOUT...
HE DRIVES FOR MISONO...
IS HE...
HURT?
LET'S TAKE HIM...
TO THE HOSPITAL.
SOB! MISONO ... SOB!
ARE YOU COMING, MAHIRU?
ACT-UALLY ...
I'M FINE.
JUST CONCENTRATE...
ON MISONO.

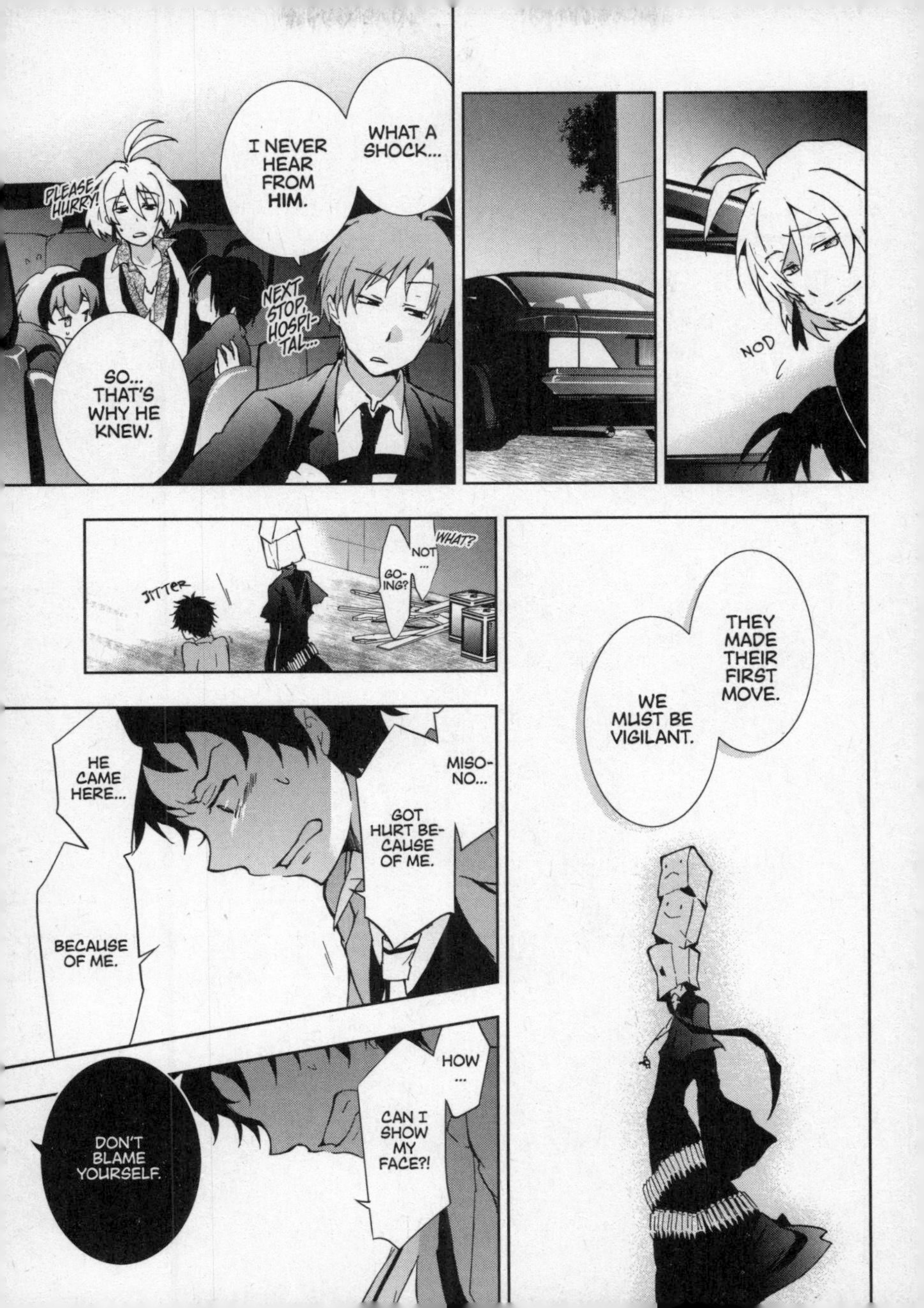
NOD
WHAT A SHOCK...
I NEVER HEAR FROM HIM.
NEXT STOP, HOSPITAL...
PLEASE HURRY!
SO... THAT'S WHY HE KNEW.
THEY MADE THEIR FIRST MOVE.
WE MUST BE VIGILANT.
WHAT?
NOT... GOING?
JITTER
MISONO...
GOT HURT BECAUSE OF ME.
HE CAME HERE...
BECAUSE OF ME.
HOW...
CAN I SHOW MY FACE?!
DON'T BLAME YOURSELF.

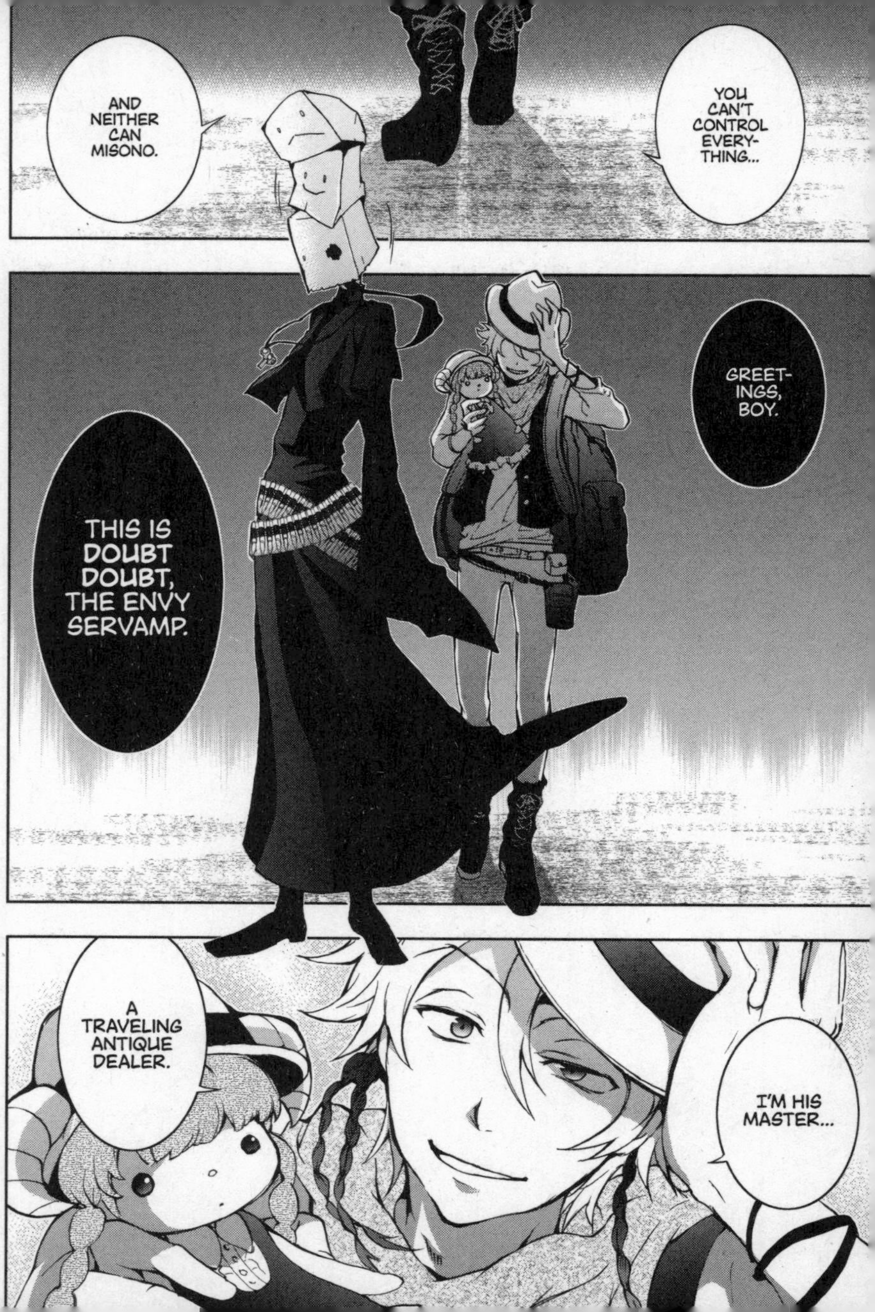
YOU CAN'T CONTROL EVERYTHING...
AND NEITHER CAN MISONO.
GREETINGS, BOY.
THIS IS DOUBT DOUBT, THE ENVY SERVAMP.
I'M HIS MASTER...
A TRAVELING ANTIQUE DEALER.

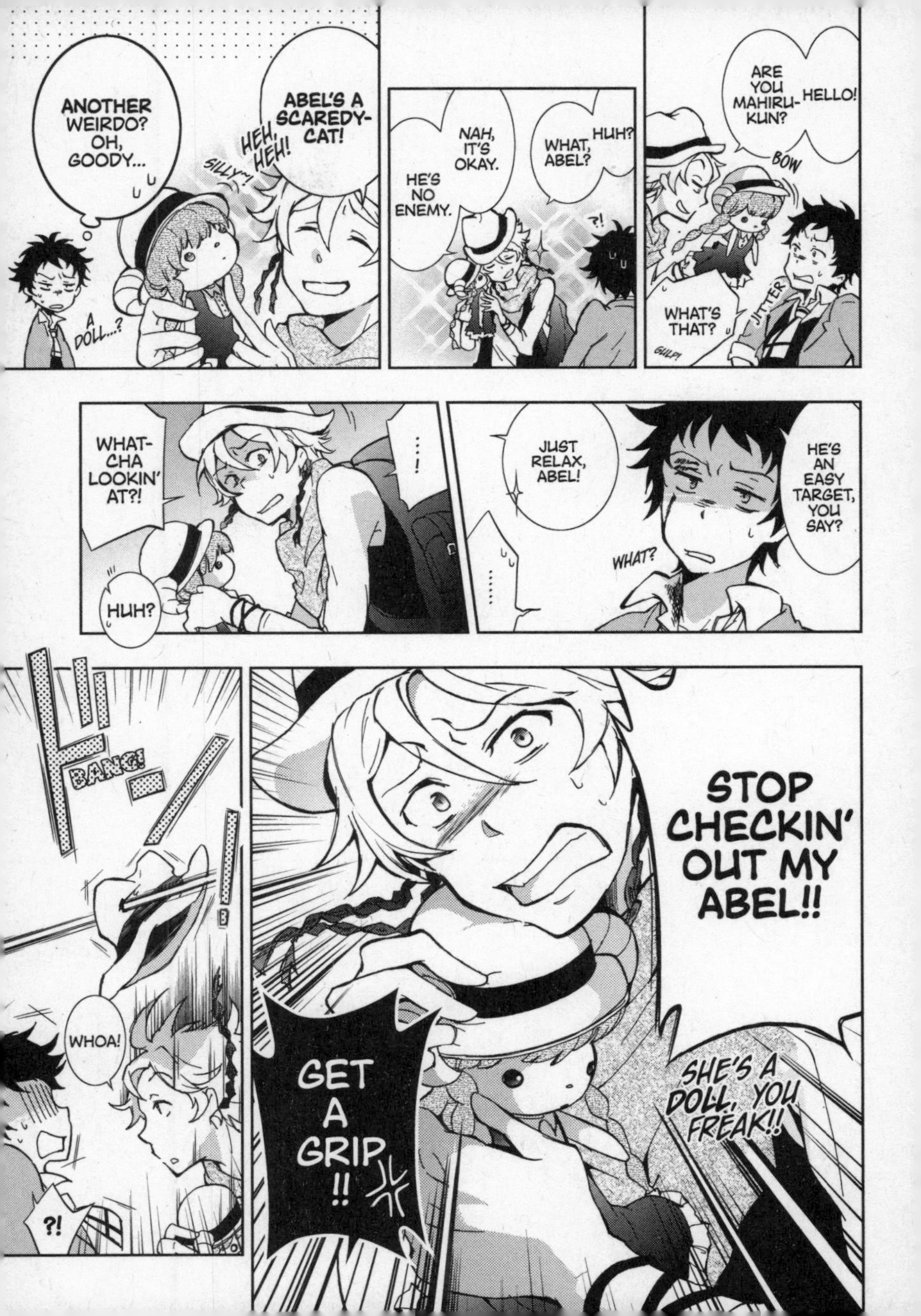
HELLO!
ARE YOU MAHIRU-KUN?
BOW
JITTER
WHAT'S THAT?
GULP!
HUH?
WHAT, ABEL?
NAH, IT'S OKAY.
HE'S NO ENEMY.
?!
ABEL'S A SCAREDY-CAT!
HEH, HEH!
SILLY~!
ANOTHER WEIRDO? OH, GOODY...
A DOLL...?
HE'S AN EASY TARGET, YOU SAY?
JUST RELAX, ABEL!
WHAT?
......
...!
WHAT-CHA LOOKIN' AT?!
HUH?
STOP CHECKIN' OUT MY ABEL!!
SHE'S A DOLL, YOU FREAK!!
GET A GRIP!!
BANG!
WHOA!
?!

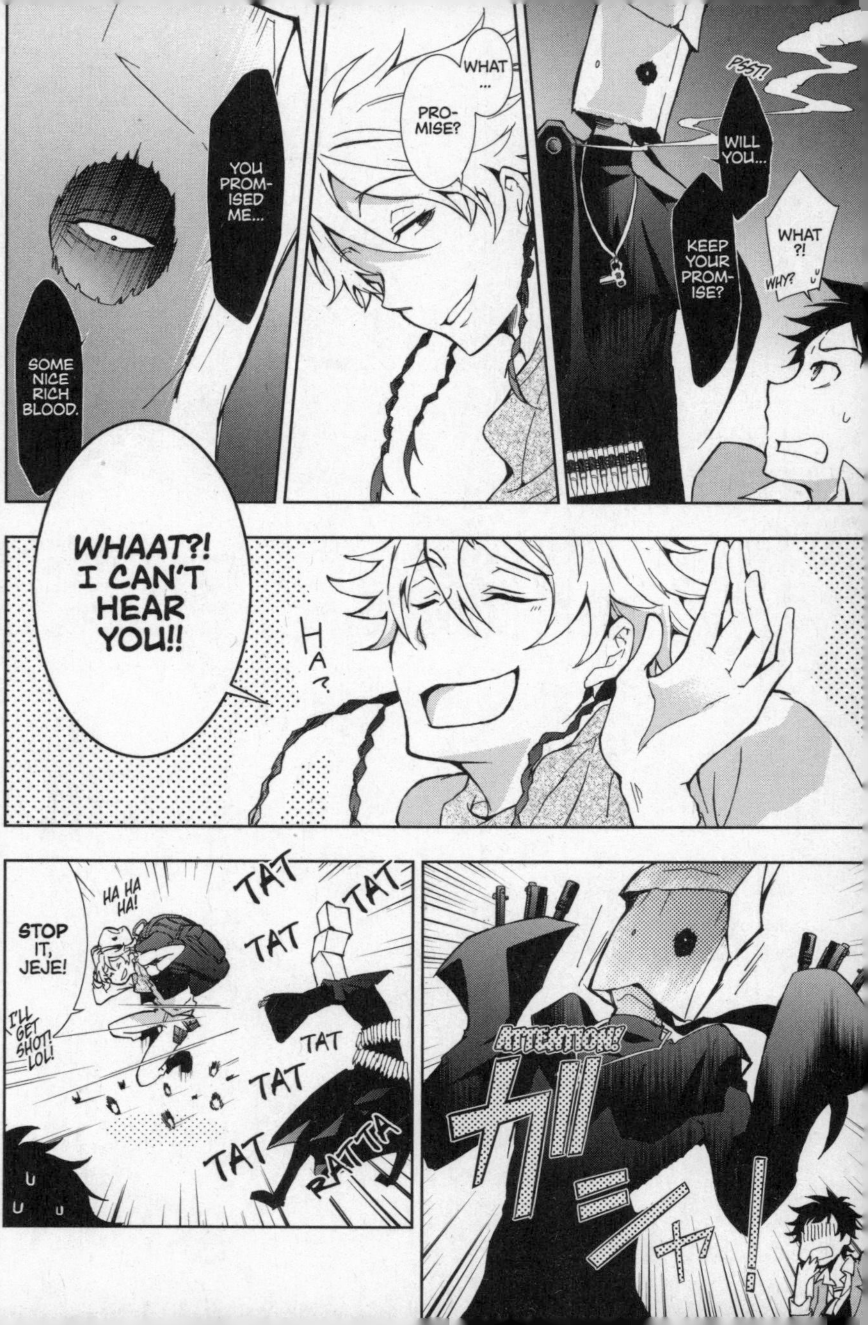
PSST!
WILL YOU...
KEEP YOUR PROMISE?
WHAT ?!
WHY?
WHAT ... PROMISE?
YOU PROMISED ME...
SOME NICE RICH BLOOD.
WHAAT?! I CAN'T HEAR YOU!!
ATTENTION!
HA HA HA!
STOP IT, JEJE!
I'LL GET SHOT! LOL!
TAT
TAT
TAT
TAT
TAT
TAT
RATTA

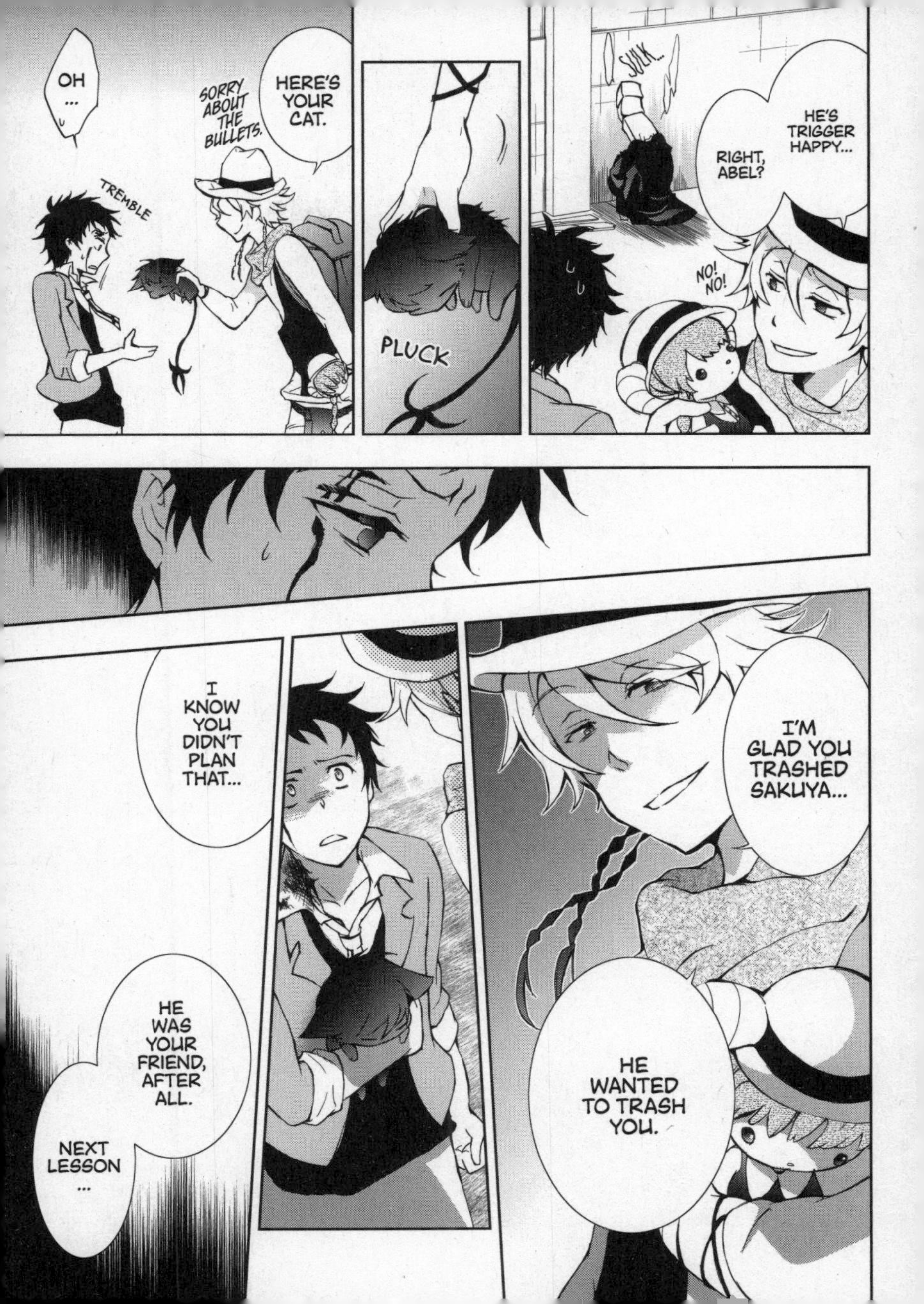
SULK...
HE'S TRIGGER HAPPY...
RIGHT, ABEL?
NO! NO!
PLUCK
HERE'S YOUR CAT.
SORRY ABOUT THE BULLETS.
OH ...
TREMBLE
I'M GLAD YOU TRASHED SAKUYA...
HE WANTED TO TRASH YOU.
I KNOW YOU DIDN'T PLAN THAT...
HE WAS YOUR FRIEND, AFTER ALL.
NEXT LESSON ...

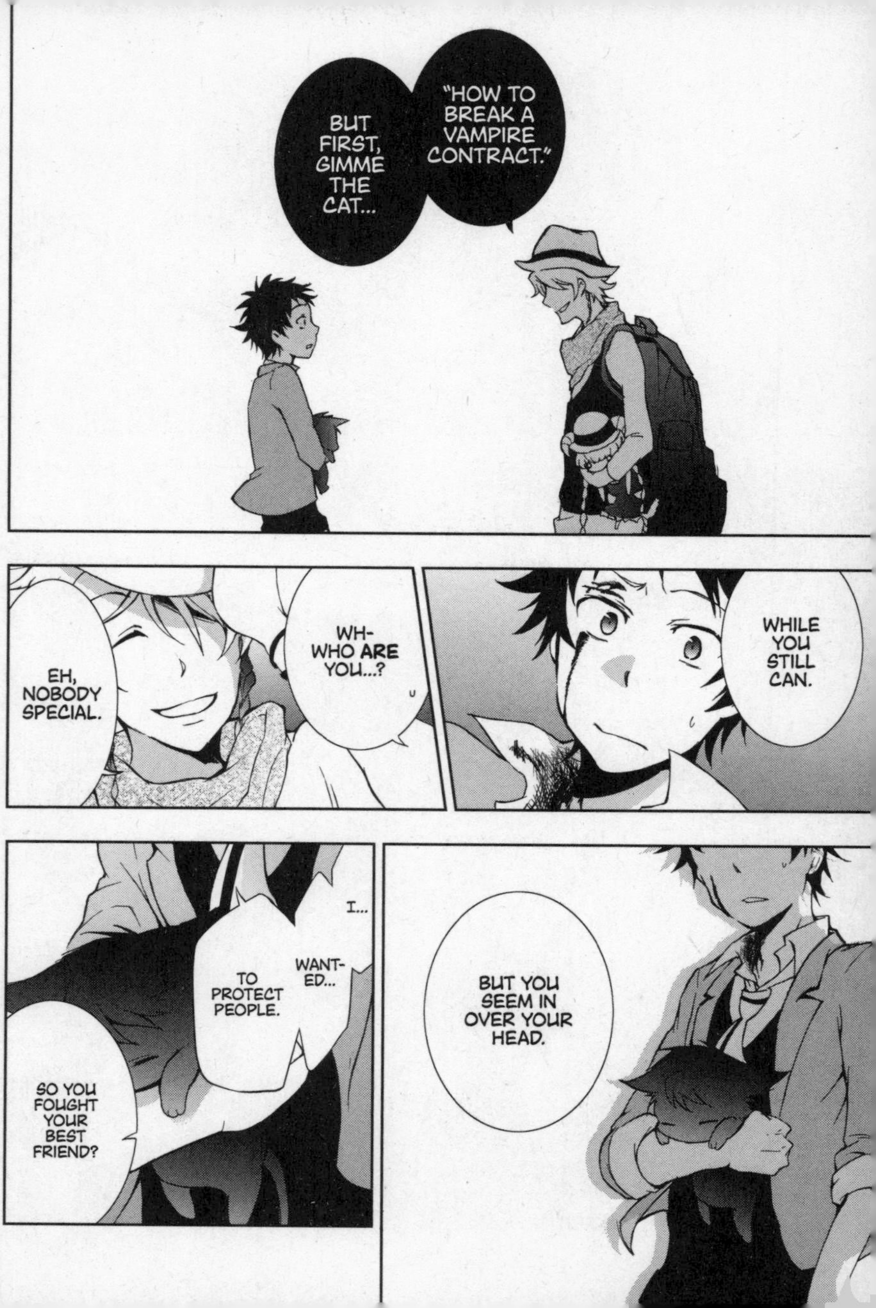
"HOW TO BREAK A VAMPIRE CONTRACT."
BUT FIRST, GIMME THE CAT...
WHILE YOU STILL CAN.
WH-WHO ARE YOU...?
EH, NOBODY SPECIAL.
BUT YOU SEEM IN OVER YOUR HEAD.
I...
WANT-ED...
TO PROTECT PEOPLE.
SO YOU FOUGHT YOUR BEST FRIEND?

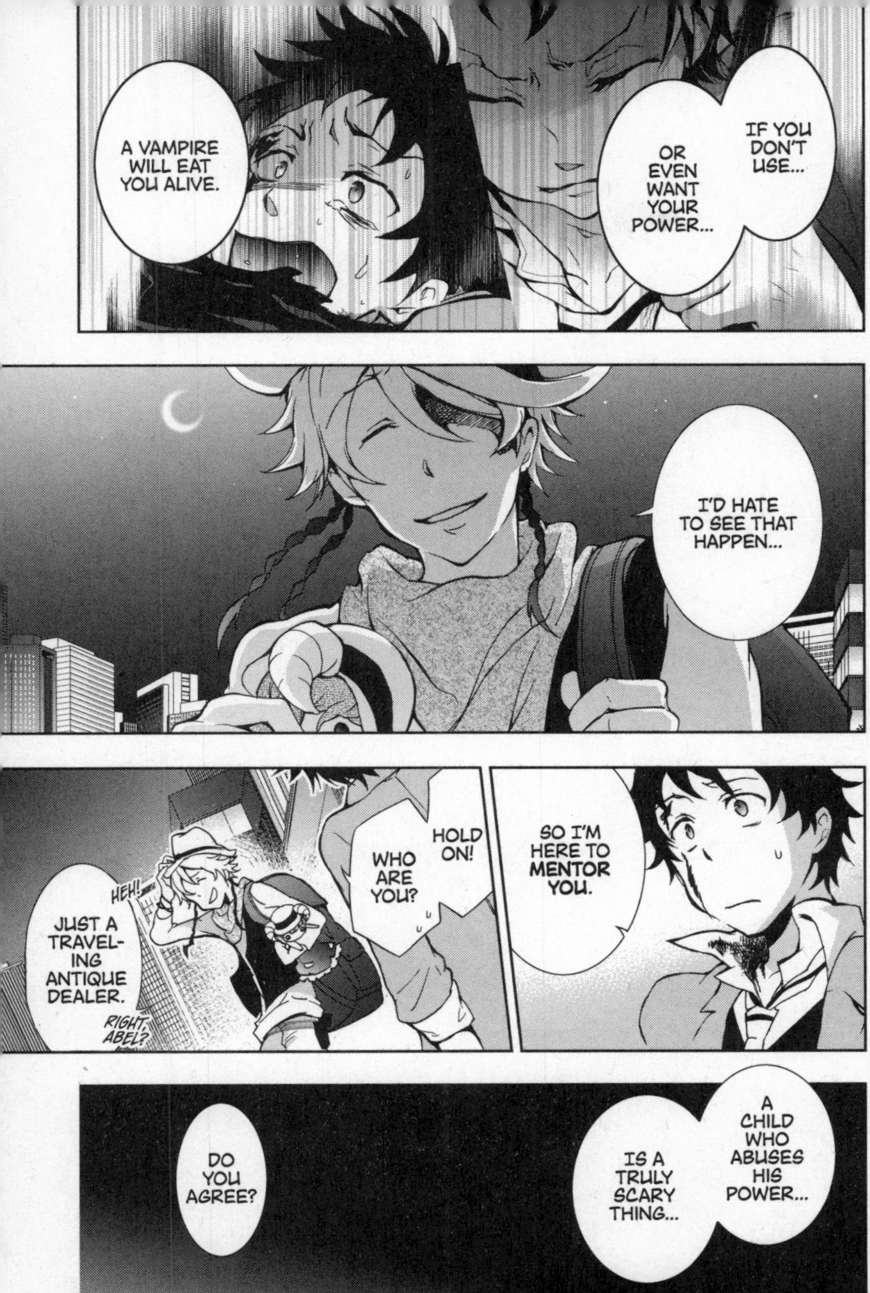
IF YOU DON'T USE...
OR EVEN WANT YOUR POWER...
A VAMPIRE WILL EAT YOU ALIVE.
I'D HATE TO SEE THAT HAPPEN...
SO I'M HERE TO MENTOR YOU.
HOLD ON!
WHO ARE YOU?
HEH!
JUST A TRAVEL-ING ANTIQUE DEALER.
RIGHT, ABEL?
A CHILD WHO ABUSES HIS POWER...
IS A TRULY SCARY THING...
DO YOU AGREE?

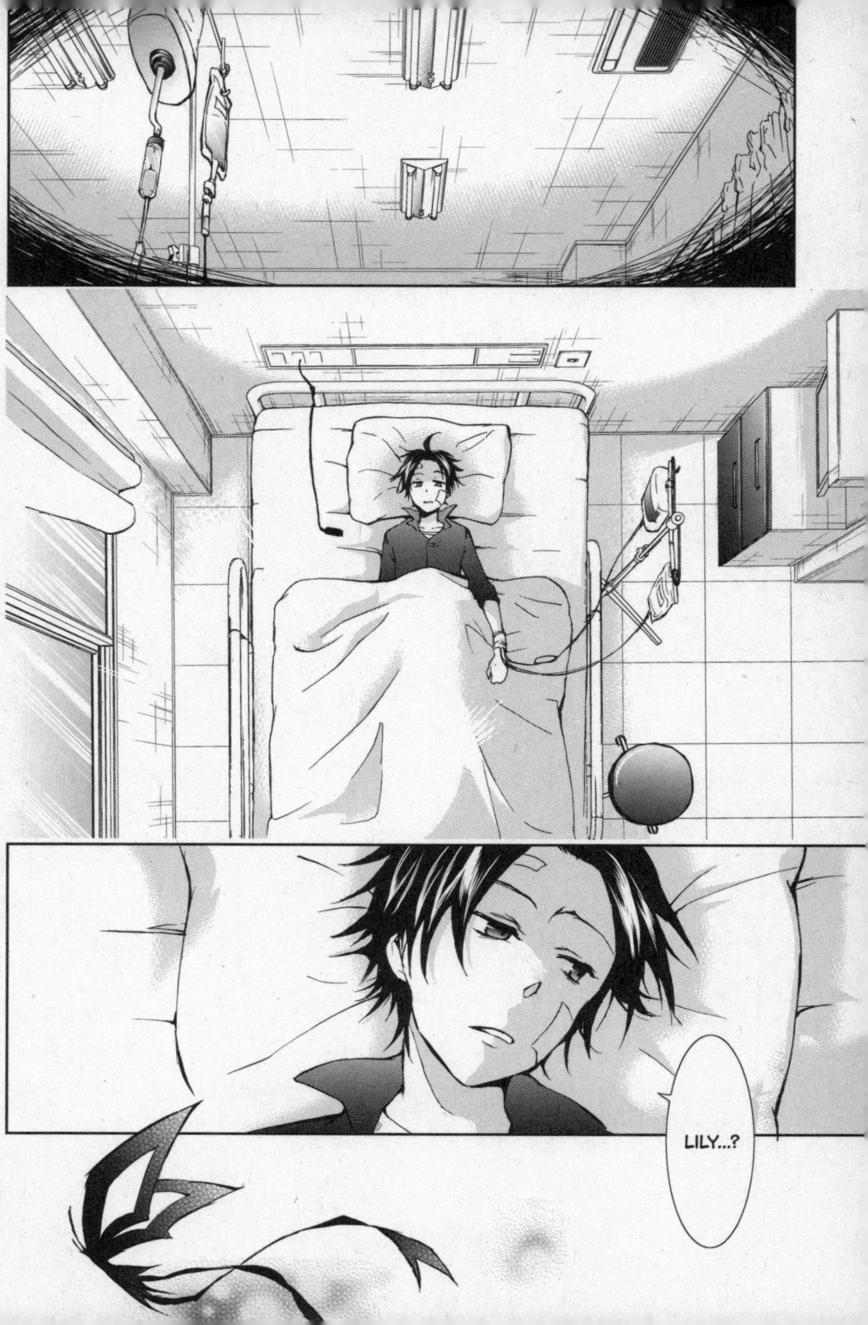
LILY...?

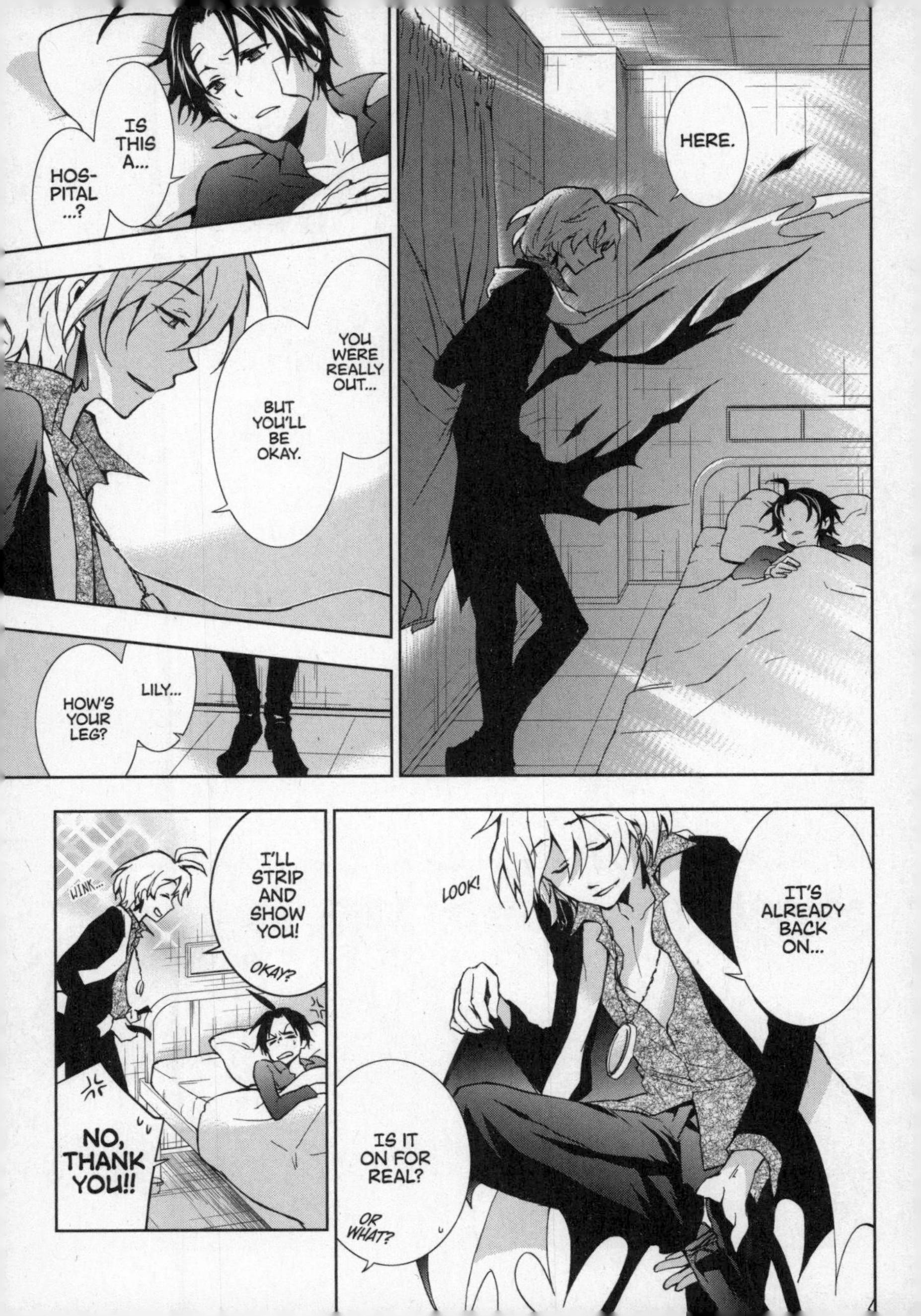
HERE.
IS THIS A... HOSPITAL...?
YOU WERE REALLY OUT...
BUT YOU'LL BE OKAY.
LILY...
HOW'S YOUR LEG?
IT'S ALREADY BACK ON...
LOOK!
IS IT ON FOR REAL?
OR WHAT?
I'LL STRIP AND SHOW YOU!
OKAY?
WINK...
NO, THANK YOU!!

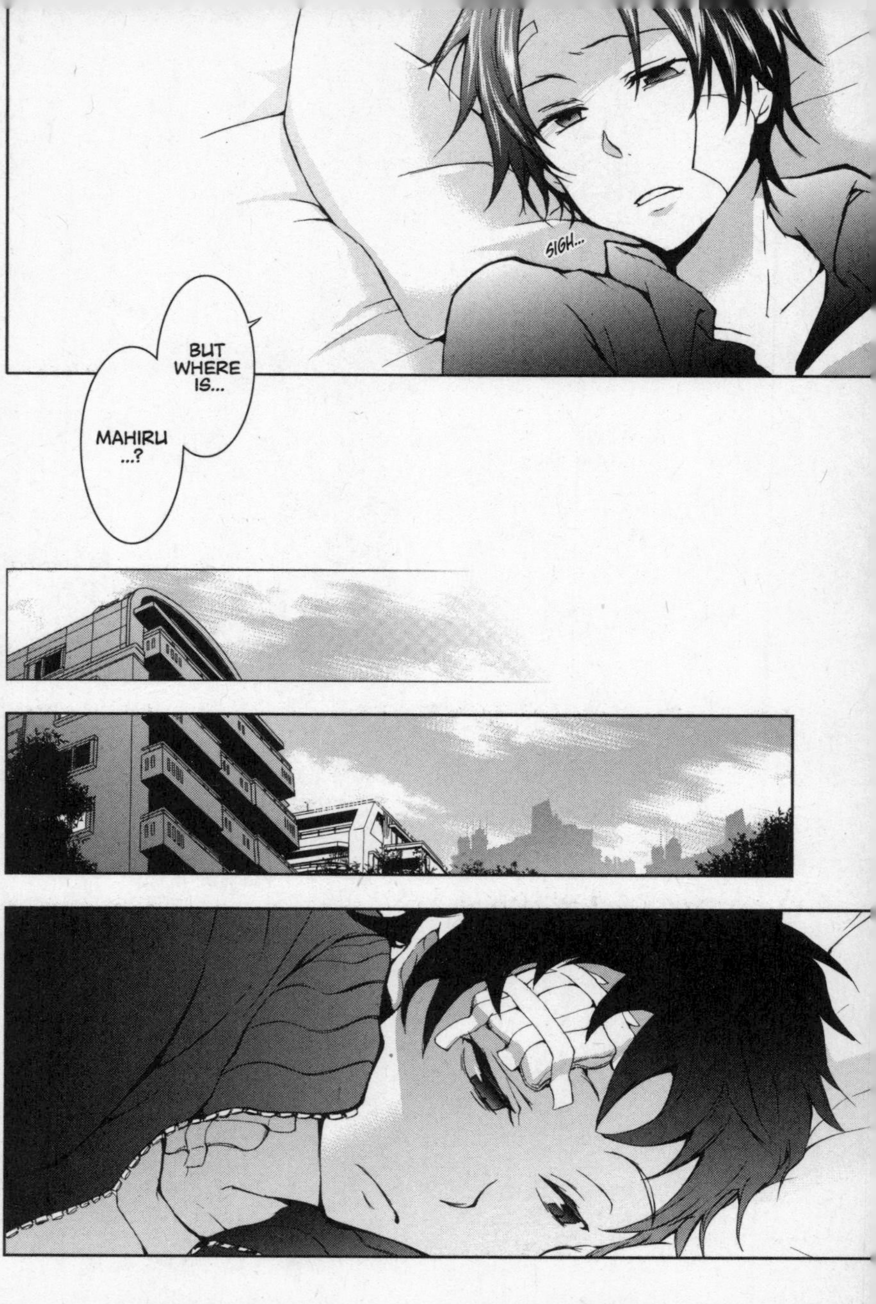
SIGH...
BUT WHERE IS...
MAHIRU ...?

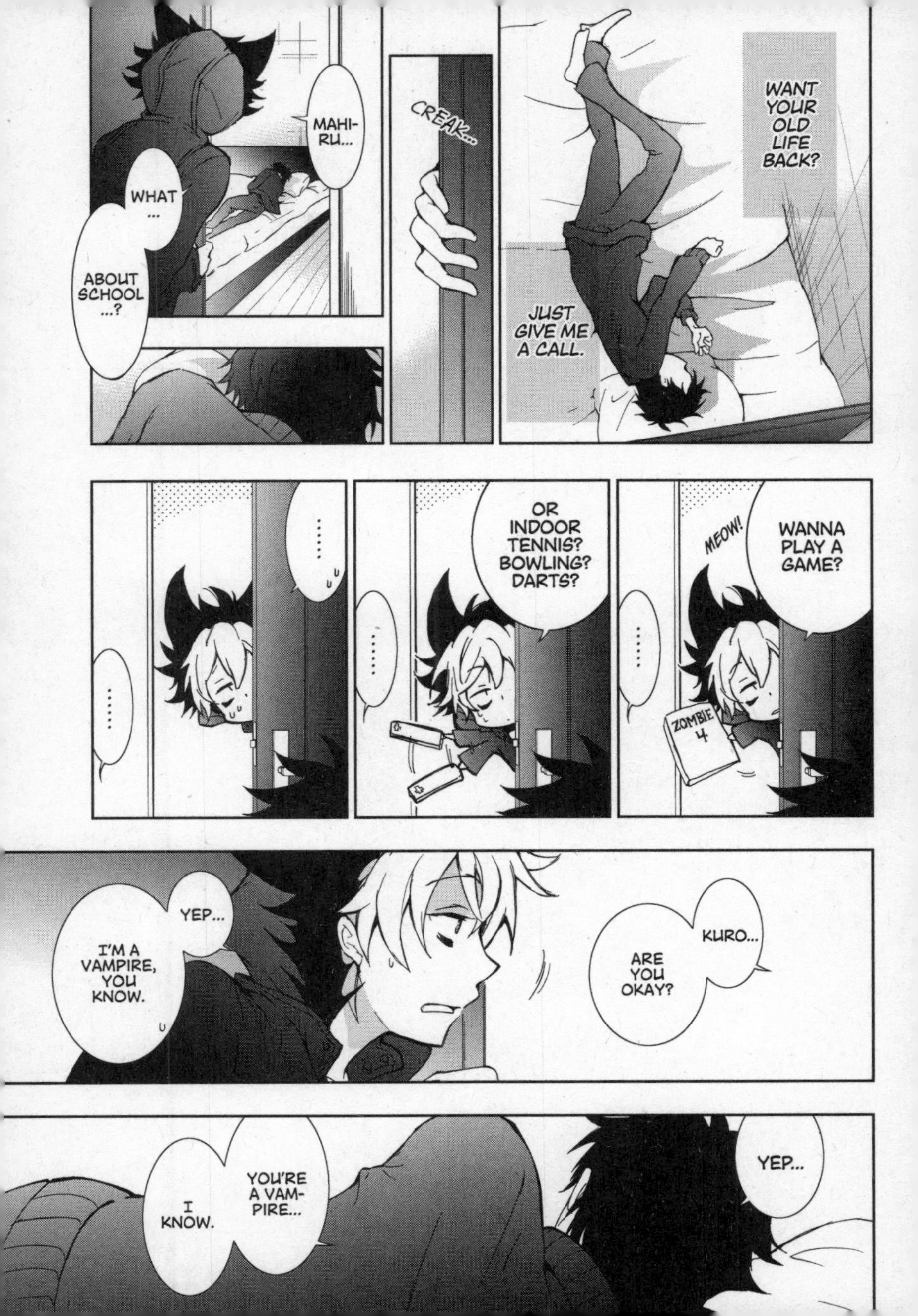
WANT YOUR OLD LIFE BACK?
JUST GIVE ME A CALL.
CREAK...
MAHI-RU...
WHAT ... ABOUT SCHOOL ...?
MEOW!
WANNA PLAY A GAME?
ZOMBIE 4
......
OR INDOOR TENNIS? BOWLING? DARTS?
......
......
......
KURO...
ARE YOU OKAY?
YEP...
I'M A VAMPIRE, YOU KNOW.
YEP...
YOU'RE A VAMPIRE...
I KNOW.

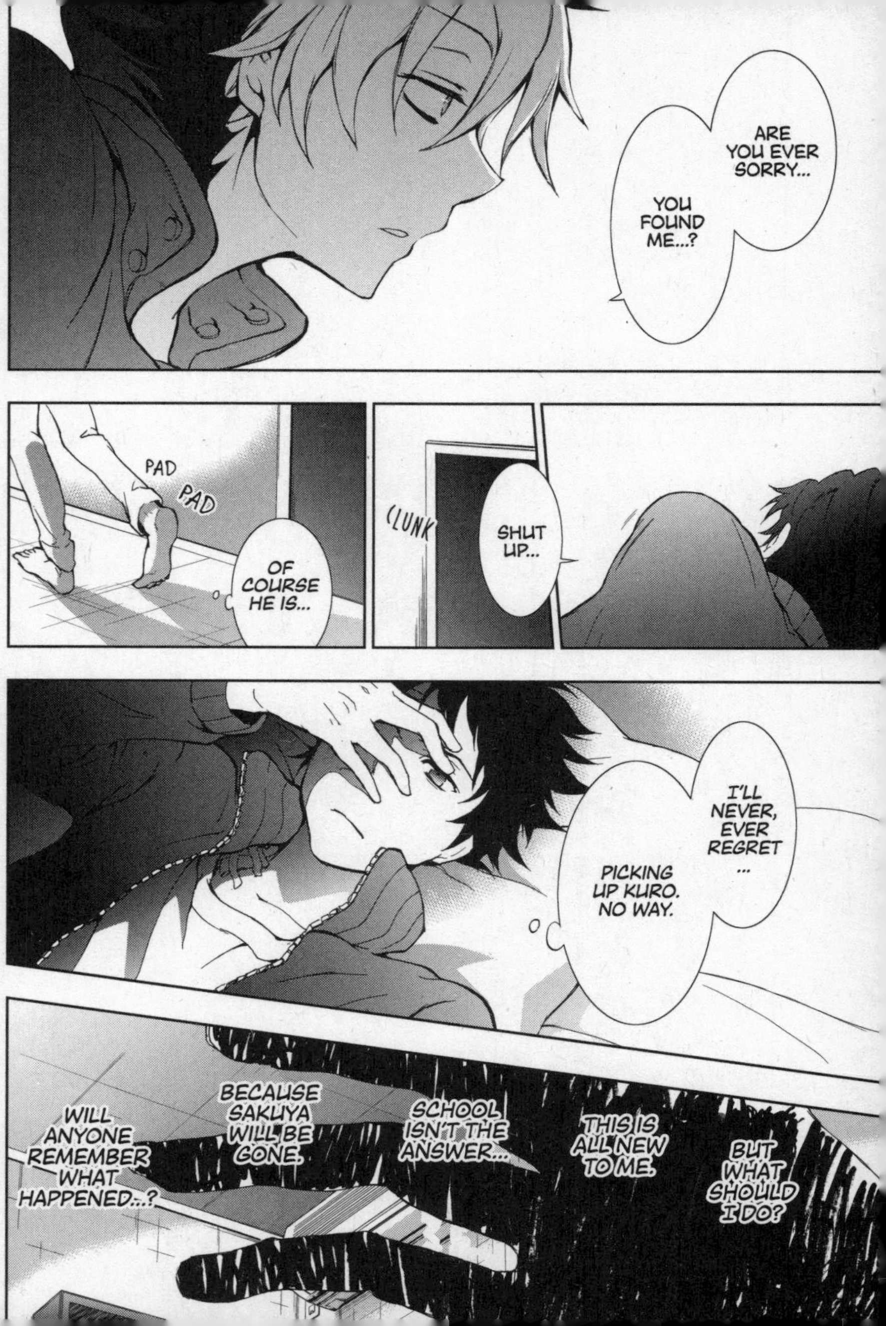
ARE YOU EVER SORRY... YOU FOUND ME...?
SHUT UP...
CLUNK
PAD
PAD
OF COURSE HE IS...
I'LL NEVER, EVER REGRET... PICKING UP KURO. NO WAY.
BUT WHAT SHOULD I DO?
THIS IS ALL NEW TO ME.
SCHOOL ISN'T THE ANSWER...
BECAUSE SAKUYA WILL BE GONE.
WILL ANYONE REMEMBER WHAT HAPPENED...?

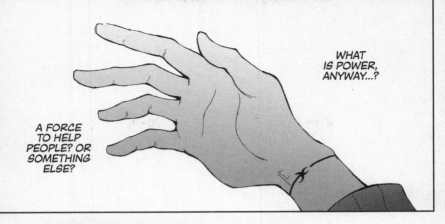

WHAT IS POWER, ANYWAY...?

A FORCE TO HELP PEOPLE? OR SOMETHING ELSE?

OH, RIGHT!

MA-HIRU!

I'M HOME!!

DING DING DONG DONG

STOMP

CLICK

SLAM

HE MUST BE AT SCH-OOL...

STOMP

STOMP

BLEEP

BLOOP

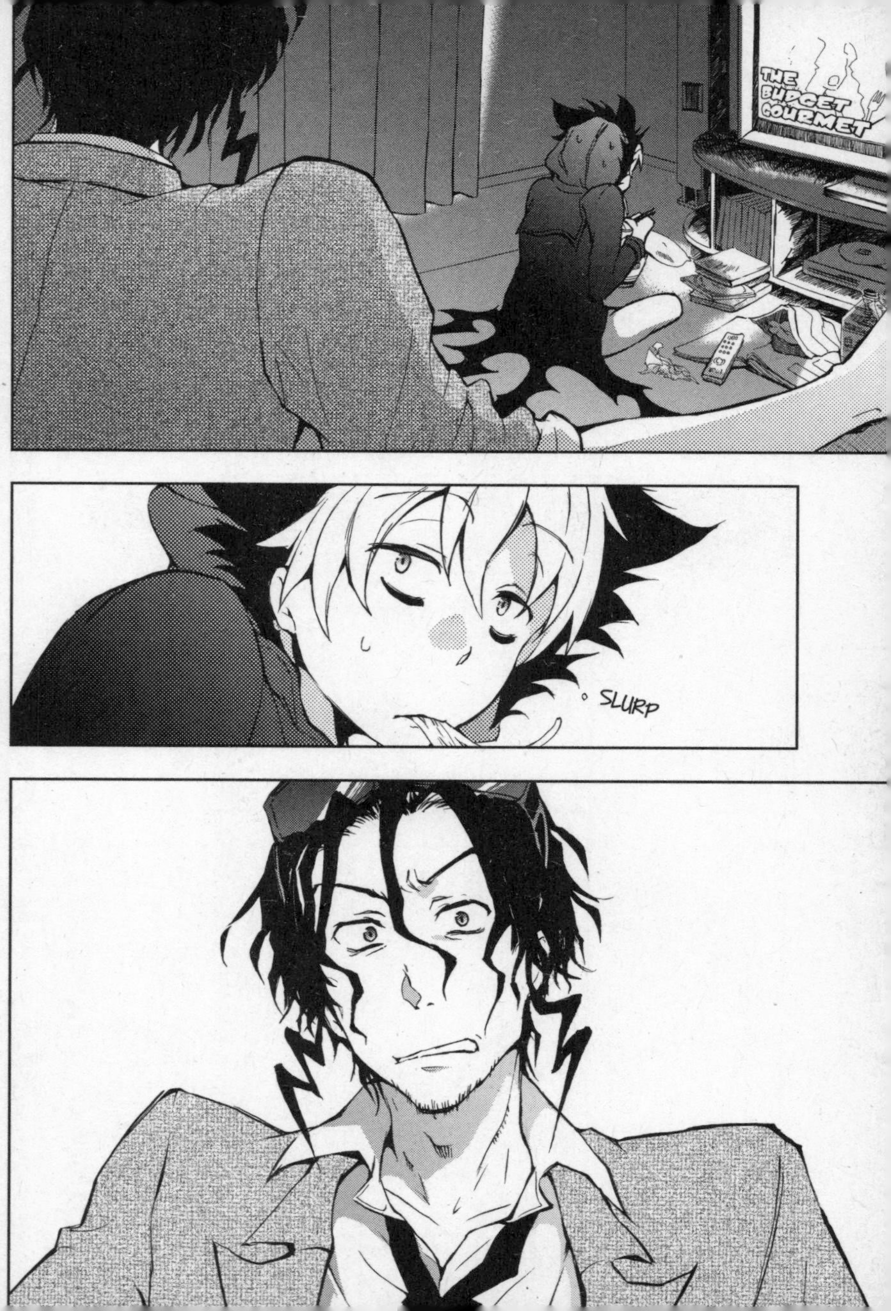
THE BUDGET GOURMET
SLURP

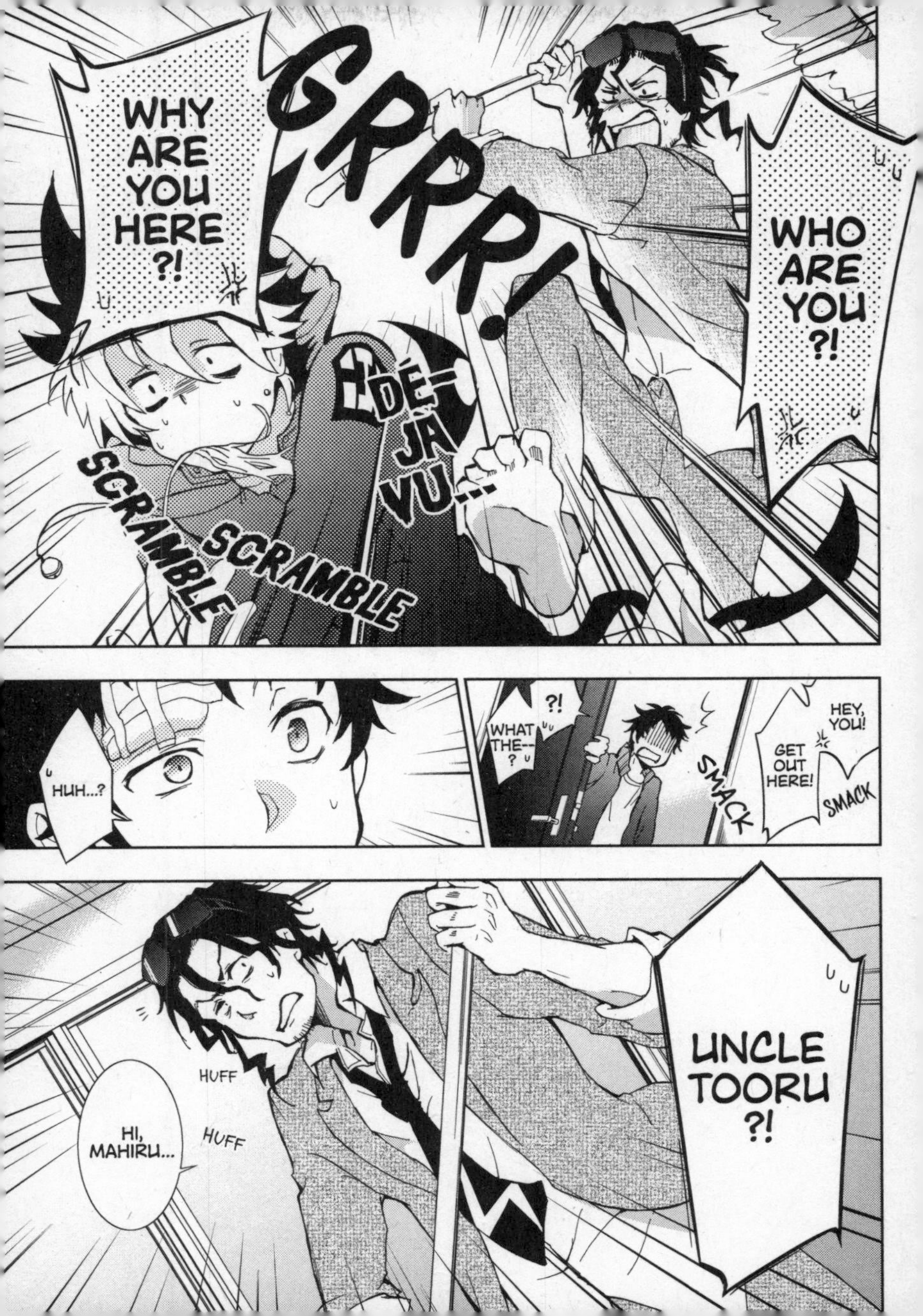
GRRR!
WHO ARE YOU ?!
WHY ARE YOU HERE ?!
DÉ-JA VU...
SCRAMBLE
SCRAMBLE
HEY, YOU!
GET OUT HERE!
SMACK
SMACK
?!
WHAT THE-- ?
HUH...?
UNCLE TOORU ?!
HUFF
HUFF
HI, MAHIRU...

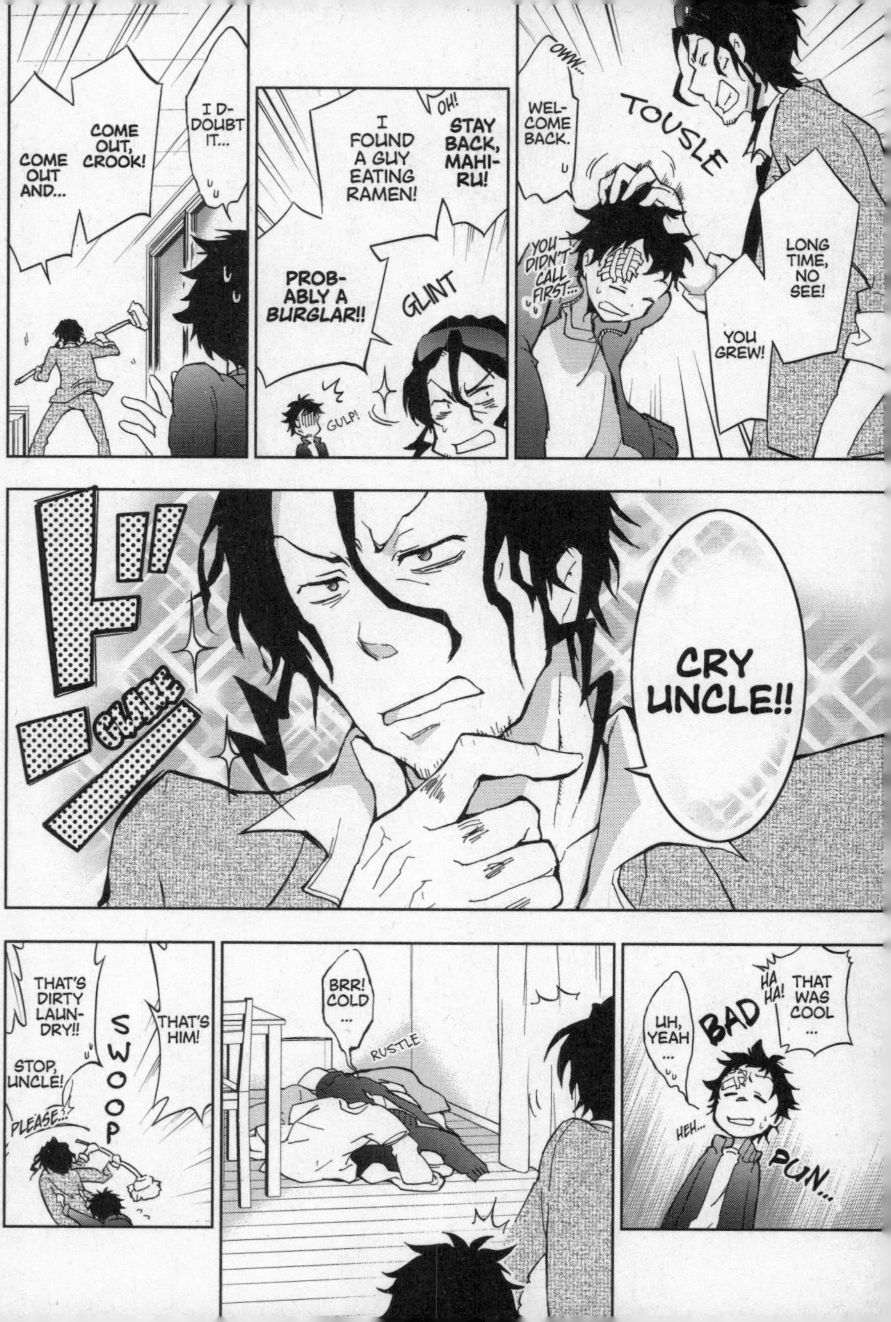
TOUSLE
OWW...
WEL-COME BACK.
LONG TIME, NO SEE!
YOU GREW!
YOU DIDN'T CALL FIRST...
OH!
STAY BACK, MAHI-RU!
I FOUND A GUY EATING RAMEN!
PROB-ABLY A BURGLAR!!
GLINT
GULP!
I D-DOUBT IT...
COME OUT, CROOK!
COME OUT AND...
CRY UNCLE!!
THAT WAS COOL...
HA HA!
BAD
UH, YEAH...
PUN...
HEH...
BRR! COLD...
RUSTLE
THAT'S HIM!
SWOOP
THAT'S DIRTY LAUN-DRY!!
STOP, UNCLE!
PLEASE...

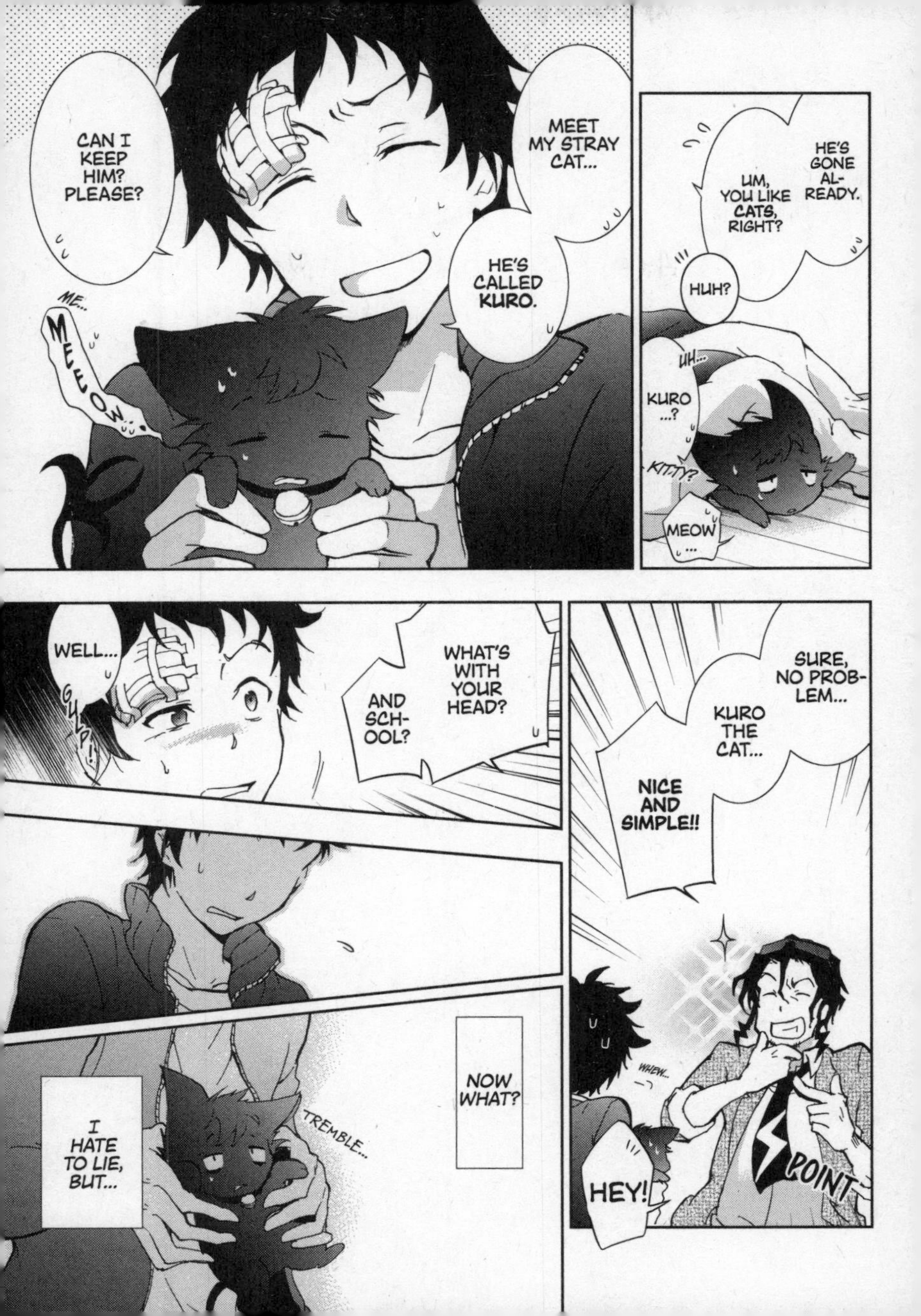
HE'S GONE AL-READY.
UM, YOU LIKE CATS, RIGHT?
HUH?
UH...
KURO ...?
KITTY?
MEOW ...
MEET MY STRAY CAT...
HE'S CALLED KURO.
CAN I KEEP HIM? PLEASE?
ME...
MEEEOW
SURE, NO PROB-LEM...
KURO THE CAT...
NICE AND SIMPLE!!
WHEW...
POINT
HEY!
WHAT'S WITH YOUR HEAD?
AND SCH-OOL?
WELL...
GULP!
NOW WHAT?
TREMBLE...
I HATE TO LIE, BUT...

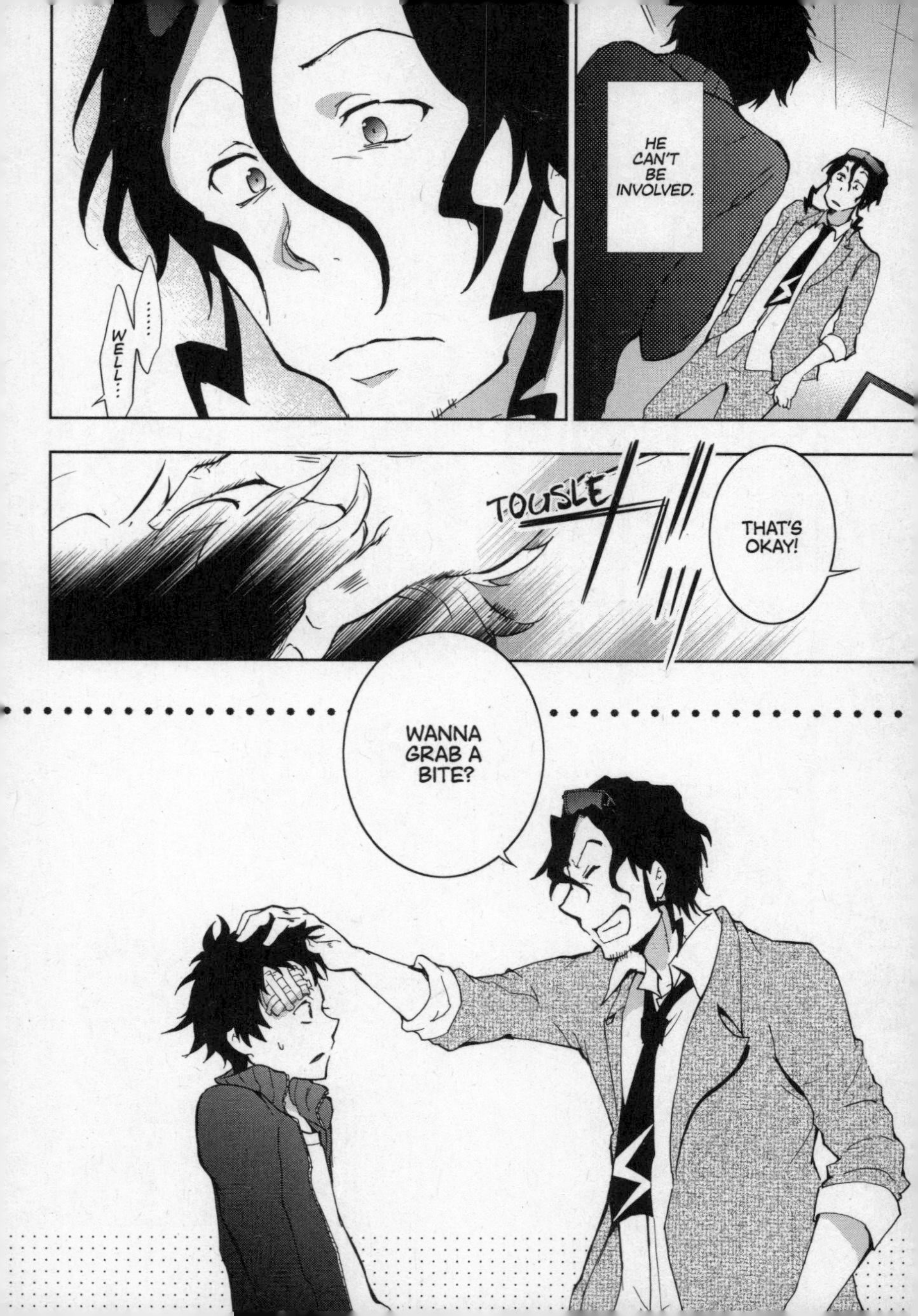
HE CAN'T BE INVOLVED.
WELL......
THAT'S OKAY!
TOUSLE
WANNA GRAB A BITE?

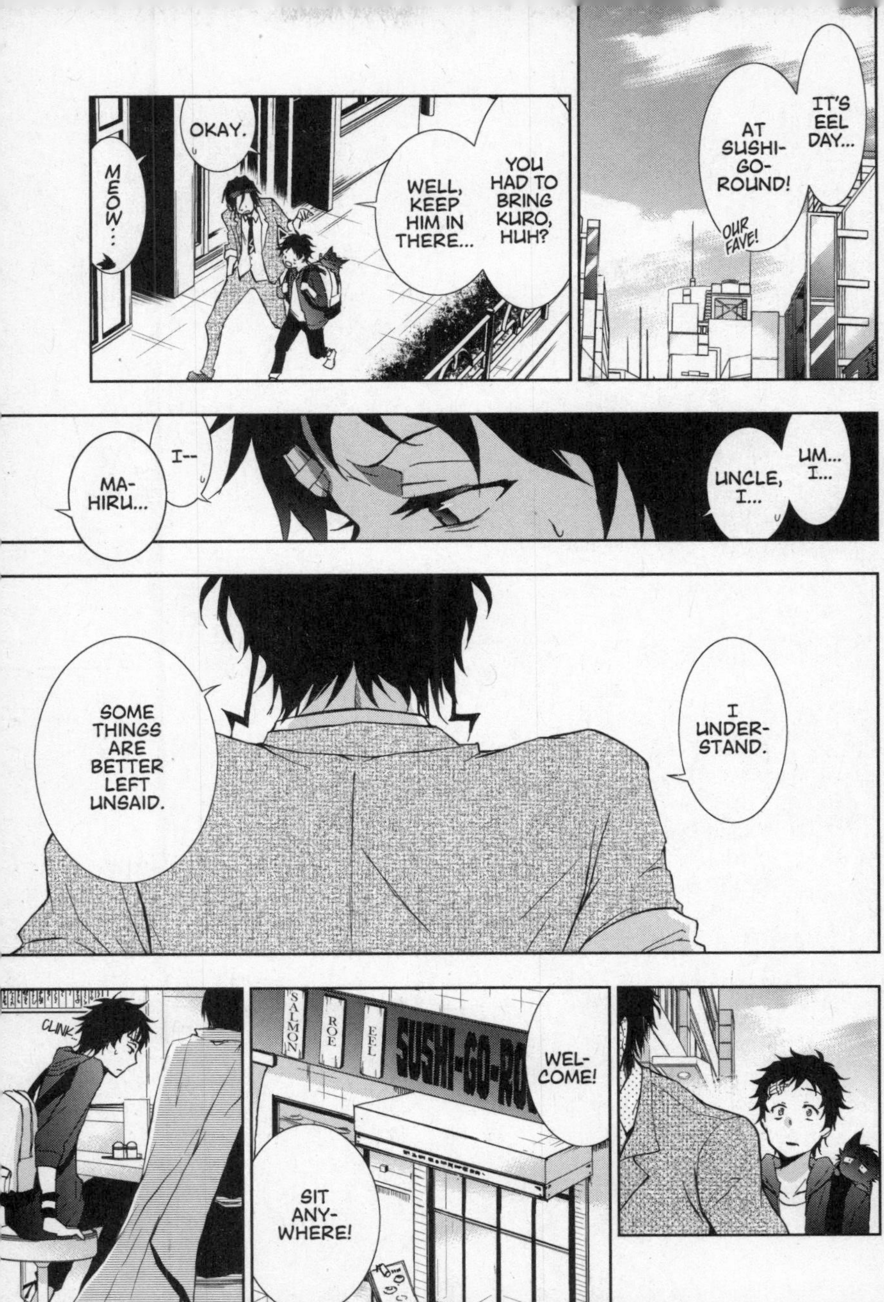
IT'S EEL DAY...
AT SUSHI-GO-ROUND!
OUR FAVE!
YOU HAD TO BRING KURO, HUH?
WELL, KEEP HIM IN THERE...
OKAY.
MEOW...
UM... I...
UNCLE, I...
I--
MA-HIRU...
I UNDER-STAND.
SOME THINGS ARE BETTER LEFT UNSAID.
SALMON
ROE
EEL
SUSHI-GO-RO
WEL-COME!
SIT ANY-WHERE!
CLINK...

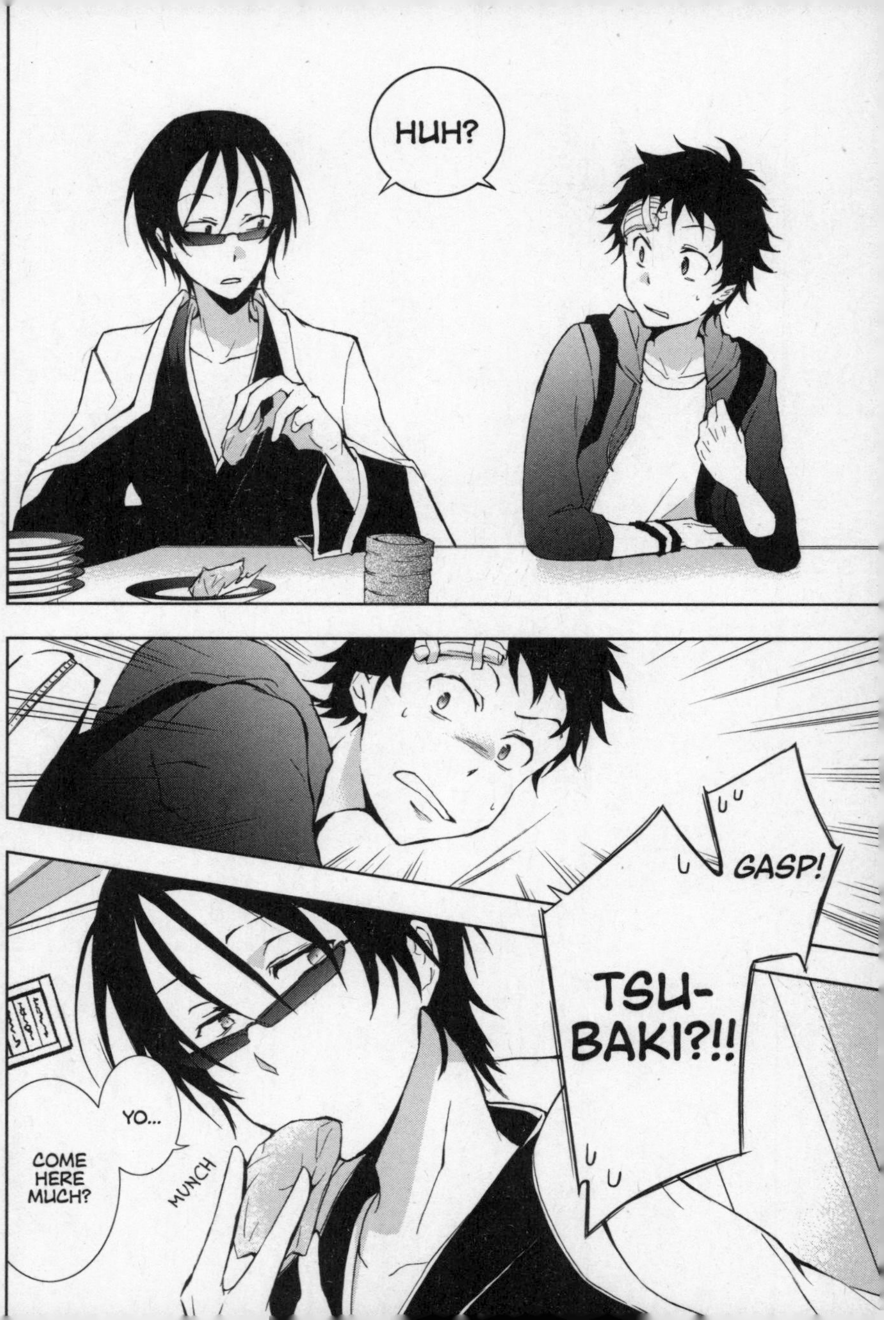
HUH?
GASP!
TSU-BAKI?!!
YO...
COME HERE MUCH?
MUNCH

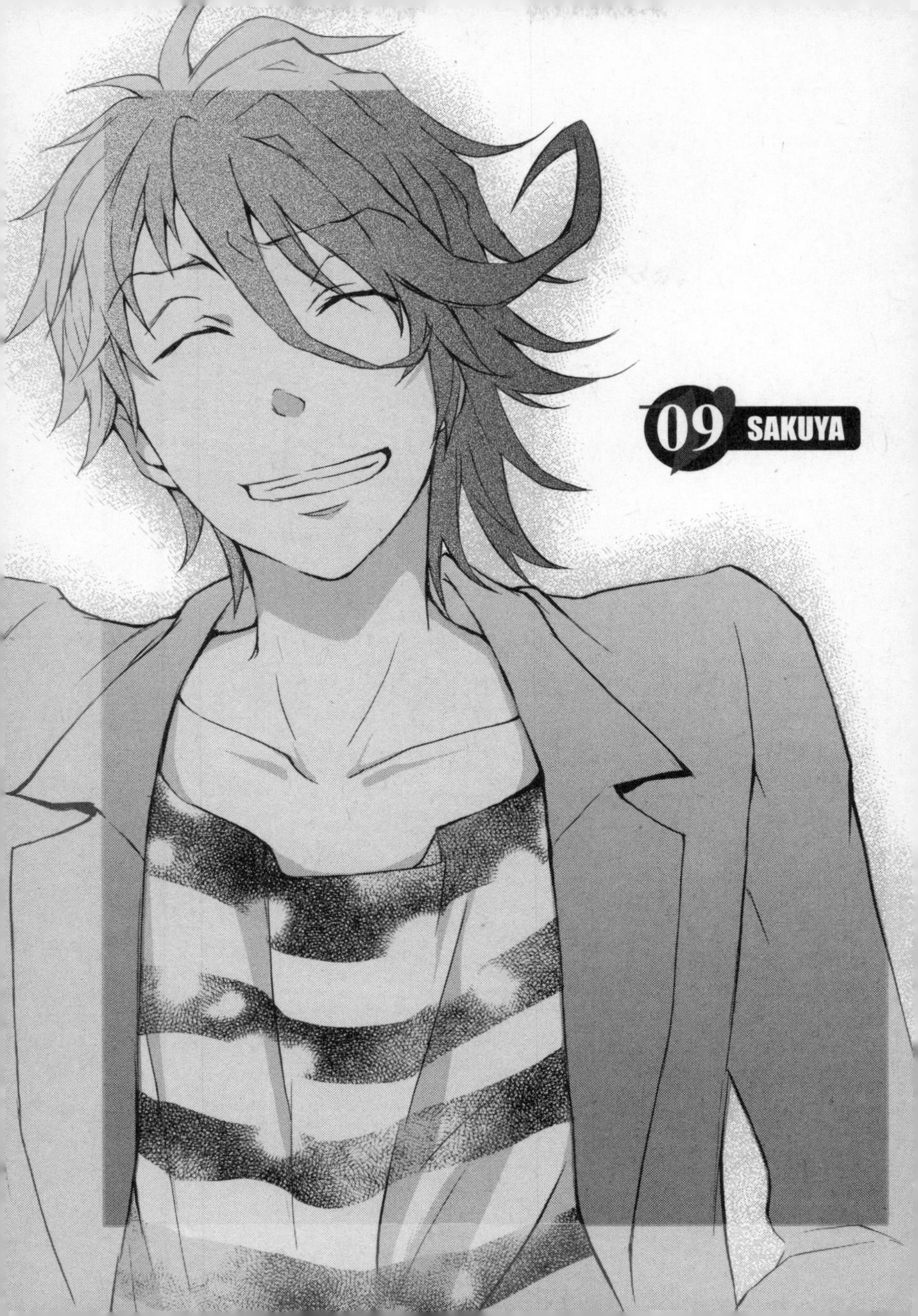
09 SAKUYA

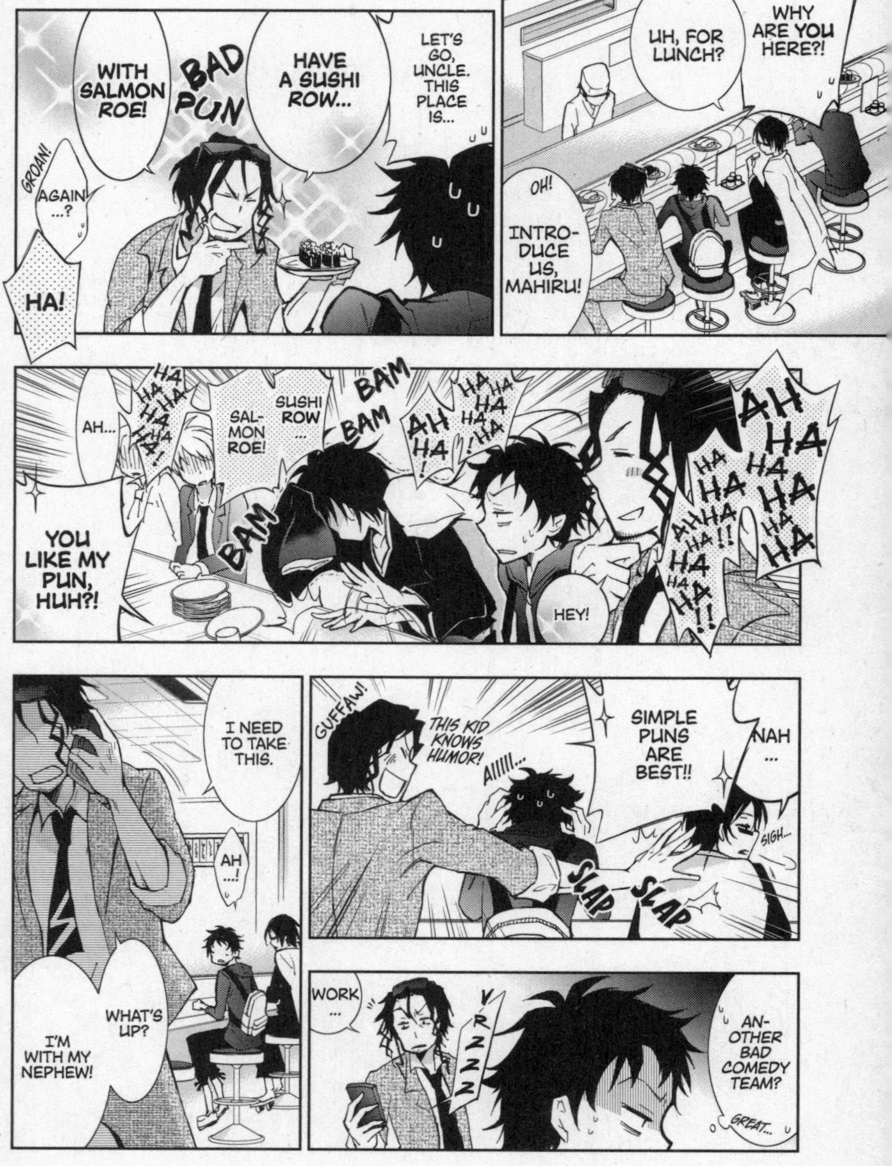
WHY ARE YOU HERE?!
UH, FOR LUNCH?
OH!
INTRODUCE US, MAHIRU!
LET'S GO, UNCLE. THIS PLACE IS...
HAVE A SUSHI ROW...
BAD PUN
WITH SALMON ROE!
GROAN!
AGAIN ...?
HA!
AH HA HA HA HA HA HA HA HA
AH HA HA HA!!
HEY!
AH HA!
HA HA HA HA HA!
BAM BAM BAM
SUSHI ROW ...
SALMON ROE!
HA HA HA HA HA!
AH...
YOU LIKE MY PUN, HUH?!
NAH ...
SIGH...
SIMPLE PUNS ARE BEST!!
THIS KID KNOWS HUMOR!
GUFFAW!
AIIIII...
SLAP SLAP
AN-OTHER BAD COMEDY TEAM?
GREAT...
VRZZZ
WORK ...
I NEED TO TAKE THIS.
AH ...!
WHAT'S UP?
I'M WITH MY NEPHEW!

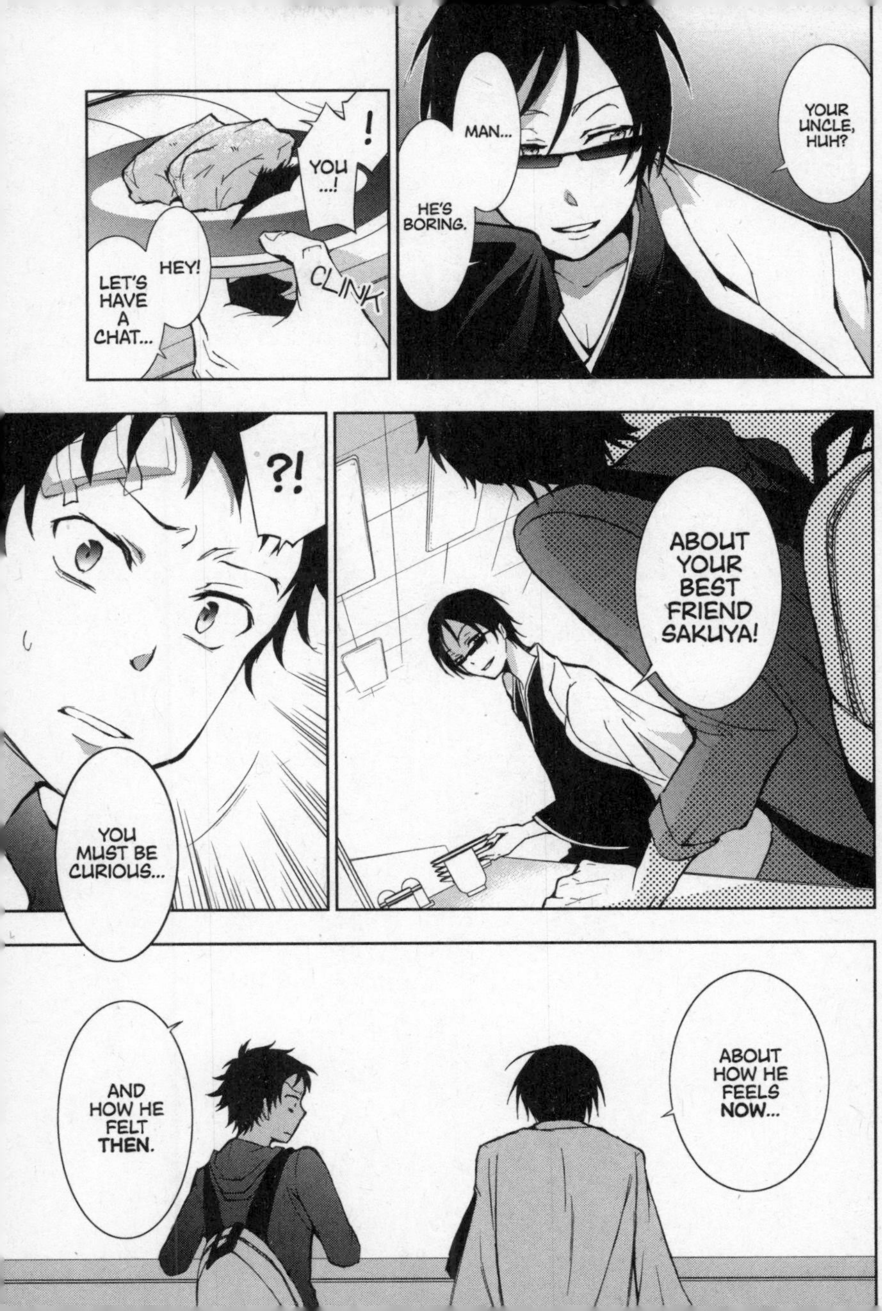
YOUR UNCLE, HUH?
MAN...
HE'S BORING.
!
YOU ...!
CLINK
HEY!
LET'S HAVE A CHAT...
ABOUT YOUR BEST FRIEND SAKUYA!
?!
YOU MUST BE CURIOUS...
ABOUT HOW HE FEELS NOW...
AND HOW HE FELT THEN.

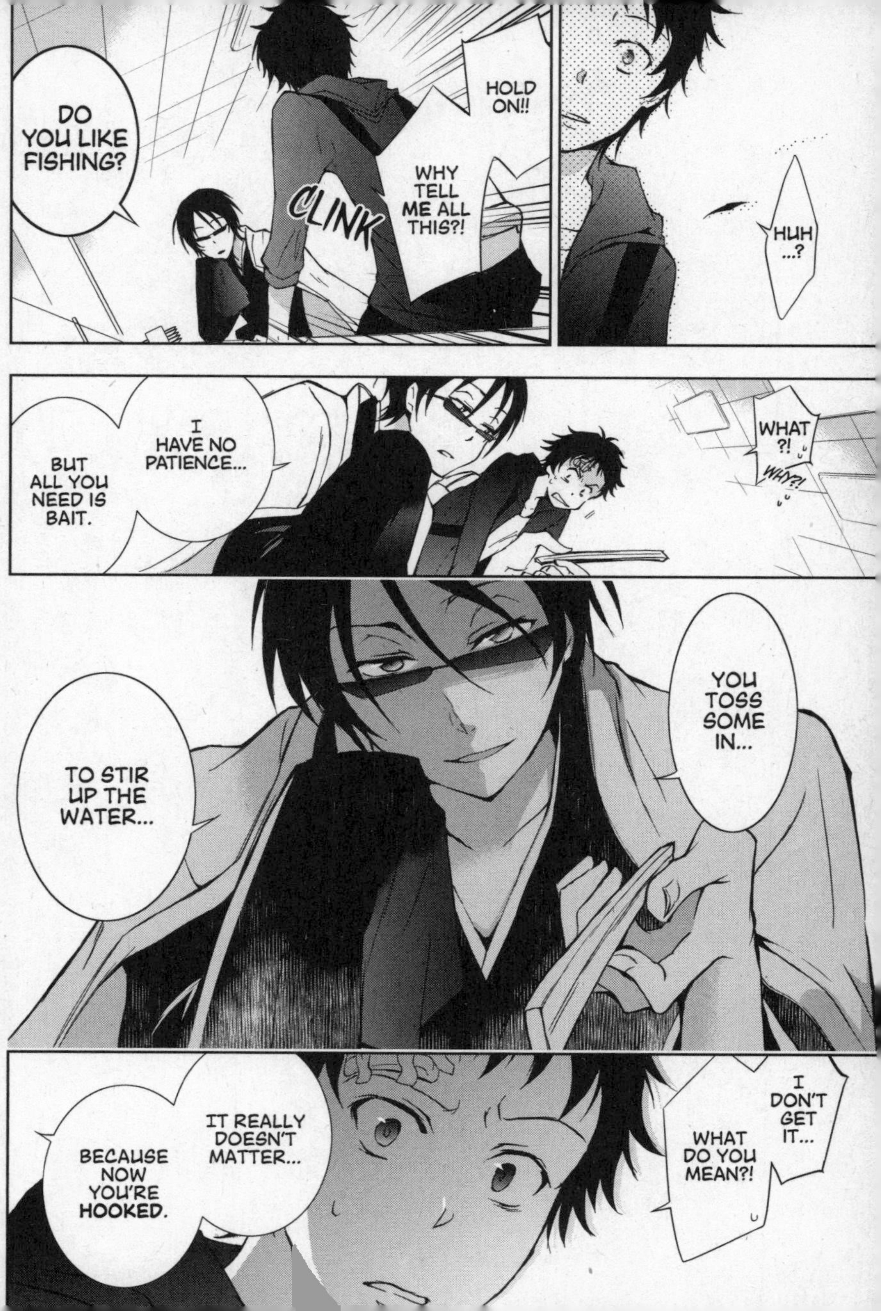
HUH ...?
HOLD ON!!
WHY TELL ME ALL THIS?!
CLINK
DO YOU LIKE FISHING?
WHAT ?!
WHY?!
I HAVE NO PATIENCE...
BUT ALL YOU NEED IS BAIT.
YOU TOSS SOME IN...
TO STIR UP THE WATER...
I DON'T GET IT...
WHAT DO YOU MEAN?!
IT REALLY DOESN'T MATTER...
BECAUSE NOW YOU'RE HOOKED.

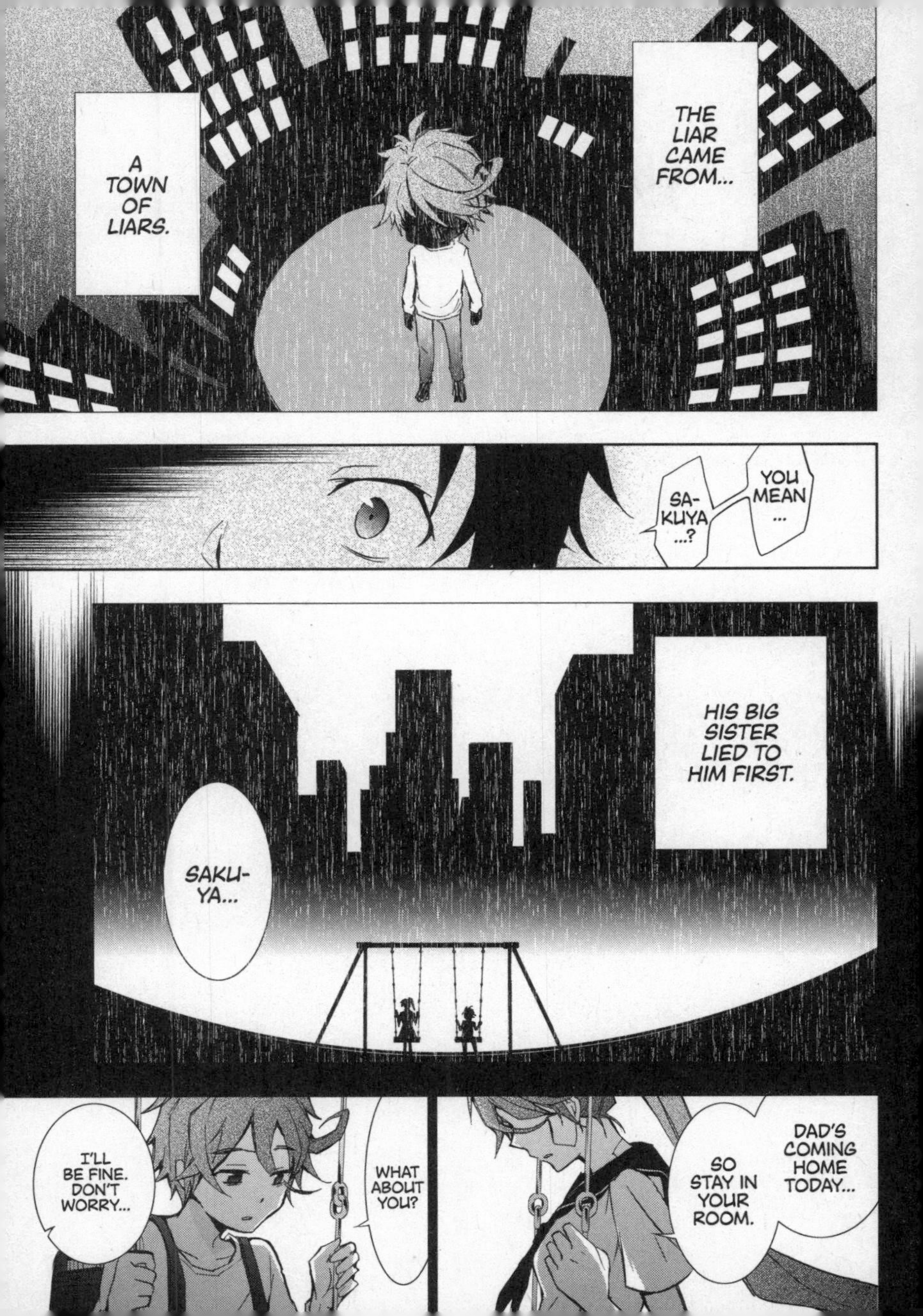
THE LIAR CAME FROM...
A TOWN OF LIARS.
YOU MEAN...
SA-KUYA...?
HIS BIG SISTER LIED TO HIM FIRST.
SAKU-YA...
DAD'S COMING HOME TODAY...
SO STAY IN YOUR ROOM.
WHAT ABOUT YOU?
I'LL BE FINE. DON'T WORRY...

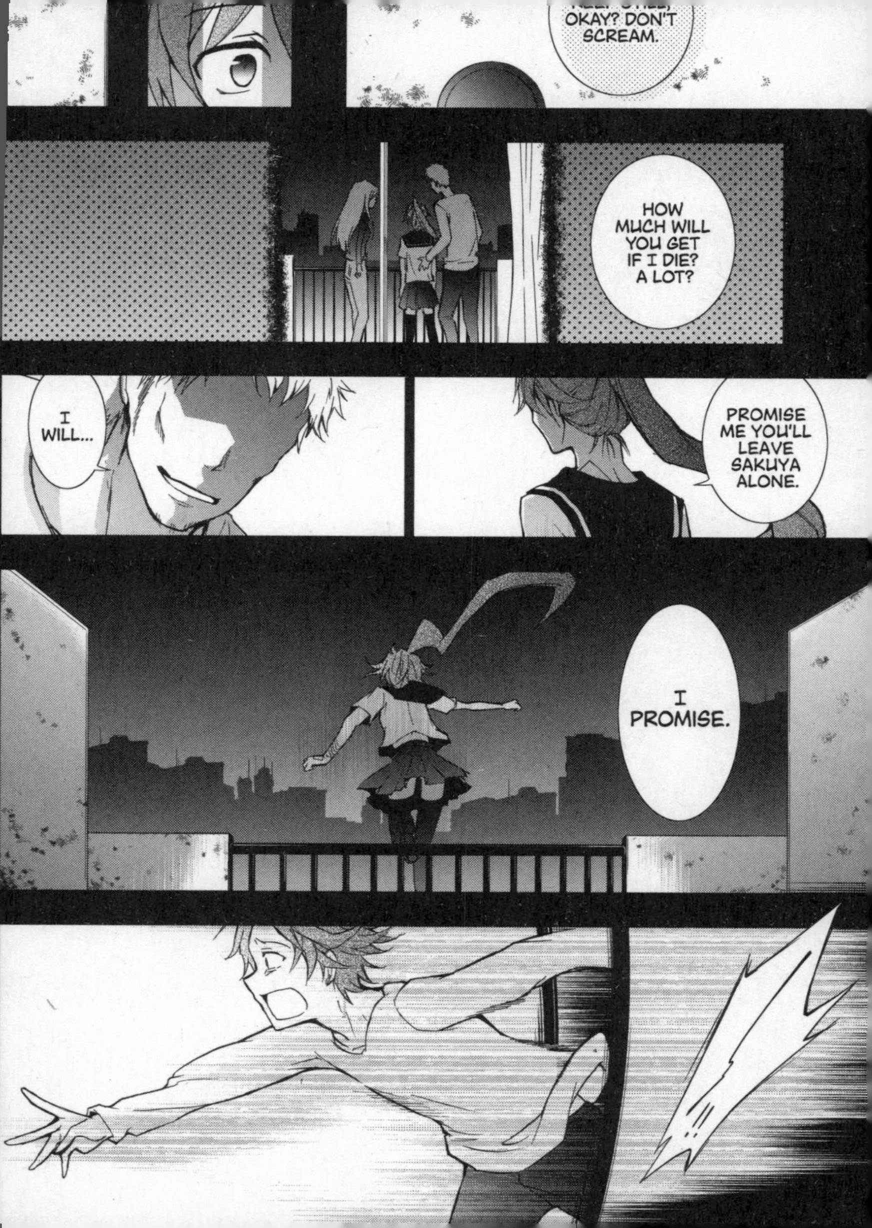

OKAY? DON'T SCREAM.
HOW MUCH WILL YOU GET IF I DIE? A LOT?
PROMISE ME YOU'LL LEAVE SAKUYA ALONE.
I WILL...
I PROMISE.

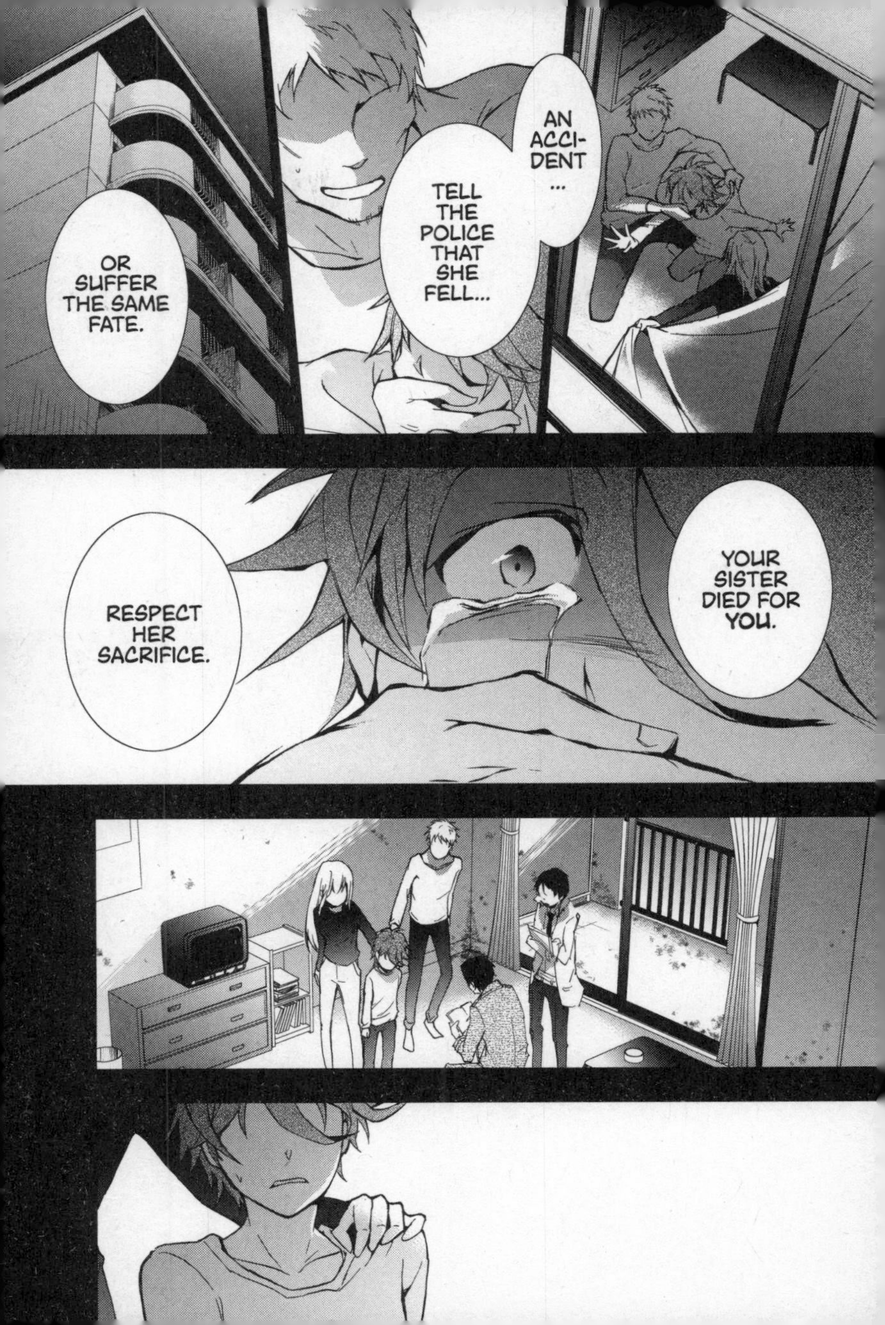
AN ACCI-DENT ...
TELL THE POLICE THAT SHE FELL...
OR SUFFER THE SAME FATE.
YOUR SISTER DIED FOR YOU.
RESPECT HER SACRIFICE.

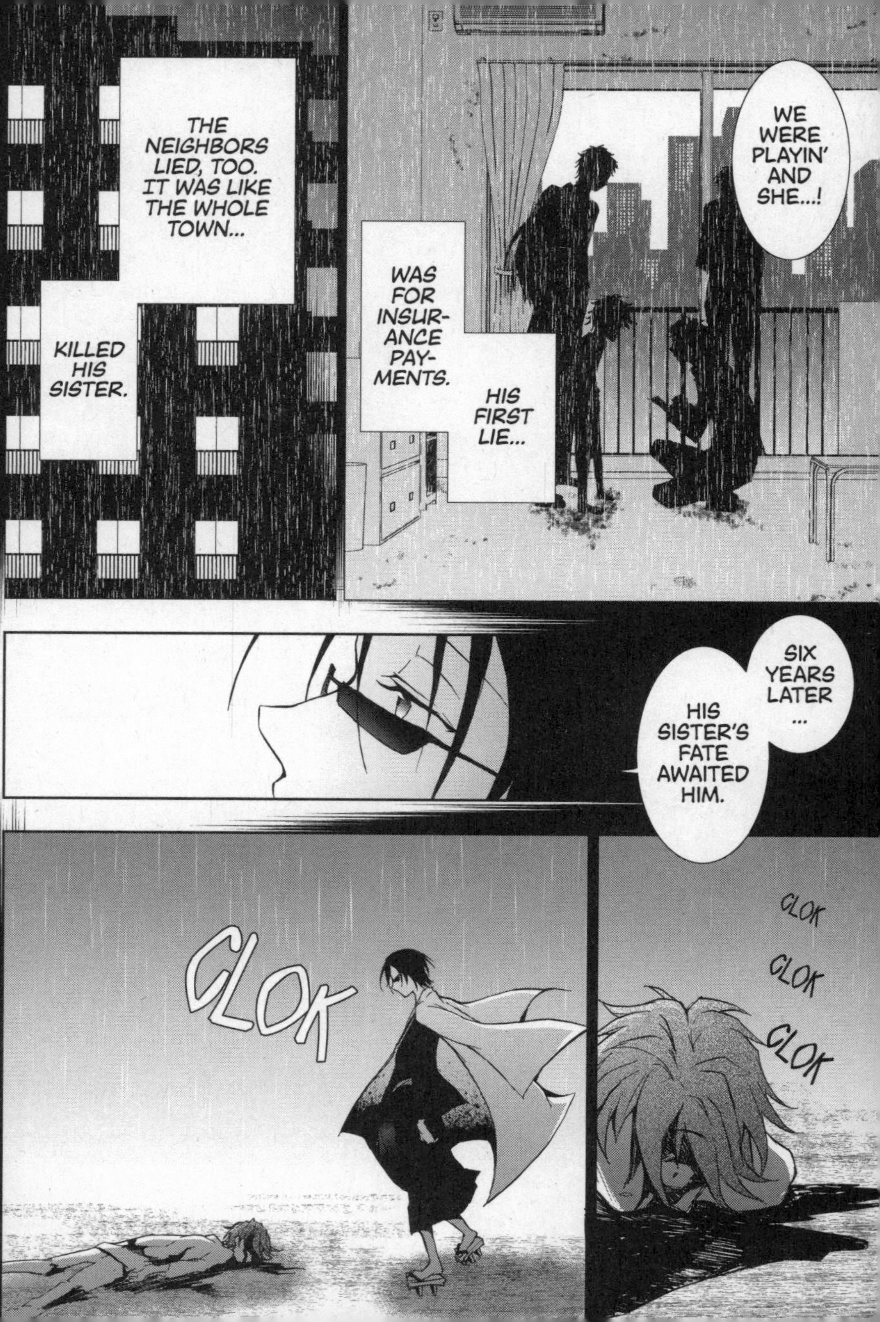

WE WERE PLAYIN' AND SHE...!
HIS FIRST LIE...
WAS FOR INSURANCE PAYMENTS.
THE NEIGHBORS LIED, TOO. IT WAS LIKE THE WHOLE TOWN...
KILLED HIS SISTER.
SIX YEARS LATER...
HIS SISTER'S FATE AWAITED HIM.
CLOK
CLOK
CLOK
CLOK

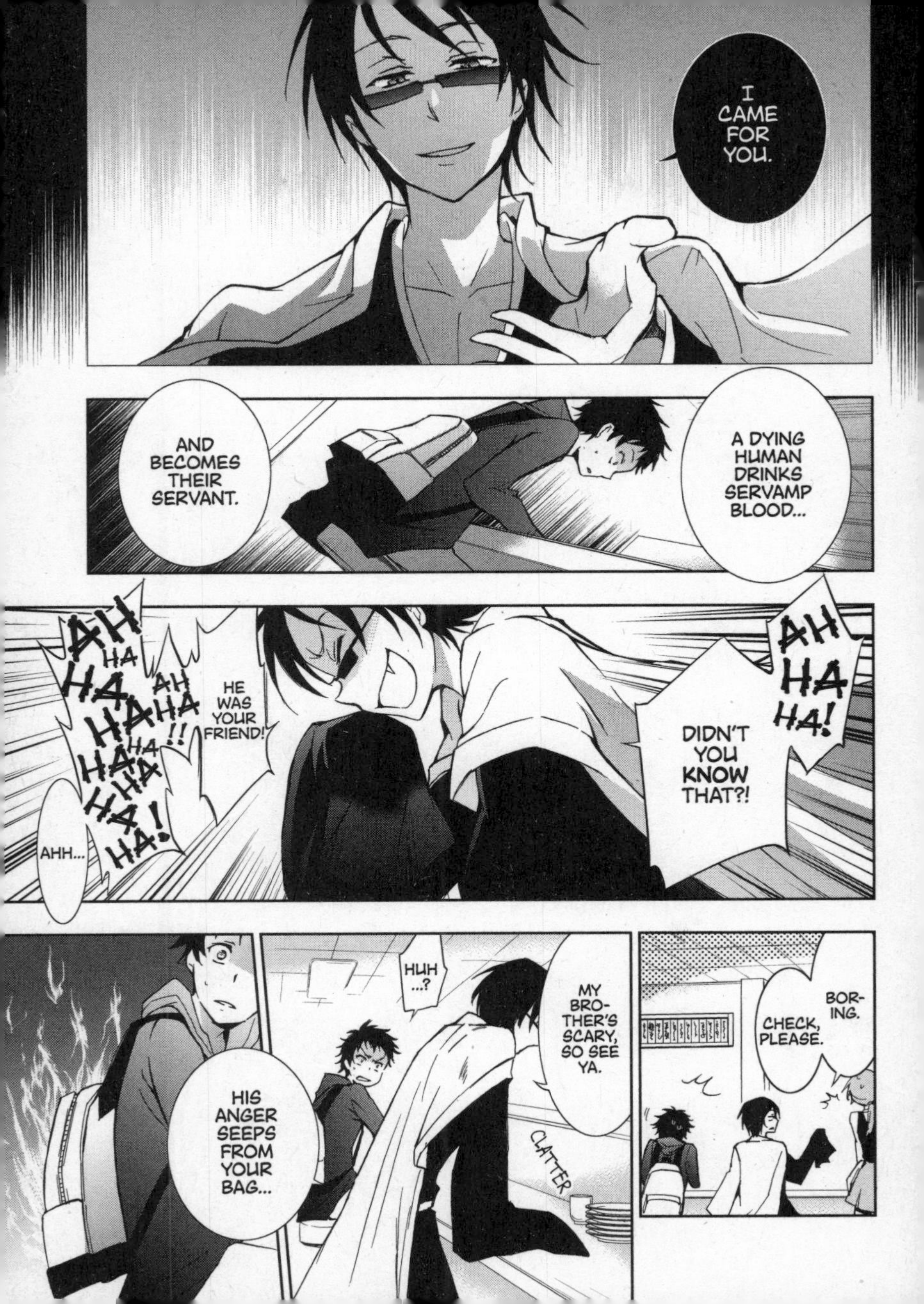
I CAME FOR YOU.
A DYING HUMAN DRINKS SERVAMP BLOOD...
AND BECOMES THEIR SERVANT.
AH HA HA!
DIDN'T YOU KNOW THAT?!
HE WAS YOUR FRIEND!
AH HA!!
AH HA HA HA HA HA HA HA HA!
AHH...
BOR-ING.
CHECK, PLEASE.
MY BRO-THER'S SCARY, SO SEE YA.
HUH ...?
CLATTER
HIS ANGER SEEPS FROM YOUR BAG...

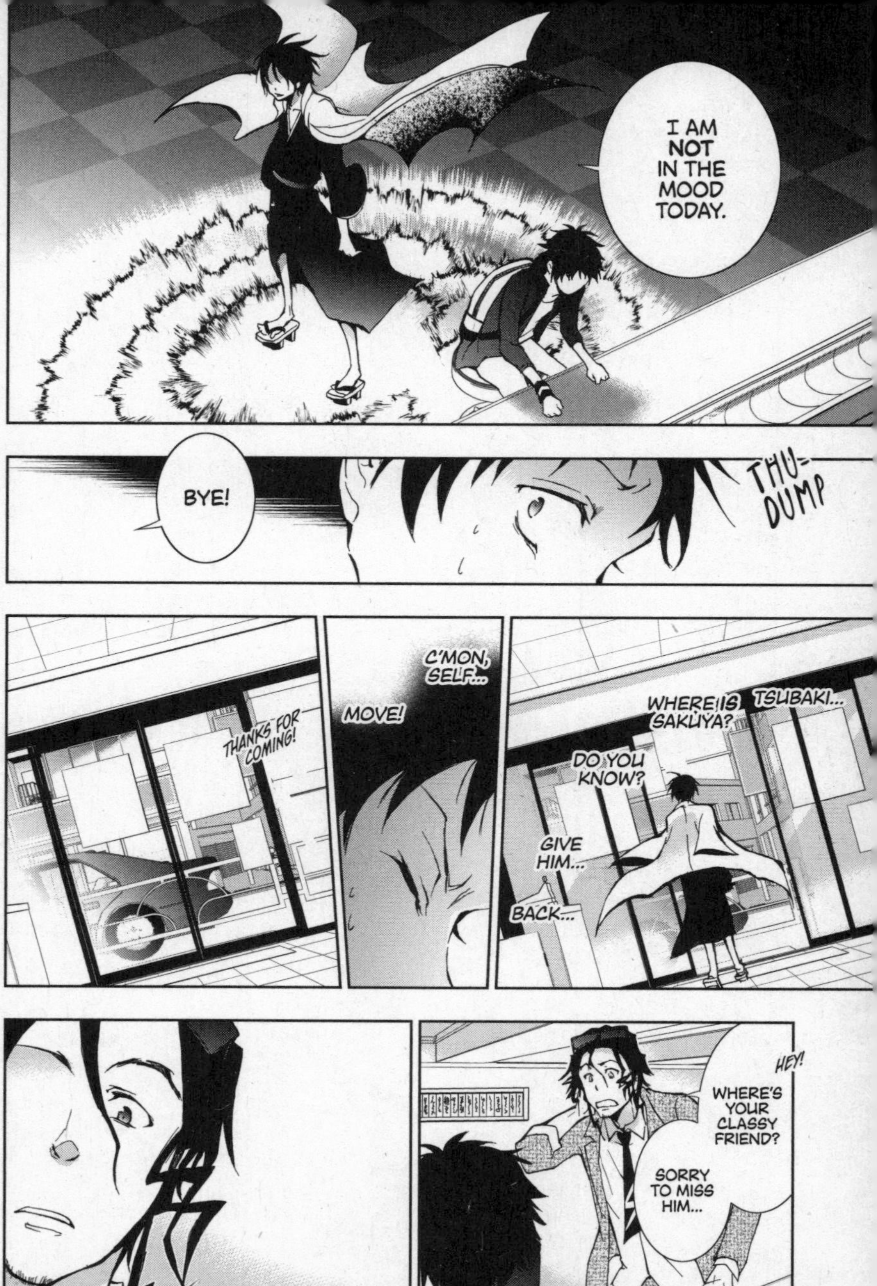
I AM NOT IN THE MOOD TODAY.
THU-DUMP
BYE!
TSUBAKI...
WHERE IS SAKUYA?
DO YOU KNOW?
GIVE HIM...
BACK...
C'MON, SELF...
MOVE!
THANKS FOR COMING!
HEY!
WHERE'S YOUR CLASSY FRIEND?
SORRY TO MISS HIM...

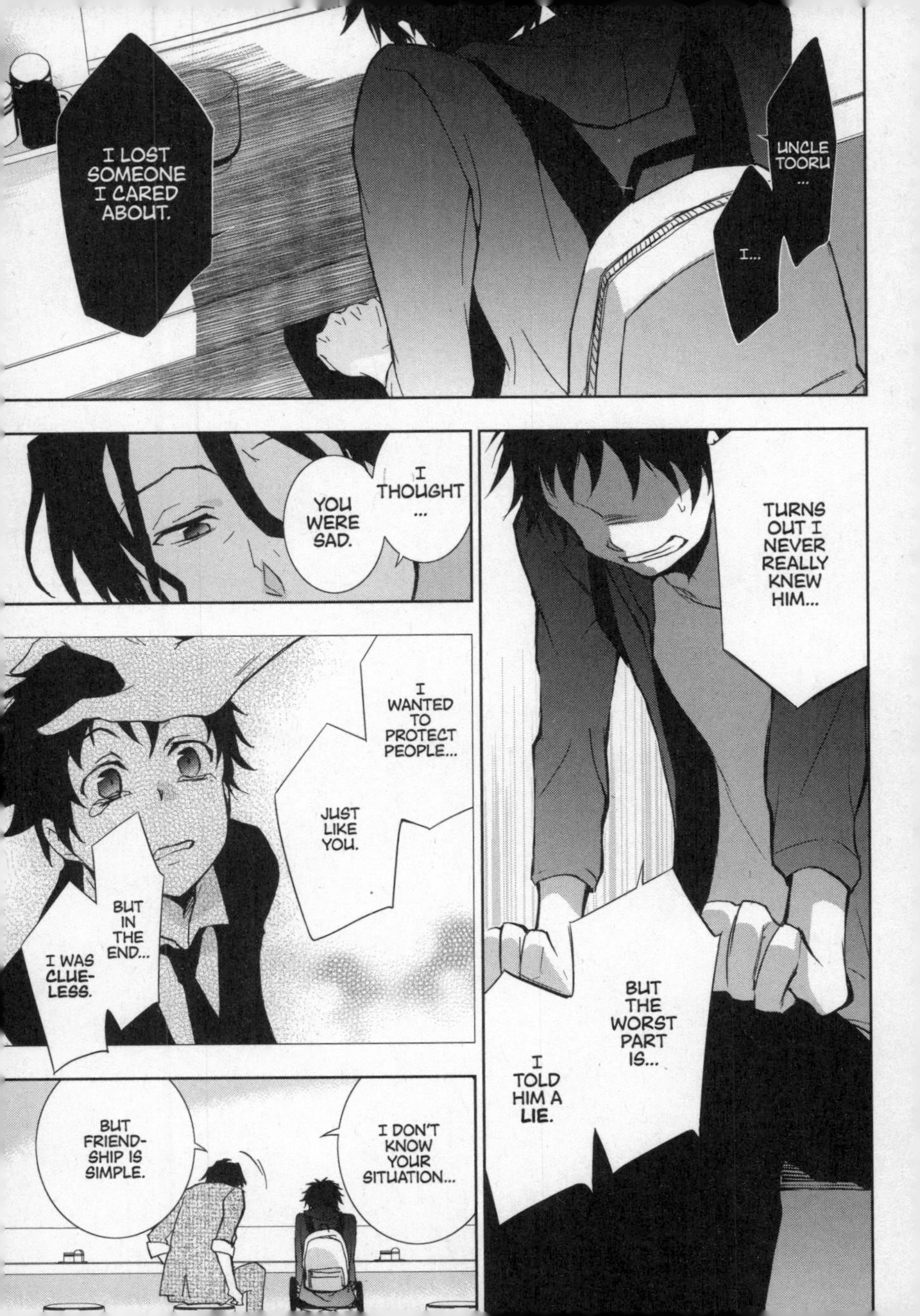
UNCLE TOORU ...
I...
I LOST SOMEONE I CARED ABOUT.
TURNS OUT I NEVER REALLY KNEW HIM...
BUT THE WORST PART IS...
I TOLD HIM A **LIE.**
I THOUGHT ...
YOU WERE SAD.
I WANTED TO PROTECT PEOPLE...
JUST LIKE YOU.
BUT IN THE END...
I WAS CLUELESS.
I DON'T KNOW YOUR SITUATION...
BUT FRIENDSHIP IS SIMPLE.

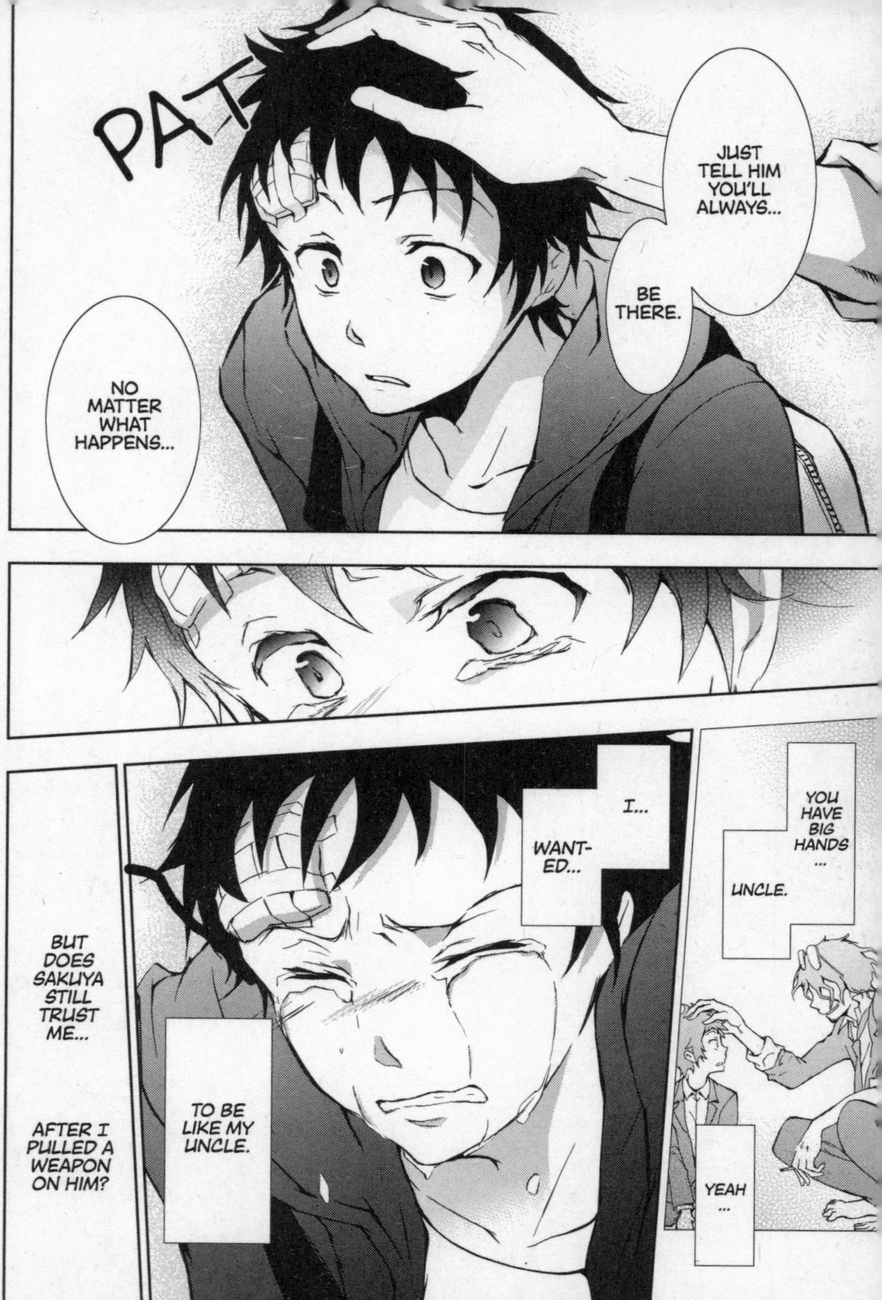
JUST TELL HIM YOU'LL ALWAYS...
PAT
BE THERE.
NO MATTER WHAT HAPPENS...
YOU HAVE BIG HANDS ...
UNCLE.
YEAH ...
I...
WANTED...
TO BE LIKE MY UNCLE.
BUT DOES SAKUYA STILL TRUST ME...
AFTER I PULLED A WEAPON ON HIM?

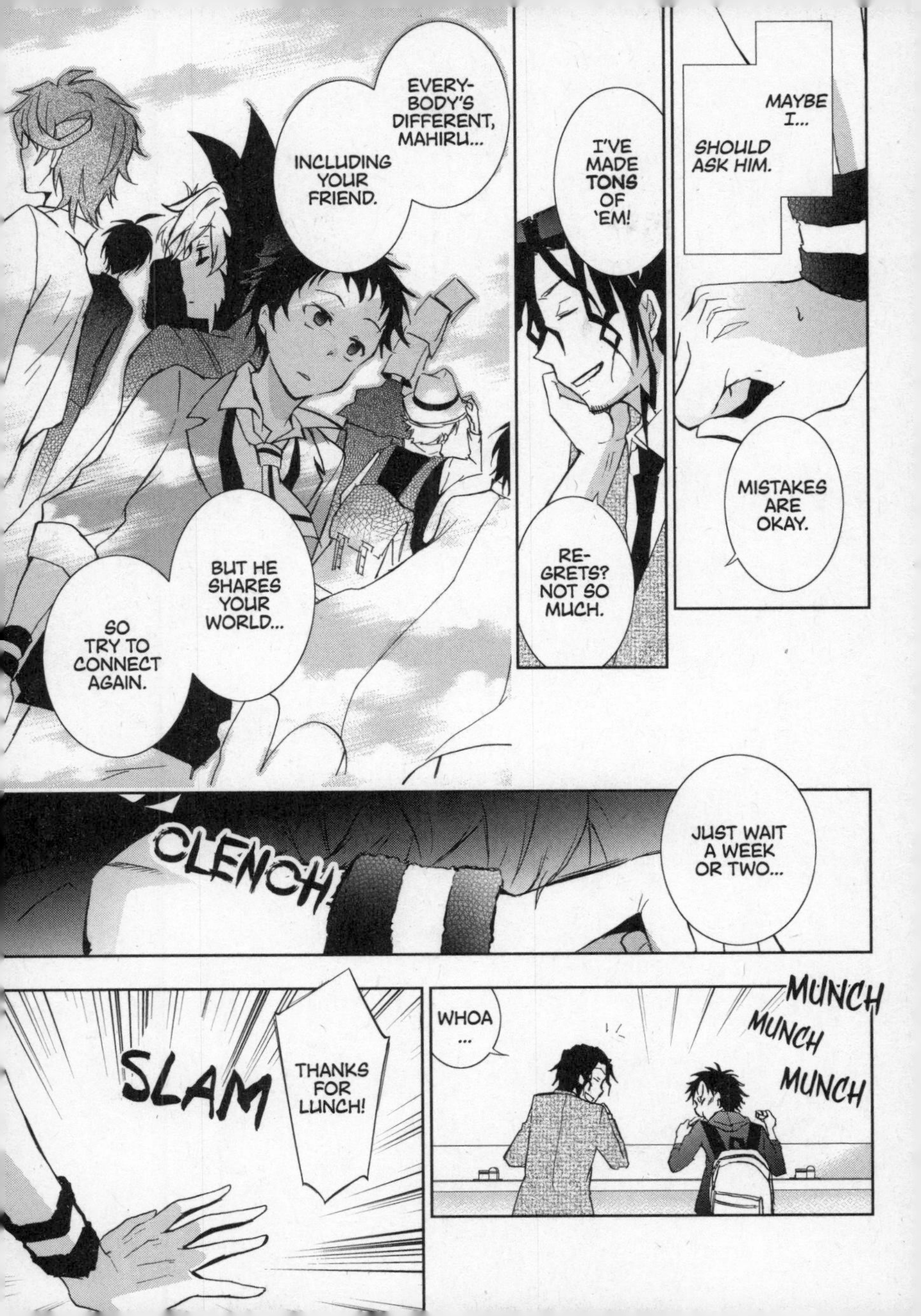
MAYBE I...
SHOULD ASK HIM.
MISTAKES ARE OKAY.
I'VE MADE TONS OF 'EM!
RE-GRETS? NOT SO MUCH.
EVERY-BODY'S DIFFERENT, MAHIRU...
INCLUDING YOUR FRIEND.
BUT HE SHARES YOUR WORLD...
SO TRY TO CONNECT AGAIN.
JUST WAIT A WEEK OR TWO...
CLENCH
MUNCH MUNCH MUNCH
WHOA ...
THANKS FOR LUNCH!
SLAM

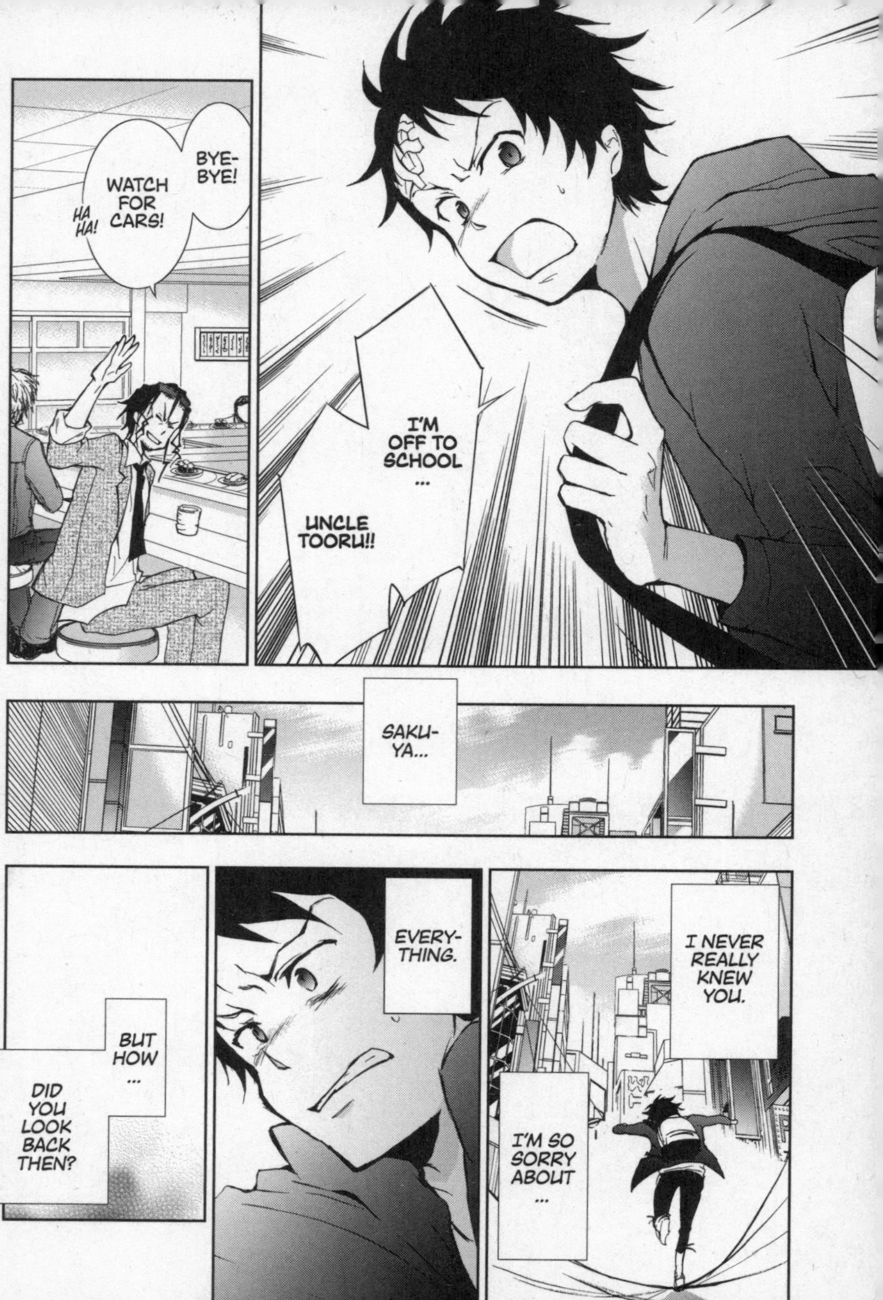
I'M OFF TO SCHOOL...
UNCLE TOORU!!
BYE-BYE!
WATCH FOR CARS!
HA HA!
SAKU-YA...
I NEVER REALLY KNEW YOU.
I'M SO SORRY ABOUT...
EVERY-THING.
BUT HOW...
DID YOU LOOK BACK THEN?

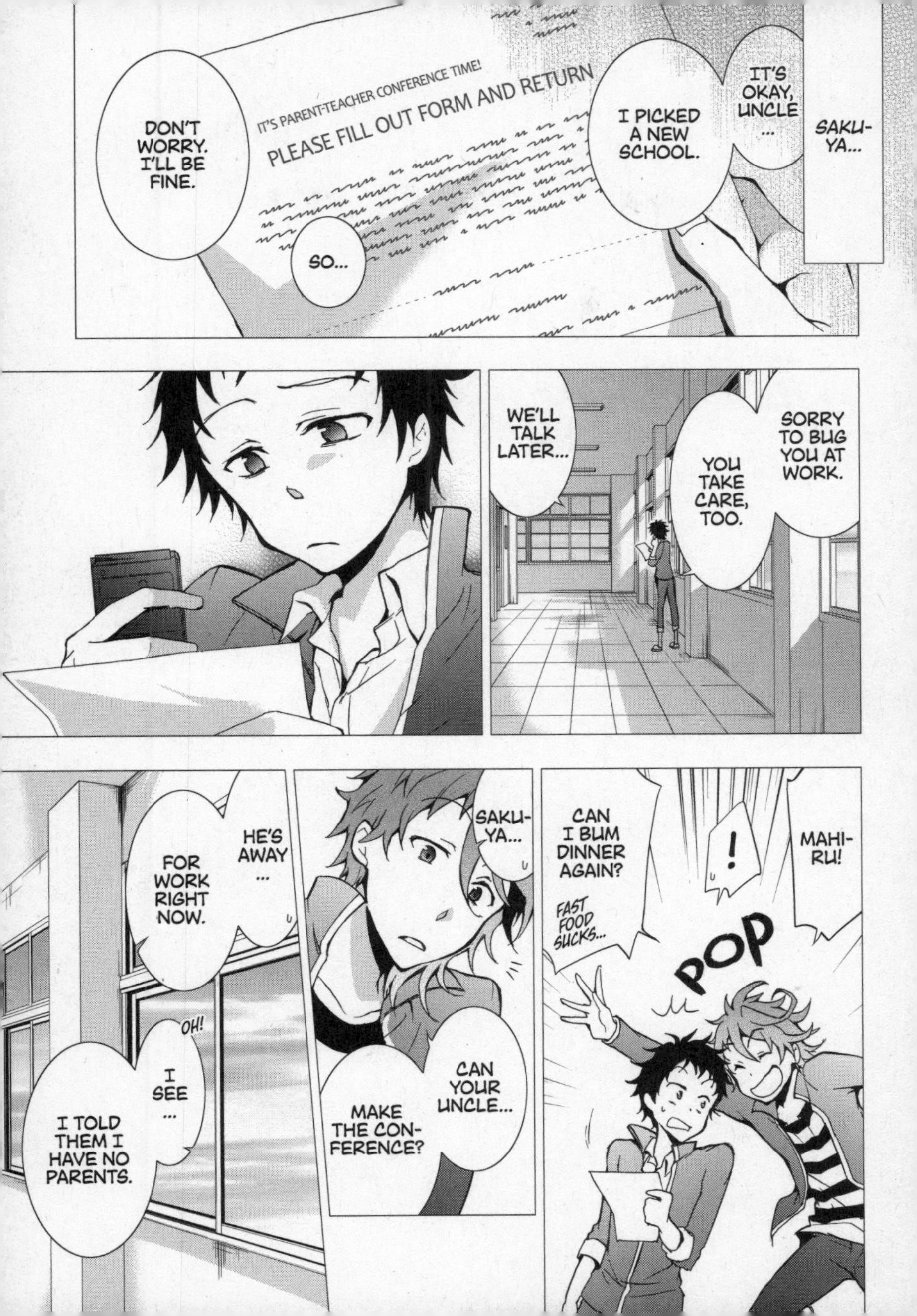
SAKU-YA...
IT'S OKAY, UNCLE ...
I PICKED A NEW SCHOOL.
IT'S PARENT-TEACHER CONFERENCE TIME!
PLEASE FILL OUT FORM AND RETURN
DON'T WORRY. I'LL BE FINE.
SO...
SORRY TO BUG YOU AT WORK.
YOU TAKE CARE, TOO.
WE'LL TALK LATER...
MAHI-RU!
!
CAN I BUM DINNER AGAIN?
FAST FOOD SUCKS...
POP
SAKU-YA...
CAN YOUR UNCLE...
MAKE THE CON-FERENCE?
HE'S AWAY ...
FOR WORK RIGHT NOW.
OH!
I SEE ...
I TOLD THEM I HAVE NO PARENTS.

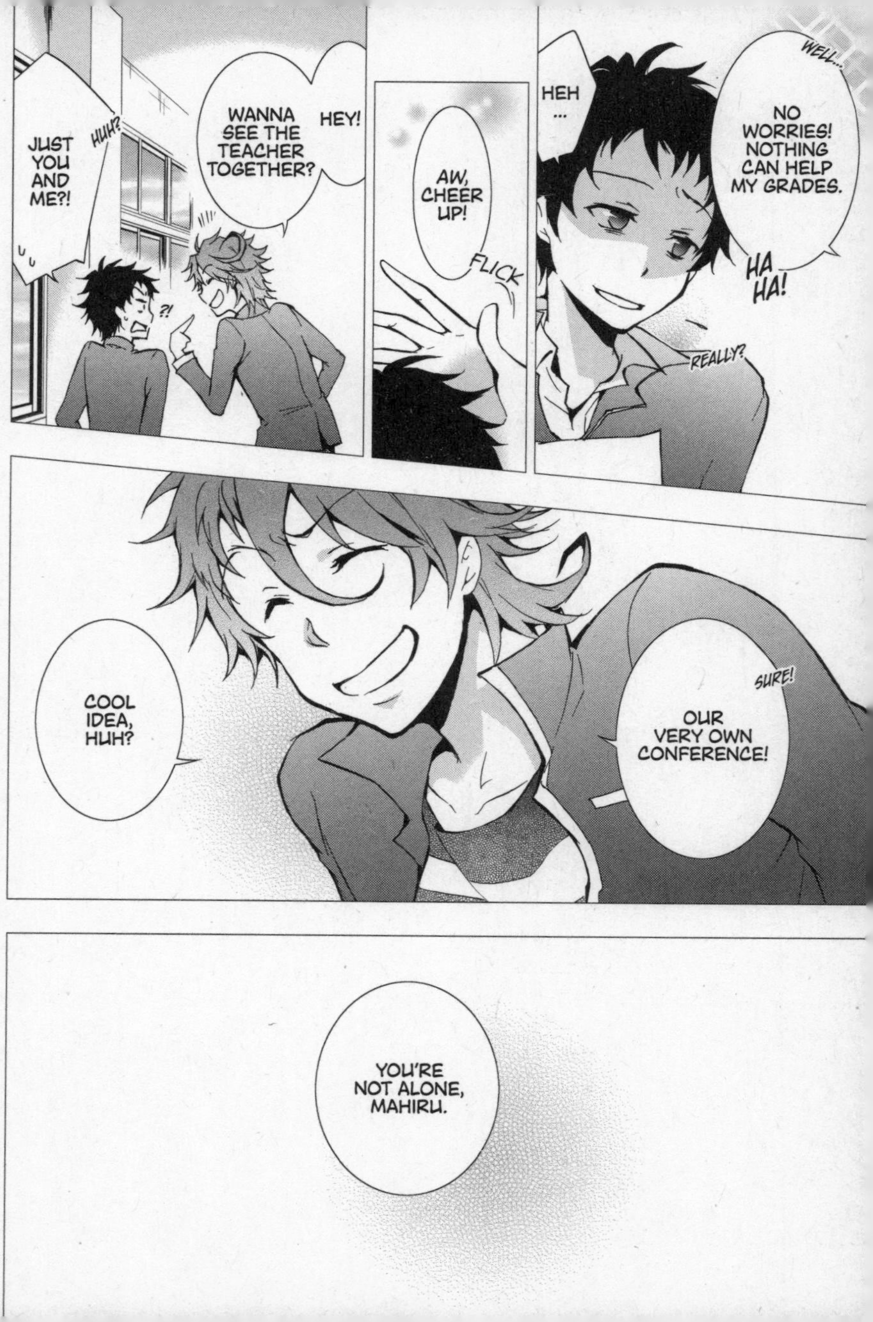
WELL...
NO WORRIES! NOTHING CAN HELP MY GRADES.
HEH ...
HA HA!
REALLY?
AW, CHEER UP!
FLICK
HEY!
WANNA SEE THE TEACHER TOGETHER?
HUH?
JUST YOU AND ME?!
?!
SURE!
OUR VERY OWN CONFERENCE!
COOL IDEA, HUH?
YOU'RE NOT ALONE, MAHIRU.

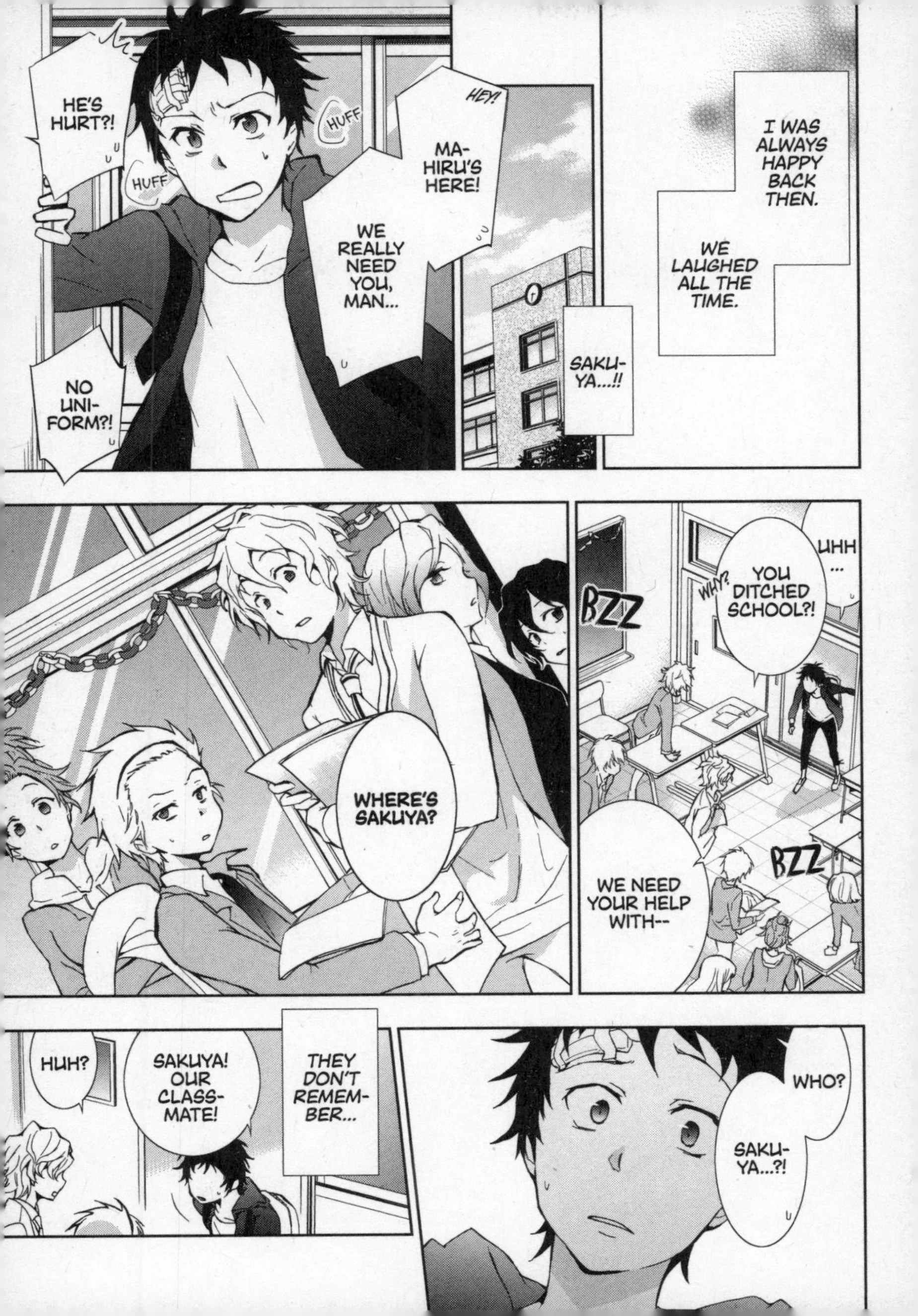
I WAS ALWAYS HAPPY BACK THEN.
WE LAUGHED ALL THE TIME.
SAKU-YA...!!
HEY!
MA-HIRU'S HERE!
HUFF
WE REALLY NEED YOU, MAN...
HE'S HURT?!
HUFF
NO UNI-FORM?!
UHH...
YOU DITCHED SCHOOL?!
WHY?
BZZ
WE NEED YOUR HELP WITH--
BZZ
WHERE'S SAKUYA?
WHO?
SAKU-YA...?!
THEY DON'T REMEM-BER...
SAKUYA! OUR CLASS-MATE!
HUH?

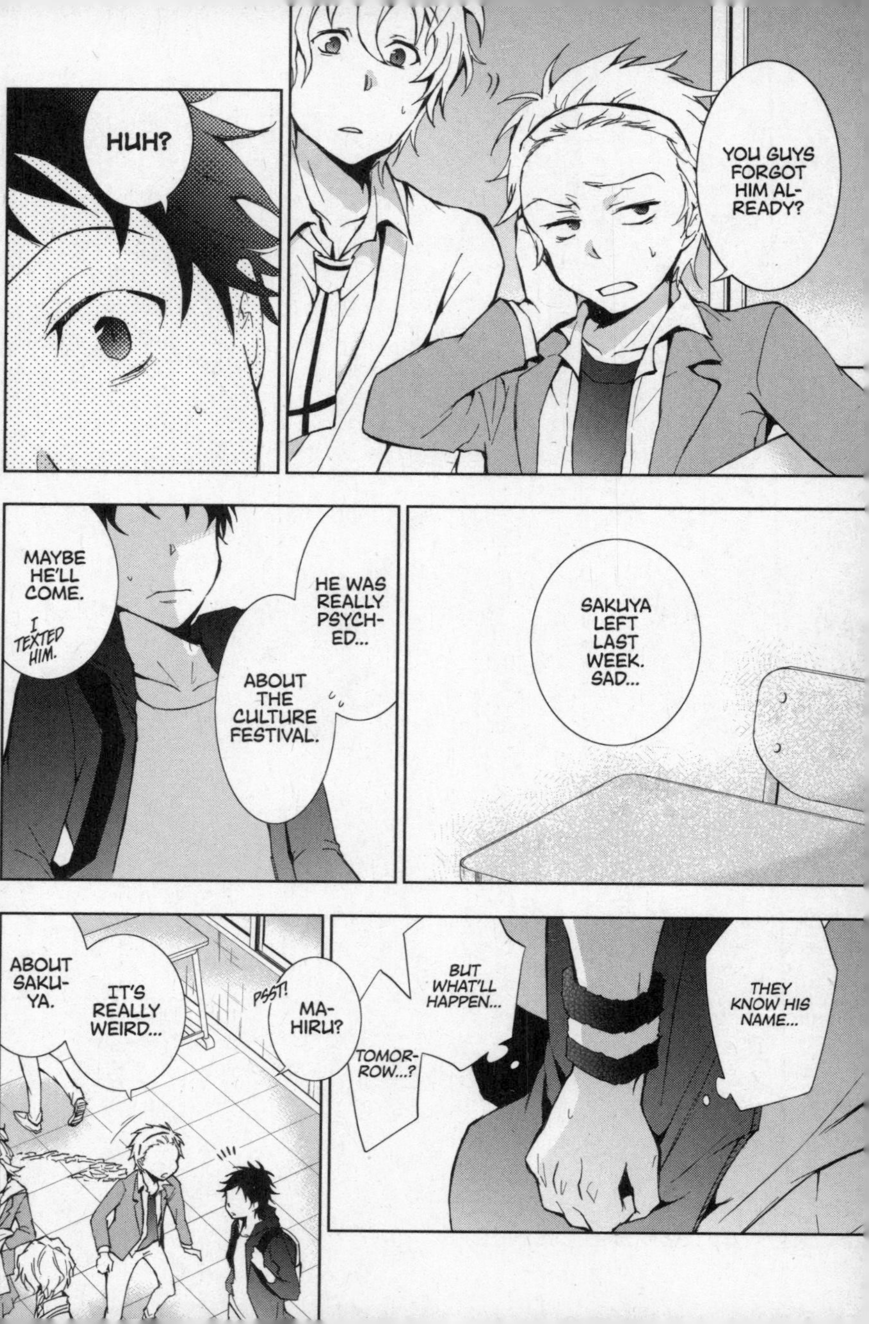
YOU GUYS FORGOT HIM AL-READY?
HUH?
SAKUYA LEFT LAST WEEK. SAD...
HE WAS REALLY PSYCH-ED...
ABOUT THE CULTURE FESTIVAL.
MAYBE HE'LL COME.
I TEXTED HIM.
THEY KNOW HIS NAME...
BUT WHAT'LL HAPPEN...
TOMOR-ROW...?
PSSST!
MA-HIRU?
IT'S REALLY WEIRD...
ABOUT SAKU-YA.

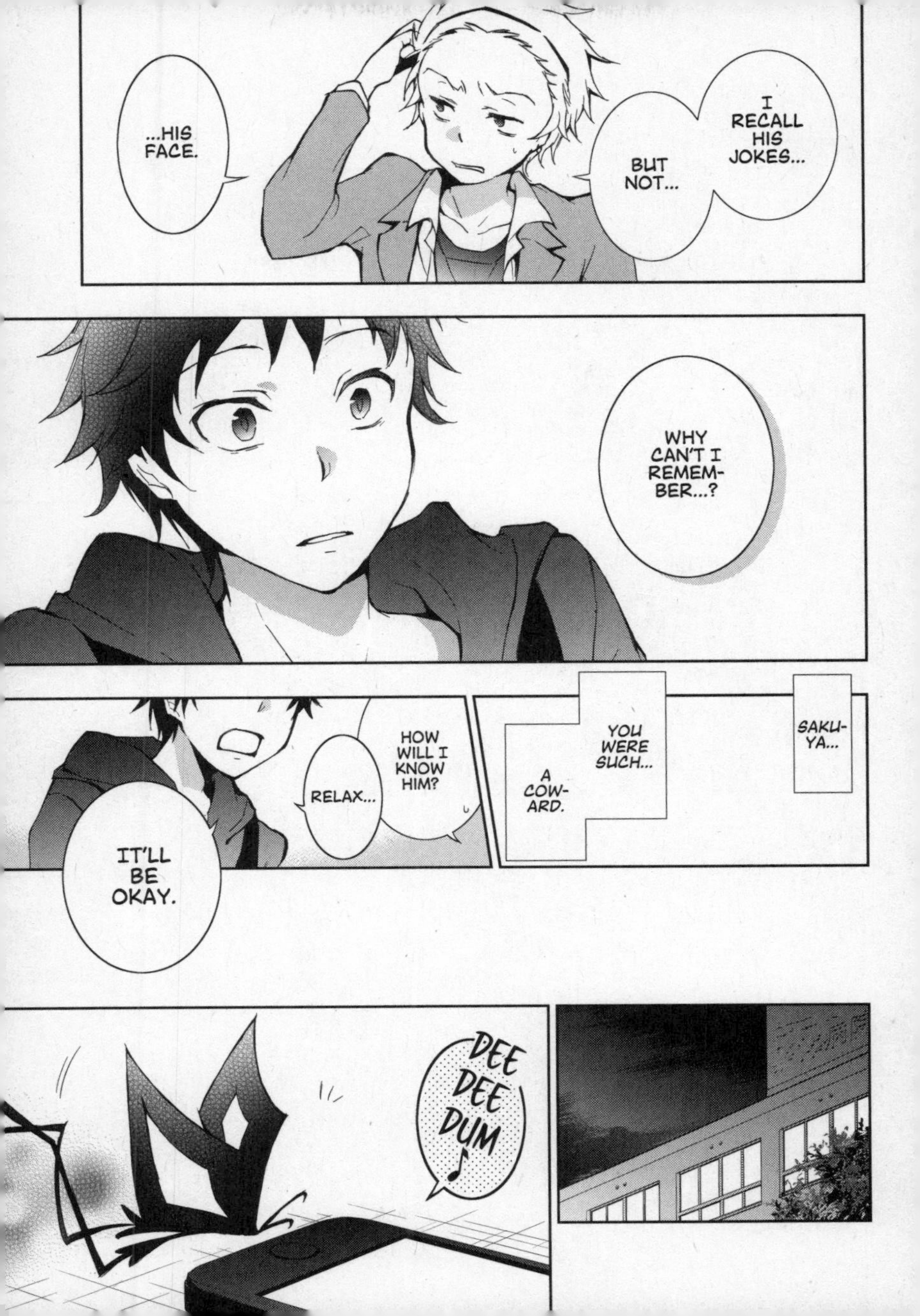
I RECALL HIS JOKES...
BUT NOT...
...HIS FACE.
WHY CAN'T I REMEM-BER...?
SAKU-YA...
YOU WERE SUCH...
A COW-ARD.
HOW WILL I KNOW HIM?
RELAX...
IT'LL BE OKAY.
DEE DEE DUM

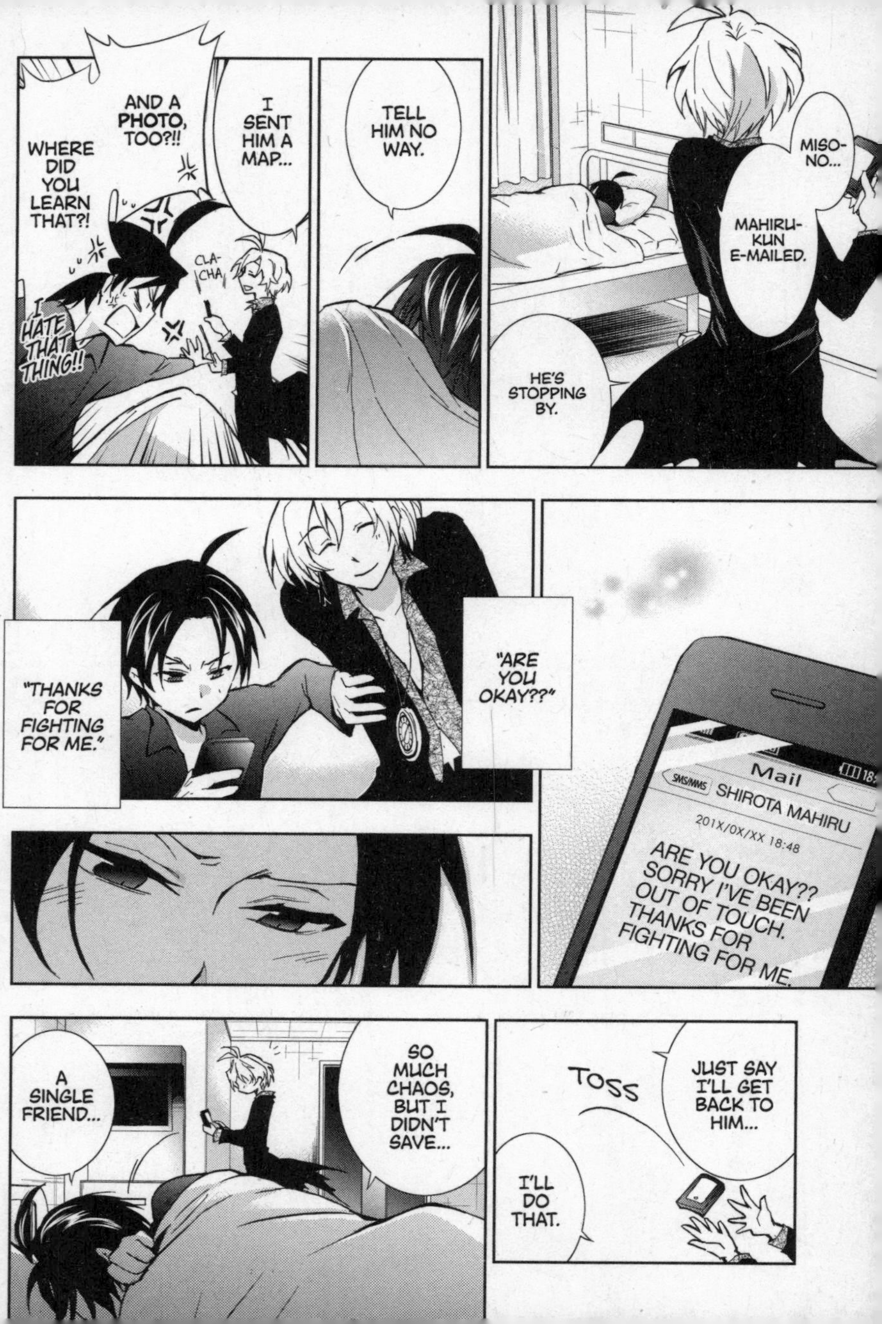
MISO-NO...
MAHIRU-KUN E-MAILED.
HE'S STOPPING BY.
TELL HIM NO WAY.
I SENT HIM A MAP...
AND A PHOTO, TOO?!!
WHERE DID YOU LEARN THAT?!
CLA-CHA
I HATE THAT THING!!
Mail
SMS/MMS SHIROTA MAHIRU
201X/0X/XX 18:48
ARE YOU OKAY?? SORRY I'VE BEEN OUT OF TOUCH. THANKS FOR FIGHTING FOR ME.
"ARE YOU OKAY??"
"THANKS FOR FIGHTING FOR ME."
JUST SAY I'LL GET BACK TO HIM...
TOSS
I'LL DO THAT.
SO MUCH CHAOS, BUT I DIDN'T SAVE...
A SINGLE FRIEND...

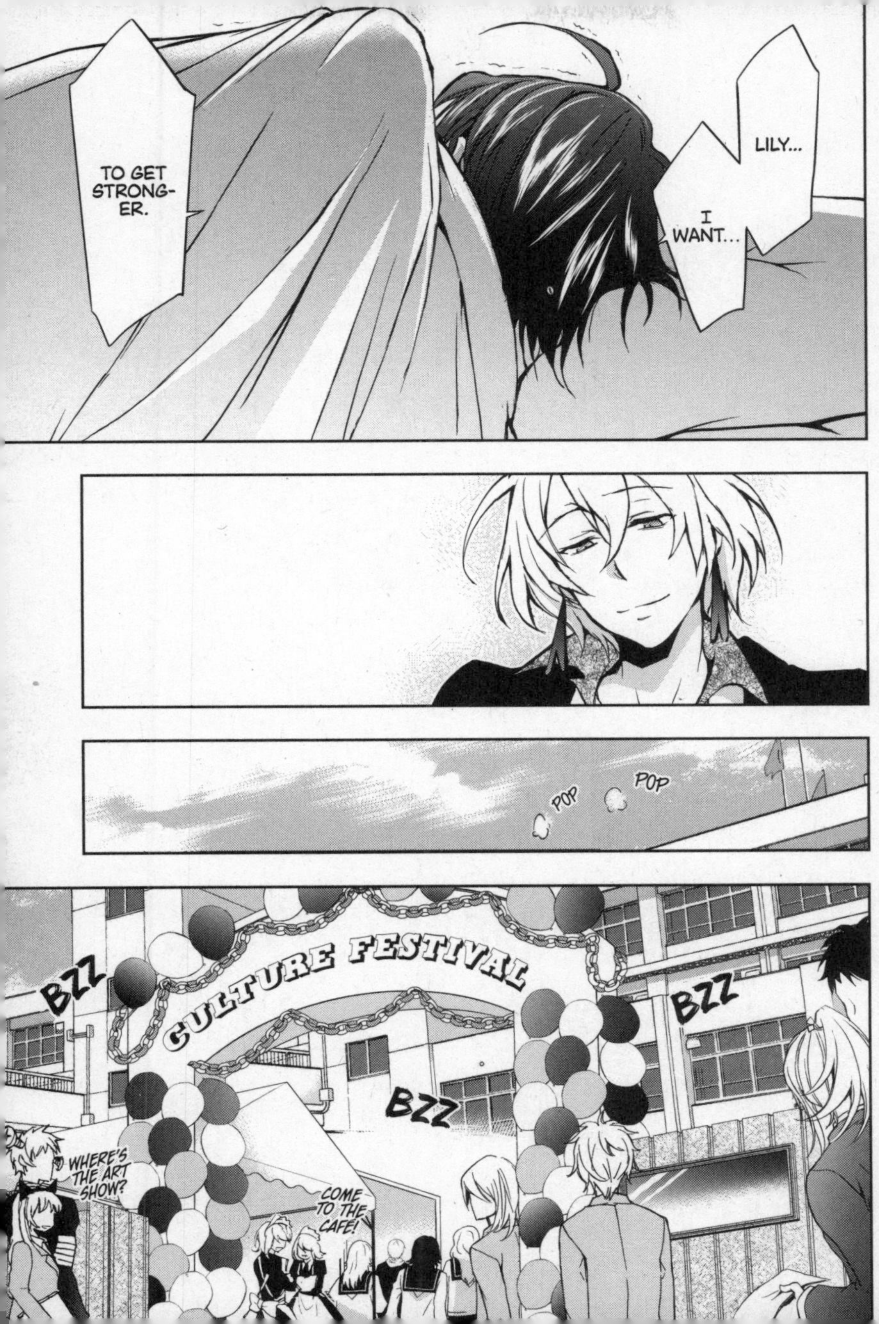
LILY...
I WANT...
TO GET STRONG-ER.
POP
POP
BZZ
CULTURE FESTIVAL
BZZ
BZZ
COME TO THE CAFE!
WHERE'S THE ART SHOW?

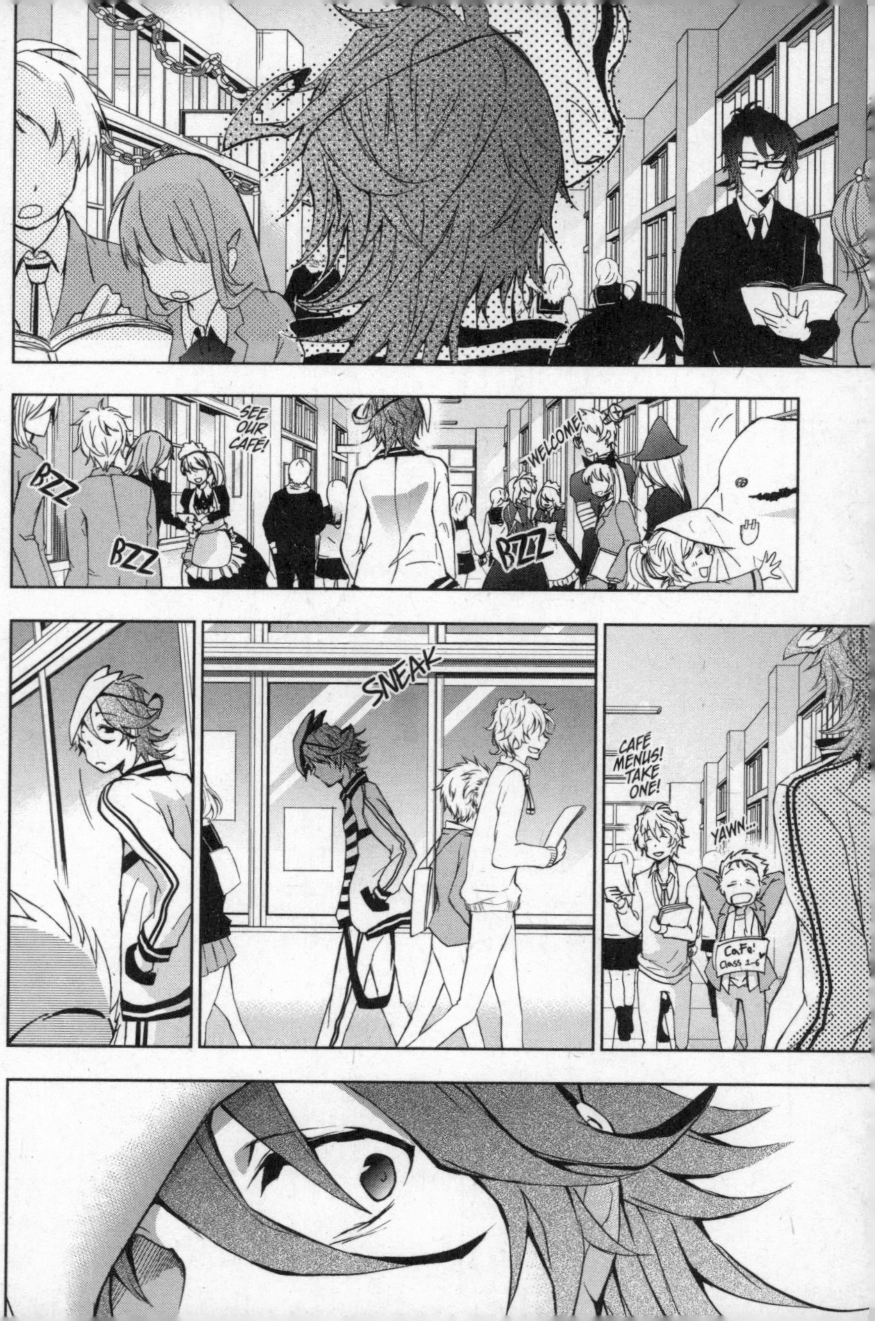
WELCOME!
SEE OUR CAFÉ!
BZZZ
BZZ
BZZ
CAFÉ MENUS! TAKE ONE!
YAWN...
Café! Class 1-6
SNEAK

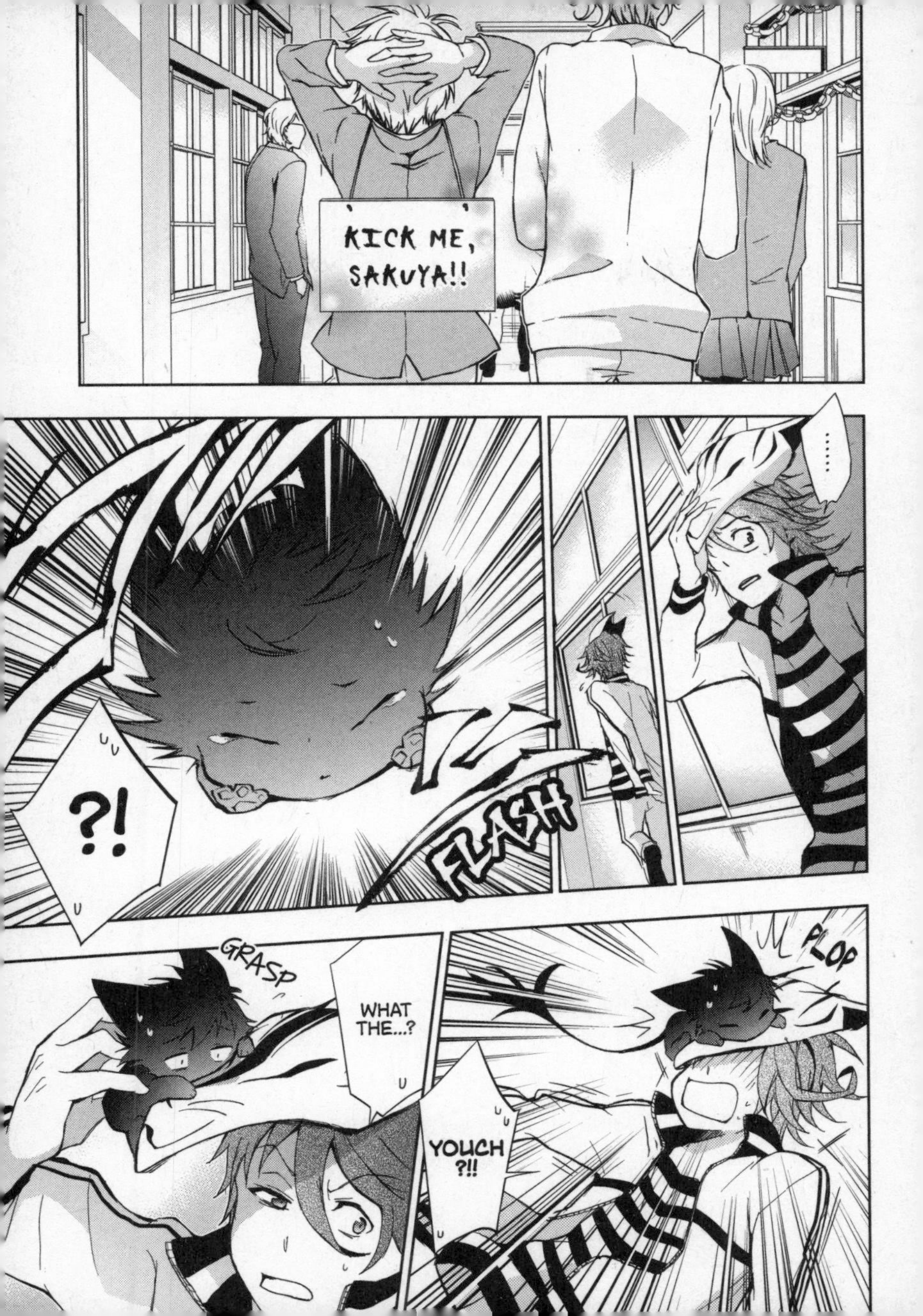
KICK ME, SAKUYA!!
......
FLASH
?!
PLOP
YOUCH ?!!
WHAT THE...?
GRASP

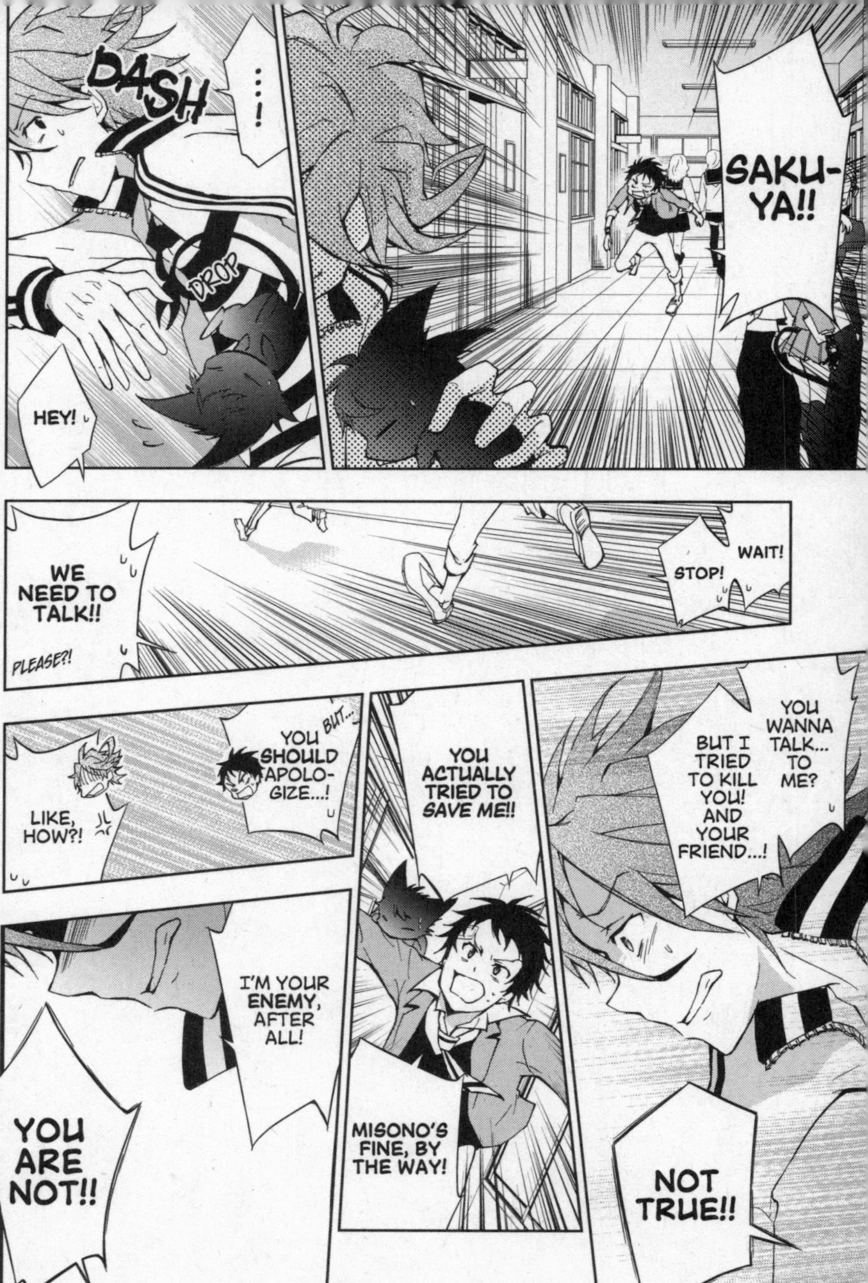

SAKU-YA!!
...!
DASH
DROP
HEY!
WAIT!
STOP!
WE NEED TO TALK!!
PLEASE?!
YOU WANNA TALK... TO ME?
BUT I TRIED TO KILL YOU! AND YOUR FRIEND...!
NOT TRUE!!
YOU ACTUALLY TRIED TO SAVE ME!!
MISONO'S FINE, BY THE WAY!
BUT...
YOU SHOULD APOLO-GIZE...!
LIKE, HOW?!
I'M YOUR ENEMY, AFTER ALL!
YOU ARE NOT!!

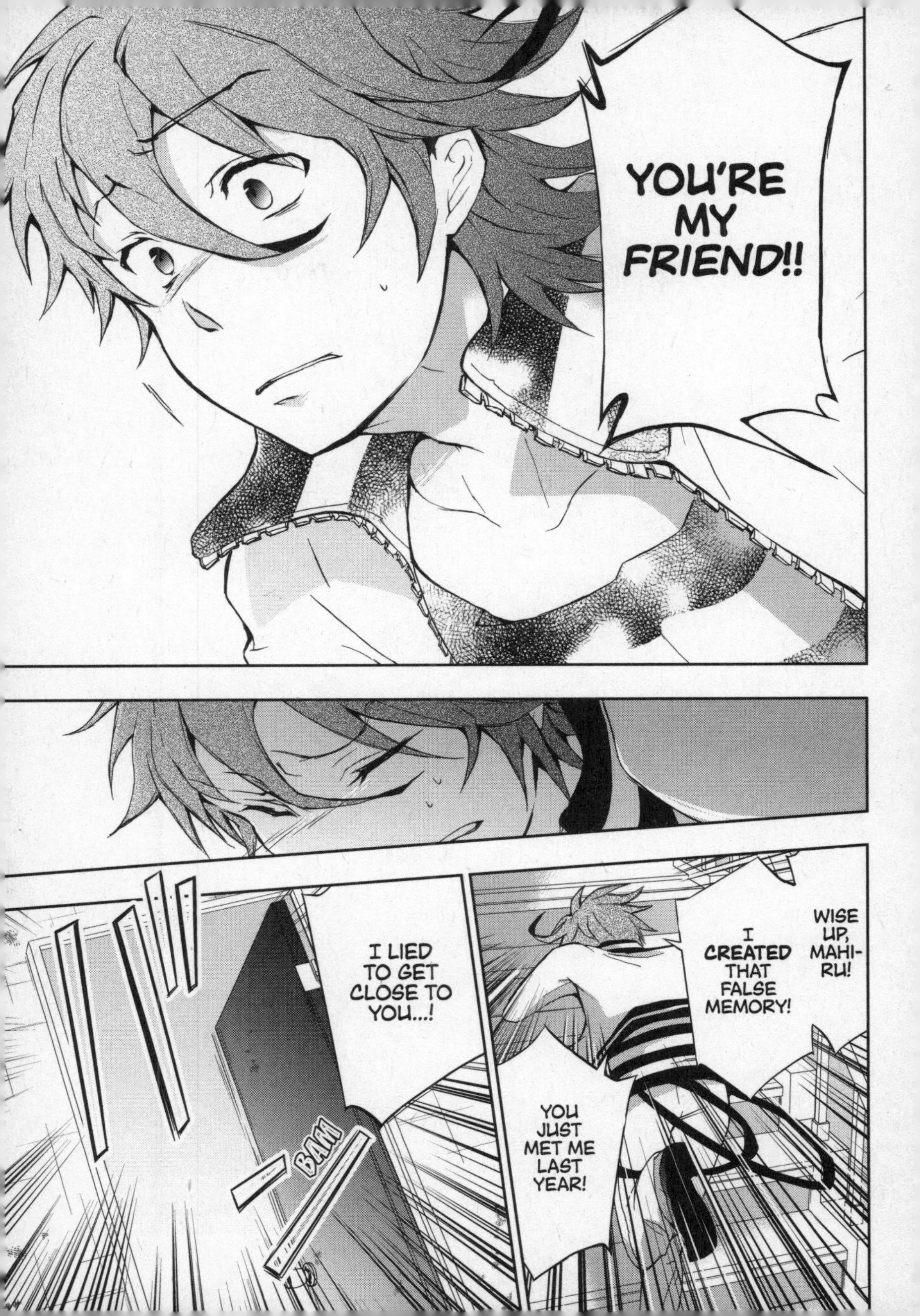

YOU'RE MY FRIEND!!
WISE UP, MAHI-RU!
I CREATED THAT FALSE MEMORY!
YOU JUST MET ME LAST YEAR!
I LIED TO GET CLOSE TO YOU...!
BAM

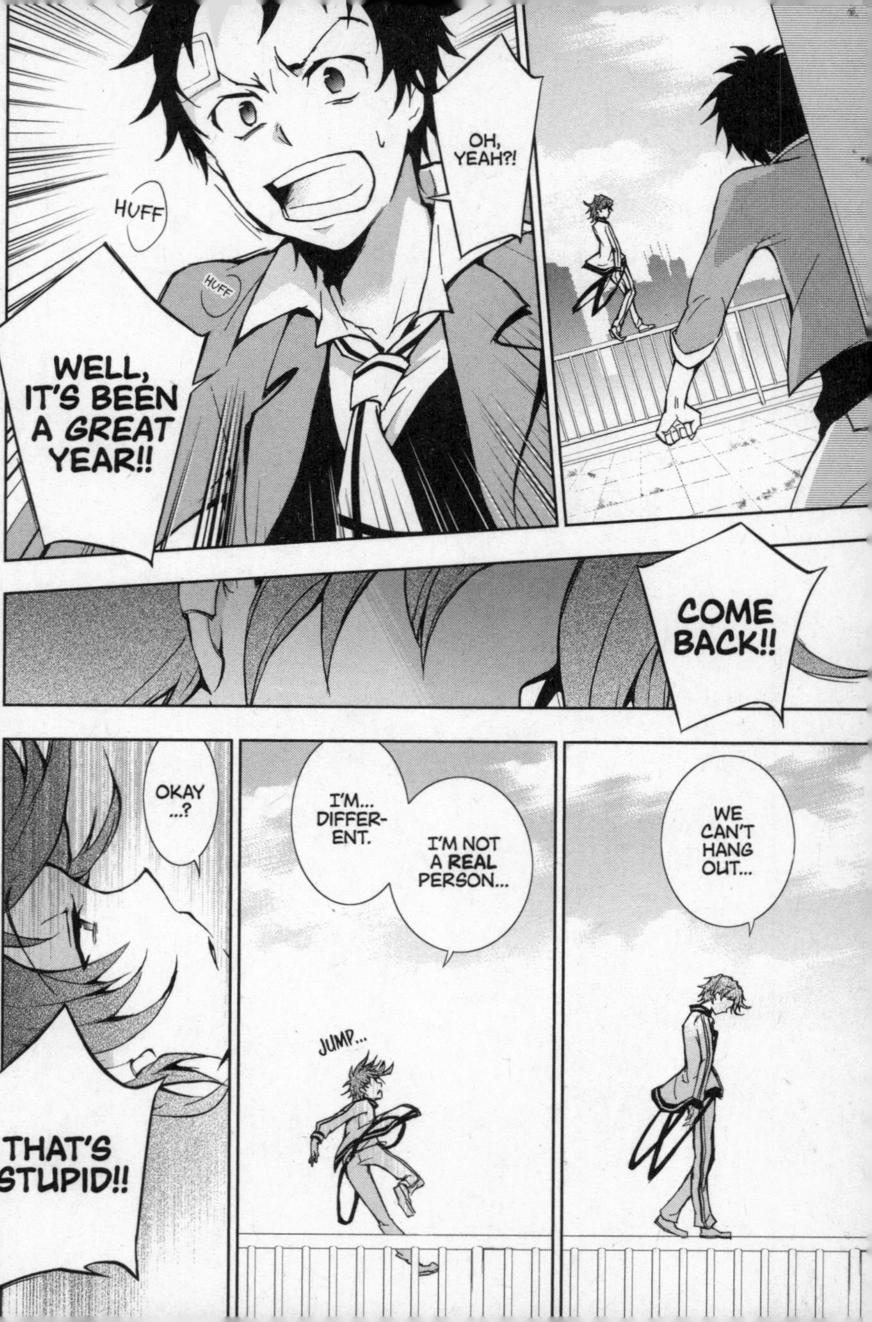
OH, YEAH?!
HUFF
HUFF
WELL, IT'S BEEN A GREAT YEAR!!
COME BACK!!
WE CAN'T HANG OUT...
I'M... DIFFER-ENT.
I'M NOT A REAL PERSON...
JUMP...
OKAY ...?
THAT'S STUPID!!

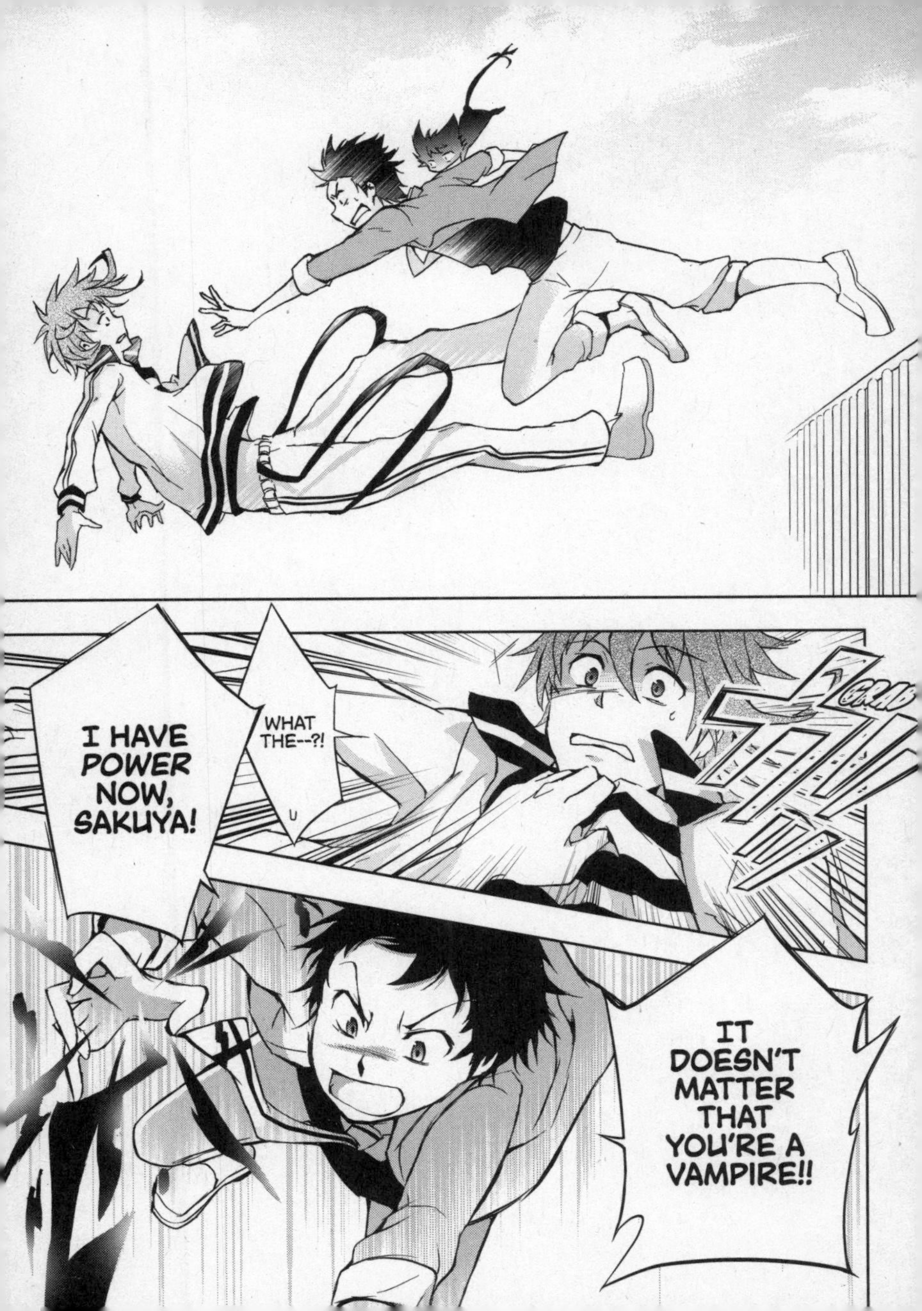
GRAB
WHAT THE--?!
I HAVE POWER NOW, SAKUYA!
IT DOESN'T MATTER THAT YOU'RE A VAMPIRE!!

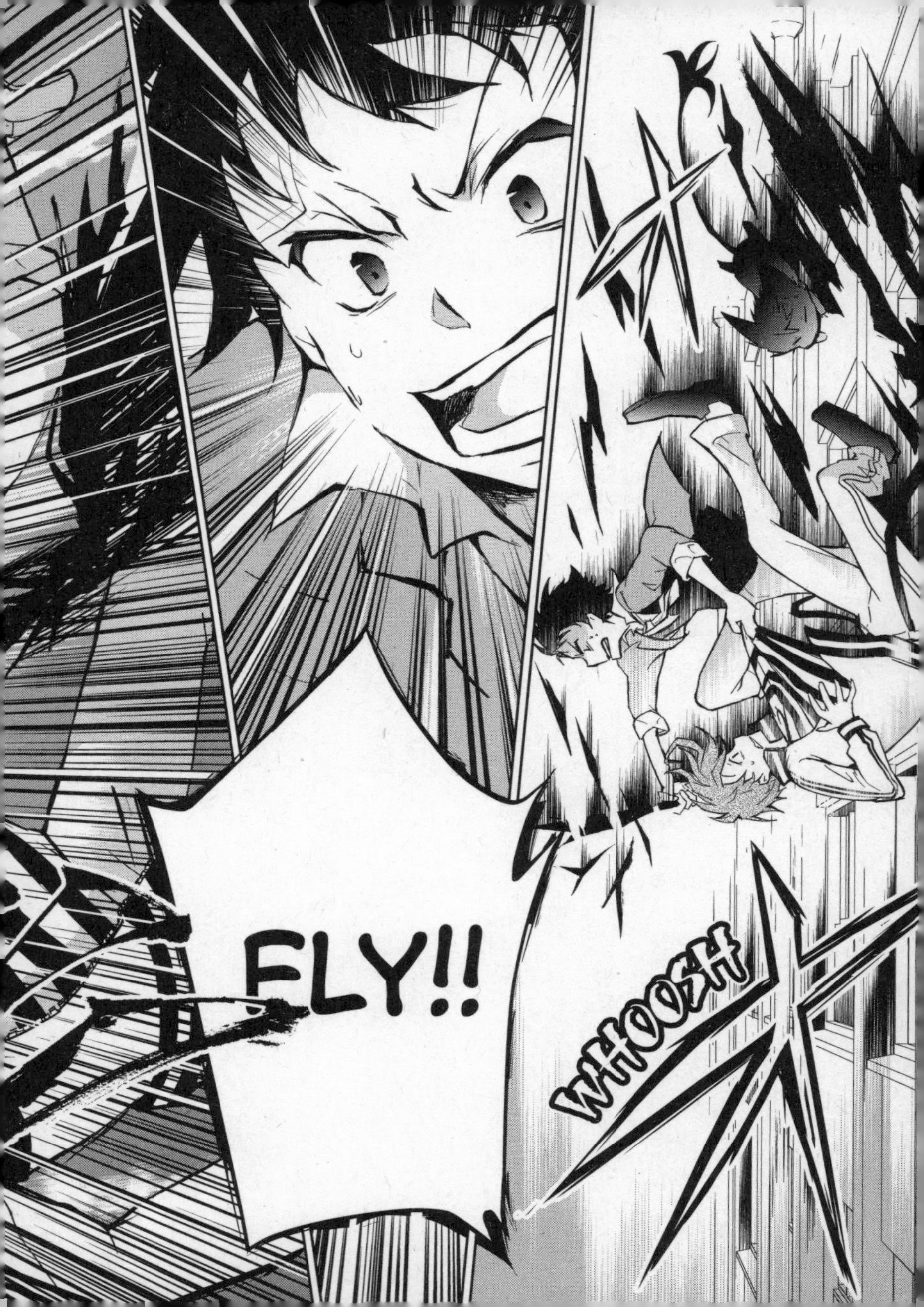
FLY!!
WHOOSH

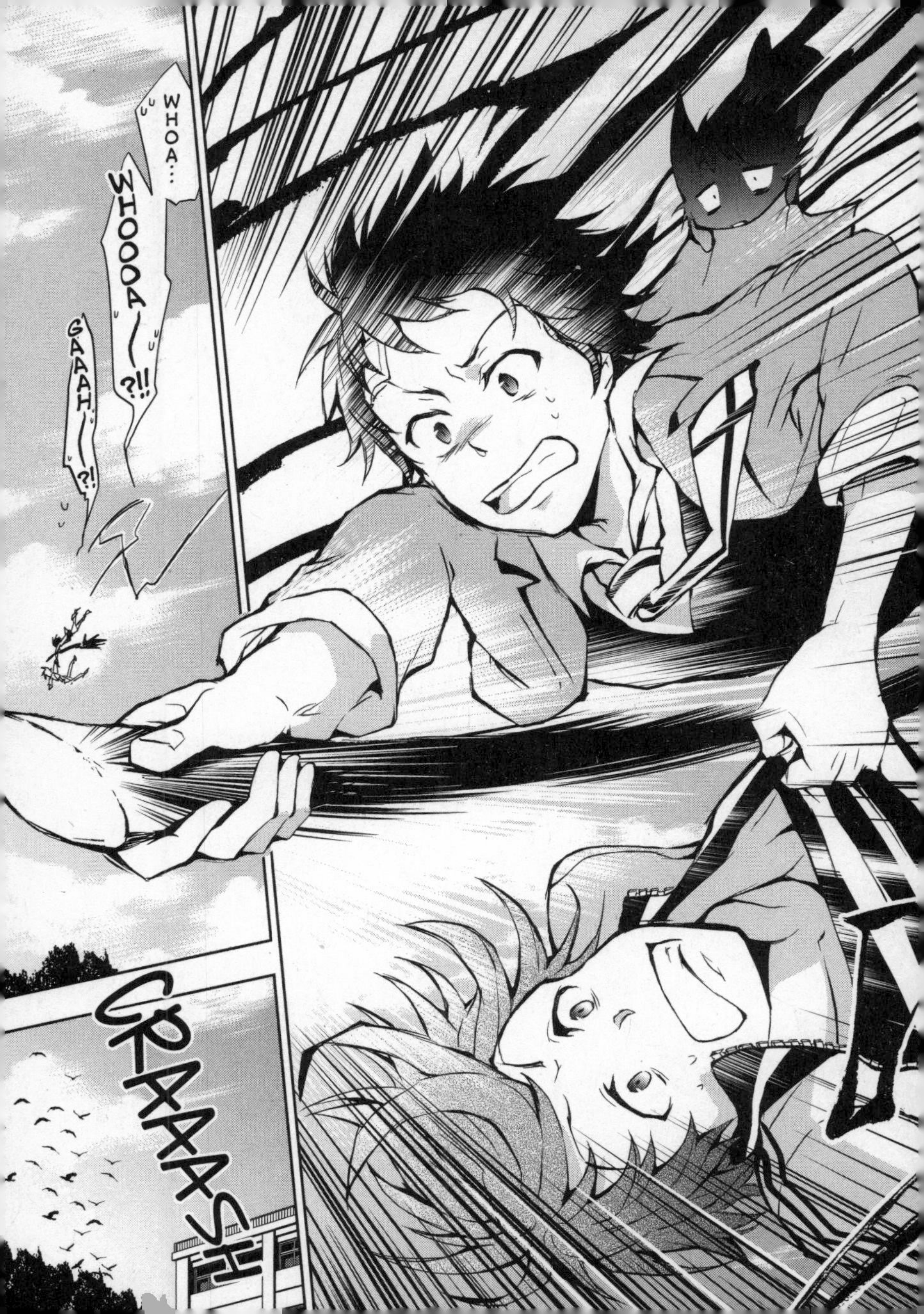

WHOA...
WHOOOA—?!!
GAAAH—?!
CRAAASH

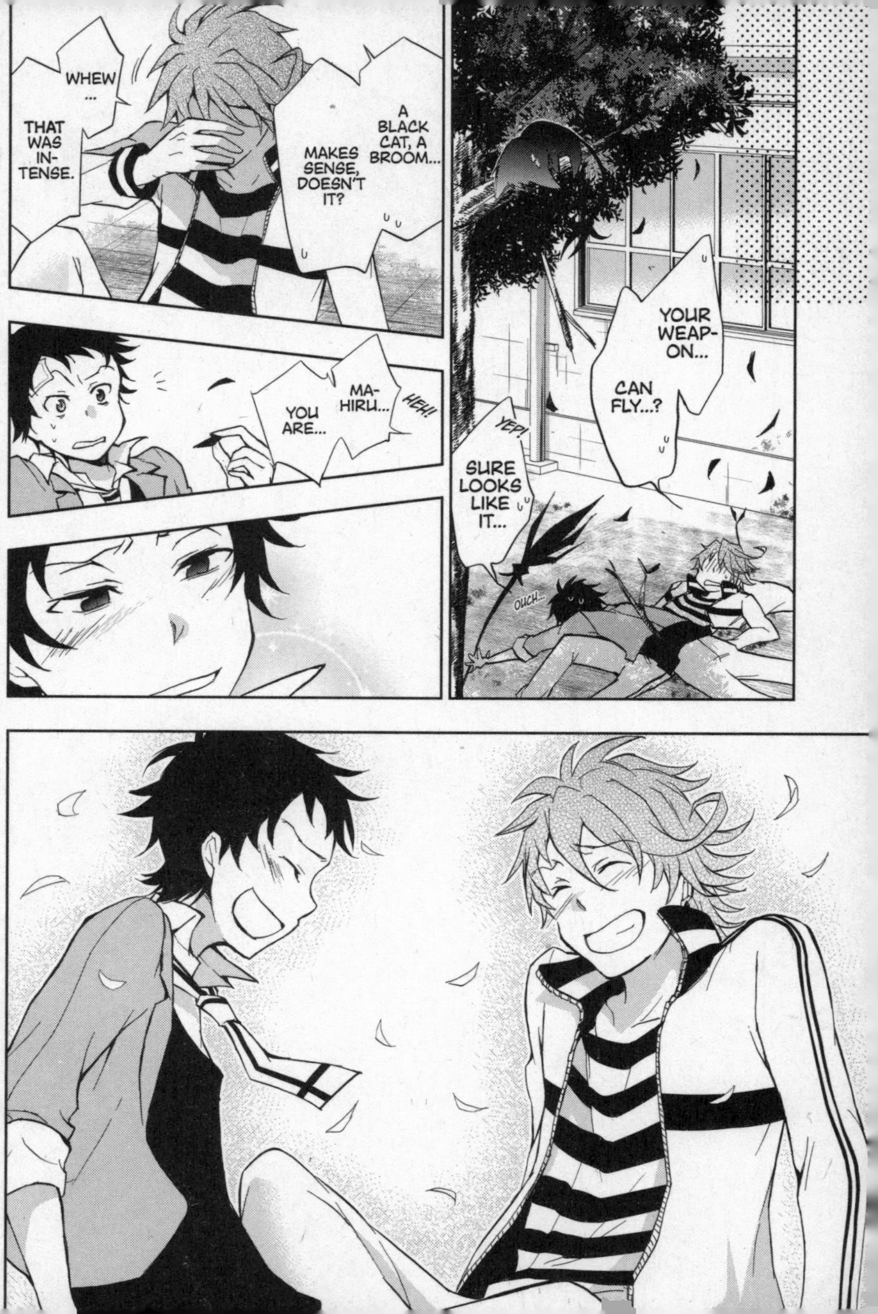
YOUR WEAP-ON...
CAN FLY...?
YEP!
SURE LOOKS LIKE IT...
OUCH...
WHEW...
THAT WAS IN-TENSE.
A BLACK CAT, A BROOM...
MAKES SENSE, DOESN'T IT?
MA-HIRU...
YOU ARE...
HEH!

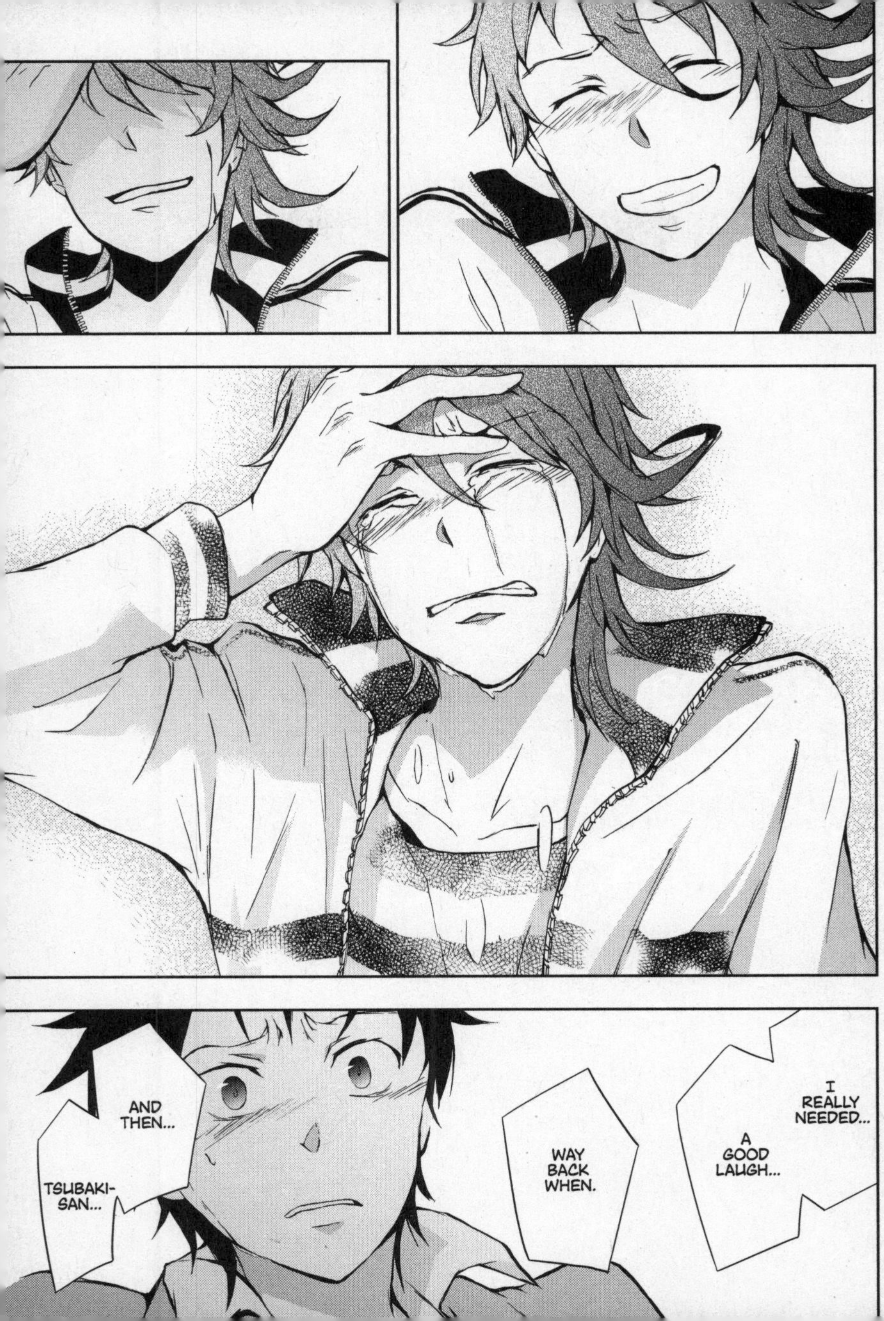
I REALLY NEEDED...
A GOOD LAUGH...
WAY BACK WHEN.
AND THEN...
TSUBAKI-SAN...

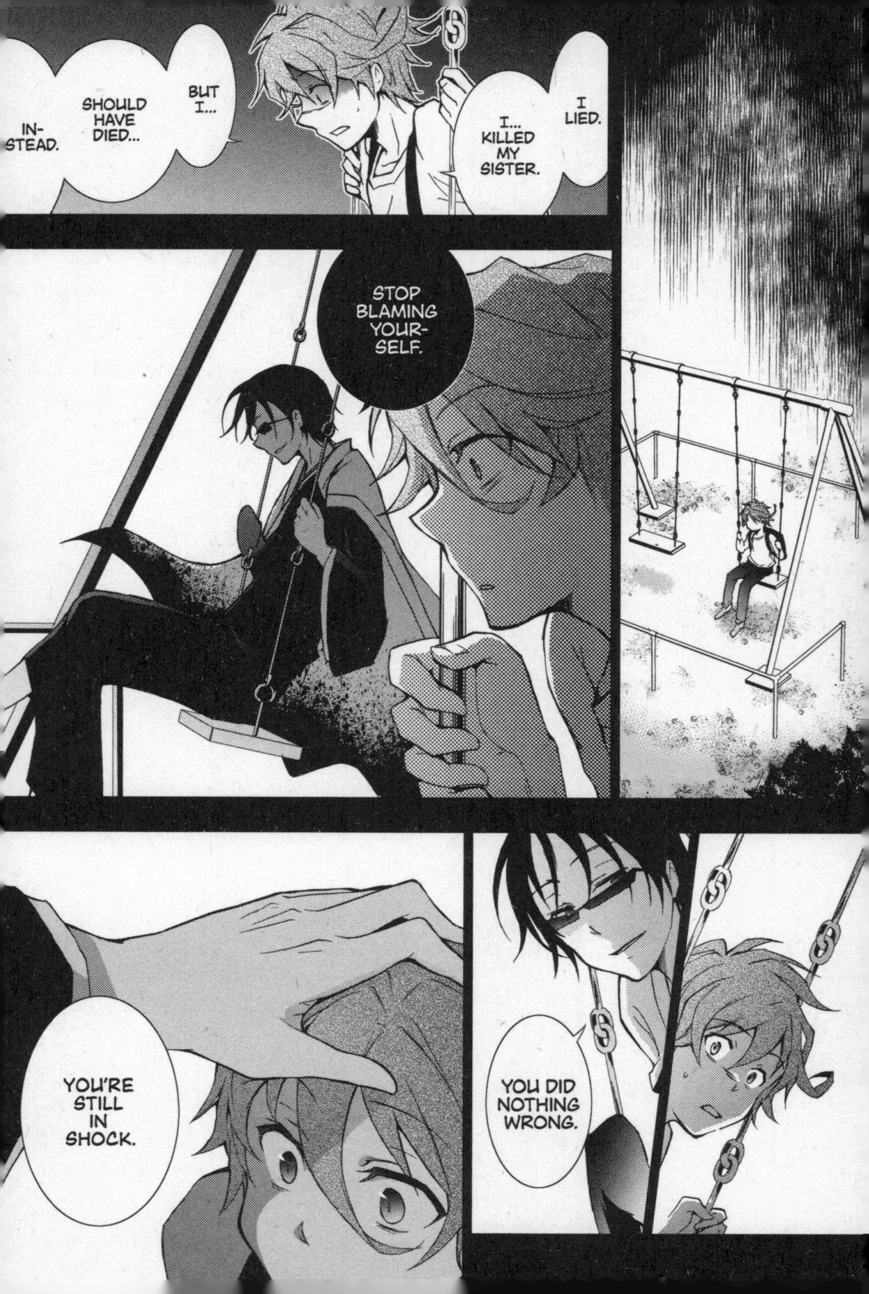
I LIED.
I... KILLED MY SISTER.
BUT I...
SHOULD HAVE DIED...
IN-STEAD.
STOP BLAMING YOUR-SELF.
YOU DID NOTHING WRONG.
YOU'RE STILL IN SHOCK.

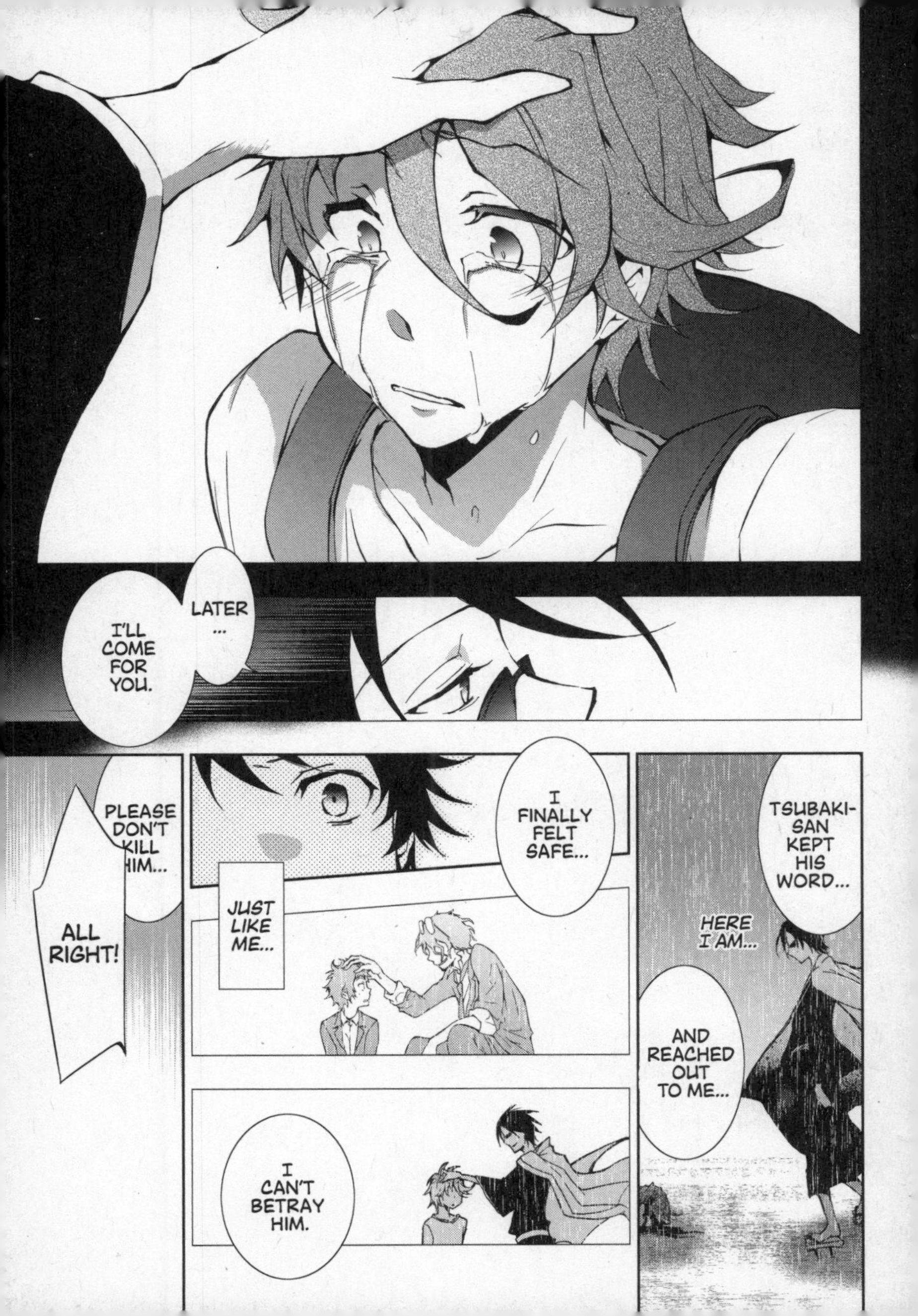
LATER... I'LL COME FOR YOU.
TSUBAKI-SAN KEPT HIS WORD...
HERE I AM...
AND REACHED OUT TO ME...
I FINALLY FELT SAFE...
JUST LIKE ME...
I CAN'T BETRAY HIM.
PLEASE DON'T KILL HIM...
ALL RIGHT!

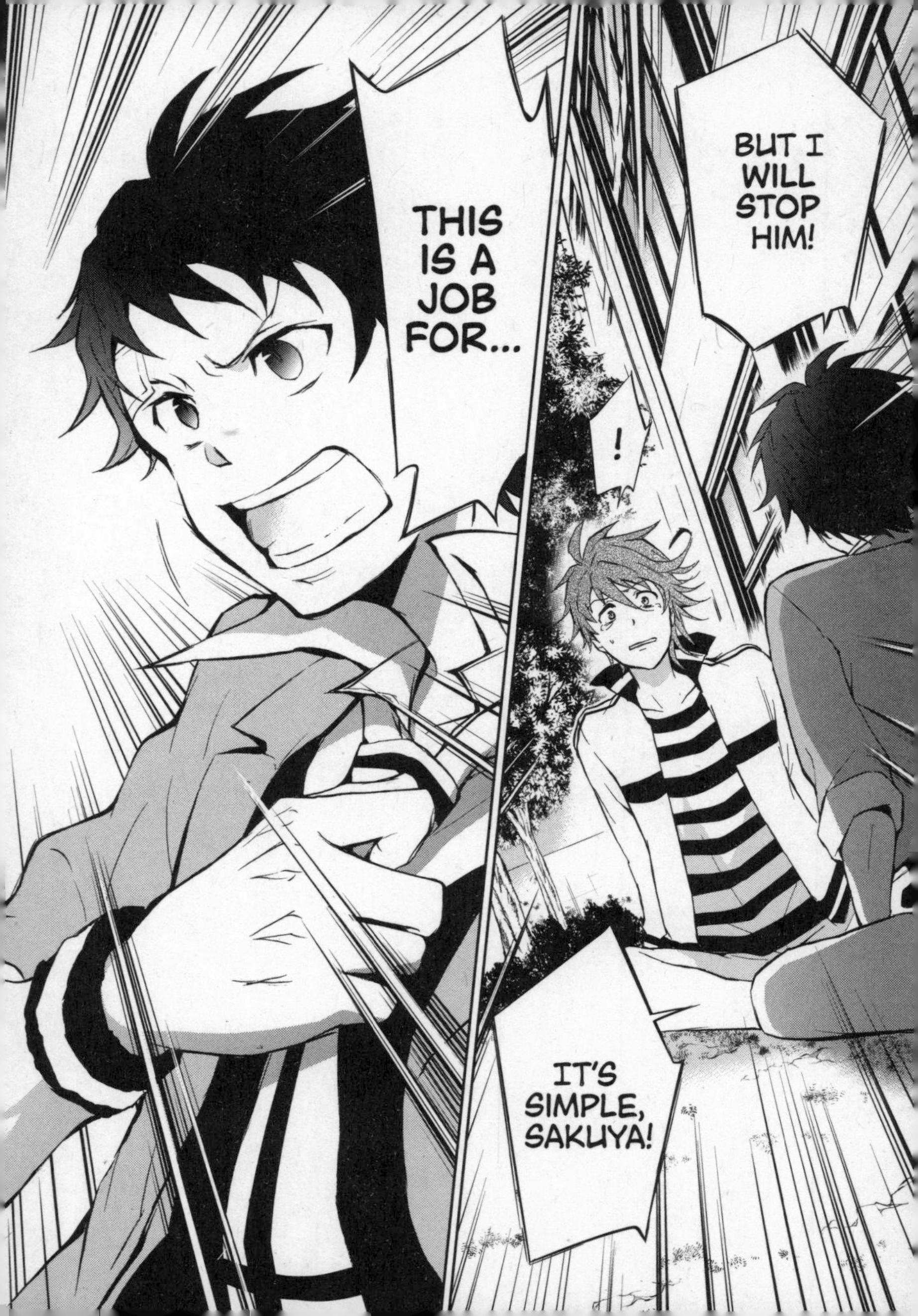
BUT I WILL STOP HIM!
!
IT'S SIMPLE, SAKUYA!
THIS IS A JOB FOR...

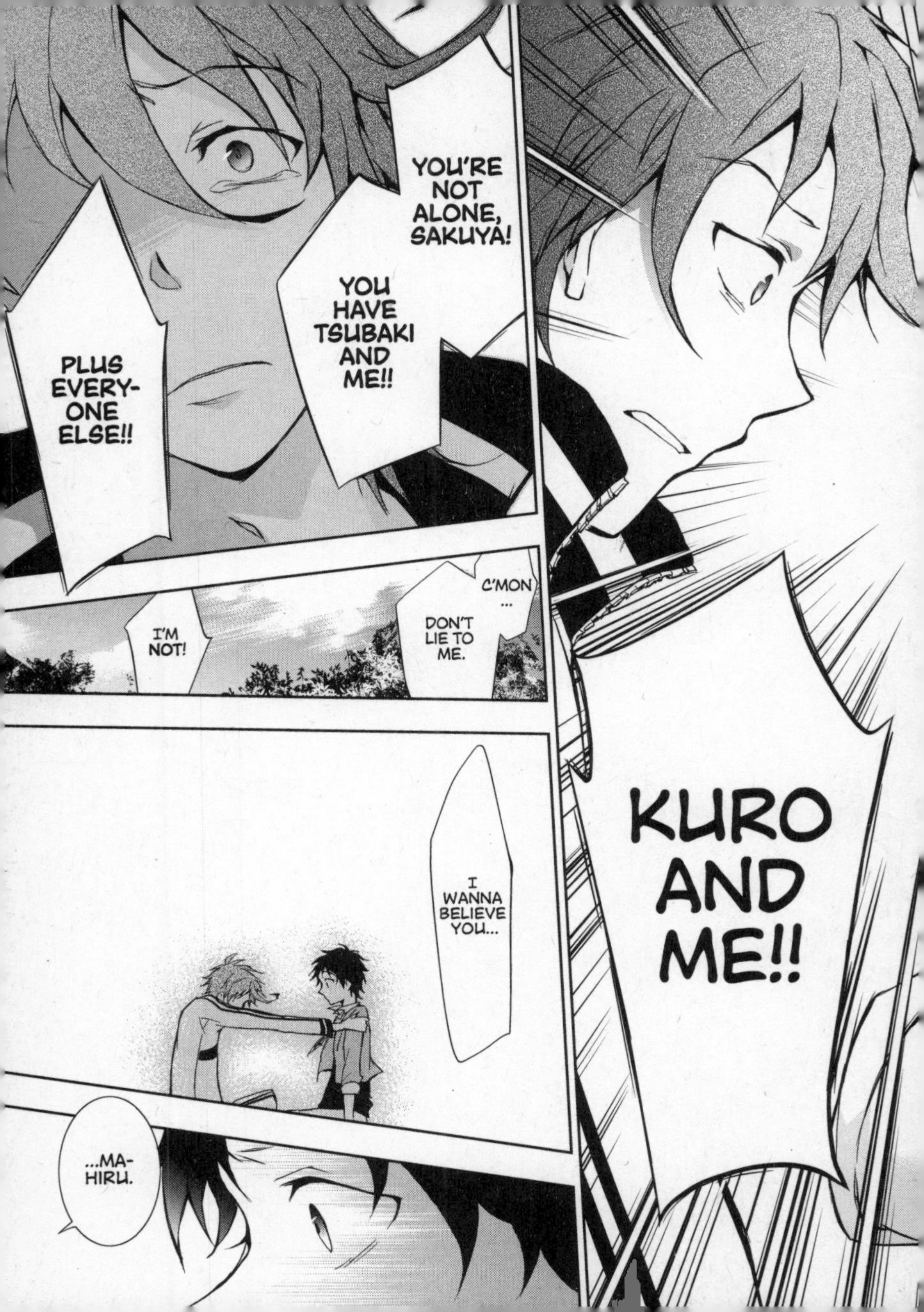
KURO AND ME!!
YOU'RE NOT ALONE, SAKUYA!
YOU HAVE TSUBAKI AND ME!!
PLUS EVERY-ONE ELSE!!
C'MON ... DON'T LIE TO ME.
I'M NOT!
I WANNA BELIEVE YOU...
...MA-HIRU.

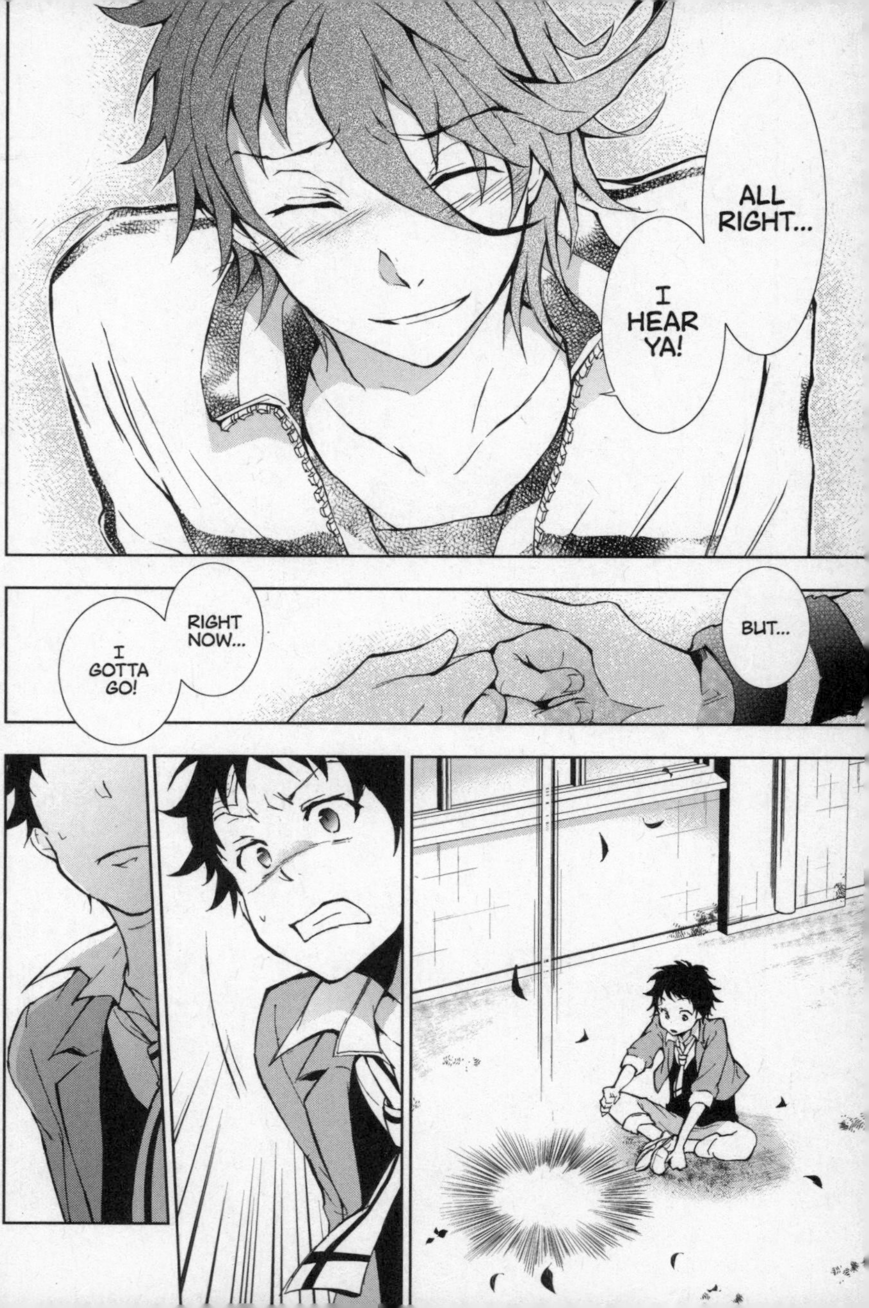
ALL RIGHT...
I HEAR YA!
BUT...
RIGHT NOW...
I GOTTA GO!

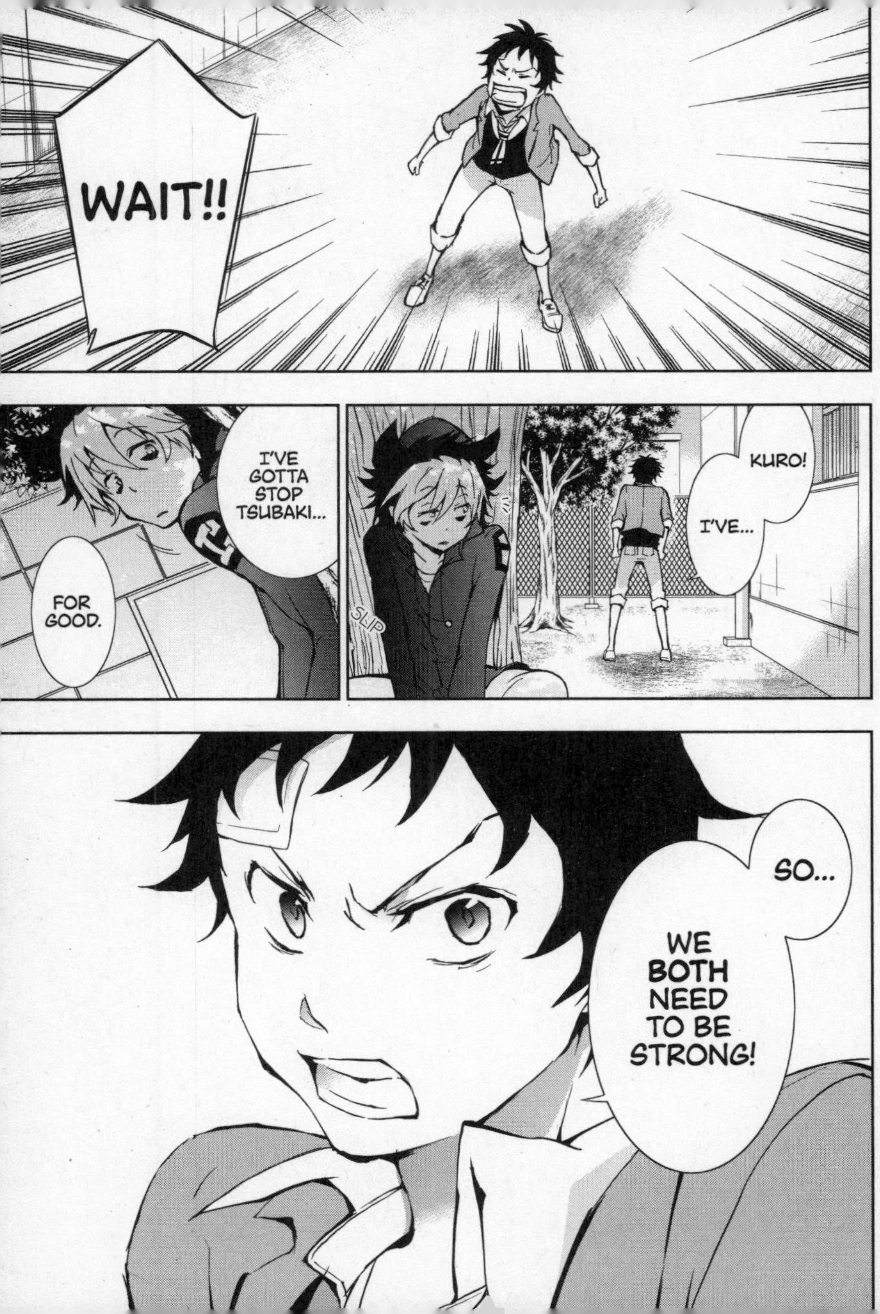
WAIT!!
KURO!
I'VE...
SLIP
I'VE GOTTA STOP TSUBAKI...
FOR GOOD.
SO...
WE BOTH NEED TO BE STRONG!

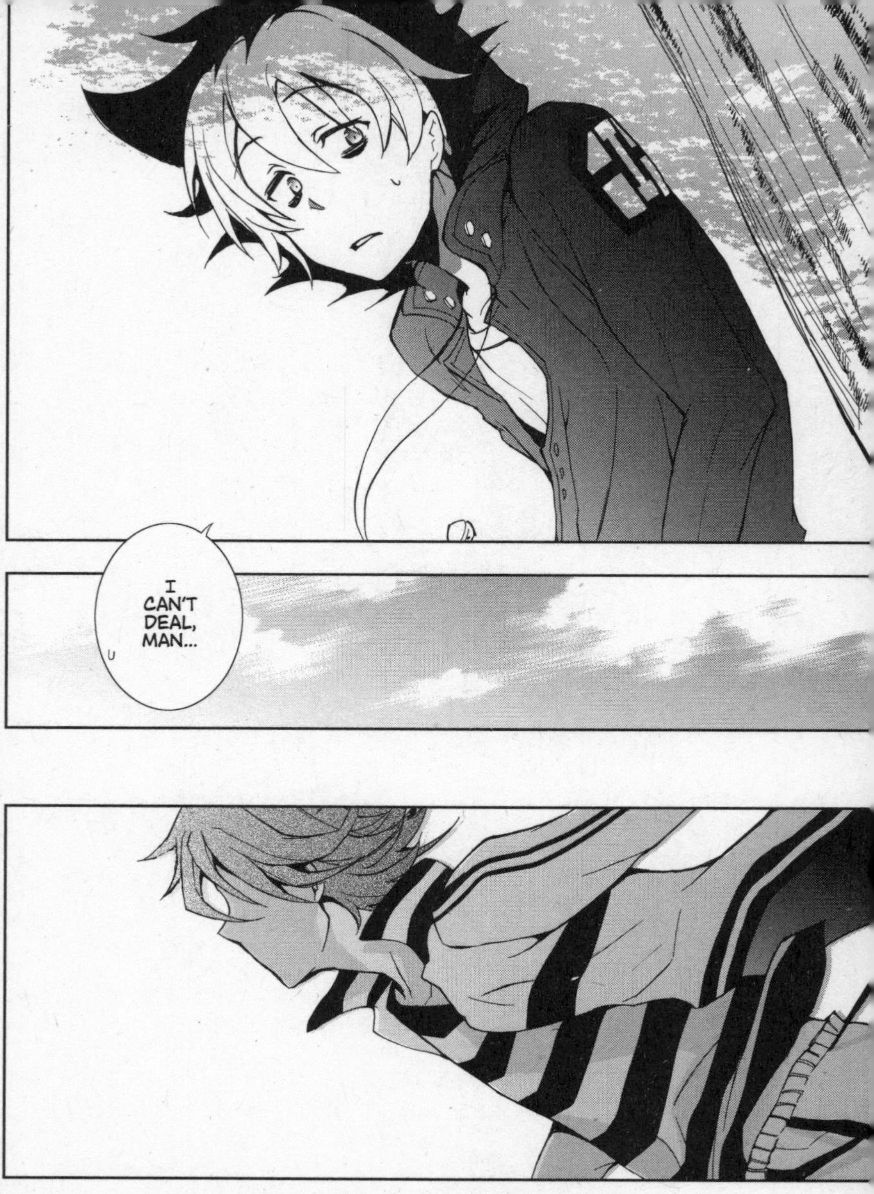
I CAN'T DEAL, MAN...

I CAME FROM A TOWN OF LIARS...

LAST YEAR, I CRASHED A MIDDLE SCHOOL, JUST FOR KICKS...

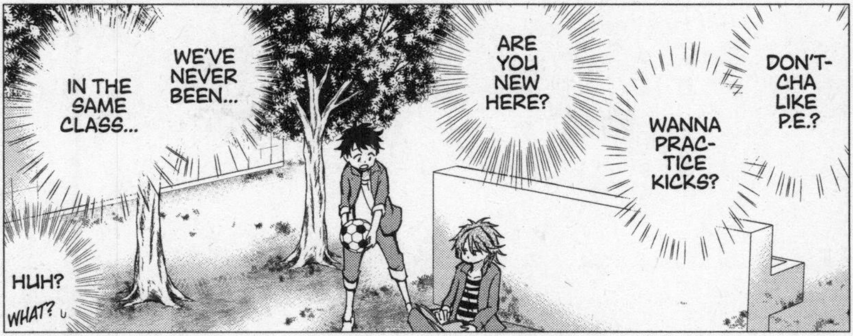
DON'T-CHA LIKE P.E.?
WANNA PRAC-TICE KICKS?
ARE YOU NEW HERE?
WE'VE NEVER BEEN...
IN THE SAME CLASS...
HUH?
WHAT?

WHAT DID I THINK WOULD HAPPEN?

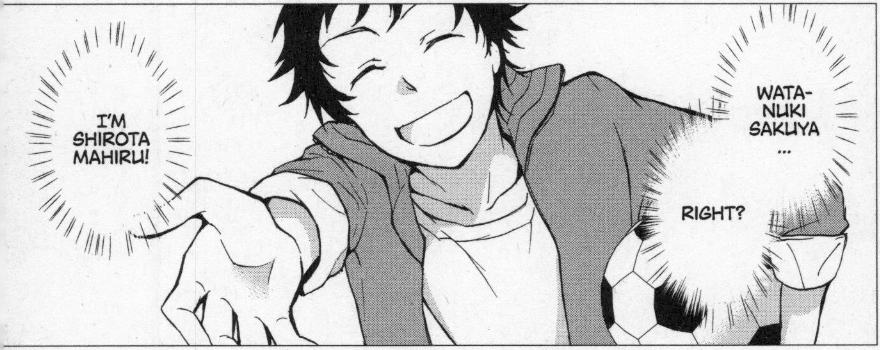
WATA-NUKI SAKUYA ...
RIGHT?
I'M SHIROTA MAHIRU!

HE SMILED, AND I INSTANTLY THOUGHT...

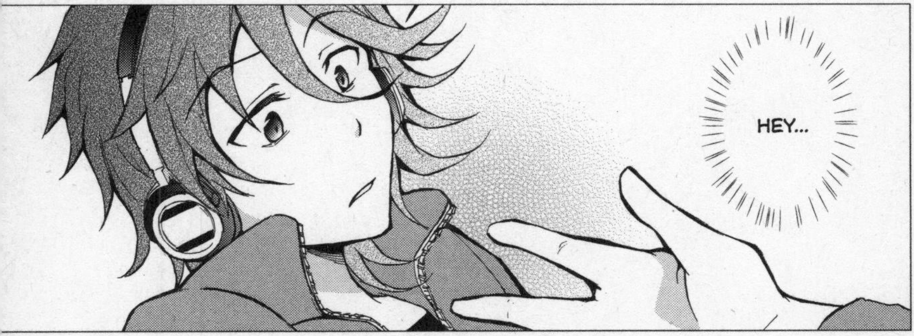
HEY...

"I WANNA BE HIS FRIEND..."

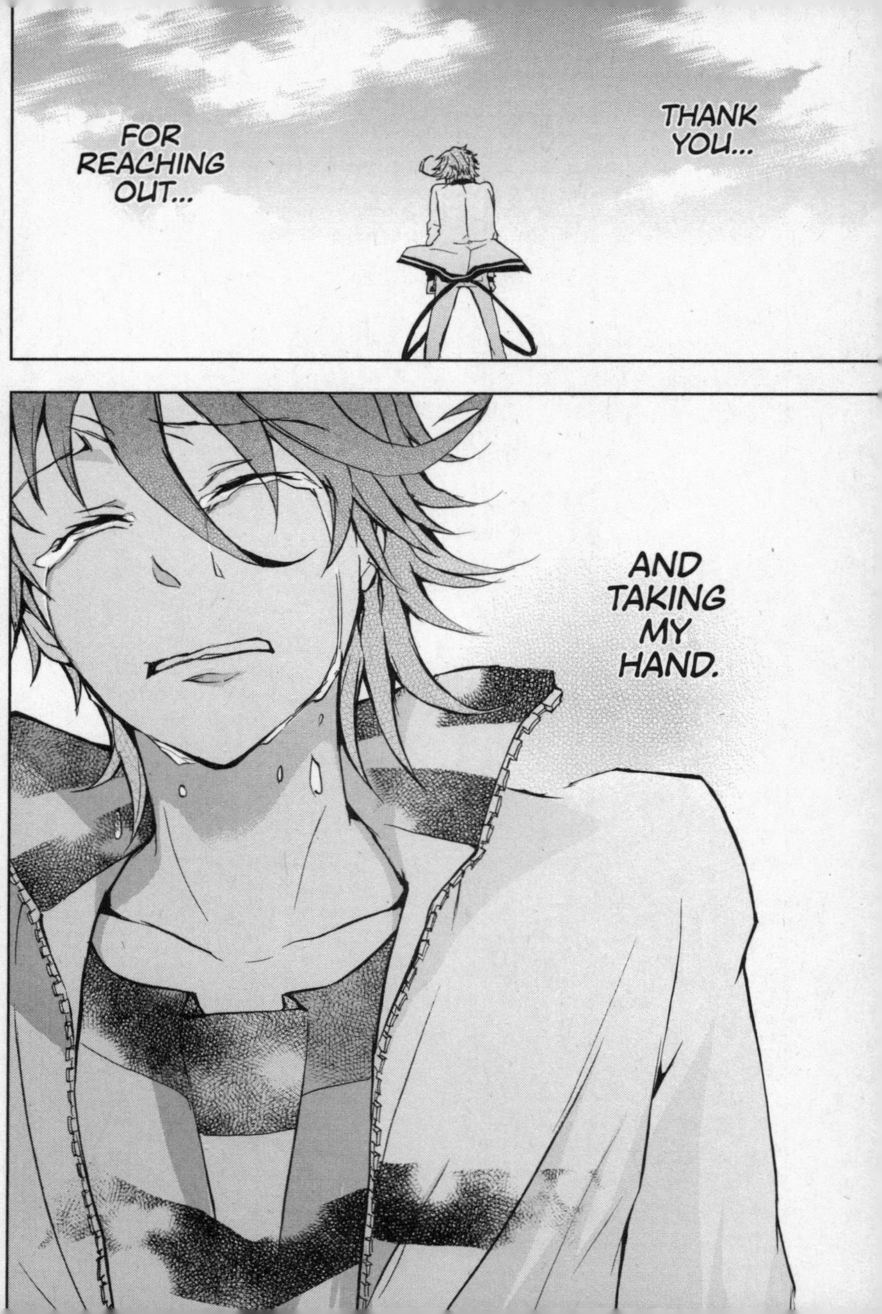
THANK YOU...
FOR REACHING OUT...
AND TAKING MY HAND.

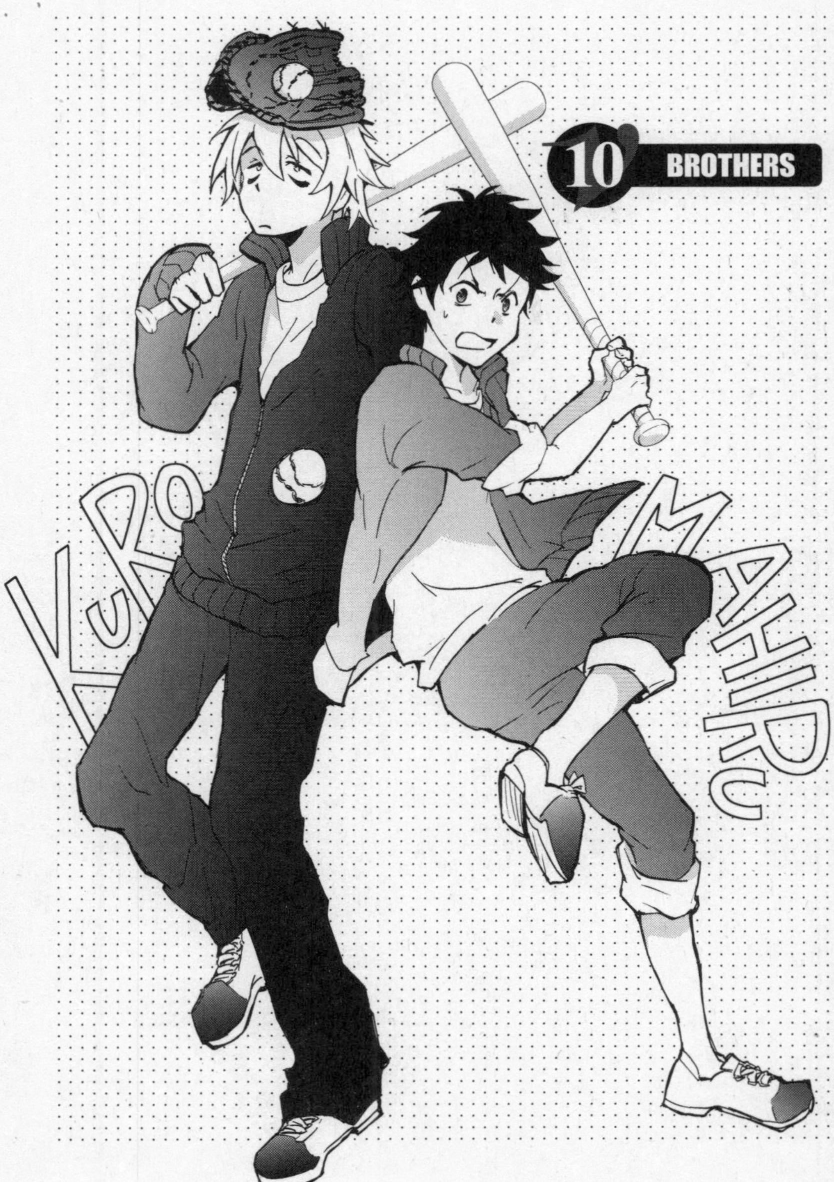
10
BROTHERS
KURO
MAHIRU

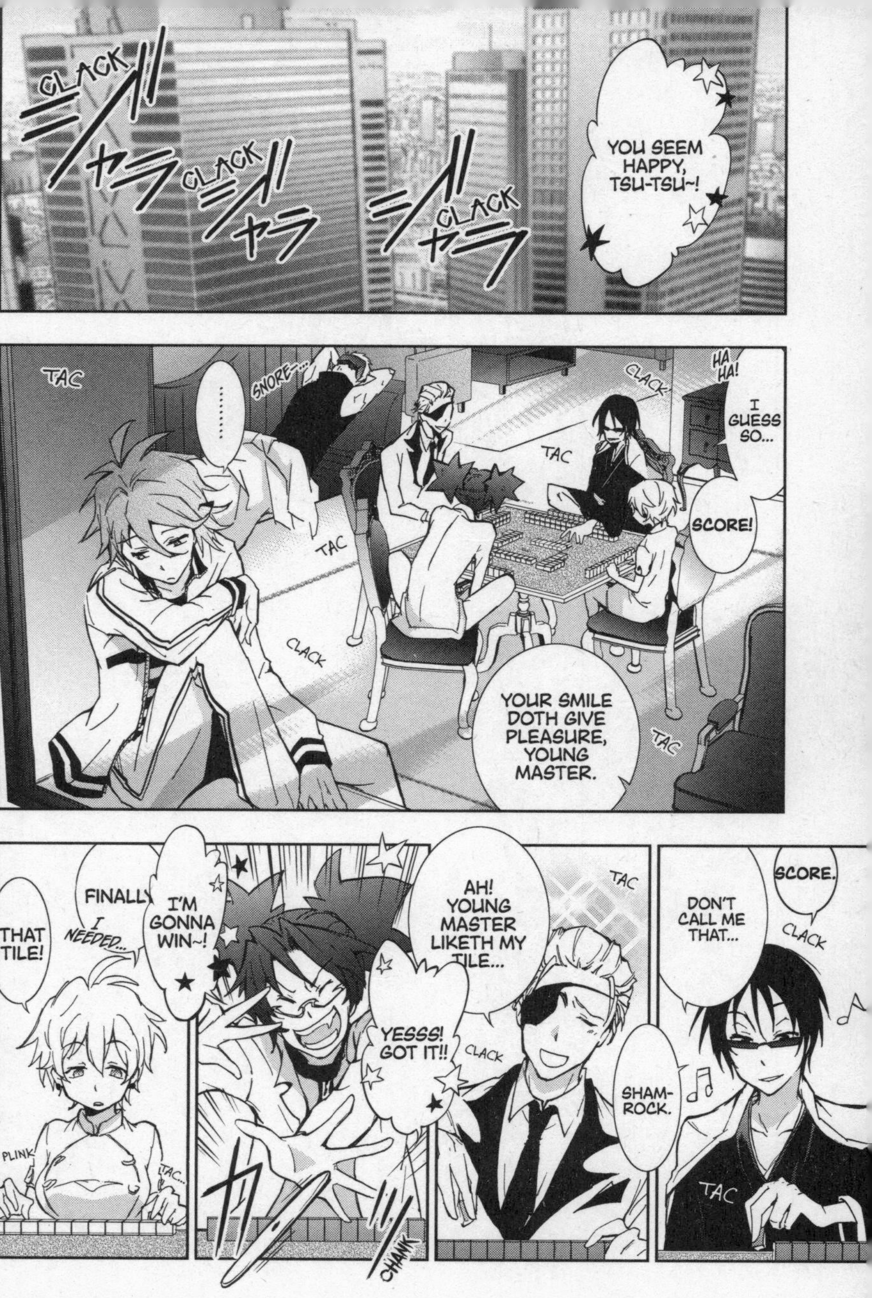
YOU SEEM HAPPY, TSU-TSU~!
CLACK
ジャラ
CLACK
ジャラ
CLACK
ジャラ
HA HA!
I GUESS SO...
CLACK
SNORE...
TAC
SCORE!
TAC
......
TAC
TAC
YOUR SMILE DOTH GIVE PLEASURE, YOUNG MASTER.
CLACK
TAC
SCORE.
DON'T CALL ME THAT...
CLACK
SHAM-ROCK.
TAC
TAC
AH! YOUNG MASTER LIKETH MY TILE...
CLACK
I'M GONNA WIN~!
YESSS! GOT IT!!
CHANK
FINALLY
I NEEDED...
THAT TILE!
PLINK
TAC...

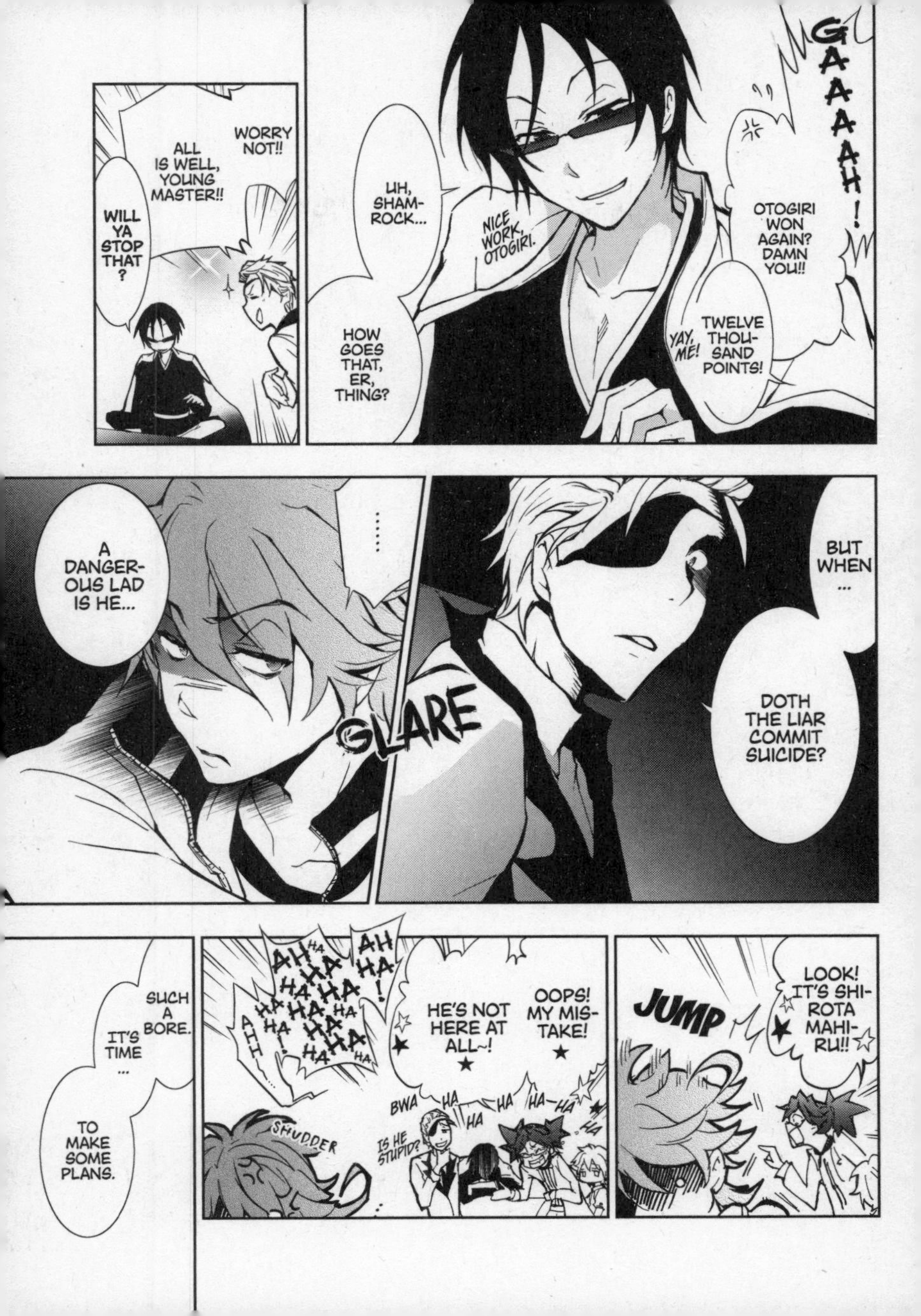
GAAAAAH!
OTOGIRI WON AGAIN? DAMN YOU!!
TWELVE THOUSAND POINTS!
YAY, ME!
NICE WORK, OTOGIRI.
UH, SHAMROCK...
HOW GOES THAT, ER, THING?
WORRY NOT!!
ALL IS WELL, YOUNG MASTER!!
WILL YA STOP THAT?
BUT WHEN...
DOTH THE LIAR COMMIT SUICIDE?
GLARE
......
A DANGEROUS LAD IS HE...
LOOK! IT'S SHIROTA MAHIRU!!
JUMP
OOPS! MY MISTAKE!
HE'S NOT HERE AT ALL~!
AH HA HA HA HA HA HA HA HA HA HA HA HA HA HA HA AH HA HA!
BWA HA HA HA HA-HA HA
IS HE STUPID?
AHH...!
SHUDDER
SUCH A BORE.
IT'S TIME...
TO MAKE SOME PLANS.

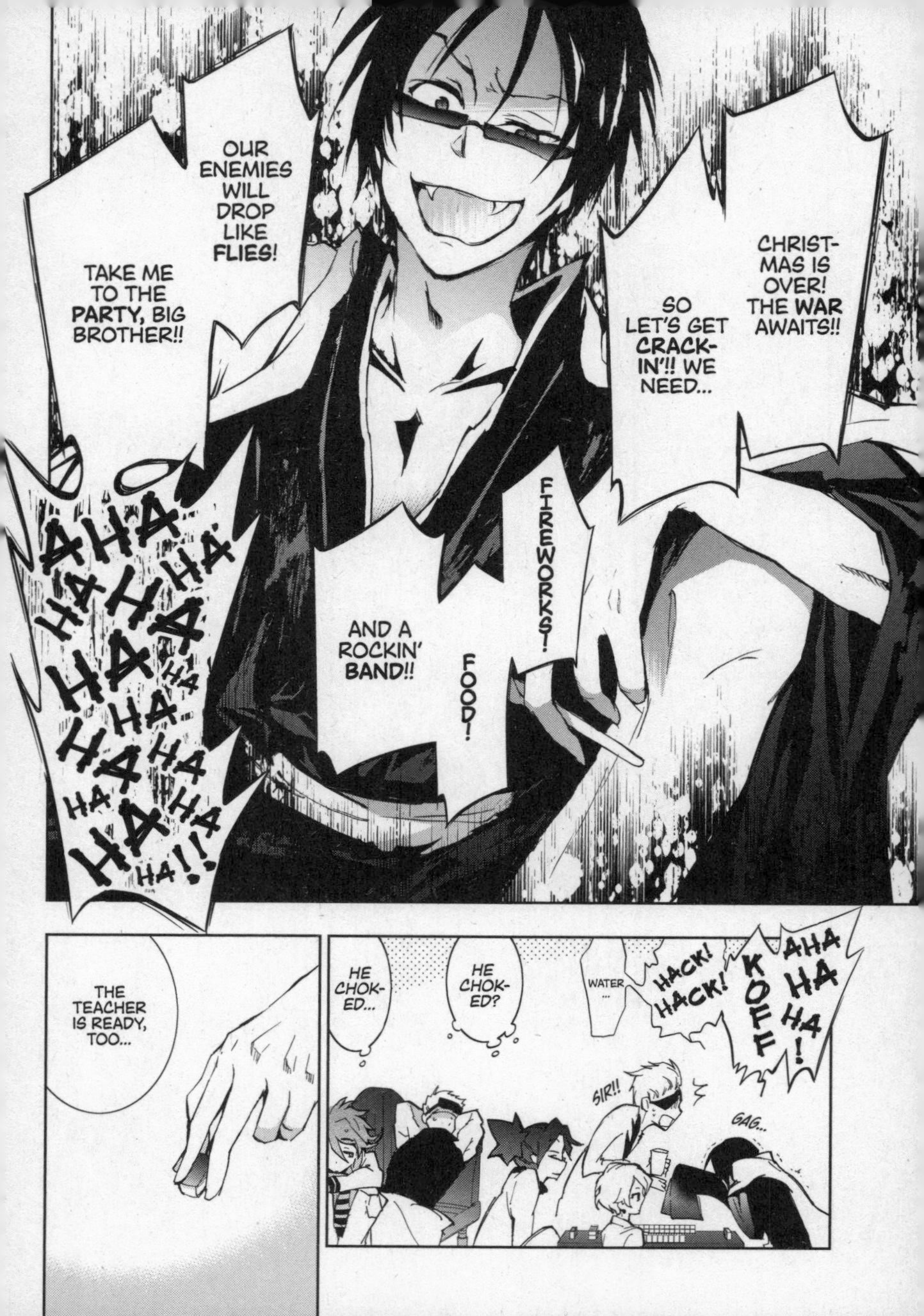
CHRIST-MAS IS OVER! THE WAR AWAITS!!
SO LET'S GET CRACK-IN'!! WE NEED...
FIREWORKS!
FOOD!
AND A ROCKIN' BAND!!
OUR ENEMIES WILL DROP LIKE FLIES!
TAKE ME TO THE PARTY, BIG BROTHER!!
AHA HA HA HA HA HA HA HA HA HA HA HA HA HA!!!
AHA HA HA HA!
KOFF
HACK! HACK!
WATER...
HE CHOKED?
HE CHOKED...
SIR!!
GAG...
THE TEACHER IS READY, TOO...

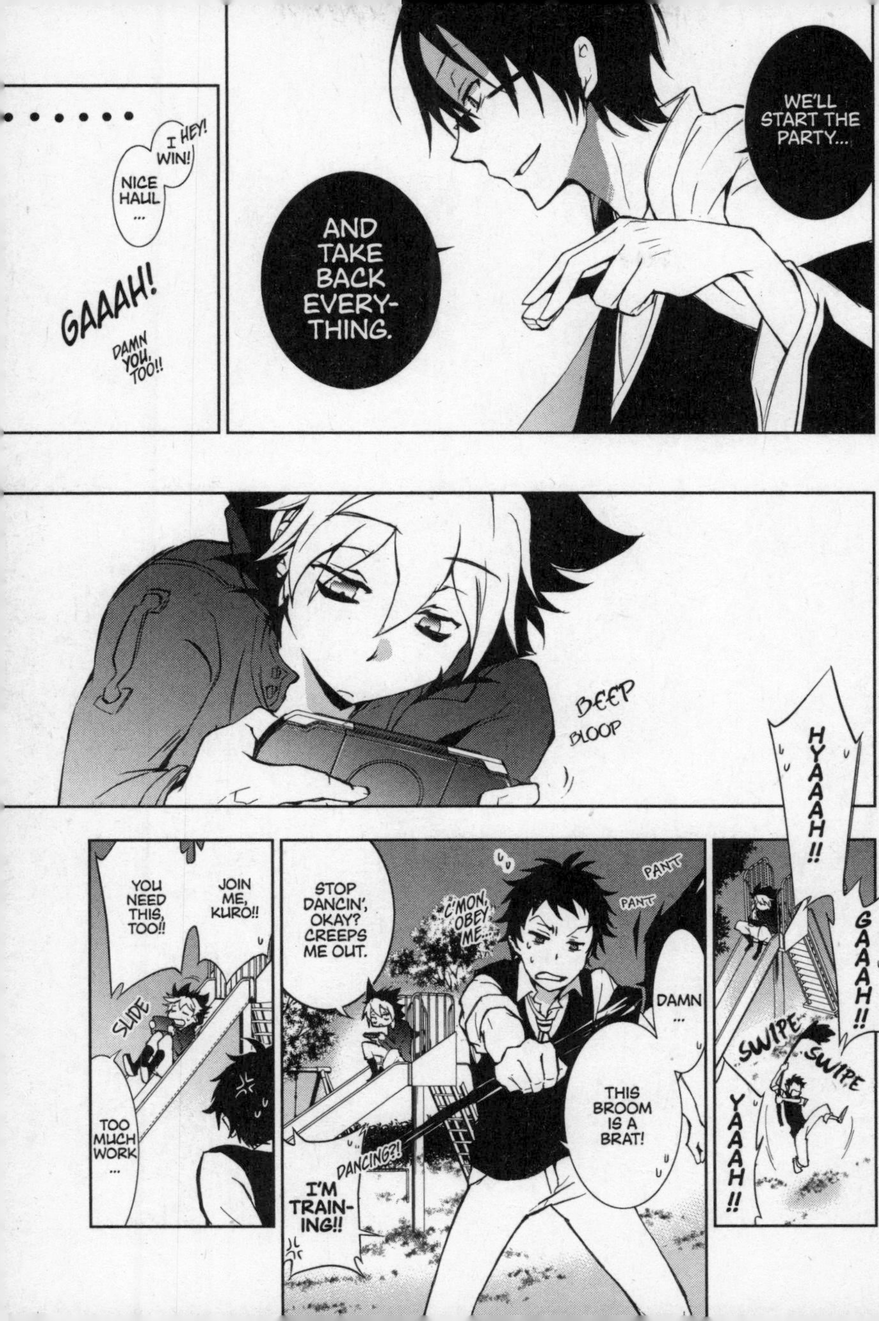
WE'LL START THE PARTY...
AND TAKE BACK EVERYTHING.
• • • • • • •
HEY!
I WIN!
NICE HAUL ...
GAAAH!
DAMN YOU, TOO!!
BEEP
BLOOP
HYAAAAH!!
GAAAAH!!
SWIPE
SWIPE
YAAAAH!!
PANT
PANT
C'MON, OBEY ME...
STOP DANCIN', OKAY? CREEPS ME OUT.
DAMN ...
THIS BROOM IS A BRAT!
DANCING?!
I'M TRAINING!!
JOIN ME, KURO!!
YOU NEED THIS, TOO!!
SLIDE
TOO MUCH WORK ...

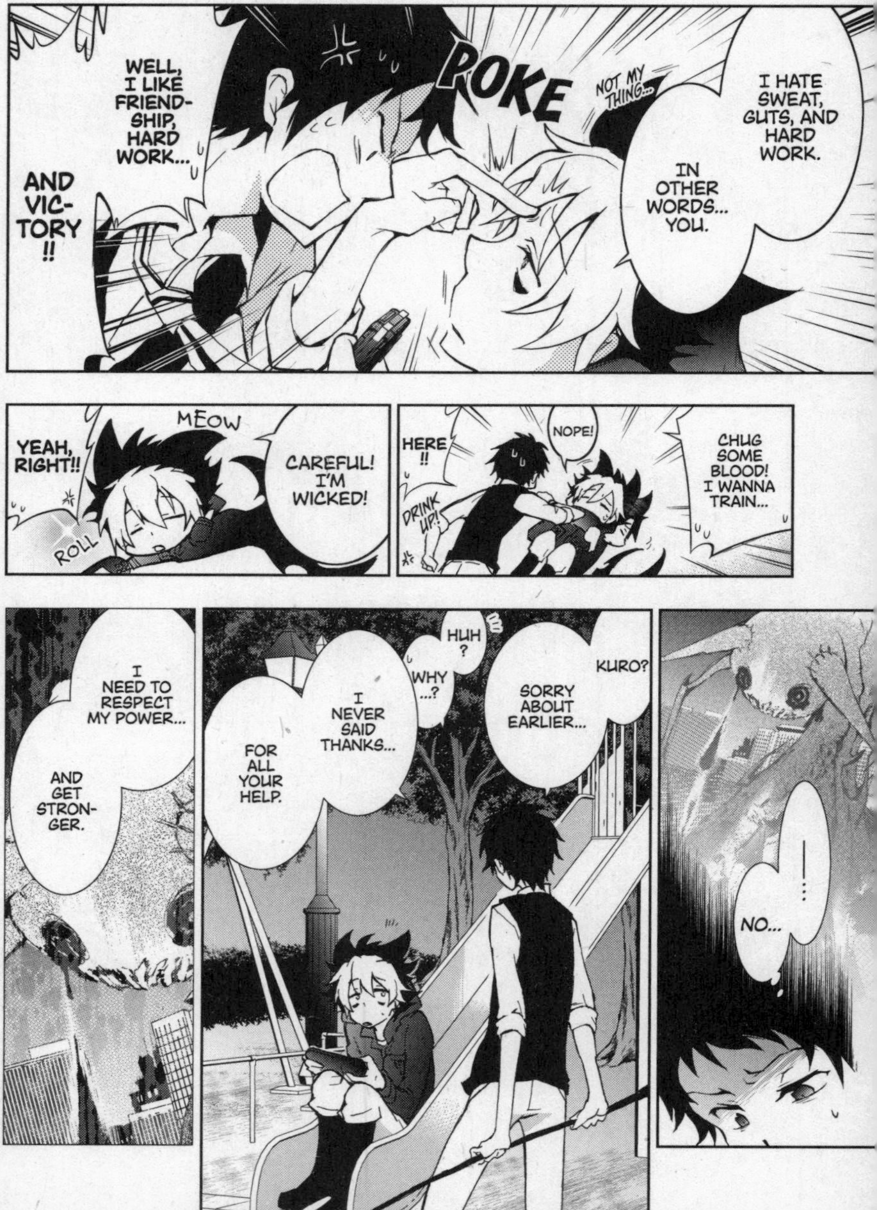
I HATE SWEAT, GUTS, AND HARD WORK.
IN OTHER WORDS... YOU.
NOT MY THING...
POKE
WELL, I LIKE FRIEND-SHIP, HARD WORK...
AND VIC-TORY!!
CHUG SOME BLOOD! I WANNA TRAIN...
NOPE!
HERE!!
DRINK UP!!
CAREFUL! I'M WICKED!
MEOW
YEAH, RIGHT!!
ROLL
...
NO...
KURO?
SORRY ABOUT EARLIER...
HUH?
WHY...?
I NEVER SAID THANKS...
FOR ALL YOUR HELP.
I NEED TO RESPECT MY POWER...
AND GET STRON-GER.

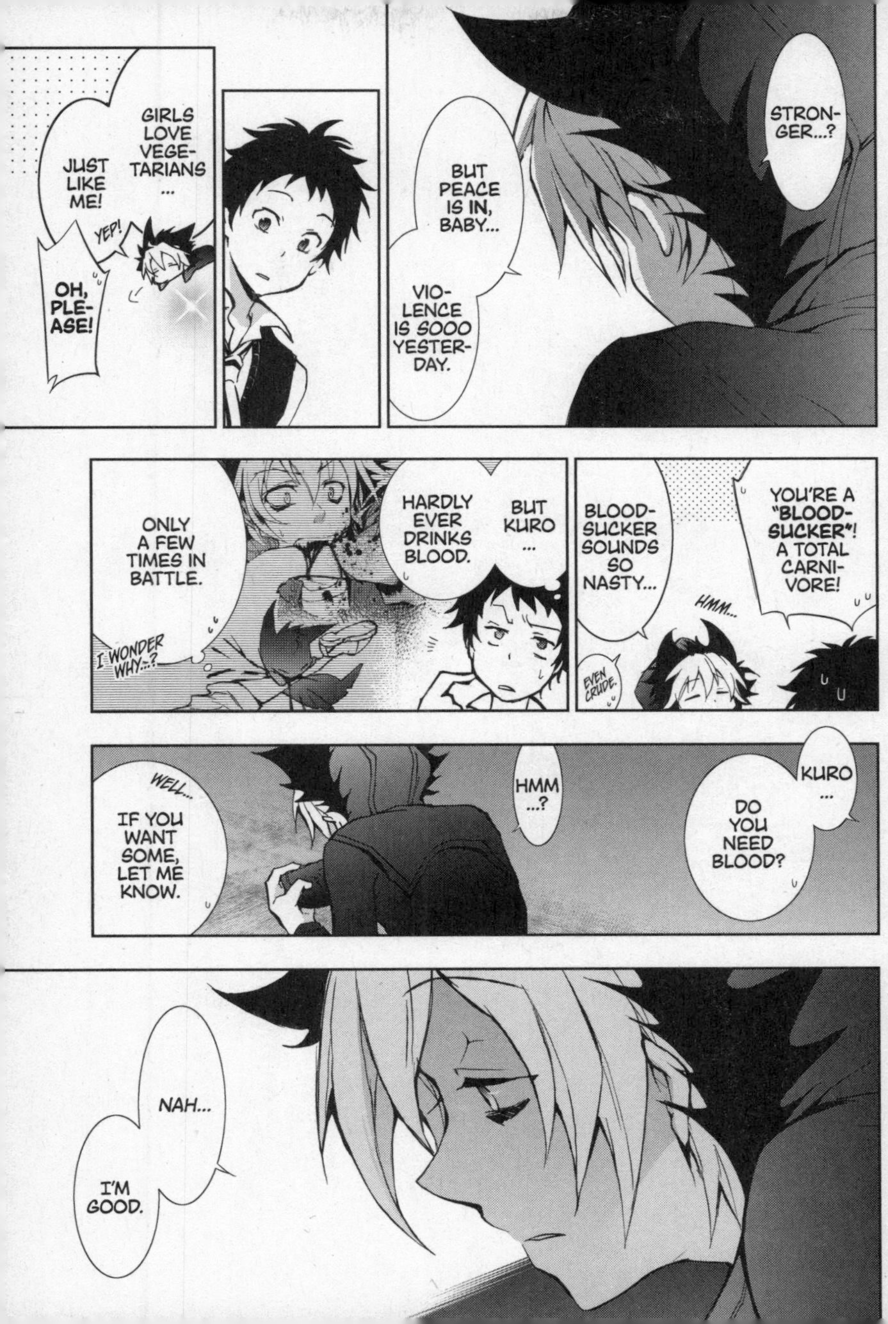
STRONGER...?
BUT PEACE IS IN, BABY...
VIOLENCE IS SOOO YESTERDAY.
GIRLS LOVE VEGETARIANS ...
JUST LIKE ME!
YEP!
OH, PLEASE!
YOU'RE A "BLOODSUCKER"! A TOTAL CARNIVORE!
HMM...
BLOODSUCKER SOUNDS SO NASTY...
EVEN CRUDE.
BUT KURO ...
HARDLY EVER DRINKS BLOOD.
ONLY A FEW TIMES IN BATTLE.
I WONDER WHY...?
KURO ...
DO YOU NEED BLOOD?
HMM ...?
WELL...
IF YOU WANT SOME, LET ME KNOW.
NAH...
I'M GOOD.

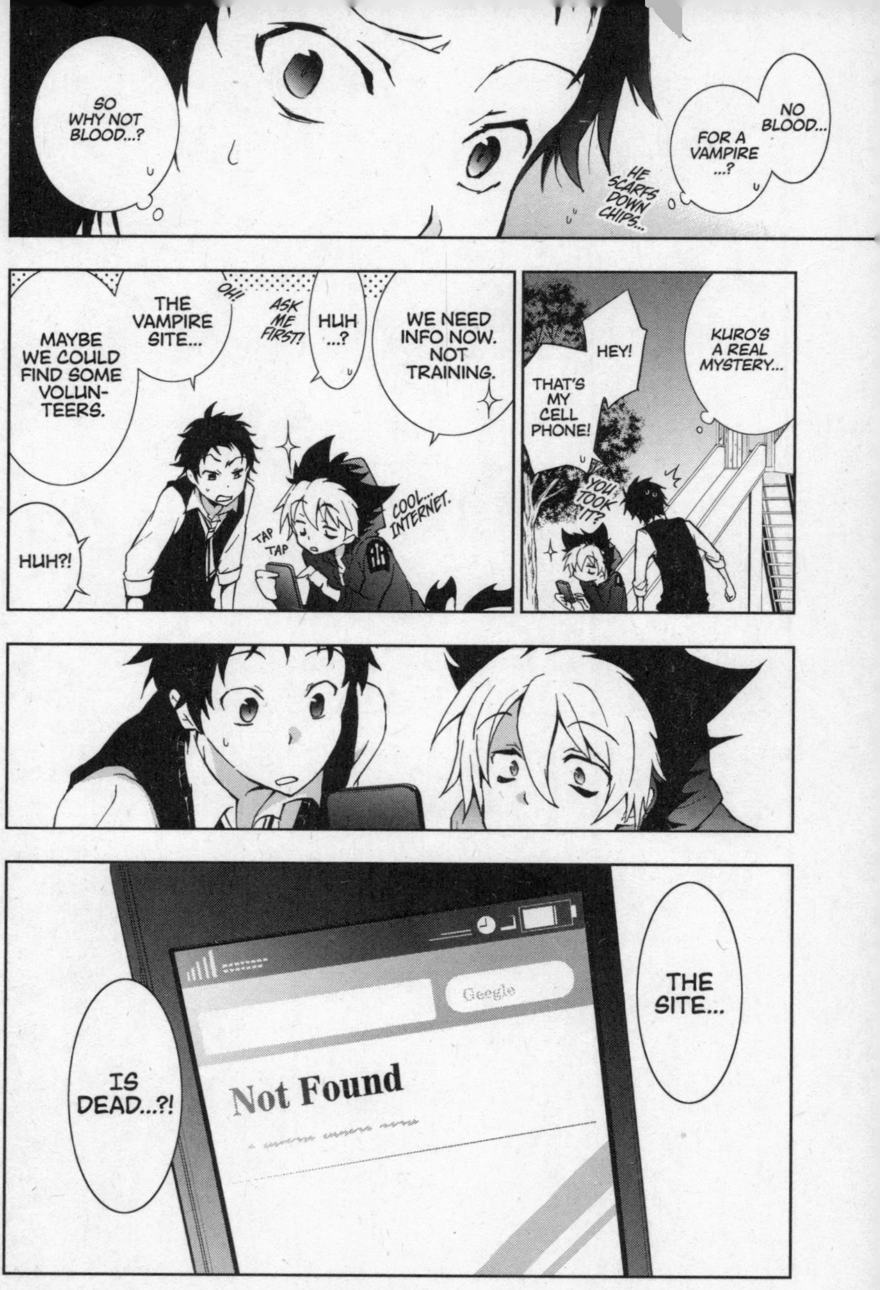
NO BLOOD... FOR A VAMPIRE ...?
HE SCARFS DOWN CHIPS...
SO WHY NOT BLOOD...?
KURO'S A REAL MYSTERY...
HEY! THAT'S MY CELL PHONE!
YOU TOOK IT?
WE NEED INFO NOW. NOT TRAINING.
HUH ...?
ASK ME FIRST!
OH!
THE VAMPIRE SITE...
MAYBE WE COULD FIND SOME VOLUN-TEERS.
COOL... INTERNET.
TAP TAP
HUH?!
THE SITE...
Geegle
Not Found
IS DEAD...?!

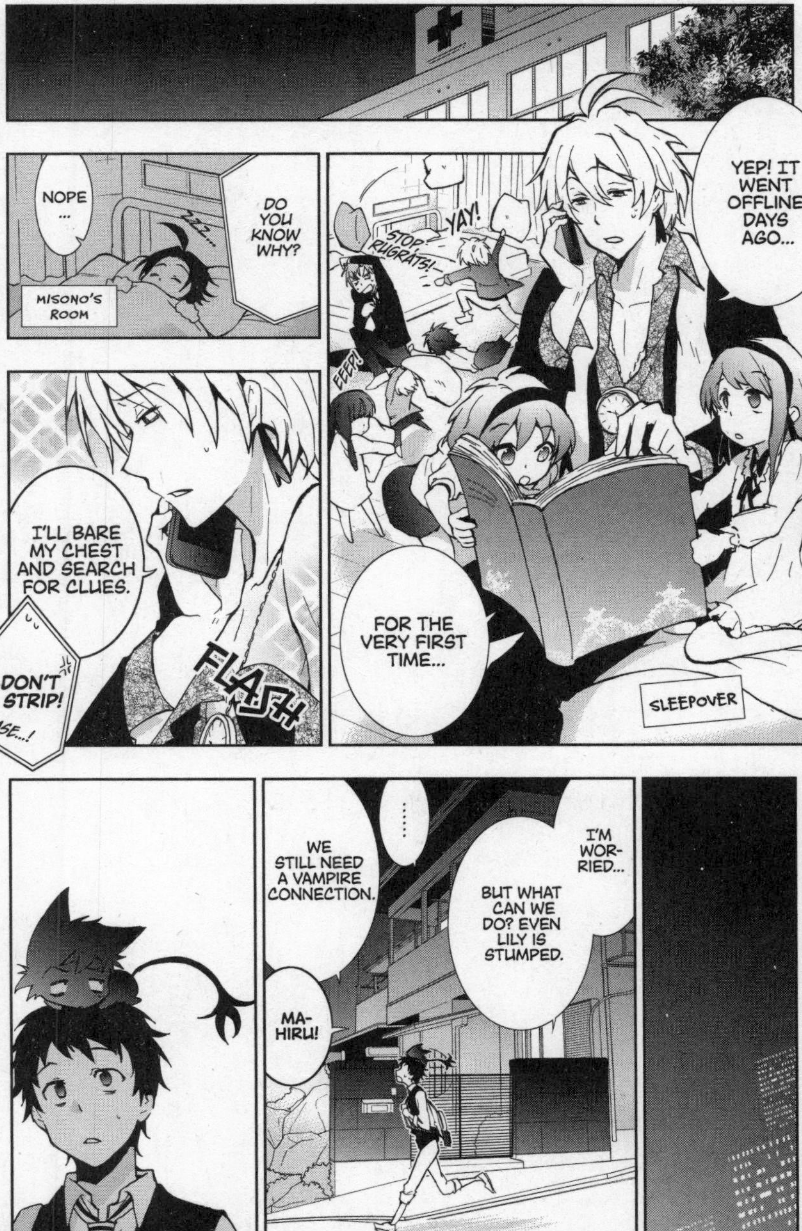
YEP! IT WENT OFFLINE DAYS AGO...
YAY!
STOP, RUGRATS!
EEEP!
FOR THE VERY FIRST TIME...
SLEEPOVER
DO YOU KNOW WHY?
NOPE ...
ZZZ...
MISONO'S ROOM
I'LL BARE MY CHEST AND SEARCH FOR CLUES.
FLASH
DON'T STRIP!
PLEASE...!
I'M WOR-RIED...
BUT WHAT CAN WE DO? EVEN LILY IS STUMPED.
......
WE STILL NEED A VAMPIRE CONNECTION.
MA-HIRU!

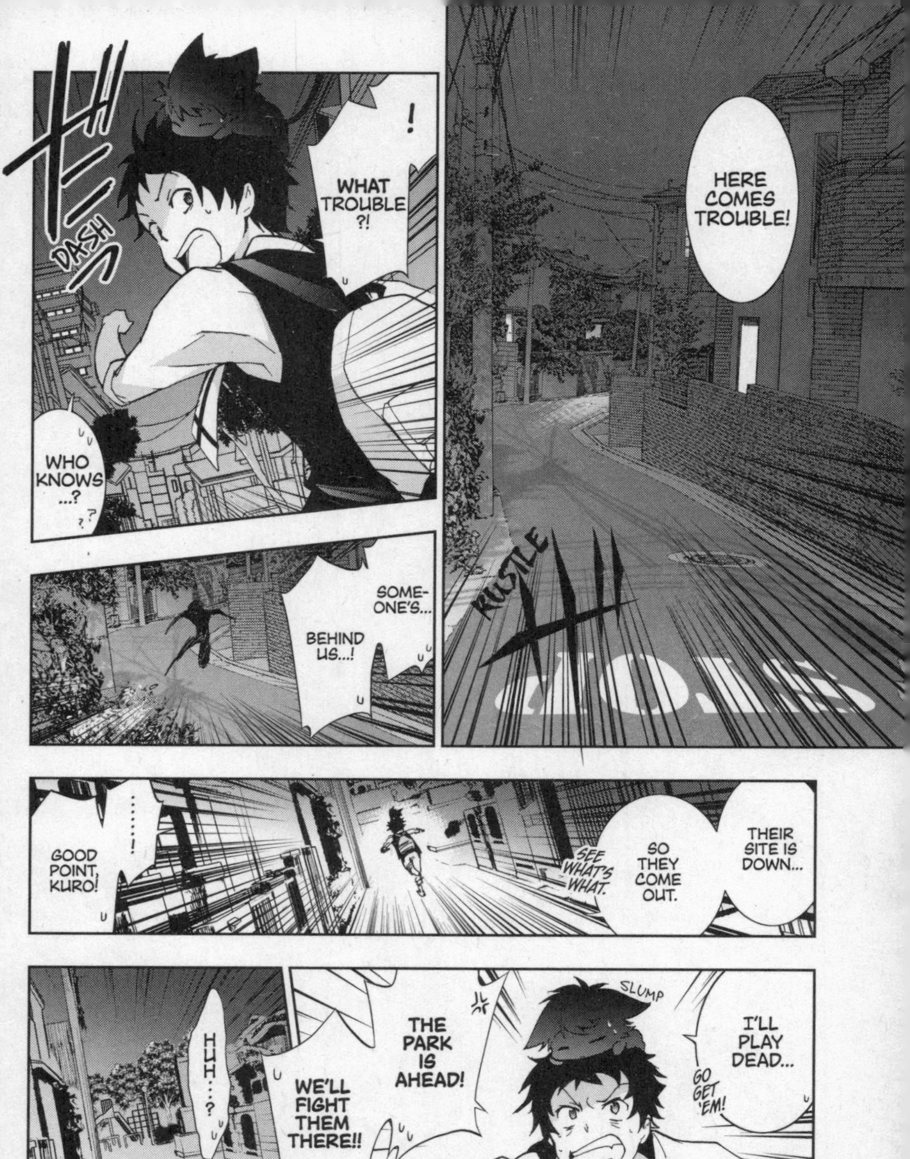
HERE COMES TROUBLE!
RUSTLE
!
WHAT TROUBLE ?!
DASH
WHO KNOWS ...?
SOME-ONE'S...
BEHIND US...!
THEIR SITE IS DOWN...
SO THEY COME OUT.
SEE WHAT'S WHAT.
......!
GOOD POINT, KURO!
I'LL PLAY DEAD...
GO GET 'EM!
SLUMP
THE PARK IS AHEAD!
WE'LL FIGHT THEM THERE!!
CLOP CLOP CLOP
CLOP CLOP CLOP
HUH...?

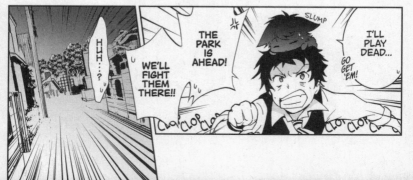

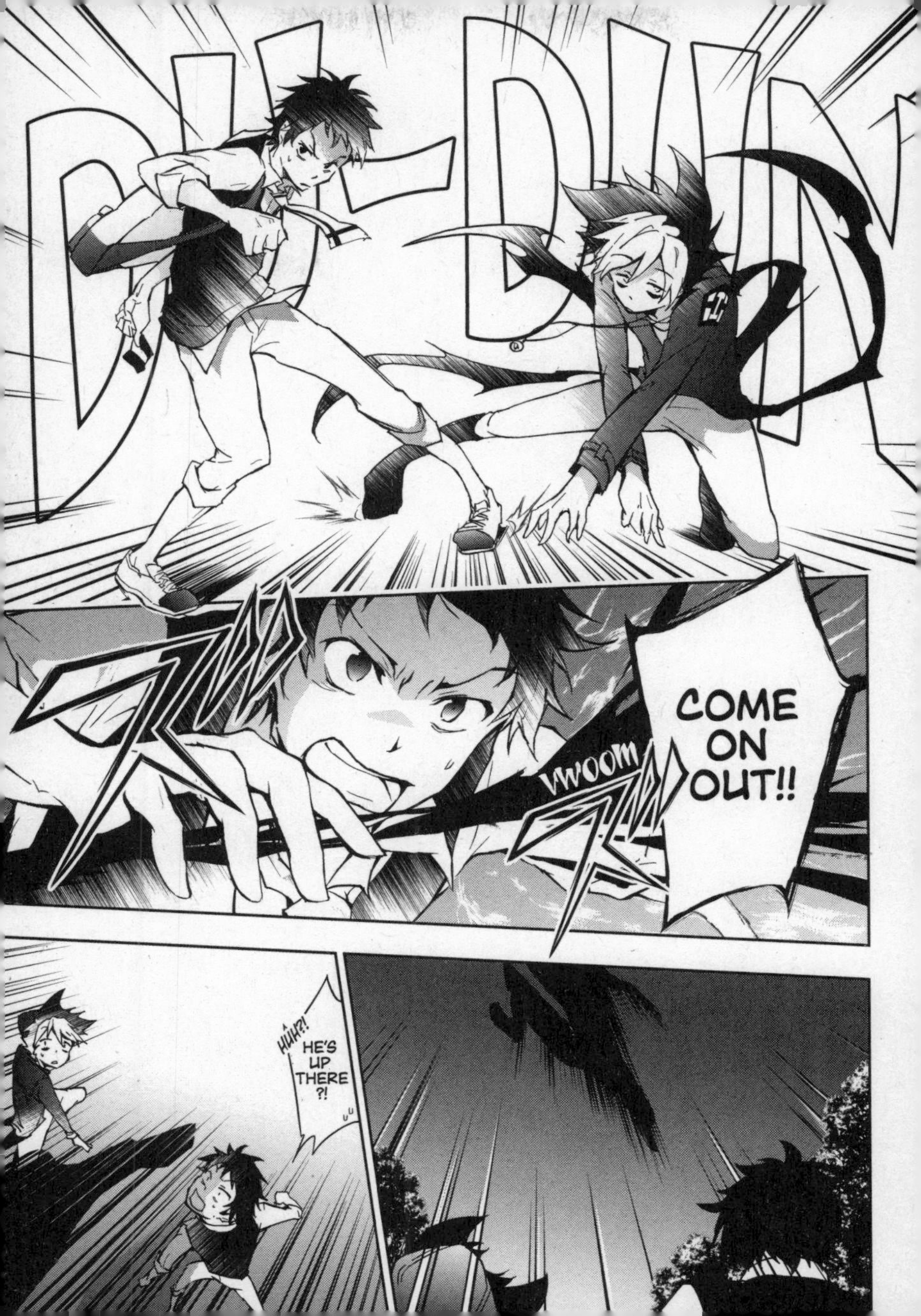
DUN DUN
COME ON OUT!!
VWOOM
HUH?!
HE'S UP THERE ?!

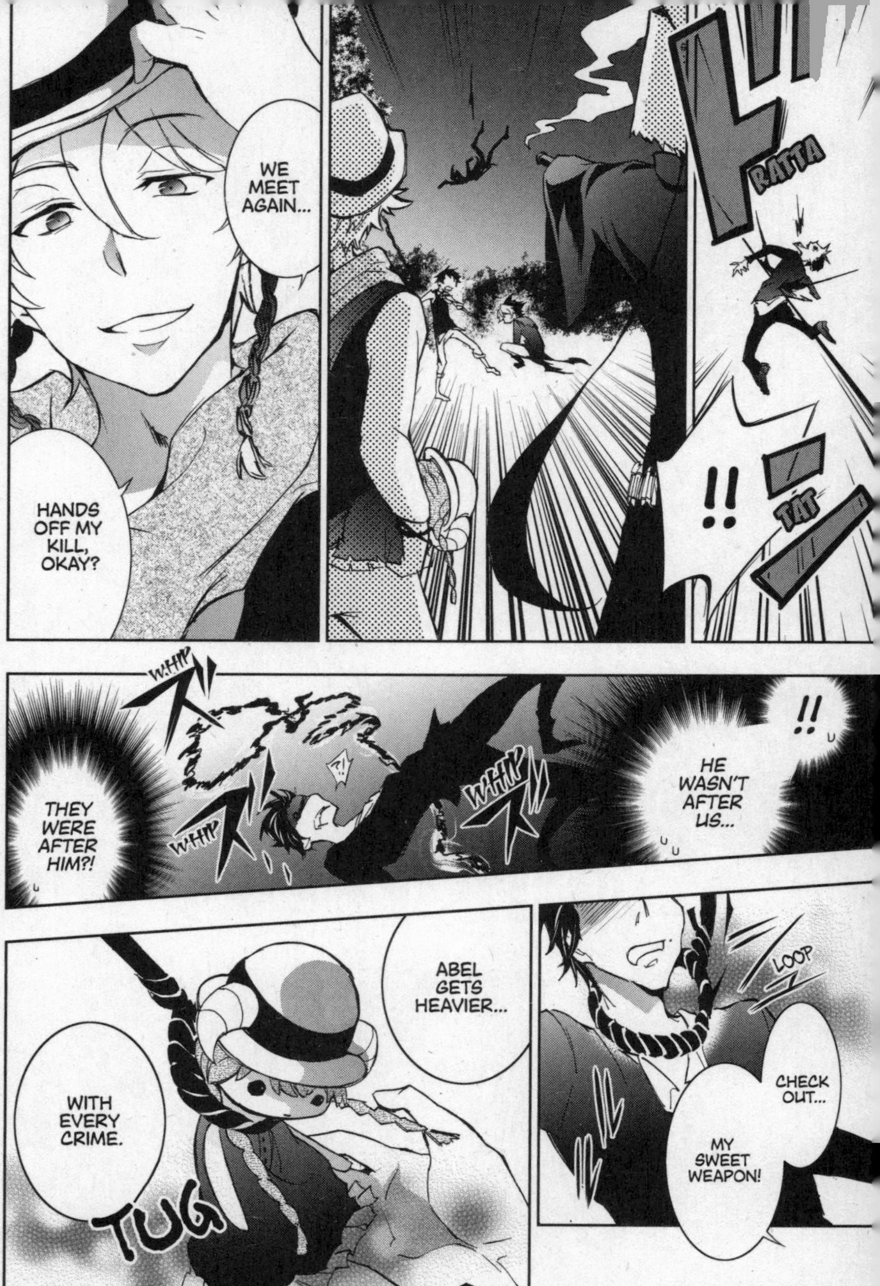
RATTA
!!
TAT
WE MEET AGAIN...
HANDS OFF MY KILL, OKAY?
!!
HE WASN'T AFTER US...
WHIP
WHIP
?!
WHIP
THEY WERE AFTER HIM?!
LOOP
CHECK OUT...
MY SWEET WEAPON!
ABEL GETS HEAVIER...
WITH EVERY CRIME.
TUG

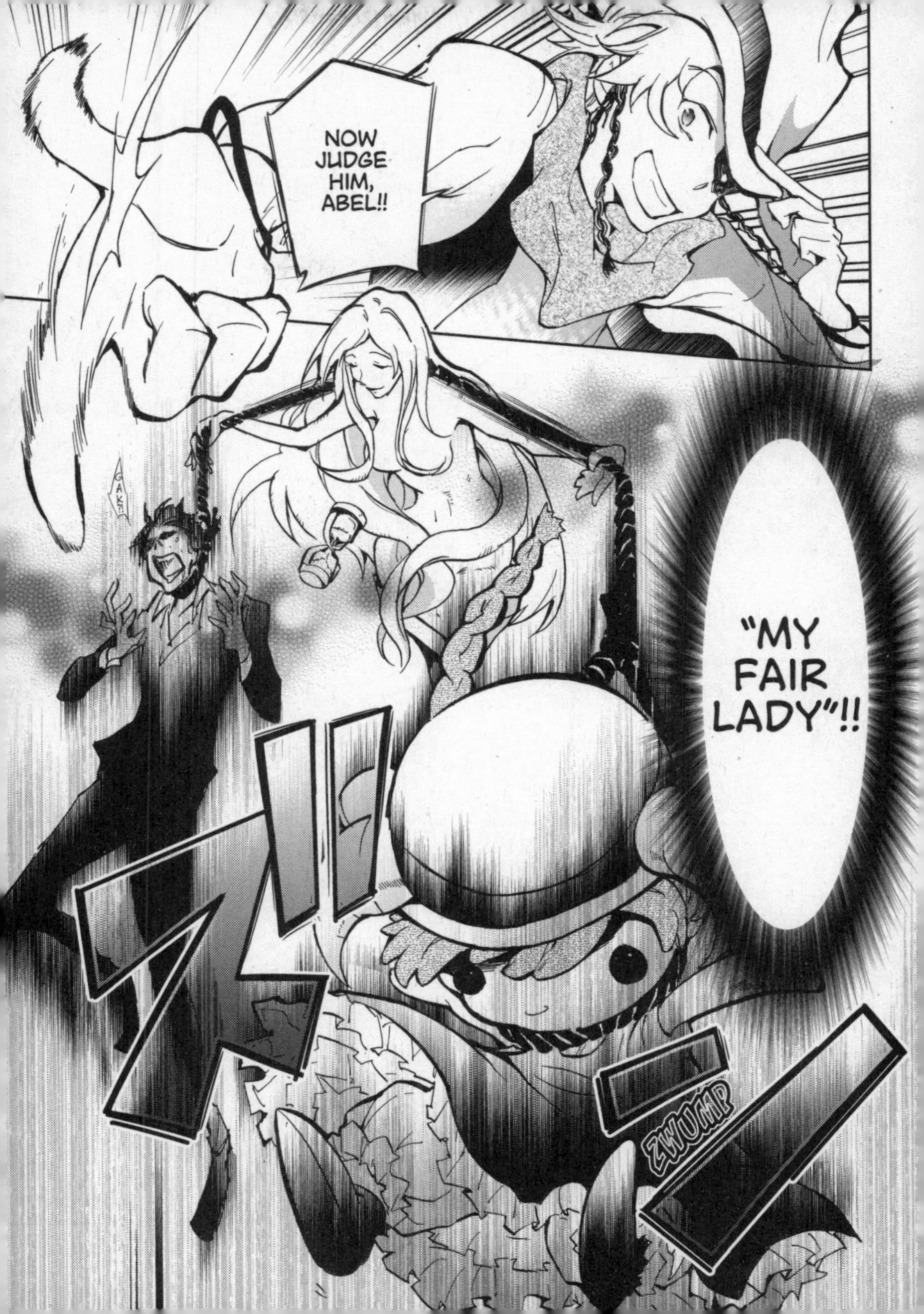
NOW JUDGE HIM, ABEL!!
"MY FAIR LADY"!!
GAK!!
ZWOMP

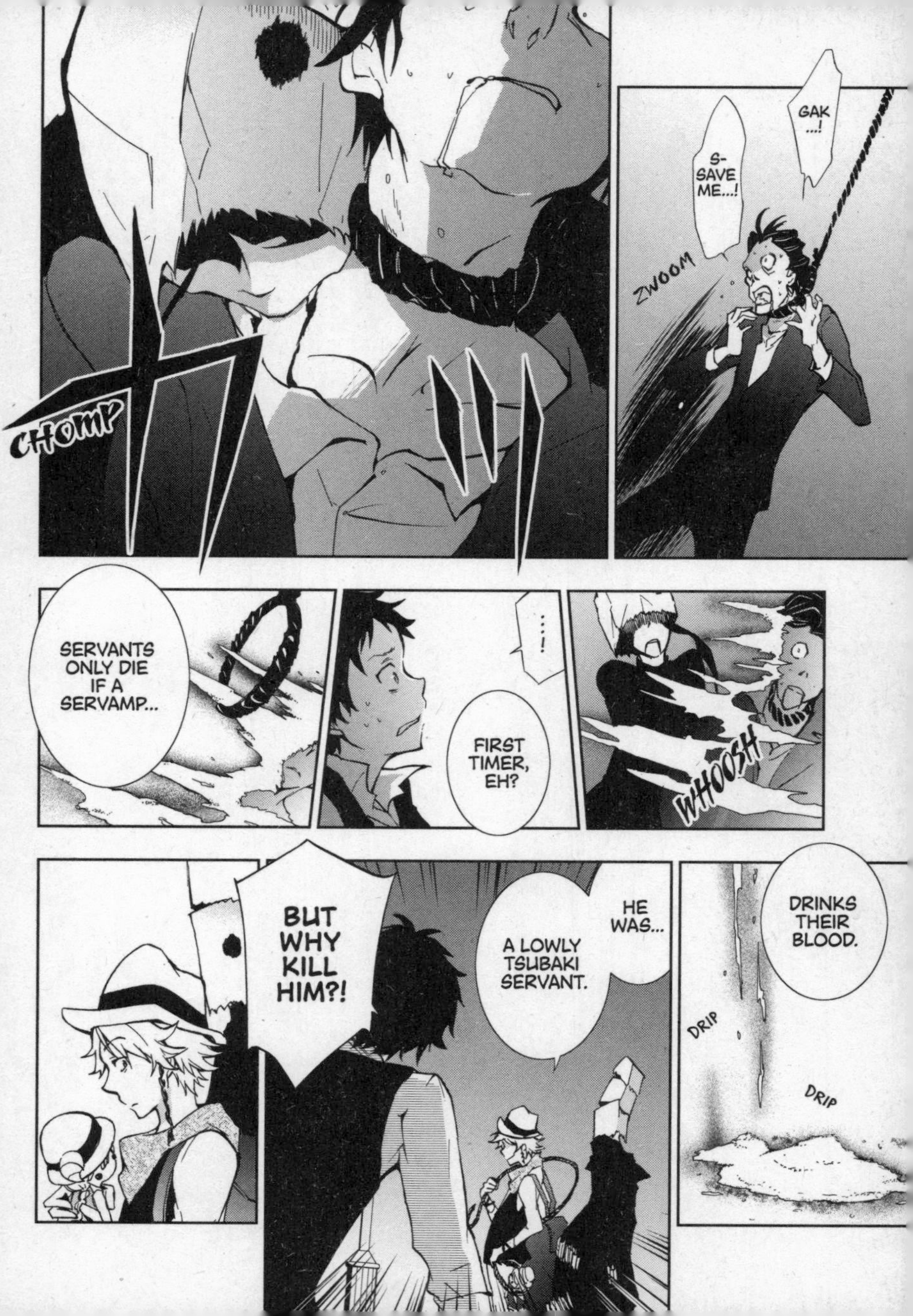
GAK ...!
S- SAVE ME...!
ZWOOM
CHOMP
WHOOSH
...!
FIRST TIMER, EH?
SERVANTS ONLY DIE IF A SERVAMP...
DRINKS THEIR BLOOD.
DRIP
DRIP
HE WAS...
A LOWLY TSUBAKI SERVANT.
BUT WHY KILL HIM?!

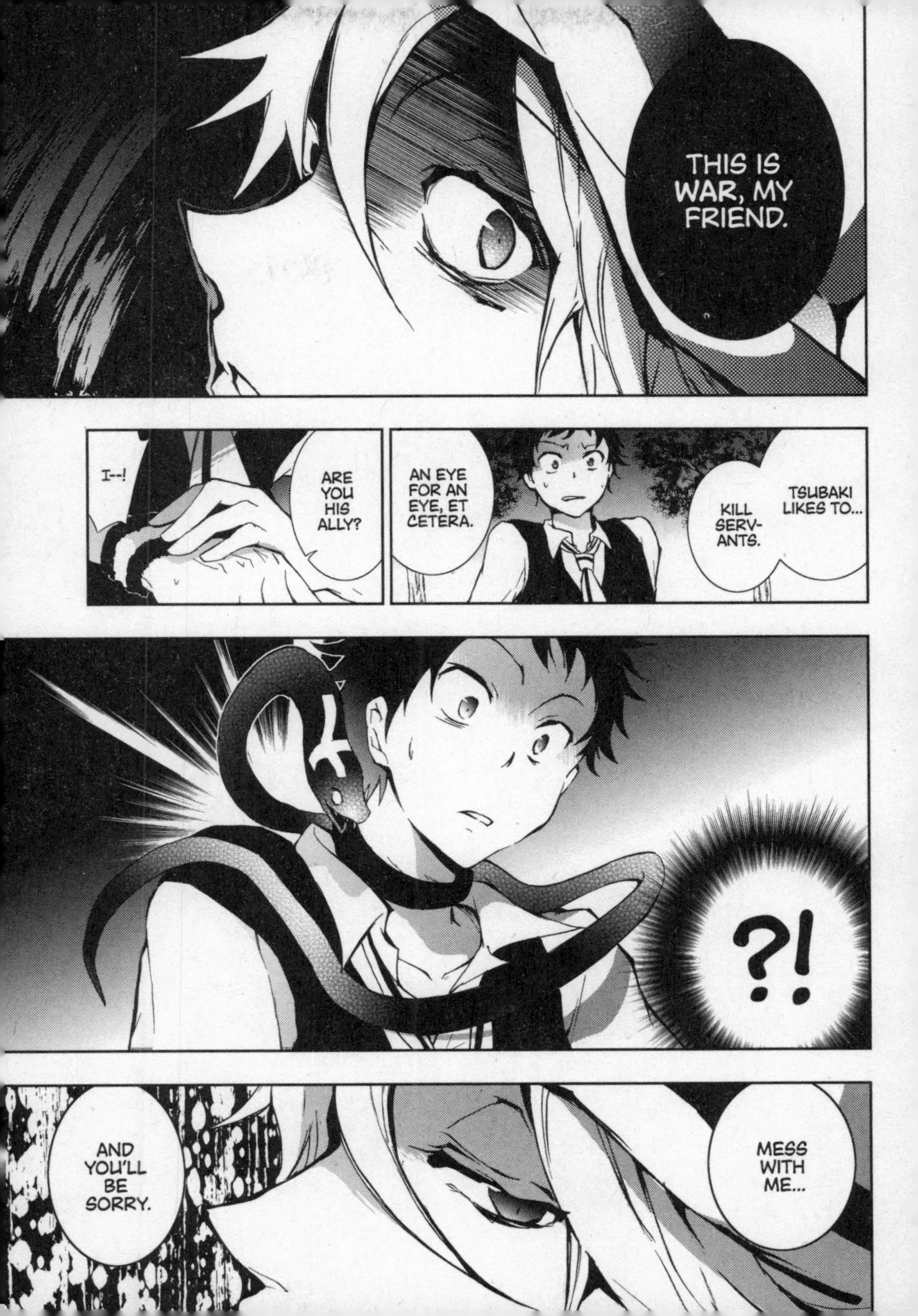

THIS IS WAR, MY FRIEND.
TSUBAKI LIKES TO...
KILL SERVANTS.
AN EYE FOR AN EYE, ET CETERA.
ARE YOU HIS ALLY?
I--!
?!
MESS WITH ME...
AND YOU'LL BE SORRY.

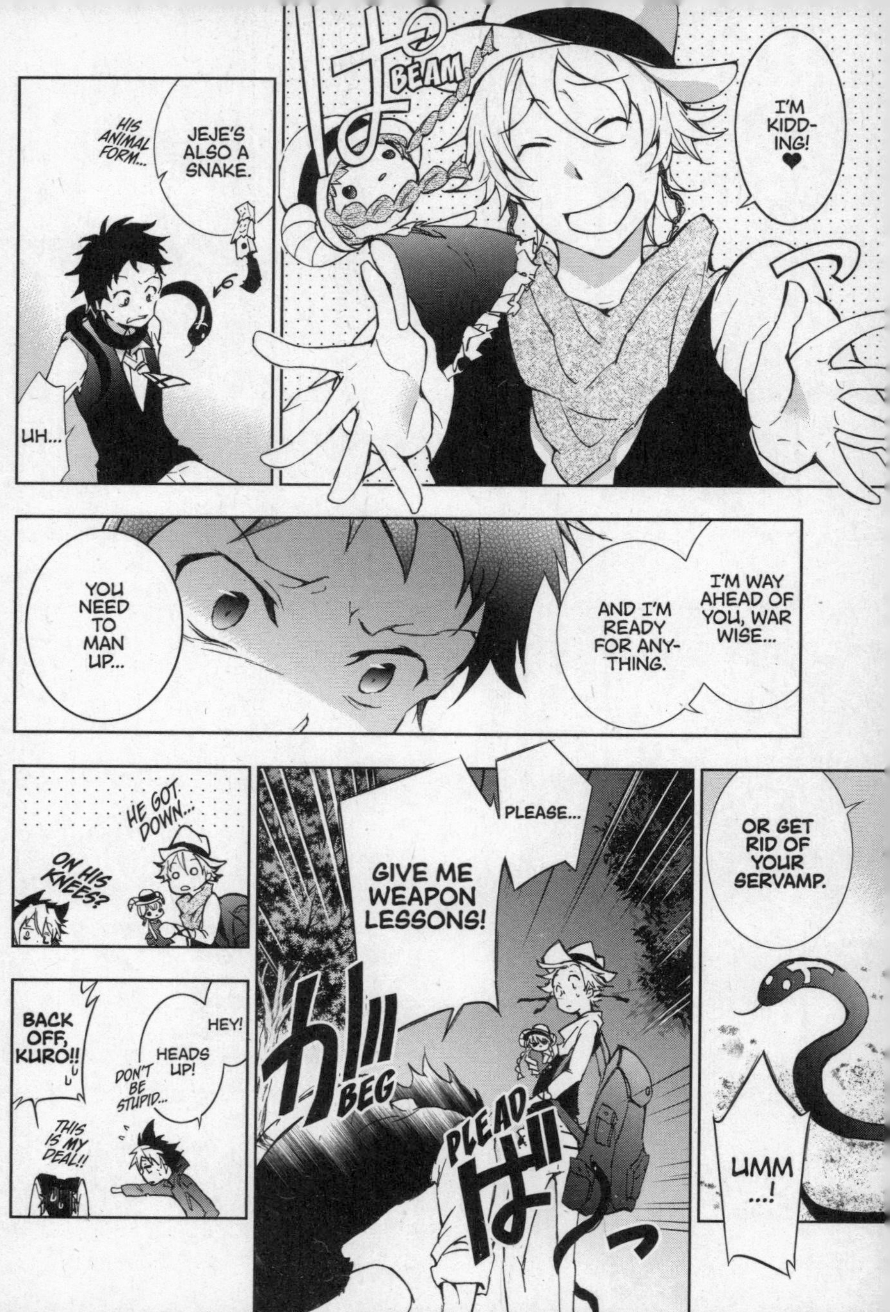
BEAM
I'M KIDDING! ♥
JEJE'S ALSO A SNAKE.
HIS ANIMAL FORM...
UH...
I'M WAY AHEAD OF YOU, WAR WISE...
AND I'M READY FOR ANYTHING.
YOU NEED TO MAN UP...
OR GET RID OF YOUR SERVAMP.
UMM...!
PLEASE...
GIVE ME WEAPON LESSONS!
BEG
PLEAD
HE GOT DOWN...
ON HIS KNEES?
HEY!
HEADS UP!
DON'T BE STUPID...
BACK OFF, KURO!!
THIS IS MY DEAL!!

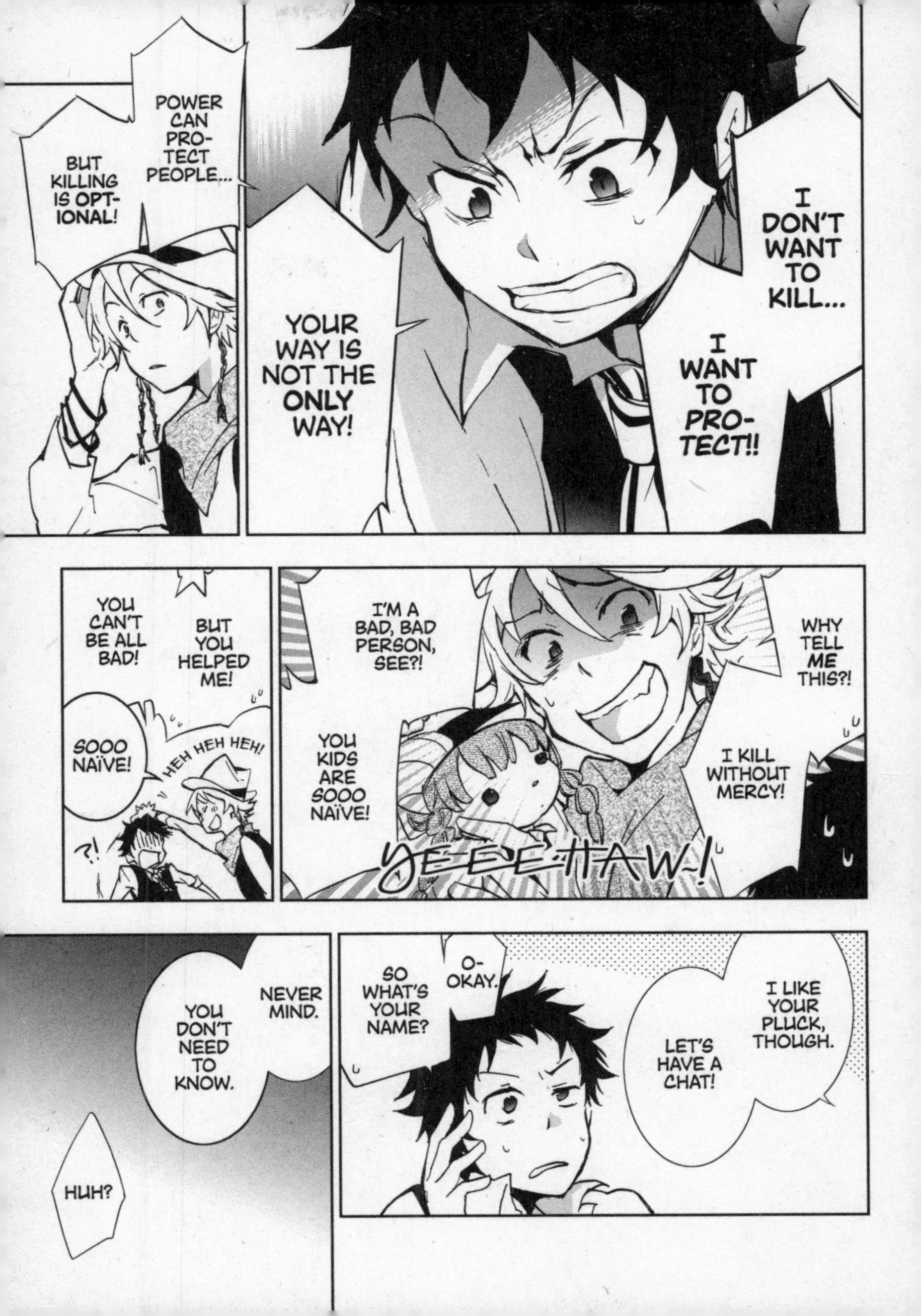
I DON'T WANT TO KILL...
I WANT TO PROTECT!!
YOUR WAY IS NOT THE ONLY WAY!
POWER CAN PROTECT PEOPLE...
BUT KILLING IS OPTIONAL!
WHY TELL ME THIS?!
I'M A BAD, BAD PERSON, SEE?!
I KILL WITHOUT MERCY!
YOU KIDS ARE SOOO NAÏVE!
YE-E-E-HAW!
BUT YOU HELPED ME!
YOU CAN'T BE ALL BAD!
HEH HEH HEH!
SOOO NAÏVE!
?!
I LIKE YOUR PLUCK, THOUGH.
LET'S HAVE A CHAT!
O-OKAY.
SO WHAT'S YOUR NAME?
NEVER MIND.
YOU DON'T NEED TO KNOW.
HUH?

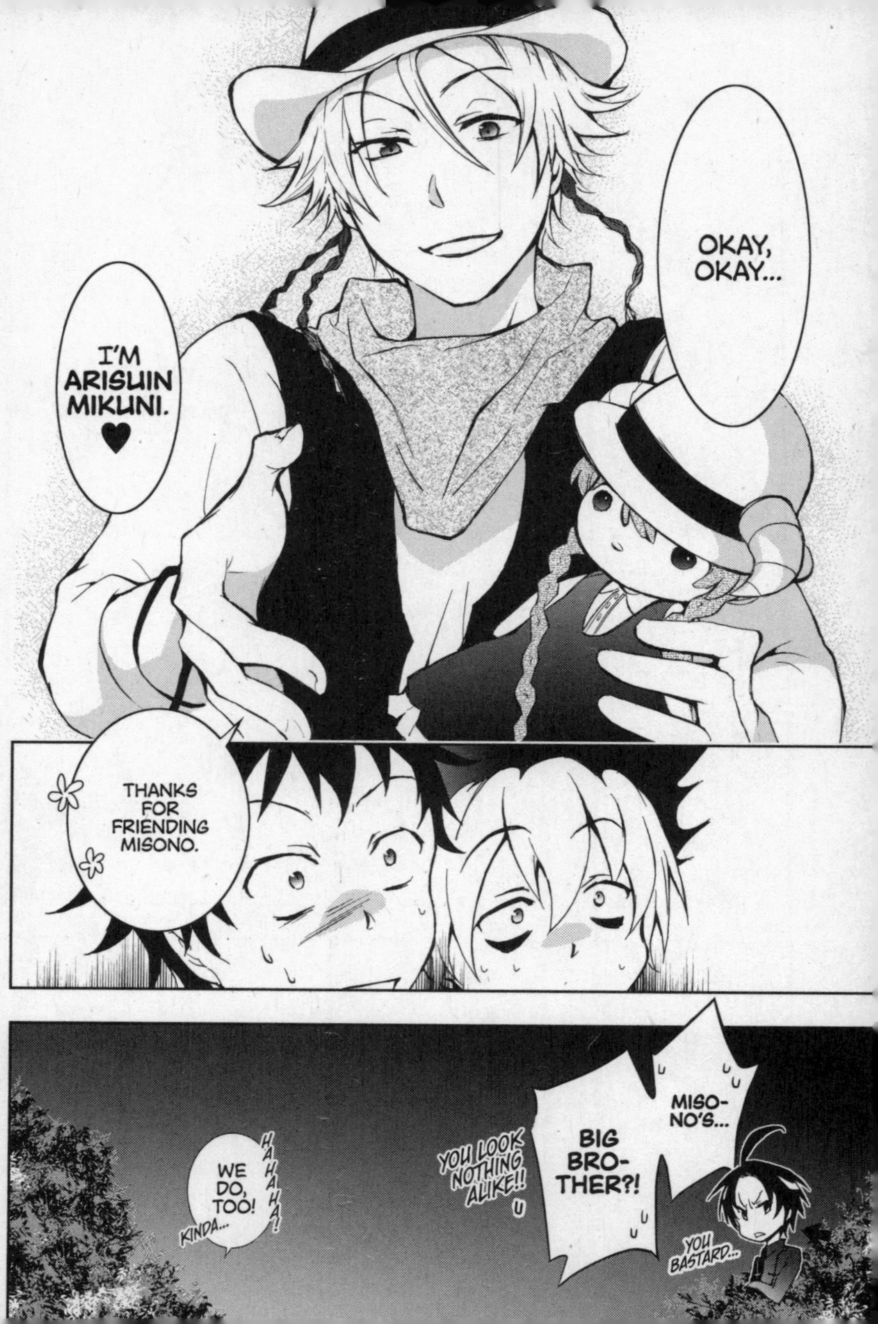
OKAY, OKAY...
I'M ARISUIN MIKUNI. ♥
THANKS FOR FRIENDING MISONO.
MISO-NO'S...
BIG BRO-THER?!
YOU LOOK NOTHING ALIKE!!
YOU BASTARD...
HAHAHA!
WE DO, TOO!
KINDA...

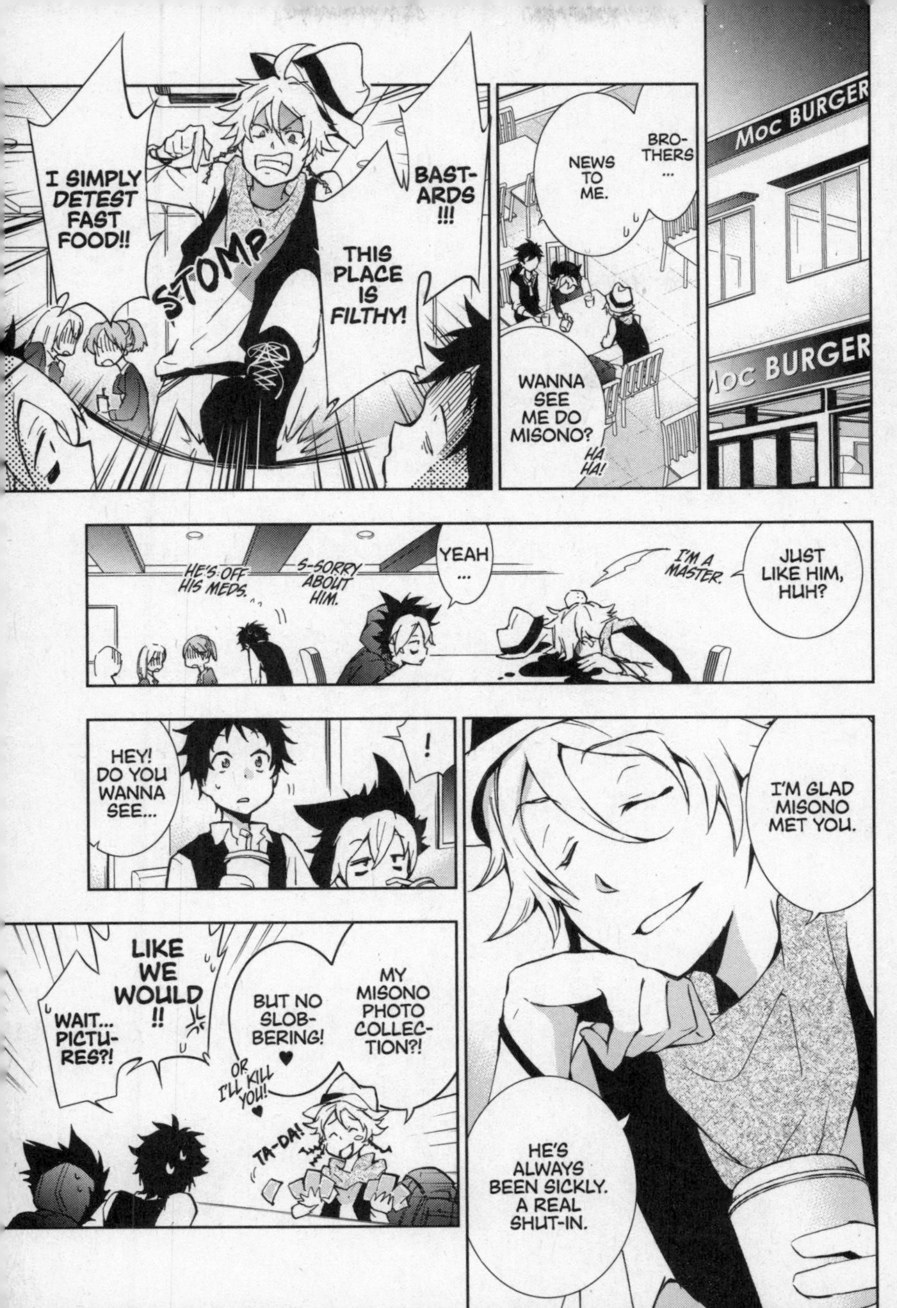
Moc BURGER
oc BURGER
BRO-THERS...
NEWS TO ME.
WANNA SEE ME DO MISONO?
HA HA!
BAST-ARDS!!!
I SIMPLY DETEST FAST FOOD!!
THIS PLACE IS FILTHY!
STOMP
JUST LIKE HIM, HUH?
I'M A MASTER.
YEAH...
S-SORRY ABOUT HIM.
HE'S OFF HIS MEDS.
I'M GLAD MISONO MET YOU.
HE'S ALWAYS BEEN SICKLY. A REAL SHUT-IN.
!
HEY! DO YOU WANNA SEE...
MY MISONO PHOTO COLLECTION?!
BUT NO SLOBBERING! ♥
OR I'LL KILL YOU! ♥
LIKE WE WOULD!!
WAIT... PICTURES?!
TA-DA!

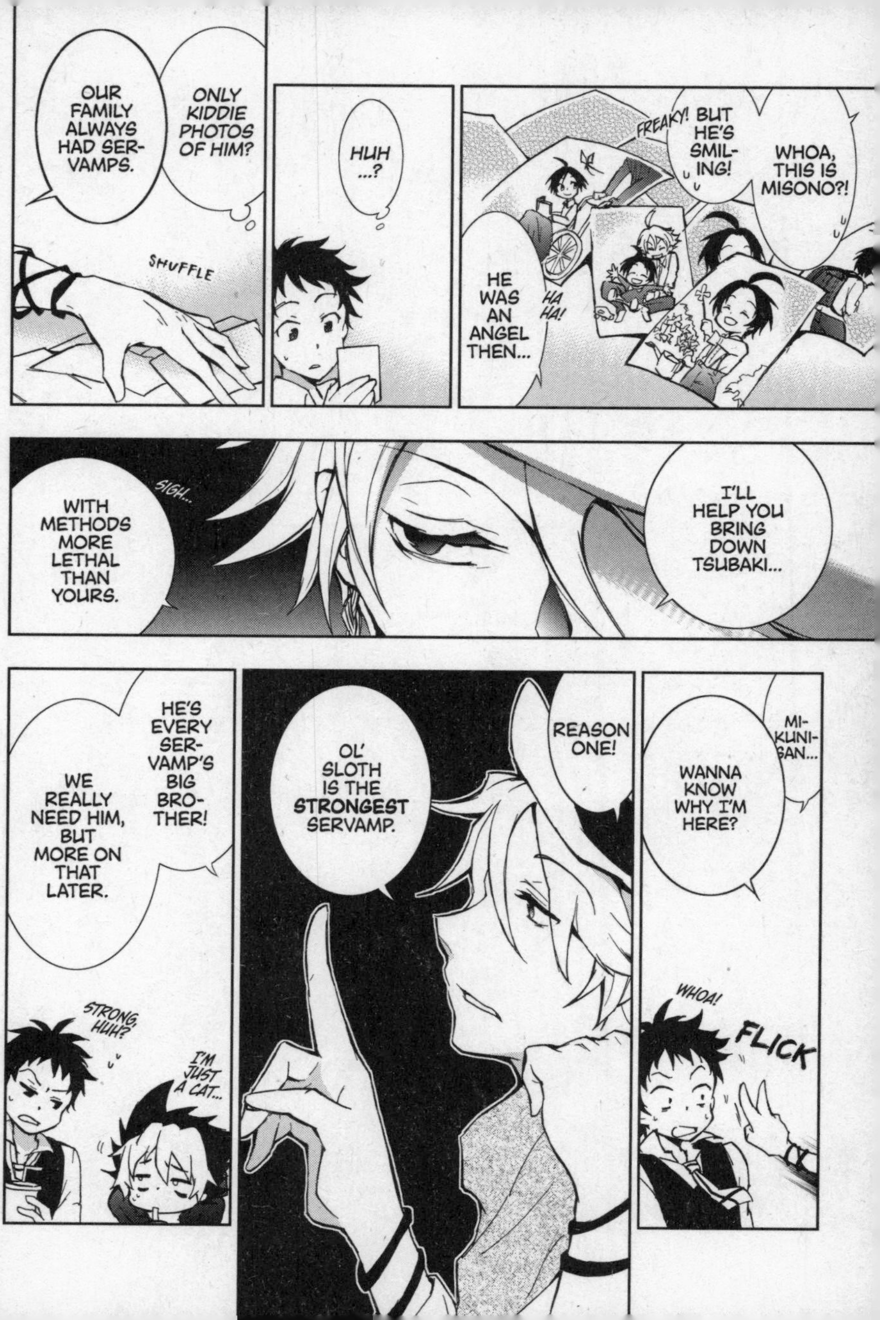
WHOA, THIS IS MISONO?!
FREAKY! BUT HE'S SMIL-ING!
HE WAS AN ANGEL THEN...
HA HA!
HUH ...?
ONLY KIDDIE PHOTOS OF HIM?
OUR FAMILY ALWAYS HAD SER-VAMPS.
SHUFFLE
I'LL HELP YOU BRING DOWN TSUBAKI...
SIGH...
WITH METHODS MORE LETHAL THAN YOURS.
MI-KUNI-SAN...
WANNA KNOW WHY I'M HERE?
WHOA!
FLICK
REASON ONE!
OL' SLOTH IS THE STRONGEST SERVAMP.
HE'S EVERY SER-VAMP'S BIG BRO-THER!
WE REALLY NEED HIM, BUT MORE ON THAT LATER.
STRONG, HUH?
I'M JUST A CAT...

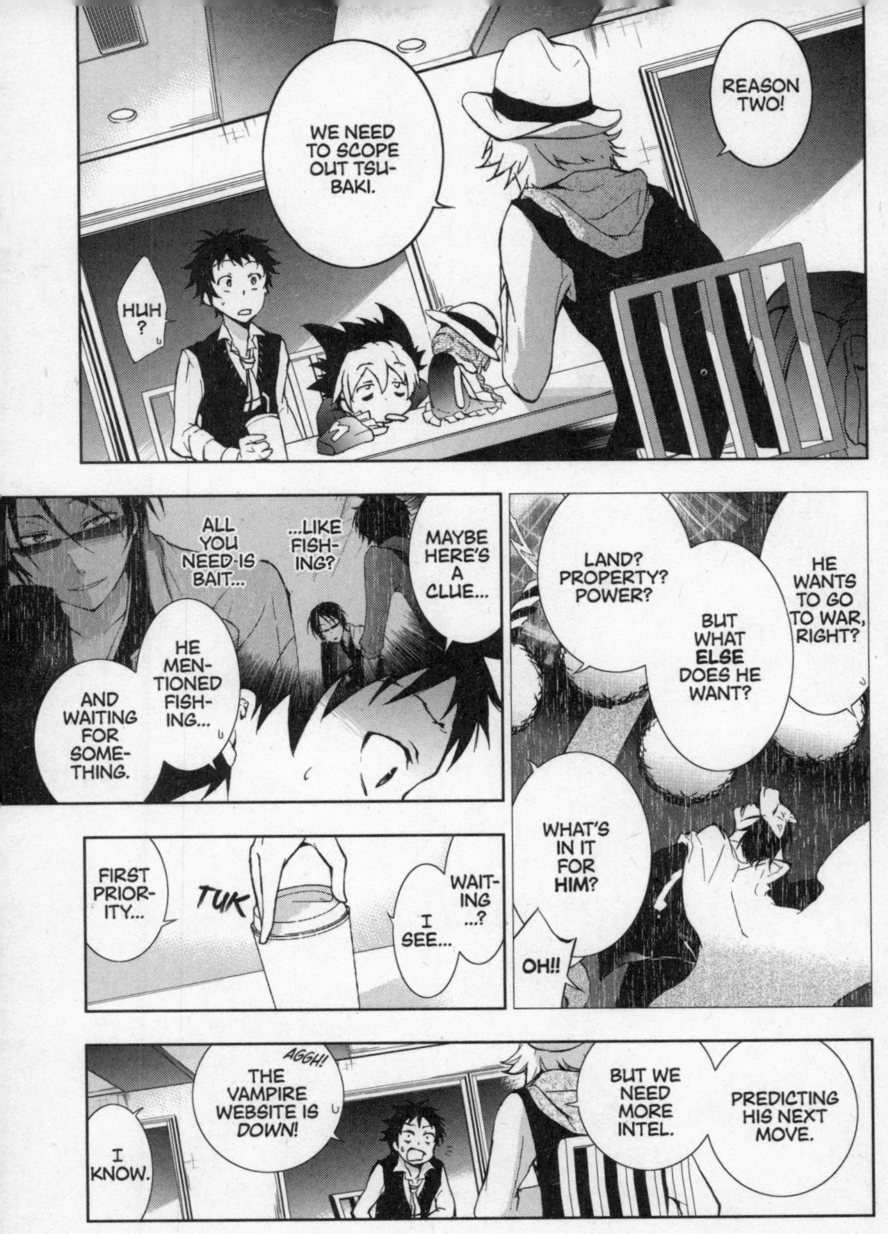
REASON TWO!
WE NEED TO SCOPE OUT TSU-BAKI.
HUH?
HE WANTS TO GO TO WAR, RIGHT?
LAND? PROPERTY? POWER?
BUT WHAT ELSE DOES HE WANT?
WHAT'S IN IT FOR HIM?
OH!!
MAYBE HERE'S A CLUE...
...LIKE FISH-ING?
ALL YOU NEED IS BAIT...
HE MEN-TIONED FISH-ING...
AND WAITING FOR SOME-THING.
WAIT-ING ...?
I SEE...
TUK
FIRST PRIOR-ITY...
PREDICTING HIS NEXT MOVE.
BUT WE NEED MORE INTEL.
AGGH!
THE VAMPIRE WEBSITE IS DOWN!
I KNOW.

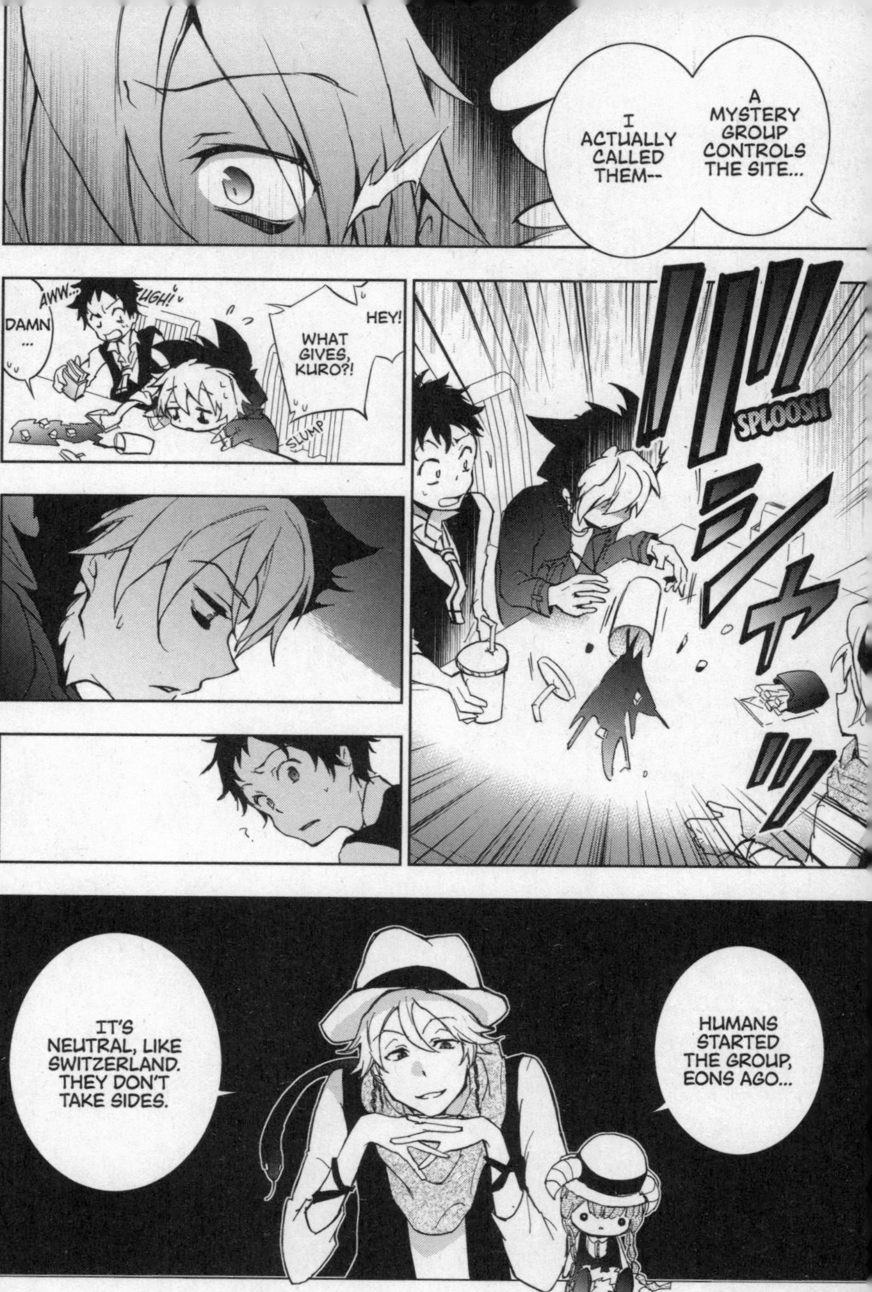
A MYSTERY GROUP CONTROLS THE SITE...
I ACTUALLY CALLED THEM--
SPLOOSH
HEY!
WHAT GIVES, KURO?!
SLUMP
UGH!
AWW... DAMN ...
HUMANS STARTED THE GROUP, EONS AGO...
IT'S NEUTRAL, LIKE SWITZERLAND. THEY DON'T TAKE SIDES.

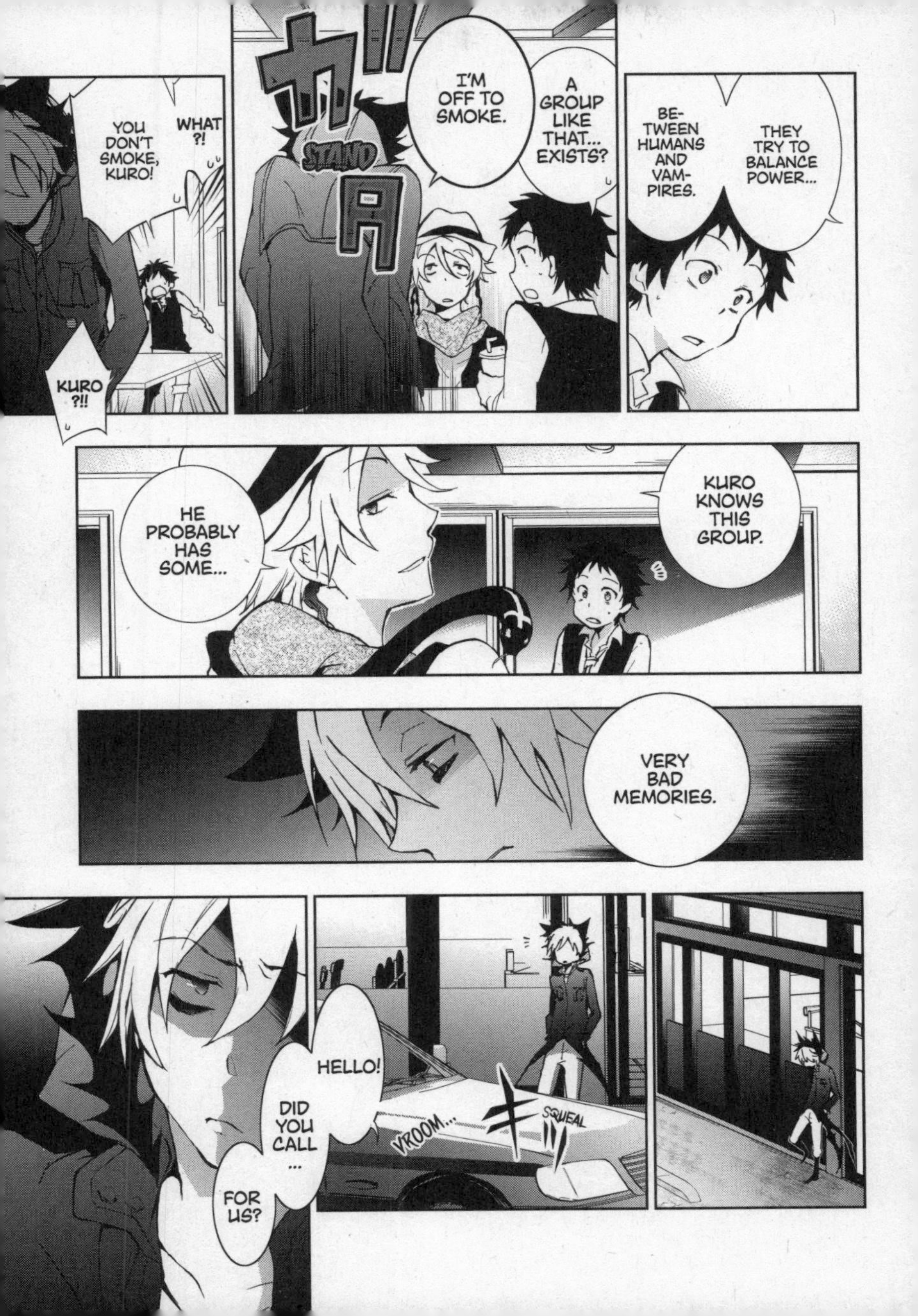
THEY TRY TO BALANCE POWER...
BE-TWEEN HUMANS AND VAM-PIRES.
A GROUP LIKE THAT... EXISTS?
I'M OFF TO SMOKE.
STAND
WHAT ?!
YOU DON'T SMOKE, KURO!
KURO ?!!
KURO KNOWS THIS GROUP.
HE PROBABLY HAS SOME...
VERY BAD MEMORIES.
SQUEAL
VROOM...
HELLO!
DID YOU CALL ...
FOR US?

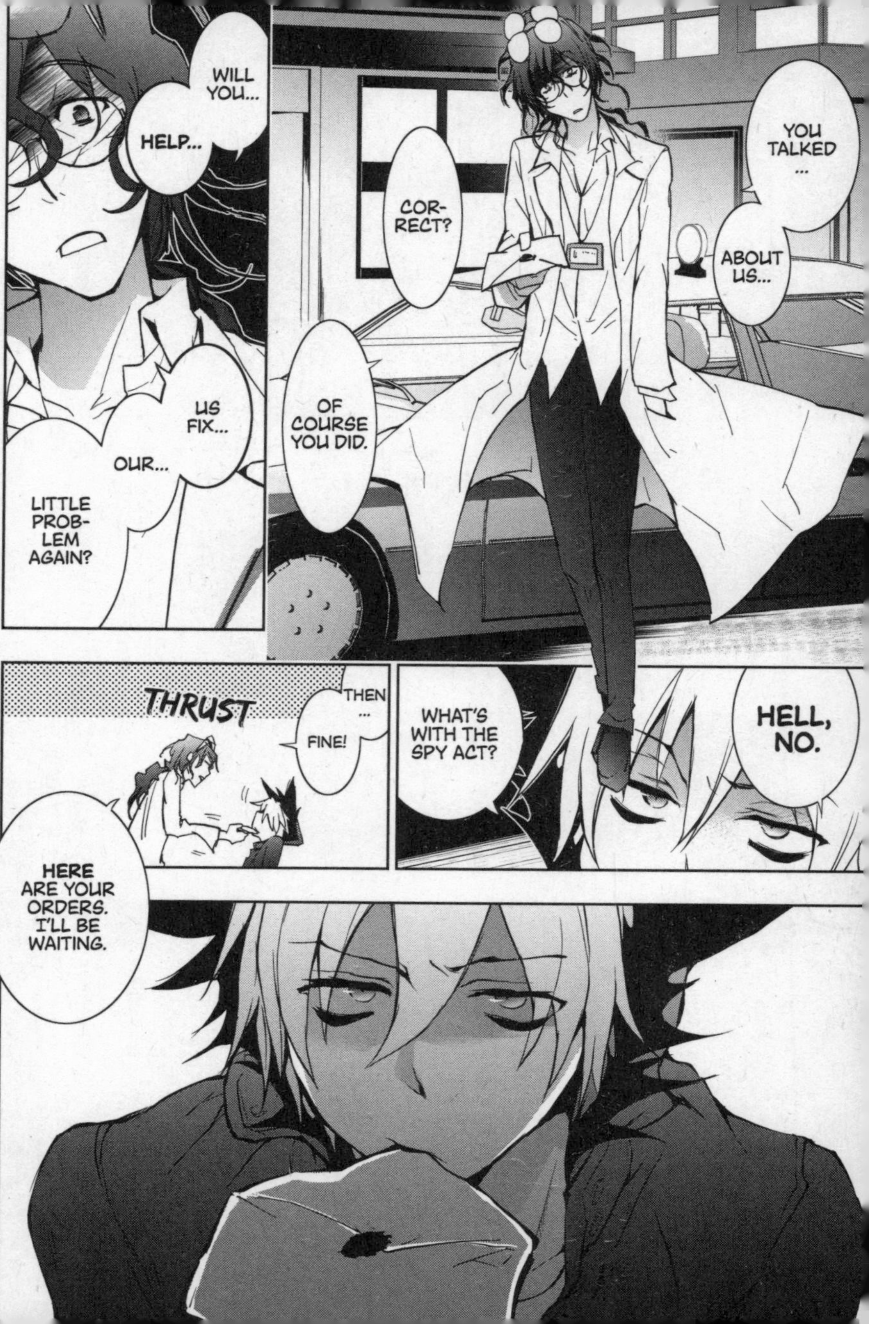

YOU TALKED ...
ABOUT US...
CORRECT?
OF COURSE YOU DID.
WILL YOU...
HELP...
US FIX...
OUR...
LITTLE PROBLEM AGAIN?
HELL, NO.
WHAT'S WITH THE SPY ACT?
THEN ...
FINE!
THRUST
HERE ARE YOUR ORDERS. I'LL BE WAITING.

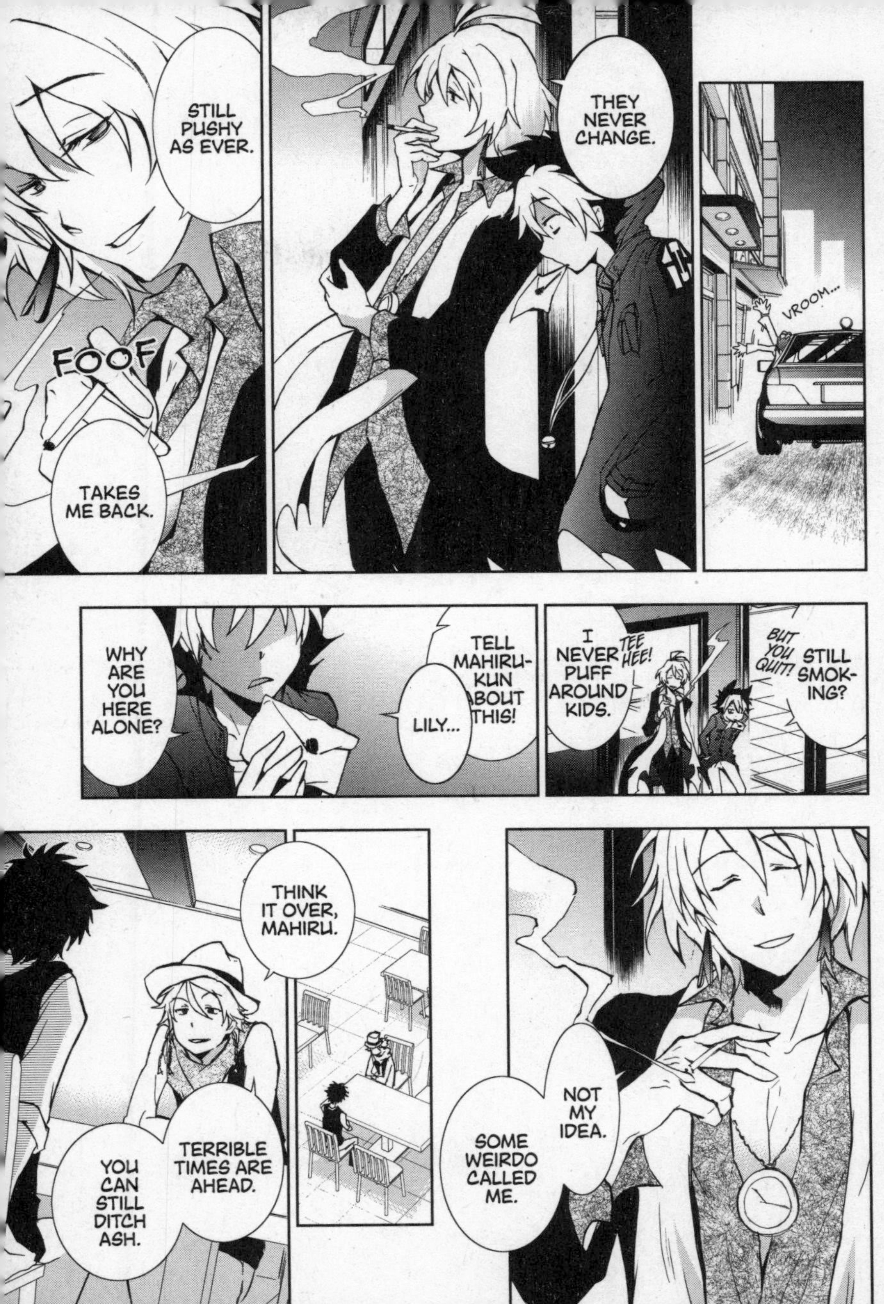
VROOM...
THEY NEVER CHANGE.
STILL PUSHY AS EVER.
FOOF
TAKES ME BACK.
STILL SMOKING?
BUT YOU QUIT!
TEE HEE!
I NEVER PUFF AROUND KIDS.
TELL MAHIRU-KUN ABOUT THIS!
LILY...
WHY ARE YOU HERE ALONE?
NOT MY IDEA.
SOME WEIRDO CALLED ME.
THINK IT OVER, MAHIRU.
TERRIBLE TIMES ARE AHEAD.
YOU CAN STILL DITCH ASH.

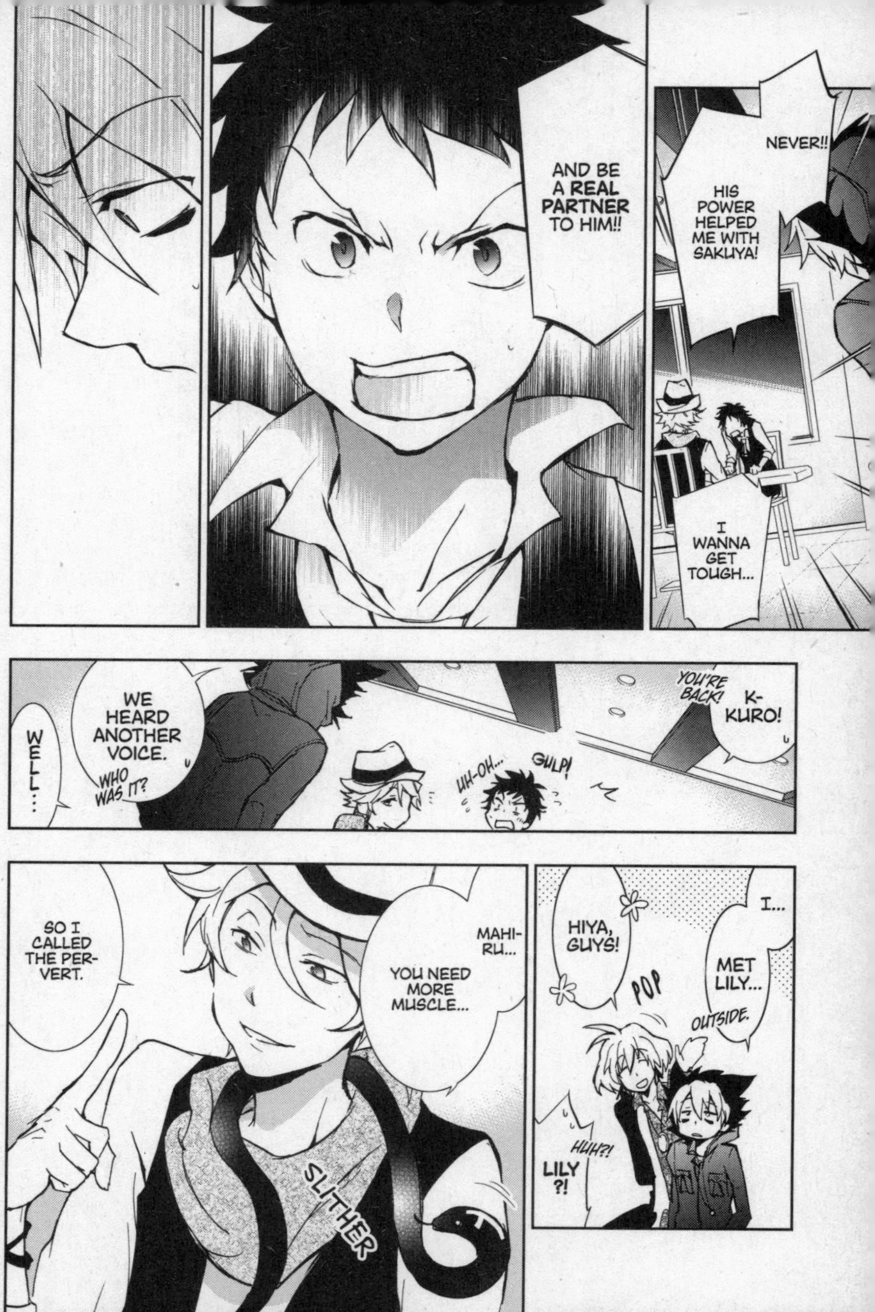
NEVER!!
HIS POWER HELPED ME WITH SAKUYA!
I WANNA GET TOUGH...
AND BE A REAL PARTNER TO HIM!!
K-KURO!
YOU'RE BACK!
GULP!
UH-OH...
WE HEARD ANOTHER VOICE.
WHO WAS IT?
WELL...
I... MET LILY... OUTSIDE.
HIYA, GUYS!
POP
HUH?!
LILY ?!
MAHI-RU...
YOU NEED MORE MUSCLE...
SO I CALLED THE PER-VERT.
SLITHER

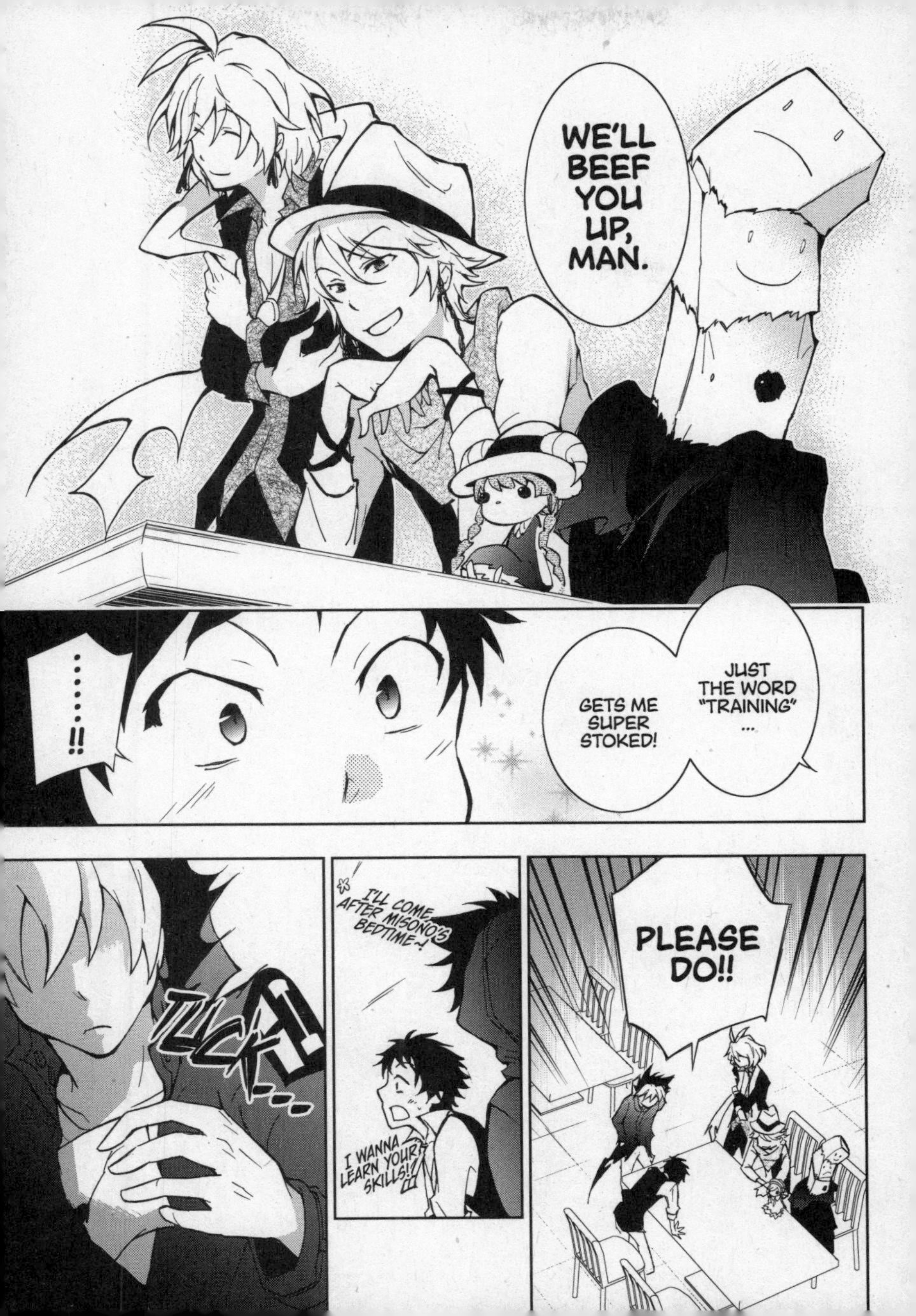
WE'LL BEEF YOU UP, MAN.
JUST THE WORD "TRAINING"...
GETS ME SUPER STOKED!
......!!
PLEASE DO!!
I'LL COME AFTER MISONO'S BEDTIME~!
I WANNA LEARN YOUR SKILLS!!
TCH...

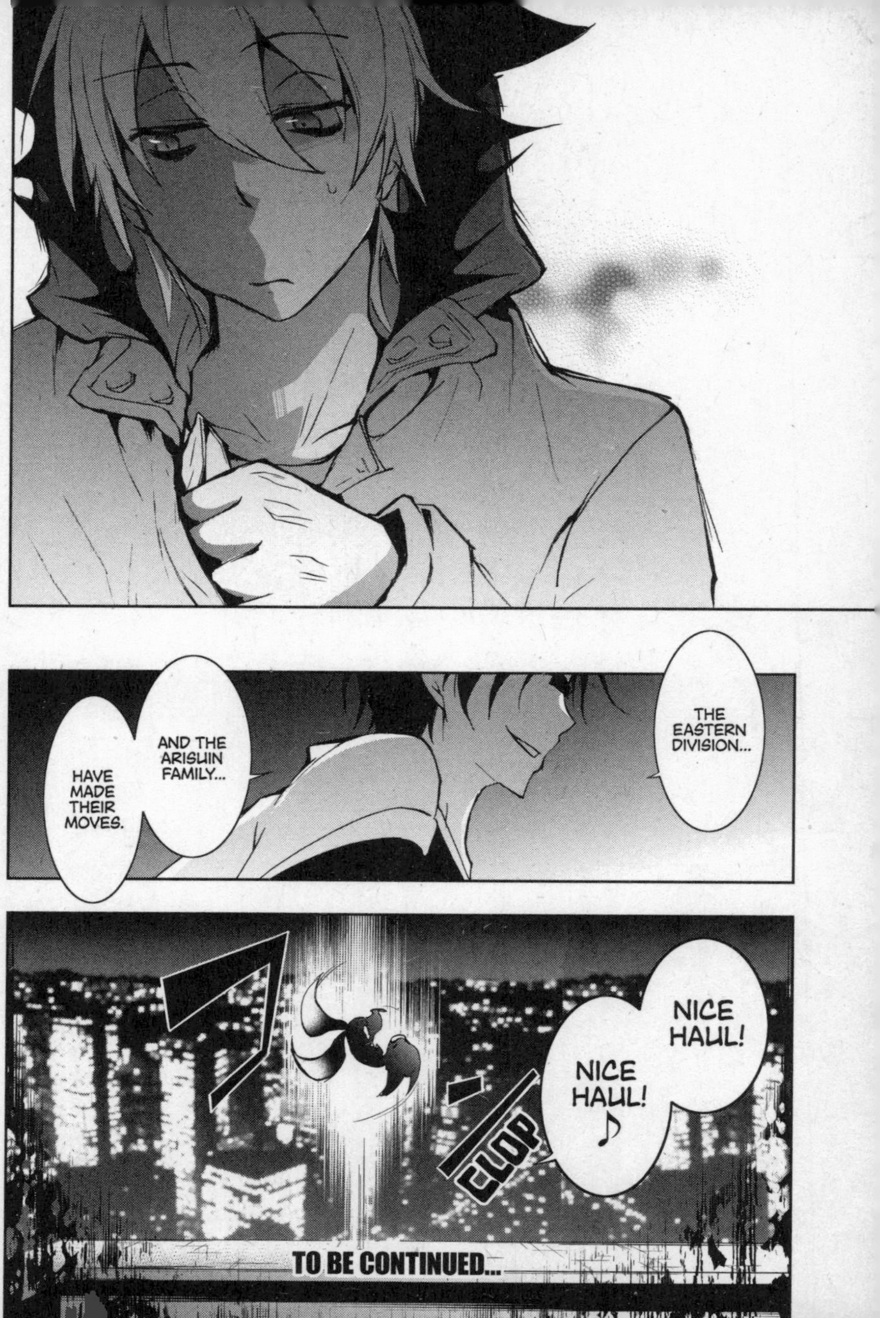
THE EASTERN DIVISION...
AND THE ARISUIN FAMILY...
HAVE MADE THEIR MOVES.
NICE HAUL!
NICE HAUL! ♪
CLOP
TO BE CONTINUED...

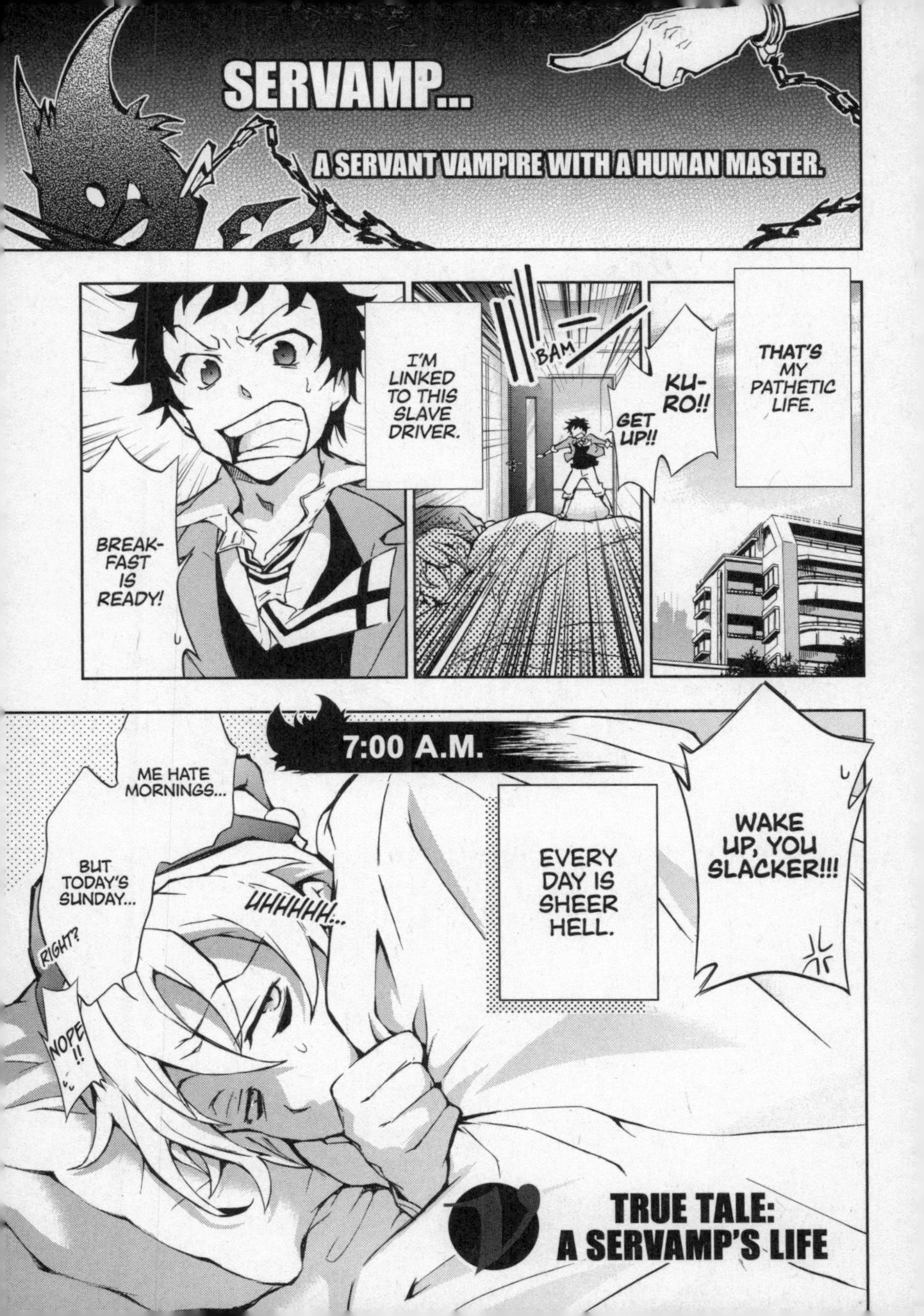
SERVAMP...
A SERVANT VAMPIRE WITH A HUMAN MASTER.
THAT'S MY PATHETIC LIFE.
KU-RO!!
GET UP!!
BAM
I'M LINKED TO THIS SLAVE DRIVER.
BREAK-FAST IS READY!
7:00 A.M.
WAKE UP, YOU SLACKER!!!
EVERY DAY IS SHEER HELL.
ME HATE MORNINGS...
BUT TODAY'S SUNDAY...
UHHHHH...
RIGHT?
NOPE!!
1
TRUE TALE: A SERVAMP'S LIFE

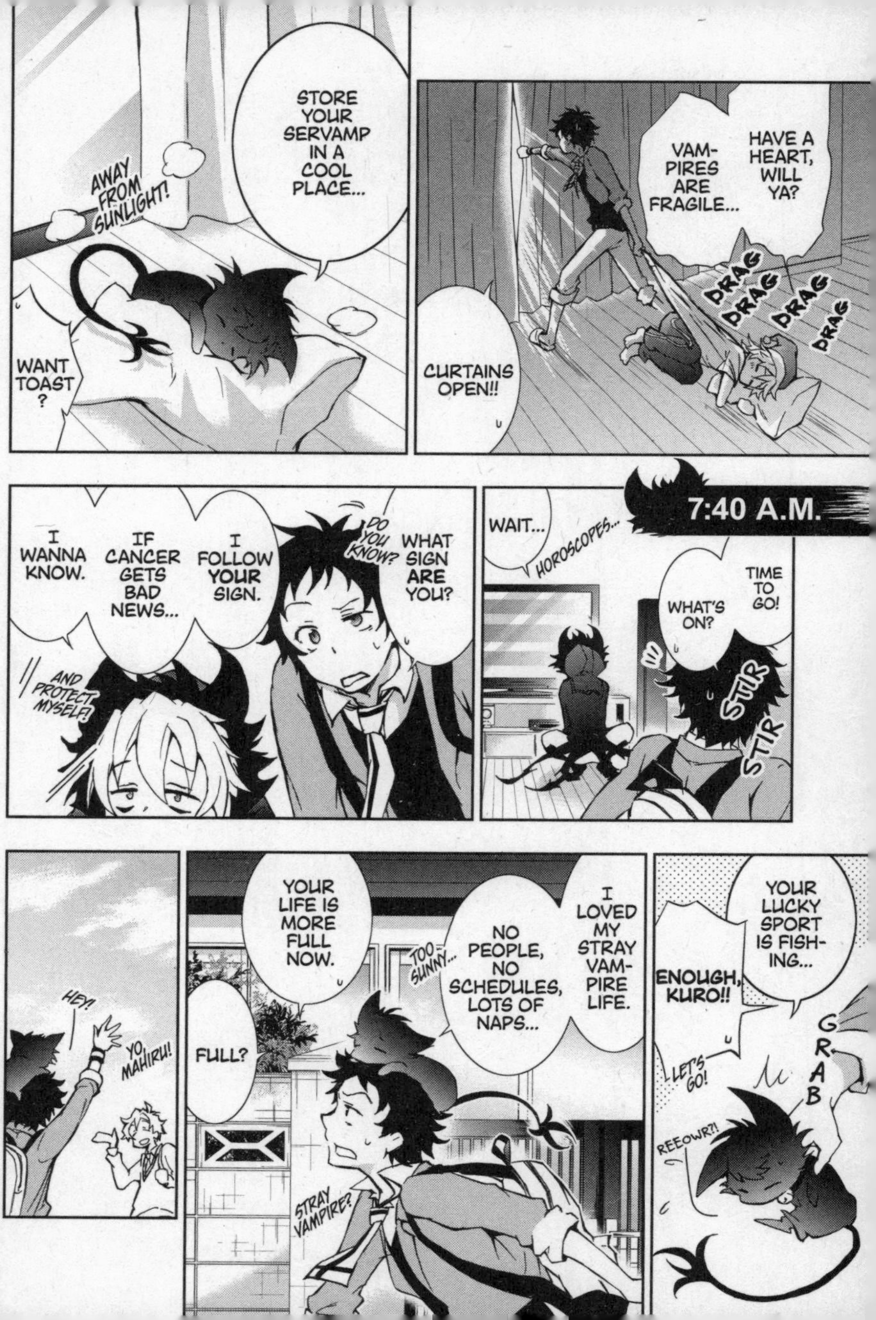
HAVE A HEART, WILL YA?
VAMPIRES ARE FRAGILE...
DRAG DRAG DRAG DRAG
CURTAINS OPEN!!
STORE YOUR SERVAMP IN A COOL PLACE...
AWAY FROM SUNLIGHT!
WANT TOAST?
7:40 A.M.
TIME TO GO!
WHAT'S ON?
WAIT...
HOROSCOPES...
STIR STIR
WHAT SIGN ARE YOU?
DO YOU KNOW?
I FOLLOW YOUR SIGN.
IF CANCER GETS BAD NEWS...
I WANNA KNOW.
AND PROTECT MYSELF!
YOUR LUCKY SPORT IS FISHING...
ENOUGH, KURO!!
LET'S GO!
GRAB
REEOWR?!
I LOVED MY STRAY VAMPIRE LIFE.
NO PEOPLE, NO SCHEDULES, LOTS OF NAPS...
TOO SUNNY...
YOUR LIFE IS MORE FULL NOW.
FULL?
STRAY VAMPIRE?
HEY!
YO, MAHIRU!

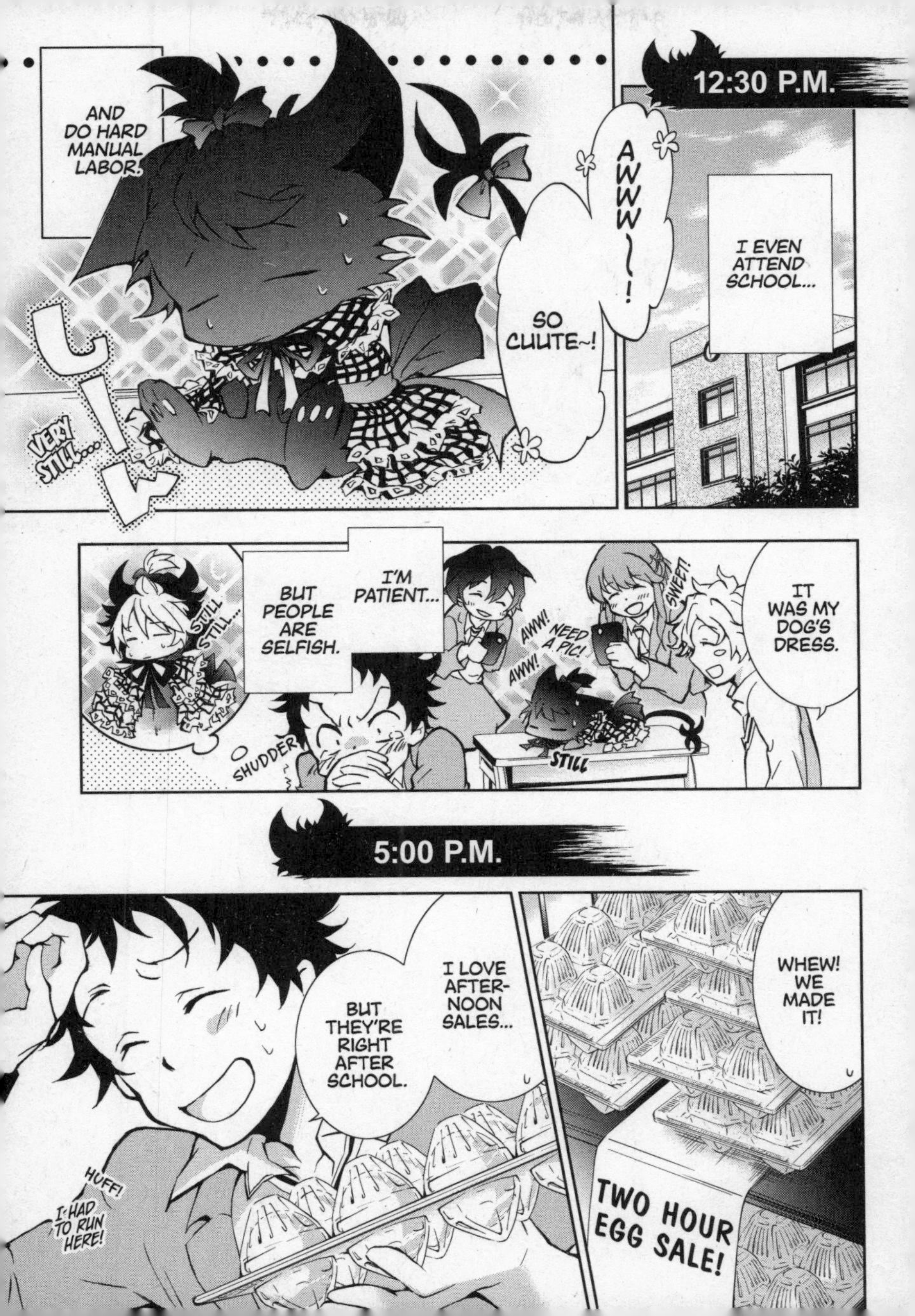
12:30 P.M.
I EVEN ATTEND SCHOOL...
AND DO HARD MANUAL LABOR.
AWWW~!
SO CUUTE~!
VERY STILL...
IT WAS MY DOG'S DRESS.
SWEET!
NEED A PIC!
AWW!
AWW!
I'M PATIENT...
BUT PEOPLE ARE SELFISH.
STILL STILL...
SHUDDER
STILL
5:00 P.M.
WHEW! WE MADE IT!
TWO HOUR EGG SALE!
I LOVE AFTER-NOON SALES...
BUT THEY'RE RIGHT AFTER SCHOOL.
HUFF! I HAD TO RUN HERE!

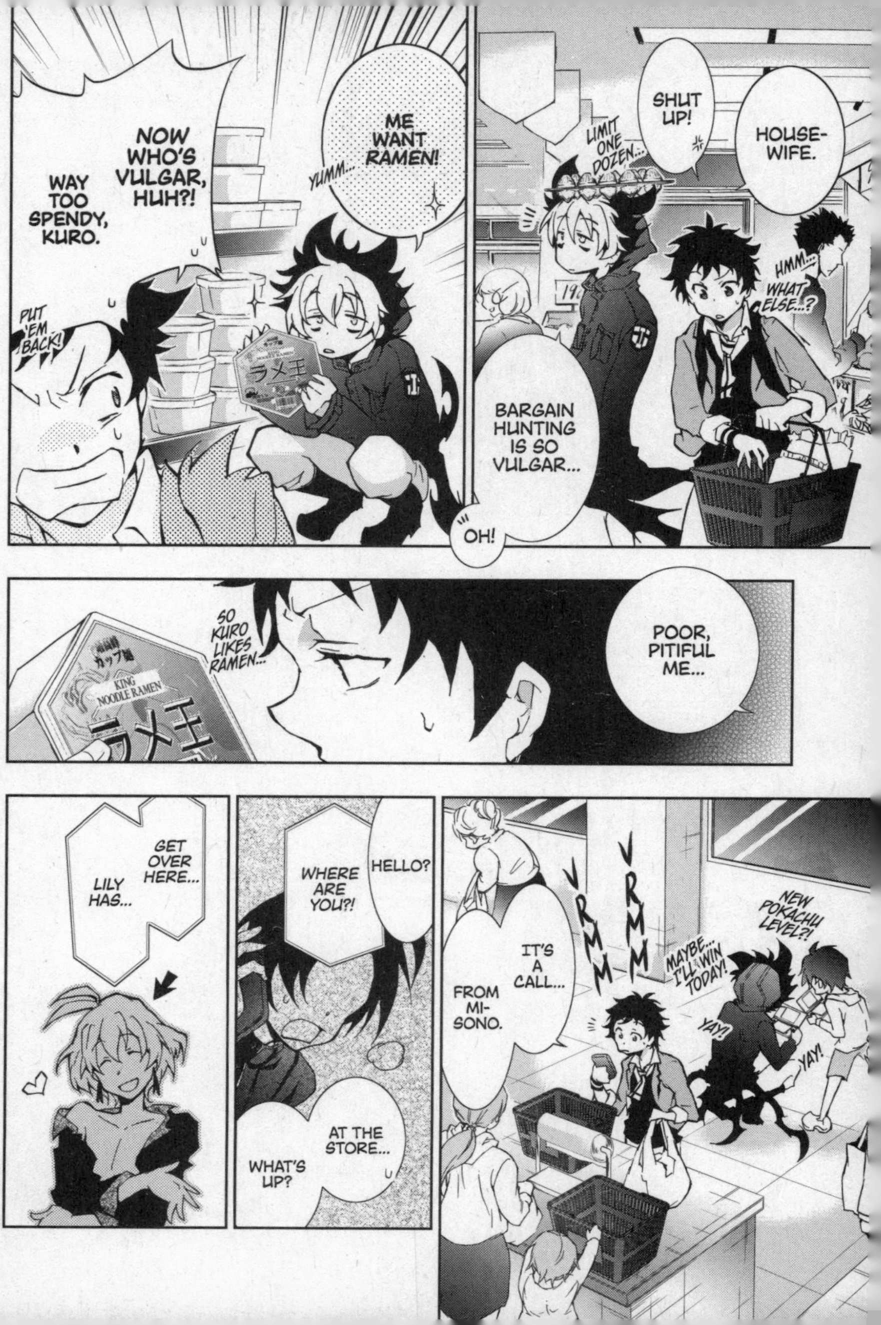
HOUSE-WIFE.
SHUT UP!
LIMIT ONE DOZEN...
HMM... WHAT ELSE...?
BARGAIN HUNTING IS SO VULGAR...
OH!
ME WANT RAMEN!
YUMM...
NOW WHO'S VULGAR, HUH?!
WAY TOO SPENDY, KURO.
PUT 'EM BACK!
POOR, PITIFUL ME...
SO KURO LIKES RAMEN...
KING NOODLE RAMEN
NEW POKACHU LEVEL?!
MAYBE... I'LL WIN TODAY!
YAY!
YAY!
VRMM
VRMM
IT'S A CALL...
FROM MI-SONO.
HELLO?
WHERE ARE YOU?!
AT THE STORE...
WHAT'S UP?
GET OVER HERE...
LILY HAS...

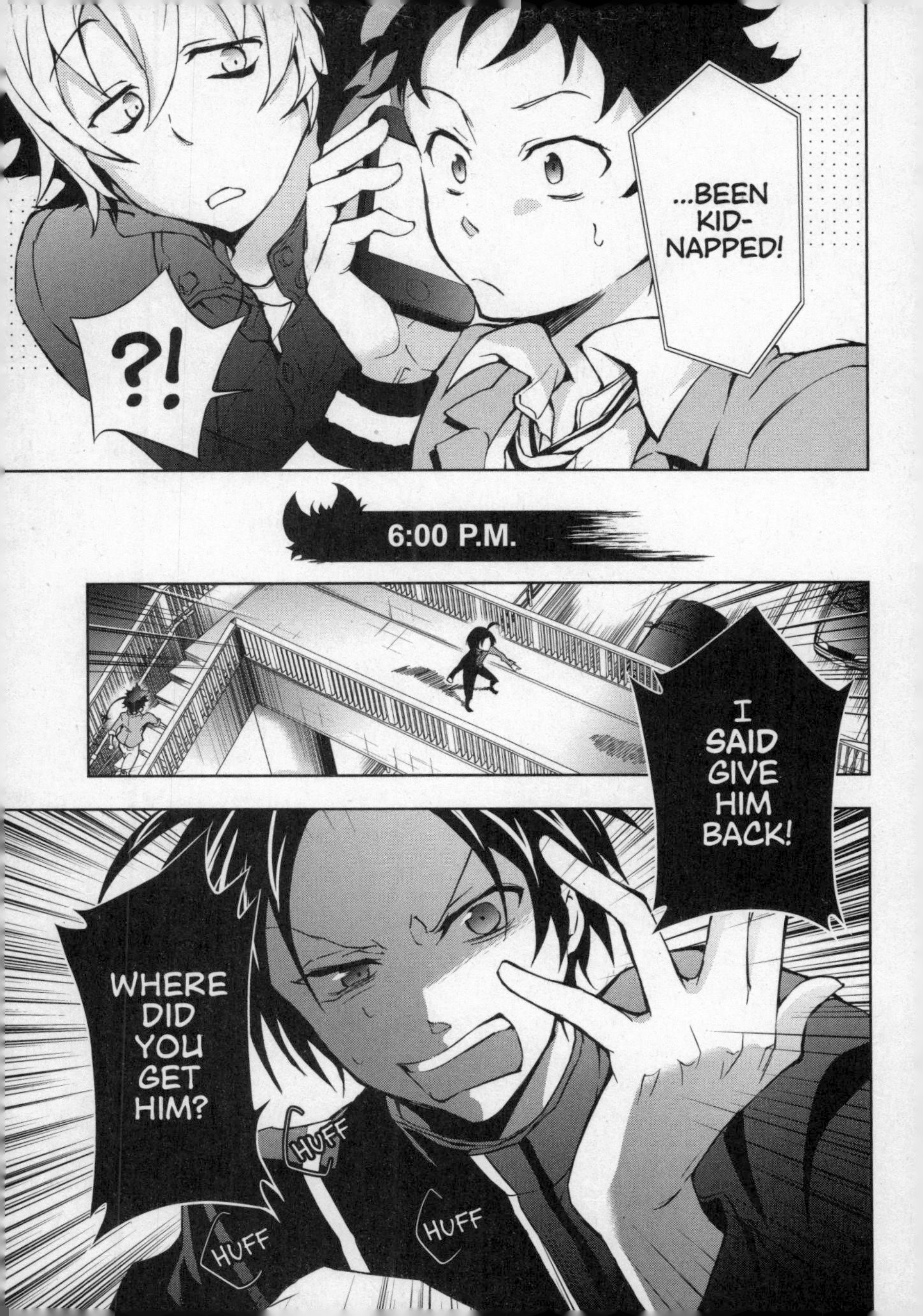
...BEEN KID-NAPPED!
?!
6:00 P.M.
I SAID GIVE HIM BACK!
WHERE DID YOU GET HIM?
HUFF
HUFF
HUFF

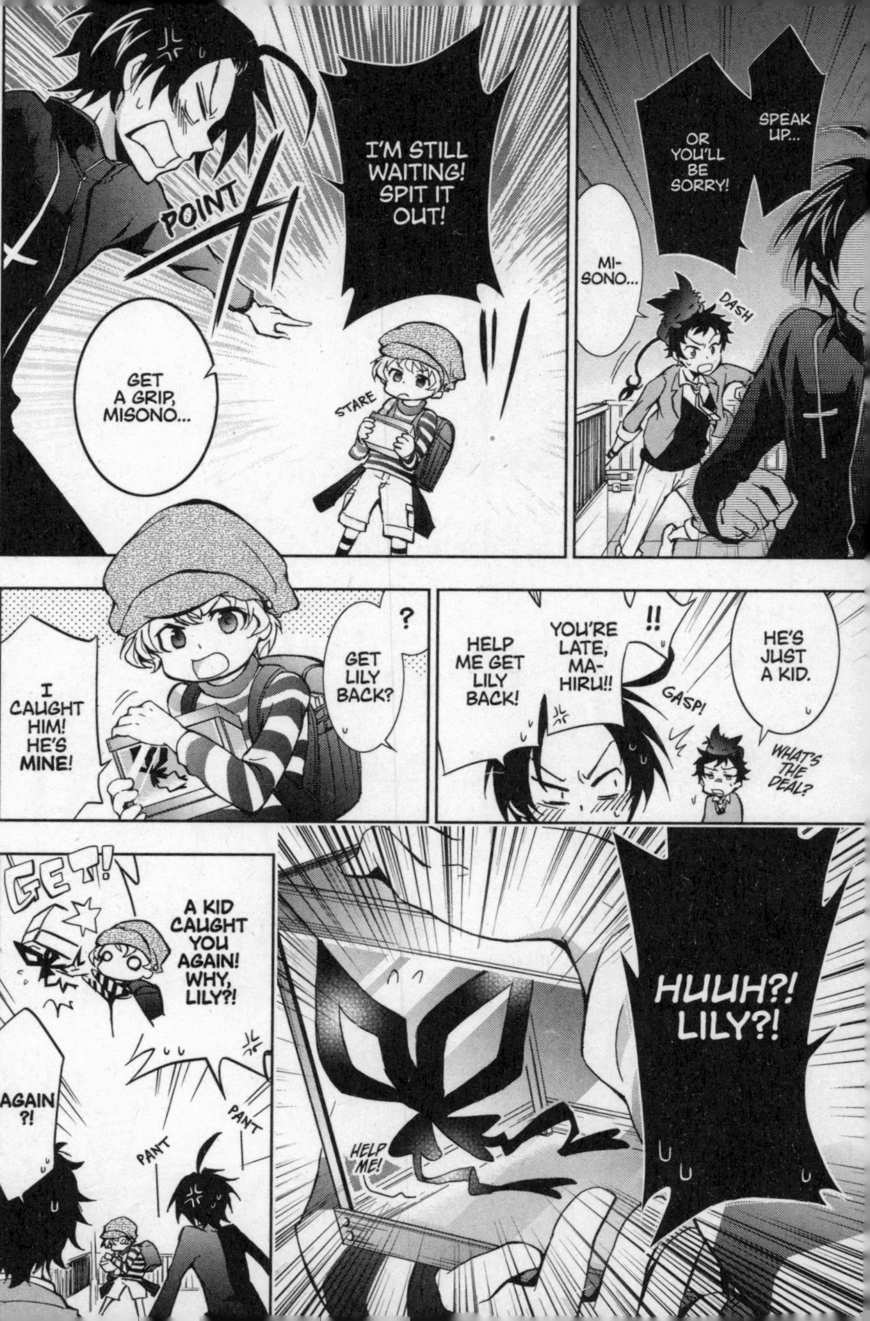
SPEAK UP...
OR YOU'LL BE SORRY!
MI-SONO...
DASH
I'M STILL WAITING! SPIT IT OUT!
POINT
GET A GRIP, MISONO...
STARE
HE'S JUST A KID.
!!
YOU'RE LATE, MA-HIRU!!
HELP ME GET LILY BACK!
GASP!
WHAT'S THE DEAL?
?
GET LILY BACK?
I CAUGHT HIM! HE'S MINE!
HUUH?! LILY?!
HELP ME!
GET!
A KID CAUGHT YOU AGAIN! WHY, LILY?!
AGAIN?!
PANT
PANT

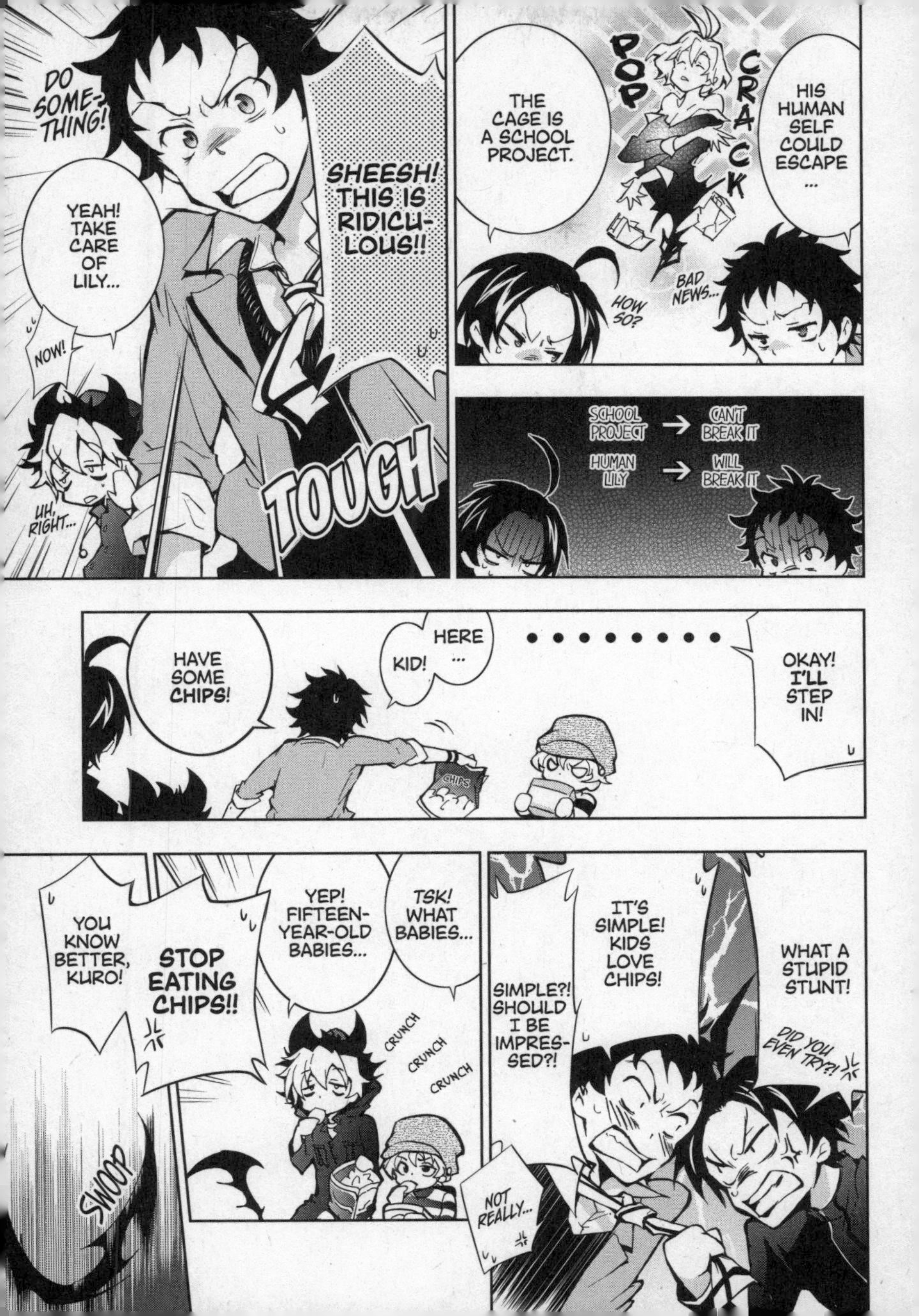

HIS HUMAN SELF COULD ESCAPE ...
CRACK
POP
THE CAGE IS A SCHOOL PROJECT.
BAD NEWS...
HOW SO?
SCHOOL PROJECT → CAN'T BREAK IT
HUMAN LILY → WILL BREAK IT
SHEESH! THIS IS RIDICULOUS!!
DO SOMETHING!
YEAH! TAKE CARE OF LILY...
NOW!
TOUGH
UH, RIGHT...
OKAY! I'LL STEP IN!
....
HERE ...
KID!
HAVE SOME CHIPS!
CHIPS
WHAT A STUPID STUNT!
DID YOU EVEN TRY?!
IT'S SIMPLE! KIDS LOVE CHIPS!
SIMPLE?! SHOULD I BE IMPRESSED?!
NOT REALLY...
TSK! WHAT BABIES...
YEP! FIFTEEN-YEAR-OLD BABIES...
STOP EATING CHIPS!!
YOU KNOW BETTER, KURO!
CRUNCH
CRUNCH
CRUNCH
SWOOP

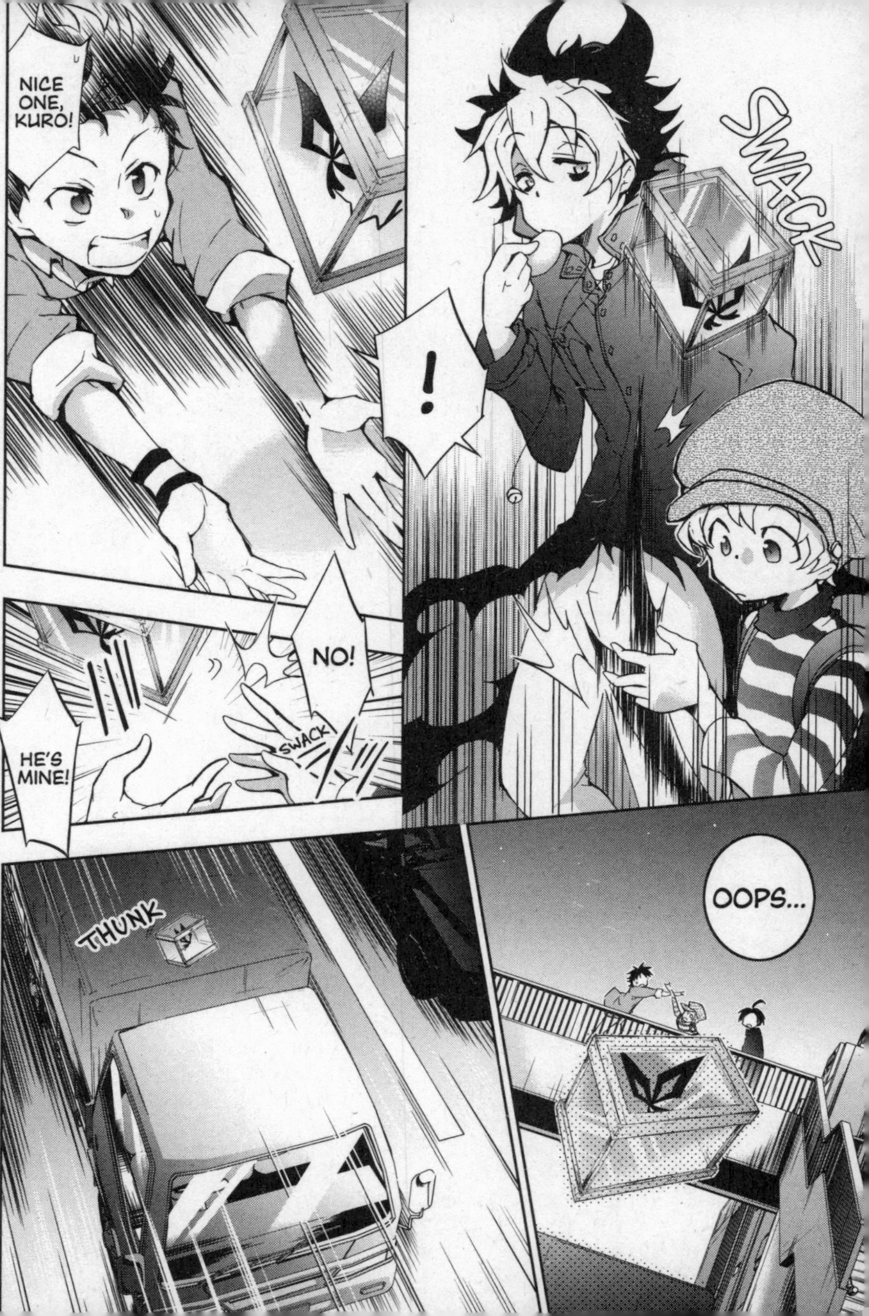
SWACK
!
NICE ONE, KURO!
NO!
SWACK
HE'S MINE!
OOPS...
THUNK

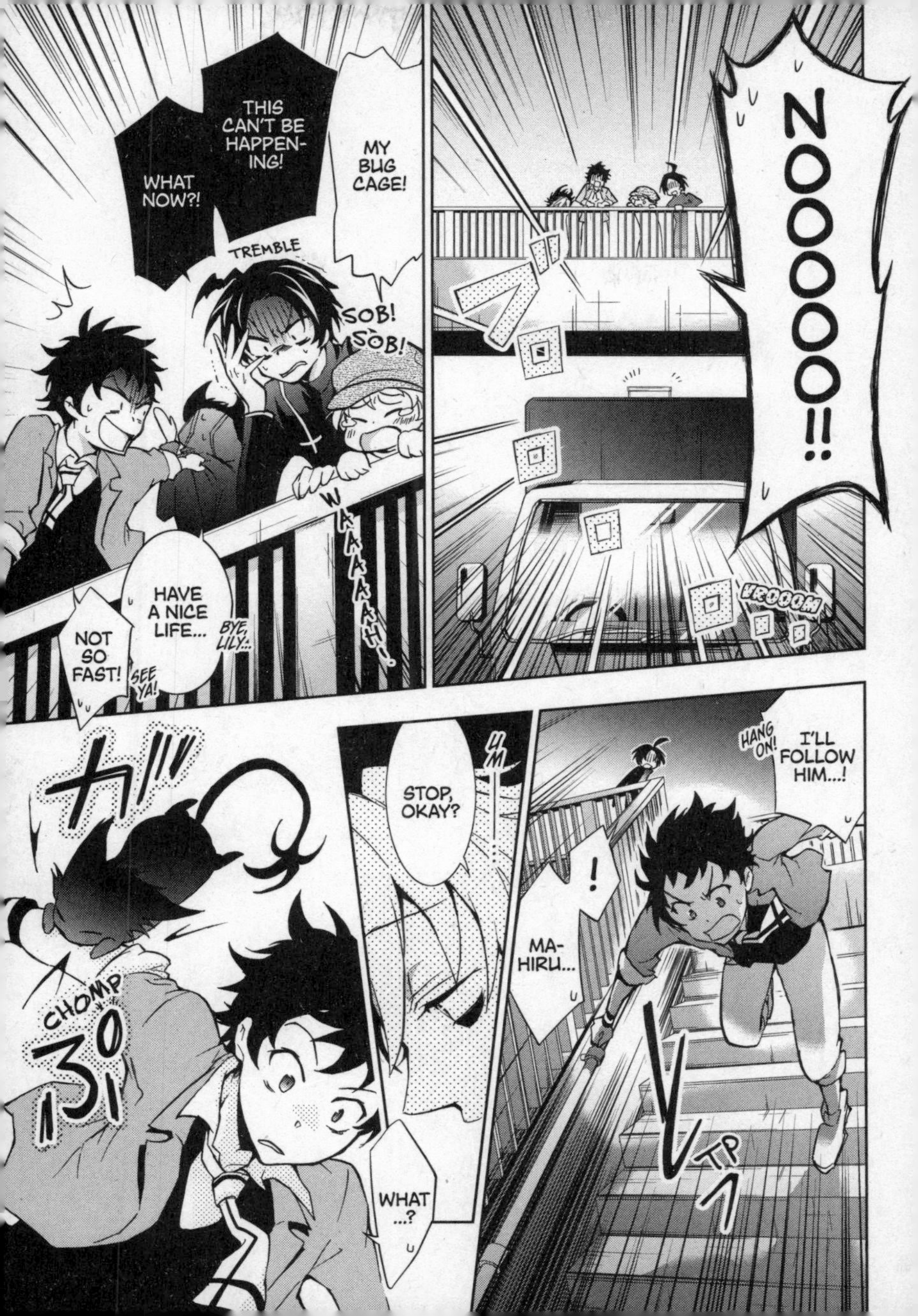
NOOOOO!!
VROOOM
MY BUG CAGE!
THIS CAN'T BE HAPPENING!
WHAT NOW?!
TREMBLE
SOB! SOB!
WAAAAAAAH!
HAVE A NICE LIFE...
BYE, LILY...
NOT SO FAST!
SEE YA!
I'LL FOLLOW HIM...!
HANG ON!
!
MA-HIRU...
TP
UM...
STOP, OKAY?
WHAT ...?
CHOMP

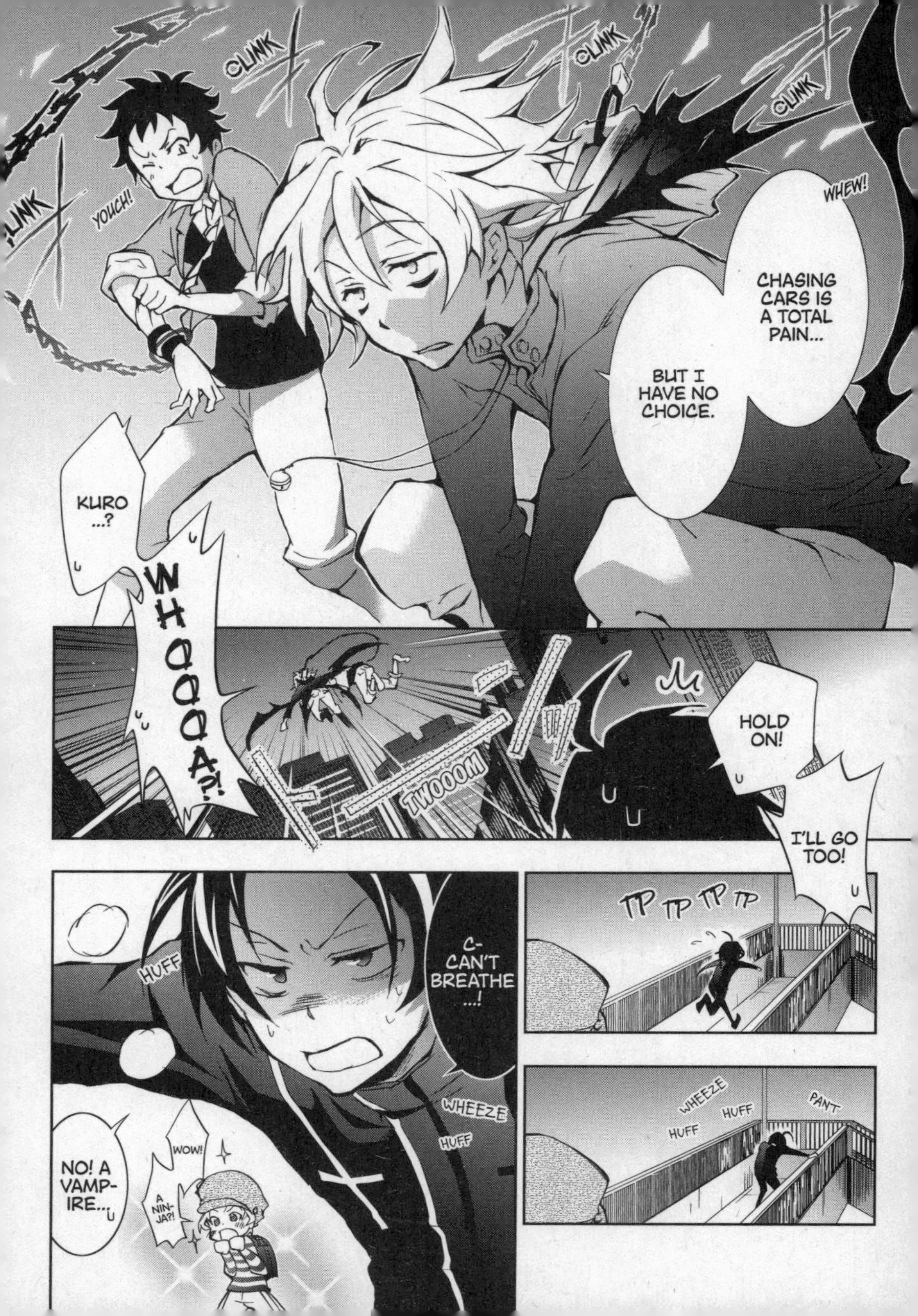
CLINK
WHEW!
CHASING CARS IS A TOTAL PAIN...
BUT I HAVE NO CHOICE.
CLINK
CLINK
YOUCH!
CLINK
KURO ...?
WHOOOOA?!
HOLD ON!
I'LL GO TOO!
TWOOOM
TP TP TP TP
PANT
HUFF
WHEEZE
HUFF
C-CAN'T BREATHE ...!
HUFF
WHEEZE
HUFF
WOW!
A NINJA?!
NO! A VAMPIRE...

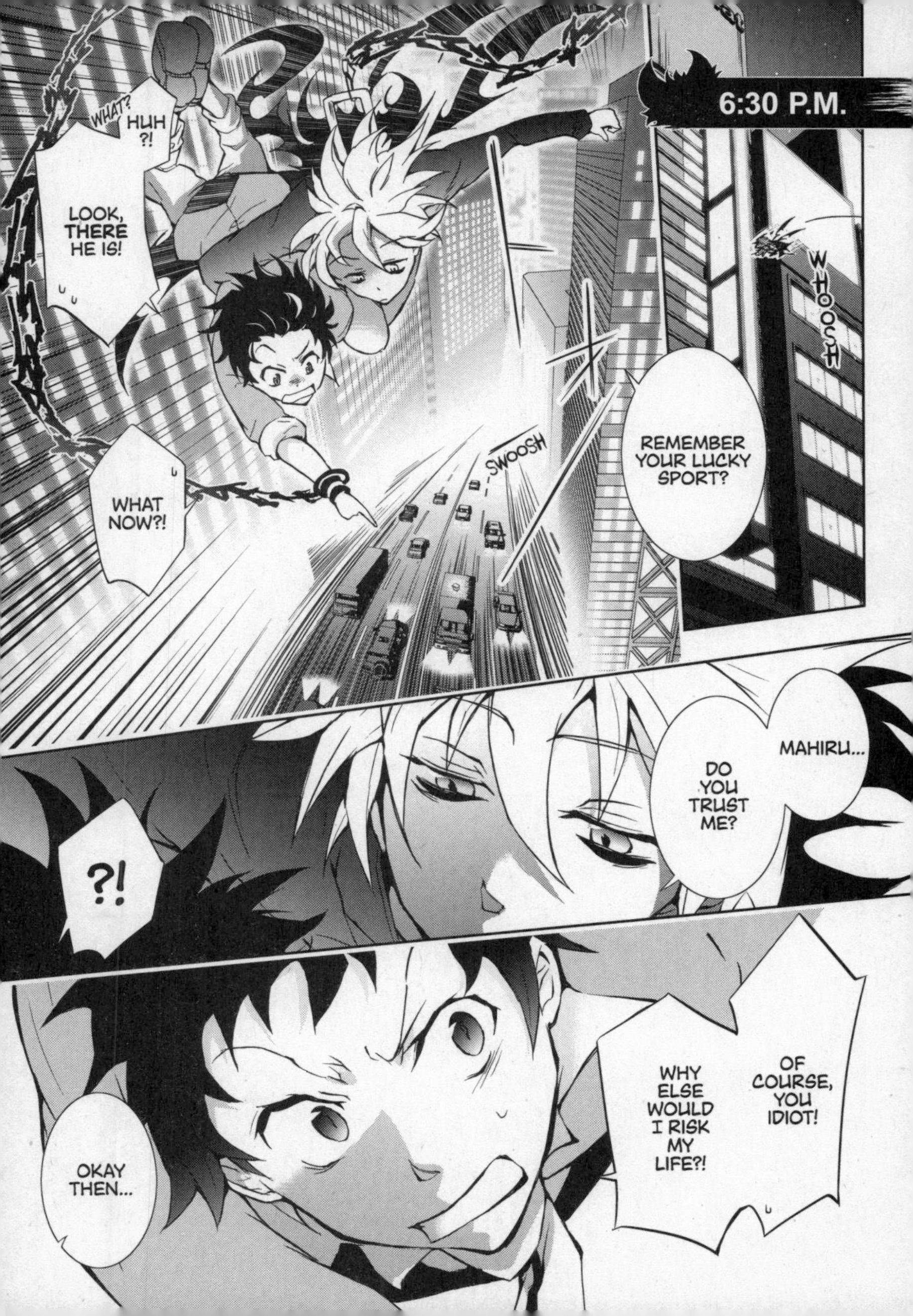
6:30 P.M.
WHOOSH
REMEMBER YOUR LUCKY SPORT?
SWOOSH
WHAT?
HUH ?!
LOOK, THERE HE IS!
WHAT NOW?!
MAHIRU...
DO YOU TRUST ME?
?!
OF COURSE, YOU IDIOT!
WHY ELSE WOULD I RISK MY LIFE?!
OKAY THEN...

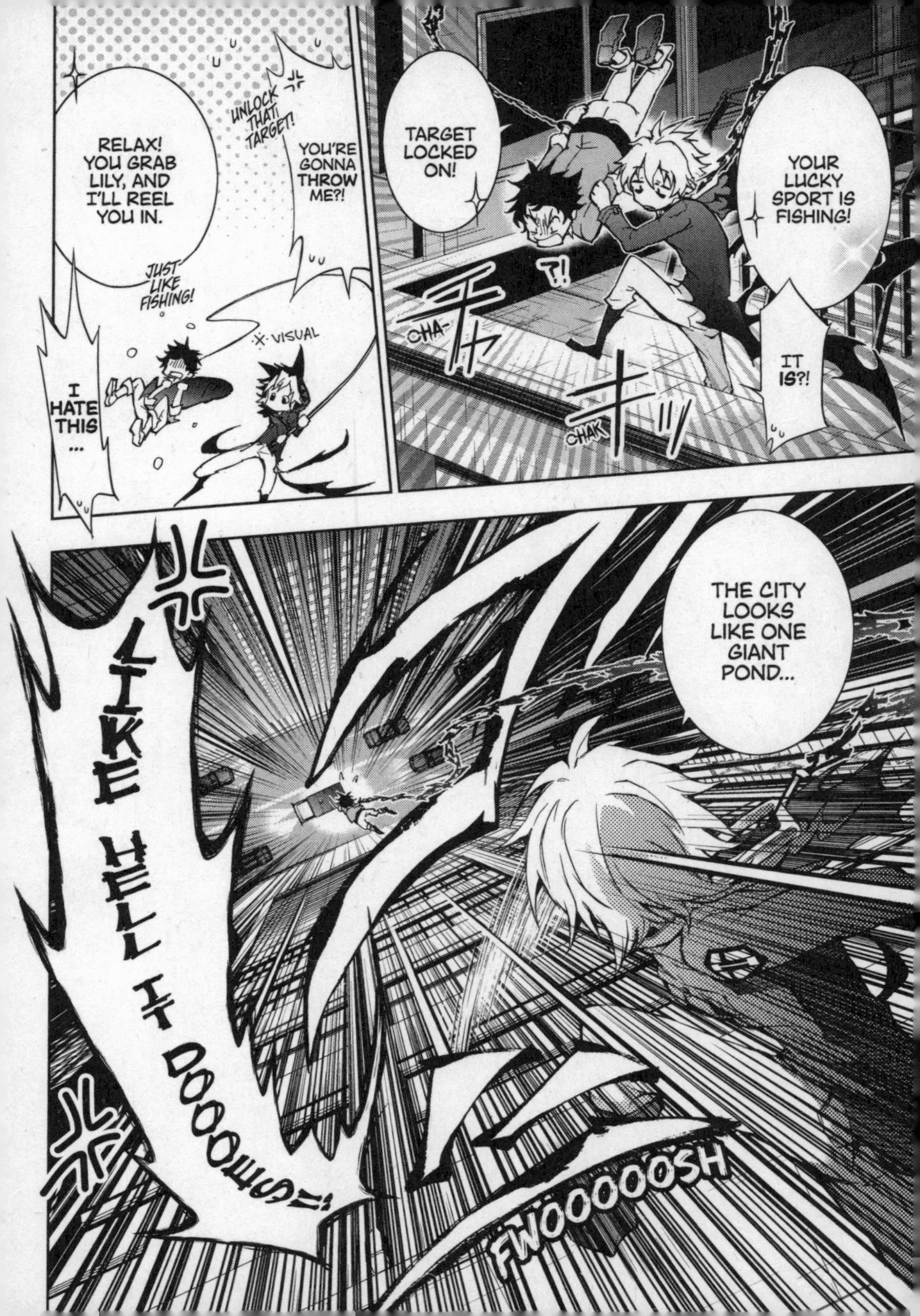
YOUR LUCKY SPORT IS FISHING!
TARGET LOCKED ON!
T?!
CHA-
CHAK
IT IS?!
YOU'RE GONNA THROW ME?!
UNLOCK THAT TARGET!
RELAX! YOU GRAB LILY, AND I'LL REEL YOU IN.
JUST LIKE FISHING!
※ VISUAL
I HATE THIS ...
THE CITY LOOKS LIKE ONE GIANT POND...
LIKE HELL IT DOOOOESS!!
FWOOOOOSH

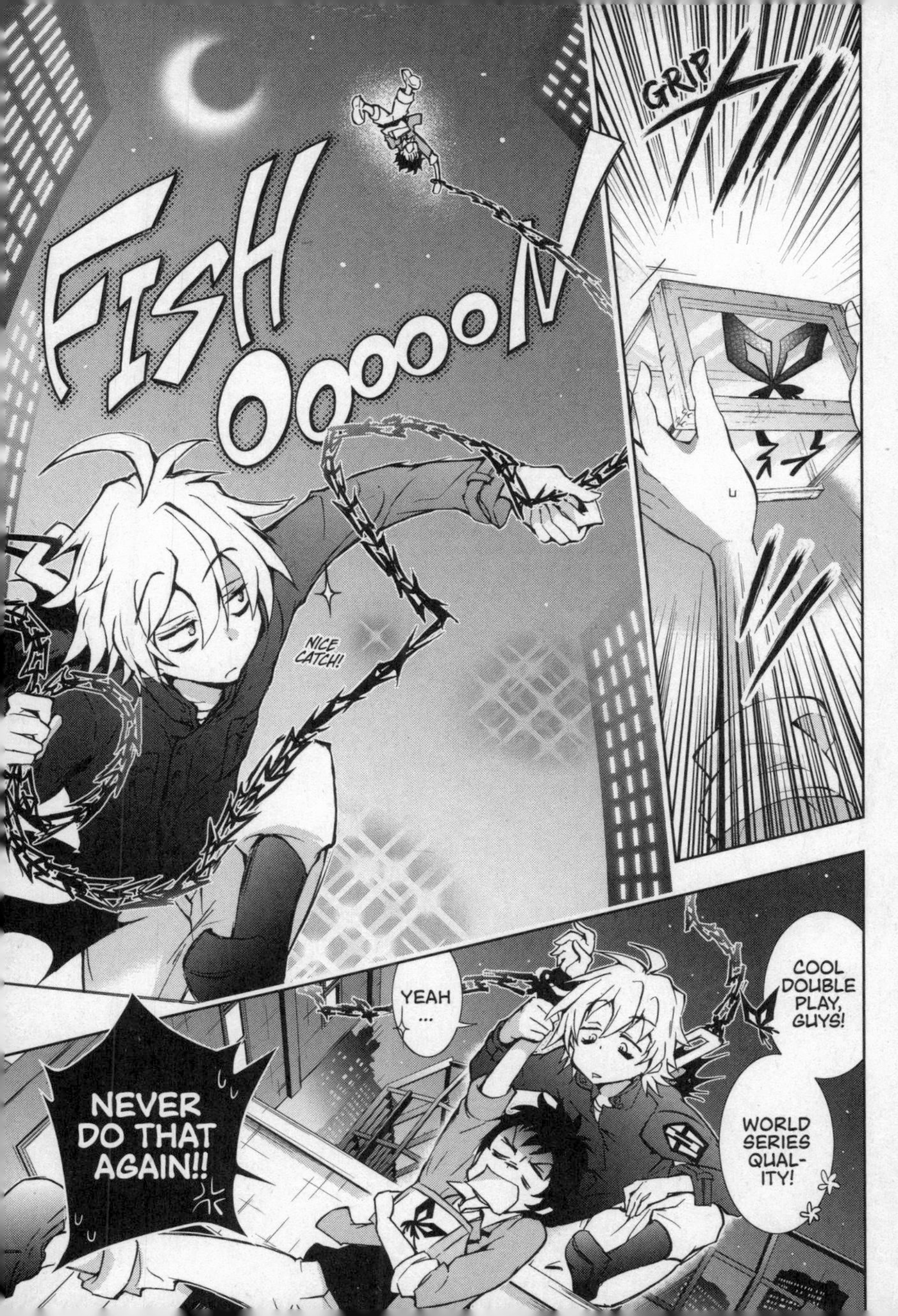
GRIP
FISH OOOOON
NICE CATCH!
COOL DOUBLE PLAY, GUYS!
WORLD SERIES QUAL- ITY!
YEAH ...
NEVER DO THAT AGAIN!!

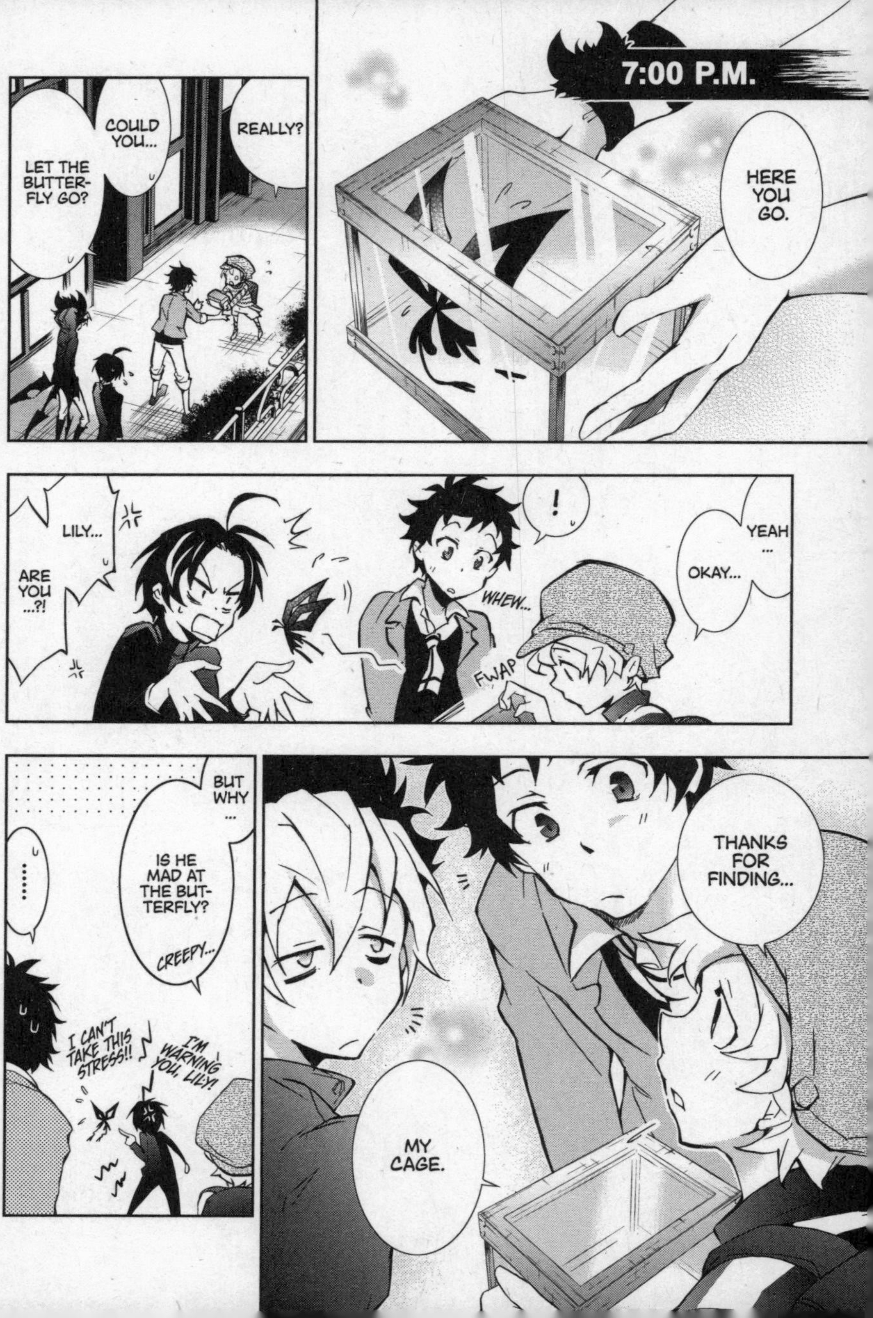
7:00 P.M.
HERE YOU GO.
REALLY?
COULD YOU...
LET THE BUTTERFLY GO?
YEAH... OKAY...
FWAP
!
WHEW...
LILY...
ARE YOU...?!
THANKS FOR FINDING...
MY CAGE.
BUT WHY...
IS HE MAD AT THE BUTTERFLY?
CREEPY...
......
I'M WARNING YOU, LILY!
I CAN'T TAKE THIS STRESS!!

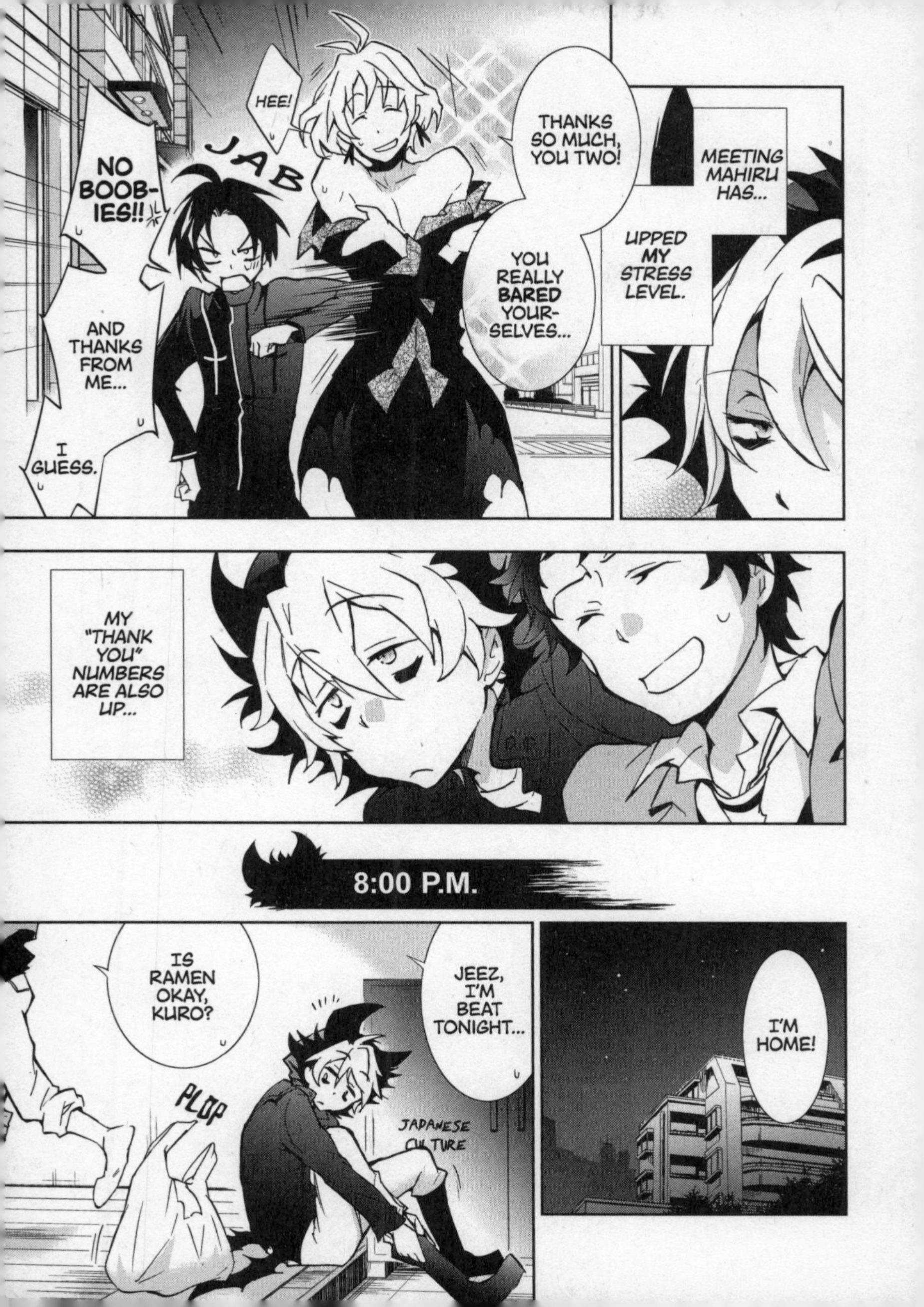
MEETING MAHIRU HAS...
UPPED MY STRESS LEVEL.
THANKS SO MUCH, YOU TWO!
YOU REALLY BARED YOUR-SELVES...
HEE!
JAB
NO BOOB-IES!!
AND THANKS FROM ME...
I GUESS.
MY "THANK YOU" NUMBERS ARE ALSO UP...
8:00 P.M.
I'M HOME!
JEEZ, I'M BEAT TONIGHT...
IS RAMEN OKAY, KURO?
PLOP
JAPANESE CULTURE

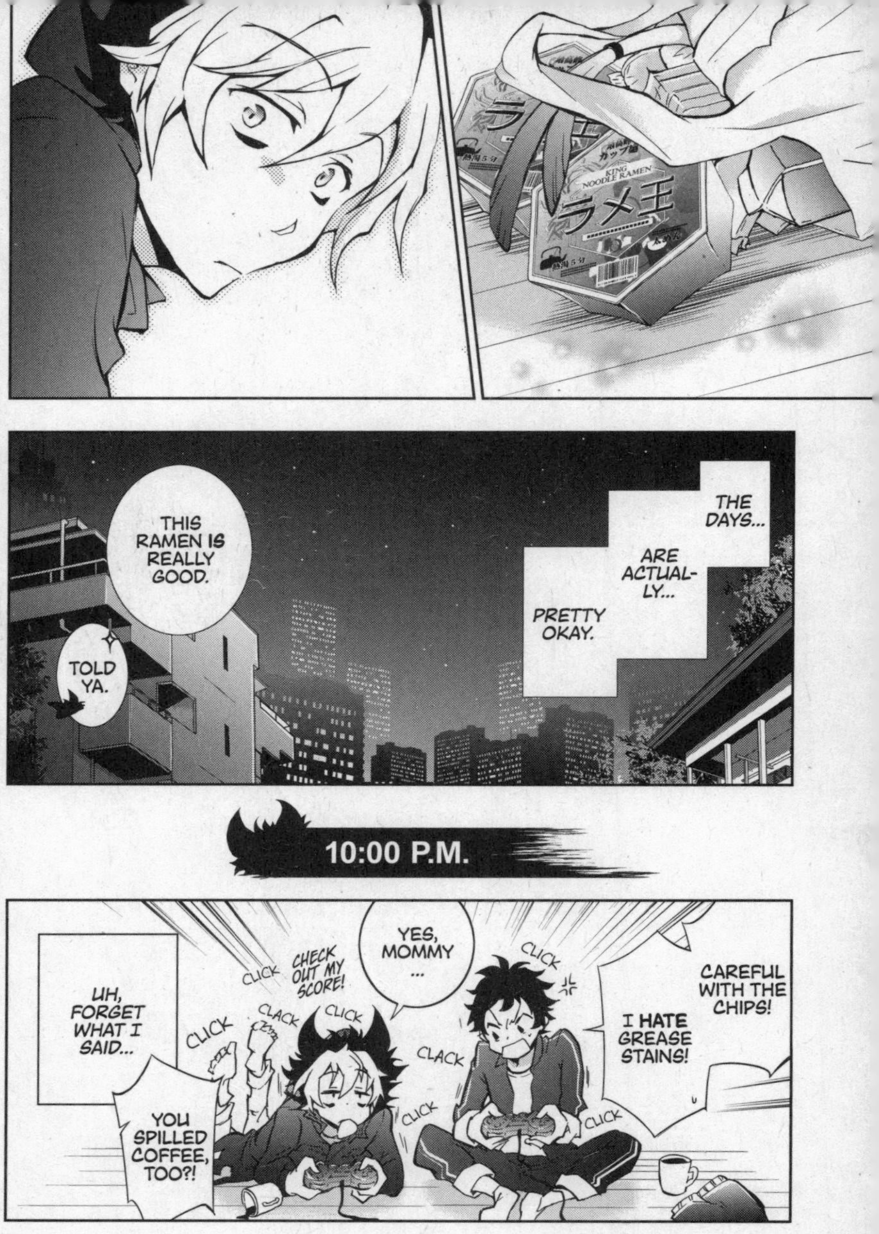
KING NOODLE RAMEN
ラメ王
THE DAYS...
ARE ACTUALLY...
PRETTY OKAY.
THIS RAMEN IS REALLY GOOD.
TOLD YA.
10:00 P.M.
CAREFUL WITH THE CHIPS!
I HATE GREASE STAINS!
CLICK
YES, MOMMY ...
CHECK OUT MY SCORE!
CLICK
CLICK
CLACK
CLACK
CLICK
CLICK
CLICK
UH, FORGET WHAT I SAID...
YOU SPILLED COFFEE, TOO?!

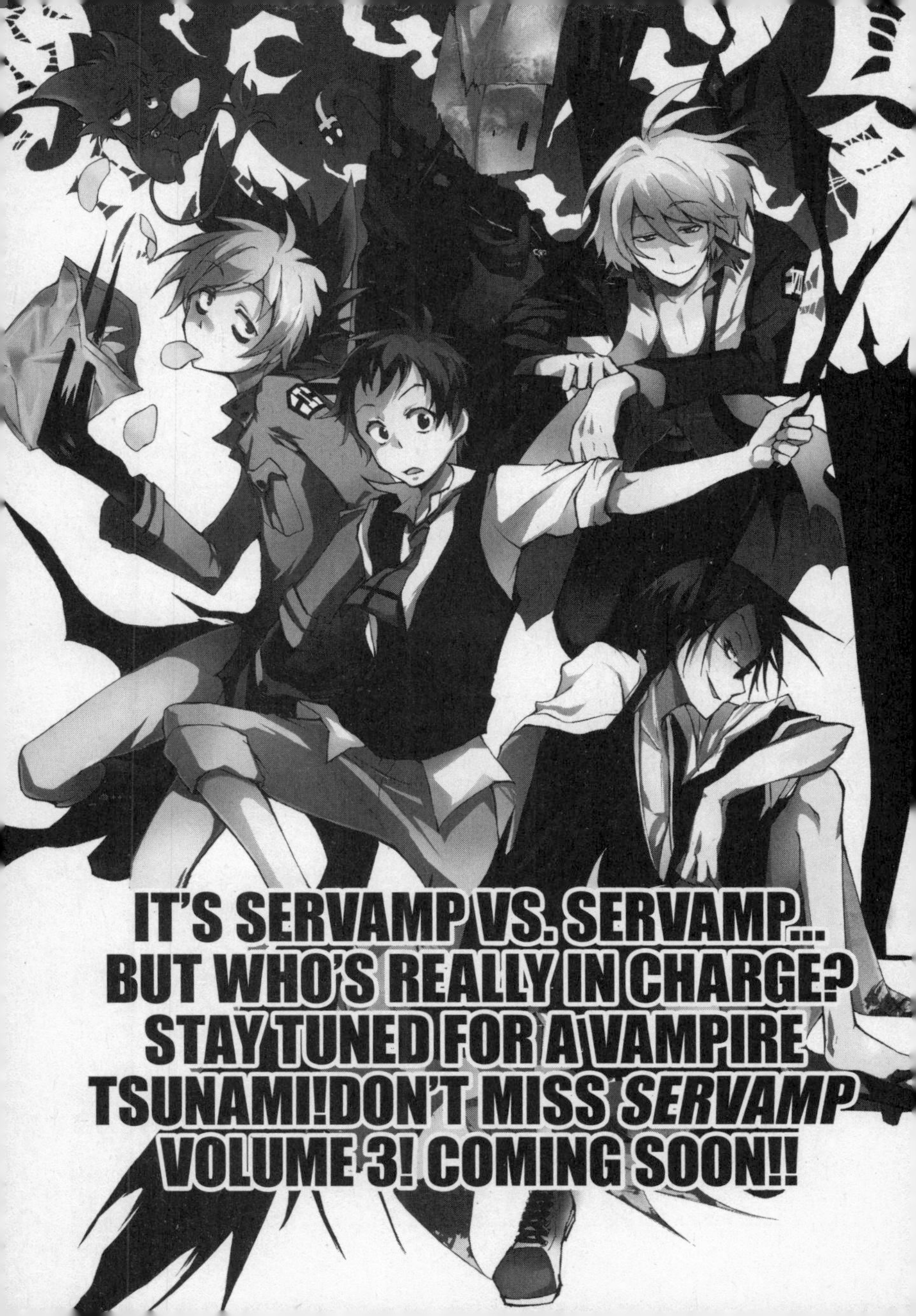
IT'S SERVAMP VS. SERVAMP...
BUT WHO'S REALLY IN CHARGE?
STAY TUNED FOR A VAMPIRE
TSUNAMI! DON'T MISS *SERVAMP*
VOLUME 3! COMING SOON!!

SEVEN SEAS ENTERTAINMENT PRESENTS

SERVAMP

story by and art by STRIKE TANAKA   VOLUME 2

TRANSLATION
Wesley Bridges

ADAPTATION
Janet Gilbert

LETTERING AND LAYOUT
Jaedison Yui

COVER DESIGN
Nicky Lim

PROOFREADER
Janet Houck
Lee Otter

ASSISTANT EDITOR
Lissa Pattillo

MANAGING EDITOR
Adam Arnold

PUBLISHER
Jason DeAngelis

SERVAMP VOL. 2
© STRIKE TANAKA 2012
Edited by MEDIA FACTORY.
First published in Japan in 2012 by KADOKAWA CORPORATION, Tokyo.
English translation rights reserved by Seven Seas Entertainment, LLC.
under the license from KADOKAWA CORPORATION, Tokyo.

Seven Seas books may be purchased in bulk for educational, business, or
promotional use. For information on bulk purchases, please contact Macmillan
Corporate & Premium Sales Department at 1-800-221-7945 (ext 5442)
or write specialmarkets@macmillan.com.

Seven Seas and the Seven Seas logo are trademarks of
Seven Seas Entertainment, LLC. All rights reserved.

ISBN: 978-1-626921-76-4

Printed in Canada

First Printing: June 2015

10 9 8 7 6 5 4 3 2 1

FOLLOW US ONLINE: *www.gomanga.com*

READING DIRECTIONS

This book reads from *right to left*, Japanese style.
If this is your first time reading manga, you start
reading from the top right panel on each page and
take it from there. If you get lost, just follow the
numbered diagram here. It may seem backwards at
first, but you'll get the hang of it! Have fun!!

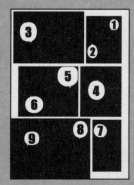